Secrets of a Billionaire

Billionaire King Series

Eva Winners

EVA WINNERS

- EVERLASTING ROMANCE FOR EVERY CENTURY -

AUTHOR'S NOTE

This book touches on some sensitive subjects and some readers might find it disturbing.

There is trigger content related to - family loss, suicide, miscarriage, violence.

Resemblance to actual persons and things living or dead, locations, or events is entirely coincidental.

If you're wondering whether I'm writing about you, I am.

Secrets of a Billionaire Playlist

PLAYLIST
https://spoti.fi/49lRjr4

Billionaire Kings Series Collection

The series covers each Ashford brother separately. While each book in the series can be read as a standalone, events and references to the other books are present in each one of these. So for best enjoyment consider giving each Ashford brother a chance. 😄

Enjoy!

Eva Winners

Note

Please note that the Russian surnames ending in -ov have an "a" added to the -ov/ -ev/ -in ending for women. Therefore, it would be Popova for women and Popov for a man.

Blurb

Winston Ashford, not exactly Prince Charming.

Arrogant. ☑
Bastard. ☑
Gorgeous. ☑

I'd mistaken him for a ten when he turned out to be a minus five. He was so beautiful but damaged beyond repair. There was no amount of understanding or love that could save a man who didn't want to be saved. So, after one night together, I gladly washed my hands of him.

Until everything went south.

My father was dead, my sister needed help, and it was time I behaved like a responsible older sister with a plan.

Unfortunately, my plan was slightly... lacking.

When I was caught red-handed stealing from my less-than-wonderful one-night stand, Winston Ashford became intent on bending me to his will.

It turned out that he was as ruthless as he was gorgeous and as cruel as he was tender.

Forced into an unwanted arrangement with the arrogant bastard —the kind that required rings—my last name became his. I became his reluctant yet, thankfully, secret wife. Unfortunately, he became the man who unknowingly held all the cards. At least we went our separate ways even if legally we were still bound together.

Six lonely years later, our paths crossed again.

There was still a darkness inside of him that scared me down to my very core.

He claimed he wanted a real marriage. That he was a changed man. But deep down, he was still the same—damaged from battling invisible scars and habits that were hard to break.

He saved me once upon a time. It was time for me to save him.

But what would happen when I wasn't enough?

Prologue
Winston

F ighting tears, I hung my head, trying not to look at my mama again. She hated going back home just as much as I did. She hated being around Father as much as the rest of us, but she was desperately trying to be strong.

I'd rather we left him and lived on our own, even in a little shack, but Mama said he would come after us. Then it'd be worse—at least for her—and I didn't want that. Not for her. She was all we had.

Father did nothing but hurt us, humiliate us.

He promised Mama he'd stop, but he always ended up breaking his promises. Every. Single. One. Of. Them.

"Let me try your dad again." Mama reached for her cell phone as we made our way down the busy downtown sidewalk, our bodyguard behind us. D.C. bustled with activity on a weekday, people going to work and visitors rushing to their next destination. "I'm sure when I explain…"

She attempted a smile and pressed the dial button, each ring making it dim a bit more. A light breeze swept through, her coconut-scented lotion drifting through the air. She always wore it—rain or shine, summer or winter—claiming it protected her skin. It was her signature scent, and I could never think of the beach without thinking about her.

Behind her, the sun shone on her dark hair, and I noticed, not for the first time, the shades of chestnut trying to fight their way out. I gave her an encouraging nod, and she rewarded me with a wink. I loved when she was like this with me, like nothing else existed, even though I knew she was trying to be brave.

She always made an effort to spend quality time with me, despite Father monopolizing every second of her day. She said it made her happy to spend time with her children, so she often pulled us out of school to play hooky with her. Today was my turn. Her warm eyes filled all the holes in my chest with love, and with the sun's rays, tiny specs of gold in them made her look like the most beautiful woman in the world. Nothing like mine. Where Royce, Kingston, and Aurora had her dark eyes, Byron and I inherited our father's eyes.

"He'll answer," she muttered under her breath, although I wasn't sure who she was trying to convince—me or herself. It was always the same, so we both knew her call would go unanswered. The part that hurt the most was seeing her pain, her disappointment.

Nothing we ever did was right by Father. Nothing pleased him. Except for his whores that made Mama feel bad. I wanted to fix it, to make her feel better, but I didn't know how.

Suddenly she turned my way with an odd, bright expression on her face and said, "We'll go to the game store."

Confusion washed over me and I blinked several times, trying to understand.

"Father said it's okay?"

She didn't answer but looked over at our bodyguard. "I'm taking my son to his favorite store."

"It's not wise, ma'am. Your husband—"

She cut him off. "He can wait a little bit longer."

But we all knew he hated waiting on anyone, especially his family. It was usually what spurred their arguments. She wanted to spend more time with us, which he hated. She wanted to spend more time on her designs, but he hated that too.

"We haven't cleared the route," he tried to reason.

There were a few more words spoken, but they didn't register. I was too excited to stop and question any of it.

When we arrived, I rushed to the new releases section with a grin on my face. My mama's soft chuckle followed closely behind, her scent wrapping me in a cloud of comfort. My brother Byron was the epitome of seriousness. I, on the other hand, was the opposite. Mama said I reminded her of Grandpa DiLustro, and whenever I asked her what she meant, she'd tell me the story of how he'd shut down the entire subway line so he could take a peaceful ride with his daughter. It wasn't until much later that I understood how he made it possible. After all, he was in Kingpins of the Syndicate, a mafia organization that had fingers in every pot.

"So this is the game, huh?" she mused, her eyes shining with humor. "To think that something in such a small box has so much of my son's attention."

"It's better than drugs and alcohol and cigarettes, Ma." A lot of kids my age did that shit, but I stayed away. Playing video games was my way of releasing steam.

She let out a strangled breath, most likely thinking about a few of my friends in particular, but the little crinkles around her eyes told me she was relieved. "I sure hope so."

I nodded seriously. "I could become a big-time player and support us all," I said, once again dreaming of a life without my father. "You could design to your heart's content. Byron can be an ass like usual, and—"

"Winston." Her soft reprimand instantly made me regret my words, and my shoulders slumped.

"Okay, he can just be his serious self. But the rest of us will have a great time. My sister and brothers can run around all day, roll in the mud if they want. We could do whatever we want." I wasn't even looking at the games anymore. All my focus was on this vision for a better future.

A soft smile curved around her lips. "That sounds lovely."

Seeing that wistful expression on her face made me determined to make it happen. I took her hand in mine and squeezed tightly. "Just wait and see, Ma. I'll take care of us all."

Twenty minutes later, we were exiting the store, my new game stored securely in my backpack. People were still rushing about, the busy street filled with pedestrians and tourists visiting the capital.

I turned my head, opening my mouth to thank Ma, when a deafening *bang* filled the air and warm liquid splattered onto my face. The bustle from the street fell away, the cloudless sky becoming something more terrifying than I could have ever imagined as blood rained down on me. Mama's body jerked, and before I could think to do anything, she was pushing me away. *Bang.*

I slumped to the ground, my knees scraping against the pavement as I tried to drag myself back to where she now lay, her gasps coming in sharper and sharper. That dark hair I knew so well was fanned out on the pavement, a puddle of crimson forming like a blood-soaked halo around her. I tried to blink, tried to catch my breath. Why couldn't I make myself move? Could this really be happening?

Screams filled the air and people ran around us—from us?—in all different directions. Meanwhile, I could only watch helplessly as the scene played out. The smell of copper replaced the coconut scent. A red stain spread slowly across Mama's shoulder and chest, over her diamond necklace. The one she loved most. The one that had belonged to her own mama.

I forced myself to crawl over, ignoring the chaos around me. Ignoring the pain in my chest and my body. Her warm whiskey eyes met mine, this time shining with pure terror and filled with tears.

"Ma," I breathed, trying to stand, to get help, but with the last of her energy, she gripped my arm and pulled me back down. Her worry for my safety outweighed everything else. "Please... please... be okay."

I rubbed at my face, yanked at my hair. Why wasn't anyone helping her? I couldn't bear a world without her. I needed her to stay. For my siblings. For me.

"It's all my fault." My lips repeated the words my brain chanted. Over and over again.

"N-not your f-fault." She was fading. Her touch was getting colder by the second. "Be g-good." I sniffled, terror taking over and making my head spin. "Don't be your father."

"I won't," I cried. "I promise."

"Be better than him," she whispered, and then she heaved as much of herself as she could off the bloodstained pavement to squeeze my arm again. I felt my heart bleeding out, right alongside my mother's body. "And never settle. Promise me."

What have I done? I shouldn't have wanted to come to the game store. I shouldn't have insisted. I shouldn't have—

"Promise me, Winston."

"I promise, Ma."

I never picked up another game. I did, however, pick up many a vice. From that day forward, my path of self-destruction was set.

That day, my father's daggers sank so deep into my flesh that I didn't know how to dig myself out.

Chapter 1
Billie

Holy Mother of God.

My panties may have caught on fire and burned to ashes. Winston Ashford was *hot*. Out-of-this-world hot.

He's a ten, I thought to myself. There was no way someone looked like that and didn't fuck like a ten. But then again, I'd had my share of disappointments. He was tall, maybe six-four. Broad shoulders and built. The standout for me though was that *je ne sais quoi* quality that demanded attention.

I hadn't met a man like him before. He wore understated, sophisticated clothing that carried an air of old money, but I got the distinct impression that he should be in combat gear, directing soldiers as they headed into battle. Again, I couldn't explain it, he just commanded power. He had an angular jaw, full lips shaped in a perfect Cupid's bow, and a strong if not slightly crooked nose, like it'd been broken before. Combine that with bronze skin and deep blue eyes, he had a presence that made a woman do a double take—or three.

Odette introduced me to Byron Ashford earlier, who in turn introduced us to his brother Winston and their friend River. My usual chatty self was tongue-tied, but that was okay because the gorgeous brother hadn't said a word either. Sweet Lord, it should be illegal to have so many good-looking guys in one room, let alone at one table.

However, Byron and River did nothing for me. Winston Ashford, on the other hand, did it *all* for me. My breath caught in my lungs as soon as I'd seen him step into Le Bar Américain.

For a moment, it was like the world stopped turning. It could have been only seconds, but it felt like hours. My heart drummed in my ears, drowning out everything and everyone else.

Almost as though he could hear my thoughts, his attention drifted my way and we locked eyes, staring at each other for a heartbeat too long. My stomach fluttered for what felt like the first time in my life. The air between us swirled, sexual tension so thick you could cut it with a butter knife.

As if perplexed and suddenly aware of the bar full of patrons, he tilted his head back and took a sip of his poison, nodding at something River must've said. For the second time tonight, I let my mind drift to how he oozed dominance. I couldn't help wondering what kind of woman captured a man who looked like a god. Or a fallen angel.

I snapped my eyes away, desperate to look anywhere but in his direction. Unfortunately, I wasn't able to keep my gaze from him for long. Under the guise of scoping out the bar and watching the dance floor heave with pulsating bodies, I snuck a glance in his direction, and that was all it took for goose bumps to erupt over my skin.

His eyes roamed his surroundings like he was bored. Like this night—the people, the music, life itself—was exhausting. He looked... done. His dark gaze was a little hard, like there was nothing here he hadn't seen before. His eyes stayed narrowed, never lingering for too long. Almost as if he was on the lookout for something.

From where I was standing by the bar top, his profile was in my line of sight. Those sharp cheekbones that looked sculpted from granite. Thick brown hair. And those piercing eyes that had the butterflies in my stomach going wild all over again.

I was hypnotized by those eyes.

Much later, I'd recall how startlingly white his shirt had been against his tanned throat. I'd swear that even the air between us had shimmered. How the din of the busy bar had faded into silence. It was as if I had wandered into a strange and compelling universe where there was no one else but me and that devilishly handsome man.

He sat at the VIP table with the two other men, but I couldn't tear my gaze away from him to check them out.

Based on the moment we shared earlier, I knew he saw something he liked. And just like before, the look in his eye now was that of a starved man. Those blue orbs caressed every inch of me before they met my own dark eyes, and then the corner of his lips tipped up in a smirk.

I should stop now and see this man for what he was: pure danger. But did I plan to listen to my own internal warnings?

No, sir, I didn't.

This type of man came around once in a lifetime, so I intended to seize the moment and make it count. *Carpe diem* and all that shit. It'd just be a onetime thing, I told myself. An experiment for a fun, memorable night.

My gaze traveled over to my sister who was dancing with Byron, the man who couldn't take his eyes off her.

Tonight belongs to us, the Swan sisters, I thought to myself.

So, I made my way to him, swaying my hips seductively. Halfway there though, I hesitated. He seemed a little... intoxicated.

And while it should have been a total turnoff, my normally steady and unaffected heart quivered in my chest, and it was enough to spur me on. There was something sad and lonely in his eyes that just drew me in.

As I got closer to him, his cologne hit me. Rich, spicy, *masculine*.

Inhaling subtly, I fought the urge to bury my face in the crook of his neck and feel his hot, smooth skin beneath my lips. And while I was melting for this man, Winston's face remained an unmoving mask as I reached the table.

"Hello, again," I greeted him. *Shit, did my voice actually tremble?* I cleared my throat before continuing. "Is this seat taken?"

He took a swallow of his drink, his eyes burning.

"Clearly not. Nobody's sitting in it," he grumbled. Okay, his snarkiness should have knocked this attraction down by at least a notch, but it didn't. Shit, why didn't it? I never put up with jerks, especially intoxicated ones. "Are you going to sit down, Billie, or hover over me?"

He remembers my name, my stupid romantic heart sang. *Although, his tone could use some improvements*, my reason warned. Maman always cautioned against my pride and high expectations, and I heeded her advice. Well, in every scenario but one.

My pride. *It will cost you everything and leave you with nothing.* Gosh, how many times did Maman say those words to me? I shook my head, pushing them away.

"Only if you ask nicely," I retorted, my voice a touch colder this time. "Clearly you haven't been taught manners."

He leaned back into his seat, relaxed and confident, his eyes almost calculating.

"Sit your needy, fuckable ass down, Billie." He flashed me a condescending smile, then added, "Please."

What the—

To my shock, my body immediately obeyed, and before I could even protest, I was sitting. Goddammit. *This motherfucking prick.*

"Now, why are you here?"

I worked a muscle in my jaw and tried to come up with a response. I certainly wasn't going to flirt with him now. Not when he was being a complete douche.

And yet, I remained sitting. I knew I should get up and leave, but that same something in his blue eyes kept me glued to my seat. Or maybe it was just morbid curiosity that had me suddenly acting out of character.

"I was going to offer you some suggestions on what to see around here, but I can see you're one of those men who thinks they already know everything." I flashed him a smile that rivaled his own. "So I won't bother."

His smirk slipped briefly before he remembered to rearrange his mask. "Funny, because I was gonna say the same about you. Aren't we two peas in a pod."

It was obvious that he was goading me. I doubted he found much in common with me, the jerk.

I scoffed. "I'm nothing like you."

He tilted his head as though actually considering my words. "You're right. I'm rich and you're... not. You must be one of those gold-digger bunnies who chases men who can support their shopping habits."

This arrogant son of a... Anger began to pump through my blood, my ears buzzing with fury. Slightly at him, but mostly at myself for not being smart enough to stand up and turn on my heel. I needed to get the hell out of there.

I shifted my body, ready to leave this asshole behind, when his eyes locked with mine. There it was again. Something feral and cagey in the depths of his ocean gaze. He *wanted* me to get fired up, to leave him here. So, I stayed, but not without snapping back at him.

"My ass might be fuckable, but yours isn't." *Take that, Mr. Asshole.*

His face broke out into a broad smile. "Thank God for that."

I rolled my eyes. "You're a conceited prick. You know nothing about me, and how much money I have is none of your concern."

"But you still want me to fuck you," he drawled with that confident smile. My heart beat faster as my anger boiled dangerously close to erupting. I inhaled a deep breath, needing to get myself under control. His eyes leisurely traveled over my body, and I wondered what he was thinking. I couldn't read the expression in his eyes. "Now what does that say about you?"

I stared at him, sitting there all cold and unemotional while my own emotions skyrocketed.

"If you signed over your fortune, however measly it is, I still wouldn't touch you with a ten-foot pole. You see, I'm allergic to the likes of you."

"Likes of me?" he snickered. "Rich, good-looking, capable of fucking your brains out. You meant that kind? Trust me, Billie, you want me."

"No, I fucking don't," I hissed. "And just so you know, the French make love. So why in the world would I entertain giving it up for a crude, rude American?"

Hopefully he didn't pick up on the fact that I was half American too. Or that I frequently traveled to the States to assist with fashion shows and wedding dress alterations. In fact, wedding gowns were my area of expertise. One day, I'd combine that with diamond design, and I'd be golden. Dad and Odette had the brains, while I was more the creative one. Together, we were a well-balanced family.

"A crude, rude American, huh?" he echoed in a bored tone. He tilted his chin to the open sky, where stars twinkled above us. I loved this section of the Américain, it was the perfect place to get fresh air amongst a sea of loose bargoers. I studied the smug look on his face that he didn't even bother hiding, and it pissed me off even more when my body refused to react with any semblance of self-respect and dignity. Instead, my insides clenched with each second that passed... almost as if this was our foreplay.

I mentally slapped myself. I needed to have my head examined. Why did he have to be so damn gorgeous?

He leaned over, his scent of aftershave swirling with the top-shelf vodka in his highball glass. He threw me a slow and sexy smile, and my traitorous pussy throbbed. Then he was cupping my face in his hand, and the only thing I was able to do was to get lost in his gaze as a wave of arousal swept through me.

God, I wanted him. I'd never wanted another man so much.

"You and I both know that you want me to fuck you. Admit it. You want to suck my cock, Billie," he murmured darkly. The image of the two of us naked flashed in my head, me on my knees, him on a chair, legs spread wide while I deepthroated him like a woman possessed. He'd lose his mind, and then he'd be following me around like a damn puppy, begging for more. I couldn't resist smirking smugly. Yeah, I wanted to suck his cock.

"You want me to bend you over and fuck you senseless. In. Every. Hole." The insinuation made me shiver. His lips brushed over mine ever so lightly. It was barely a touch, but it lit my whole body on fire. My sex clenched, and I feared I'd orgasm from this idiotic interaction, which had to be a testament to my far-too-long period of abstinence. "Except, my temptress, I'm afraid when morning comes, you'll be too clingy for my taste. Not to mention you'll end up heartbroken, because I don't fuck the same girl twice."

Okay, I'm back to being turned off, I lied to myself as I stared at him, my brain short-circuiting. Thankfully, I had just enough sense not to ask him to take me away from here and prove it.

"You'd have to have me once in order to deny yourself that second round. Quite frankly, you don't seem worth the effort," I rasped, anger simmering beneath my skin. My cheeks burned because *of course* the prick was right. Clingy or not, I liked having a man. "By the looks of it, you're a drunk too. A pitiful one." He stared at me with a bored expression, as if to say that clearly none of my words were getting to him. "Honestly, with your obvious alcohol problem, your dick probably doesn't even function properly."

Take that, asshole.

He grinned, his expression remaining dark. "Trust me, sweetheart. My dick works perfectly fine. Unfortunately, it will never be satisfied by a single woman. He likes variety too much and is easily bored." Was this guy seriously talking about his penis in the third person?

Despite wanting to scoff at his overinflated ego, images of Winston in the midst of an orgy, being worshiped by two or more women, flashed through my mind. I didn't think I was into sharing, but they still managed to make me ache with want.

My eyes dropped to his lips, then trailed down his body. It would be hard to miss that he was all muscle, his fancy clothes hiding rock-hard abs and who knew what else. I swallowed, envisioning this man naked.

"Eyes up here." His voice startled me, and to my horror, I realized I was staring at his crotch. Shit, what was wrong with me?

I shot him a glare, hating that I found everything about this man sexy. Well, everything but his mouth. Although—

"Hey, I'm going," my sister announced in French, showing up at my side suddenly and startling me. I turned my attention from the sexy asshole to her, noting the red blush staining her cheeks.

"I'm out too," Byron chimed in. "River too."

"Okay," I replied warily, all my built-up anger at Winston's words forgotten as I studied my sister.

"You okay?" Odette questioned, and I had to take a calming breath before answering so I didn't blurt out my desire to kill Winston Ashford in cold blood.

"Yes, everything is *parfait*."

My eyes darted to Winston and we shared a fleeting gaze, but then we both remembered ourselves and quickly looked away.

"Want me to stay with you?" my sister, always the thoughtful one, offered.

I shook my head.

"Absolutely not." I could handle Winston all on my own, thank you very much. I stood and pecked my sister on the cheek. "I'm going back to my table. See you later." I leaned closer. "Be safe."

Turning back to Winston, I put on the fakest, most polite smile I could muster and said, "Have a pleasant evening, Mr. Ashford. I hope your boredom doesn't shrivel your dick too badly."

And with that, I walked away with my head held high, back to where all our friends sat.

Le Bar Américain's iconic views of the French Riviera had no trouble attracting locals and tourists alike, all looking for a good time. Tonight, the breeze swept through the terrace, warm and soothing. Sapphire and ruby lights glimmered from pergolas, illuminating the cobblestone area with every strobe. The music reverberated throughout the air, but all I heard was the drumming in my ears and pulse of my heart.

Back at my usual table, I ordered my signature drink, a strawberry daiquiri, and when it was placed in front of me a few minutes later, I took a long sip, relishing the silky trail it took down my throat.

"So, guess who has an invitation to the Scandalous Temptation event?" Tristan asked enthusiastically. Tristan and Odette were in their first year at Stanford and had become good friends. The guy was a hoot. His sister—a doctor at George Washington back in the States —was here with him. She wasn't a hoot, not by a long shot.

My eyebrows scrunched. "How did you manage that? I've lived here for years and still haven't managed to get in."

Tristan flashed me a wicked grin and showed me the virtual invitation with a barcode on his phone. "When you have friends in high places..."

His words drifted off, but I knew what was left unspoken: we might never get the chance again. It was a once-in-a-lifetime opportunity, and who was I kidding? I had nothing better to do. *Adventure, here I come,* I thought with a self-satisfied huff, pleased with the turn of events.

Winston Ashford was no longer a thought, even though I could still feel his searing dark blue eyes like a burning tingle on my skin. I flicked a look at the mirror behind the bar and saw him staring at me. The desire to meet his gaze once more was immense and shocked me to my core. I had never experienced such an immediate physical attraction before, yet I still found a way to resist the urge.

Winston Ashford was hardly the only fish in the sea. Who wanted a drunk fish anyhow?

Chapter 2
Winston

I swirled the ice in my drink, glancing at my platinum tourbillon watch. It was ten minutes past eight. Too early to call it a night; too boring to stay.

My eyes flickered to the young, blonde woman with brown eyes the color of whiskey—my poison of choice, ironically. A strange feeling tickled at the back of my mind, and I couldn't shake it off.

Probably the alcohol. I smirked.

Billie Swan.

Something about her intrigued me. The way she looked, the way she smelled, the curve of her breasts through her dress, the fire in her eyes. She was beautiful and young. *Don't forget mouthy*, I reminded myself. I hated mouthy women.

Except, it seemed my cock *did* like it—all of it—which was exactly the reason why I shouldn't touch the woman *with a ten-foot pole*, as she'd so eloquently put it earlier. She was probably more of a headache than she was worth.

Most of the eyes in this bar were trained on her, devouring her. A waitress materialized next to me, offering to take another order, but I kept my eyes on Billie.

"Whiskey," I told her. "Top shelf. Make it two."

The waitress slinked away, leaving a smog of disappointment behind her. It was always the same. The moment you presented your black Amex, they hovered, hoping for attention. Nothing could repel me more.

I leaned back in my chair and watched Billie interact with her friends. She seemed to be the center of attention. She was bubbly. Too bubbly. Too young. She was nothing like the women I was regularly attracted to, but I'd be lying if I said I didn't want to bury myself inside her soft body and listen to her moan. I'd bet she was a screamer, and if she wasn't, she surely would be with me.

I licked my lips, my eyes dipping to her slender collarbone. My skin tightened at the way her creamy skin glowed with the night's humidity.

She could only be five-six, tops. Too delicate for the likes of my rough hands. I scrubbed a hand down my stubble when she turned her head, her waist-length curtain of blonde hair falling over the swelling curve of her breasts.

Very nice, but... at thirty-two, I was already jaded. All the Ashfords were. Being the oldest, Byron had done his best to shield us, but ours was an impossible burden to carry. The only one who was remotely normal was our little sister, Aurora.

Invisible walls started to close in around me, but I was used to this feeling by now. It started when my mother died. It amplified during my time with the military. And now... it was as normal as breathing. Alcohol helped. It wasn't a healthy coping mechanism, but it didn't hurt.

From the corner of my eye, I noticed the waitress placing my order down on the table—two glasses of amber-colored liquid—before disappearing again. On autopilot, I reached for the first one and downed it in one go, then went right back to ogling the vibrant blonde with honey hair and whiskey eyes.

Fuck, maybe I should have fucked her. It would have passed the time and loosened the tension I felt knitting my muscles.

No. She was the kind of trouble I didn't need. A toy whose shine would dull with the first morning light. I had met hundreds like her—hot, greedy pussies and cold, ambitious hearts. Still... Something about her had piqued my curiosity. It wasn't her beauty or her youth.

It was the forbidden images that popped into my head. Wicked and filthy. Those long legs tangled up in silk sheets. That fucking ass. That sharp mouth shaped into a red O as she carefully and deliberately opened her legs to expose her sex to me. I could almost picture it. A swollen, soaked clit that my tongue would be eager to explore. I hated to admit it, but every inch of her was perfection.

My blood rushed to my groin and I sat up straight, ignoring my body's demand that I go after her. Make her mine.

Instead, I reached for my other whiskey and downed it as she threw her head back and laughed, the melodious sound reaching me across the bar. Her group huddled closer, whispering, while Billie's gaze wandered idly around the terrace until her eyes collided with my punishing stare.

And just like the first time our eyes locked, my breath was punched out of my body. I wanted to possess her. Own her. *Fuck it all.*

I stood and made my way out of that godforsaken bar, heading to the only place in the vicinity that would quench my thirst.

An invite-only after-party was being hosted in my home. Scandalous Temptation, as it was so aptly named.

And I was about to take full advantage of all that it had to offer.

Chapter 3
Billie

"It will be freaky," Tristan claimed. "You know how much I love freaky."

I was always up for a party, but Tristan was sex on legs. The man changed women like he changed his underwear. Actually, scratch that. Probably more frequently, seeing as I'd known him to be with three different girls in a single day—more than once.

I had nothing better to do, so I'd decided to tag along. I quickly ran home, changed into a long, black silk slip dress, and paired it with strappy black heels. I twisted my hair up into a sleek chignon-style bun. A swipe of red lipstick and some smoky eyeshadow, and I was ready for some action.

I didn't need the likes of Winston Ashford to fulfill my fantasies.

Packing some cash into my Gucci clutch bag, I draped a silky wrap around my shoulders and called a cab. Twenty minutes later, I was at the entrance of a long driveway lined with torches that led to one of the oldest castles in the area. Built in the baroque period, the lavish architecture was evident everywhere you looked. It was a fresh, clear night, which meant that the white castle was lit up in the moonlight, as were the fancy, luxury vehicles snaking bumper to bumper along the driveway.

By the time I was standing on the grand stone steps, my anxiety was working overtime. There were rumors surrounding the parties that took place at this mansion, each of them more salacious than the last. I had my limits when it came to bedroom things, but curiosity—the kind that killed the cat and all that—had me swallowing my trepidation.

Now that I was here, my body seemed frozen in place as my nerves danced along my spine, causing me to hesitate. Suddenly, I wished I'd just come along with Tristan rather than insisting on going home to change. *Oh, this vanity will be the death of me one day.*

I walked up a short flight of steps to a towering set of black doors and rang the doorbell.

When they swung open, my mouth dropped. A butler—an honest-to-God butler—in a vintage uniform who looked like he was plucked straight from the set of *Downton Abbey* greeted me.

The man's eyes traveled over me, masking any expression. "*Votre invitation, mademoiselle.*"

A nervous giggle almost escaped me, but I stifled it, and a glimmer of a smile surfaced on his face. I reached for the invitation Tristan gave me and held it out for him, my hand trembling with nerves. He nodded politely and stood aside to allow me in.

Inhaling deeply, trying not to think about all the things that could go wrong, I entered the narrow space. I stifled a gasp when I turned the corner and it opened up to a room unlike anything I'd ever seen before. It was beyond opulent, and the scent of candles enveloped me. Everywhere I glanced, old money stared back. An iron chandelier holding ornate candles lit the hundreds-year-old tile, and it took everything in me not to spin around in a full circle and imagine a future here.

On the walls hung a *Madonna and Child*, which I refused to believe was an original even though my instincts warned that it was, right next to a provocative painting that portrayed an orgy. The contrast was bizarre, but something told me that was intentional.

Classical music and voices reached me, although I couldn't see anyone. I turned to the butler, who had appeared at my side.

"Thank you," I said breathlessly, suddenly feeling nervous.

"Phone?"

I blinked, confused. "Excuse me?"

"Your cell phone," the butler explained. "No electronic devices are allowed past this point."

"Oh."

A flicker of unease slithered up my spine, but I handed over my phone and received a small numbered token in return.

He pointed to the hallway to my left. "Enjoy your evening."

I took a deep breath and continued onward, following the sound of music until I arrived at the arched doorway.

The moment I stepped inside, I found myself in a kind of medieval wonderland. Hundreds of candles lit up every surface. Red rose petals adorned the marble floors.

A man in a similar getup as the butler suddenly materialized in front of me. He looked ridiculous, his belly protruding and his arms pulling at the seams of his too-tight cuffs. He stepped aside, giving me a full view of the grand ballroom behind him.

There were men and women dressed in silks and satins, laughing and drinking. Women in lavish gowns and men in black tuxedos danced and flirted. Champagne glasses stood beneath a tower of flowing bubbles that was laid out like a fountain. At the head of the room, a ten-piece orchestra performed, dressed in... Was that lingerie?

Holy fucking shit.

The energy in the room was electric, full of anticipation. A waiter carrying a tray of champagne ambled past, and I took a glass, promptly draining the tall flute. The bubbles hit the back of my throat as I returned the empty glass to the tray and snagged another two. I took in the extravagance, wide-eyed and unsure of where to go from here. The party was in full swing, and I felt like a voyeur.

I started toward the wall of open French doors leading out onto a candlelit terrace, hoping I'd spot Tristan or someone else I recognized.

Just as I started to wonder whether it was a seriously bad idea to come here, the music stopped and midnight struck, reminding me of *Cinderella*. Suddenly the cool air stilled and so did the crowd as gongs sounded in the silence.

With the last gong, some of the men and women turned to face each other. For a moment, there was nothing. Just deafening silence and the thundering of my heart. And then, they started to touch each other in a frenzy—kissing, grinding, and undressing like time was of the essence. In what felt like seconds, their clothes were pooled around their feet, leaving the women in only their heels and the men completely naked.

Holy fucking shit!

My eyes widened as I watched the naked guests reach for each other again. The orchestral music turned seductive while the writhing mass turned feverish. The music mixed with moans and groans as some started what could only be described as a performance.

A woman lowered herself onto a velvet chaise as two men poured champagne over her, licking the liquid from her ivory skin. She parted her legs, and one of them dropped to his knees, burying his face in her pussy. Behind them, a woman was bent over a piano while her partner rammed into her. In the farthest corner, a woman was draped over a low table, her mouth wrapped around one man's cock, sucking him down greedily, as another man fucked her slowly from behind.

I should have been appalled. It *was* appalling. But it was also utterly sensual. Sex and tension simmered in the air. My body tightened and hummed with desire as the wild, erotic scenes unfolded all around me.

24

I was so captured by the scene I didn't notice when someone grasped my forearm. I met the woman's gaze, beckoning me to join her and her partner. I shook my head, blushing to the roots of my scalp. I wasn't bashful by any means, but a ménage à trois was definitely not on my to-do list today. Especially if it meant two women and one guy. What was I supposed to do while the guy pleasured the other woman? Watch?

Oh hell no. Thank you very much, but I'll pass.

Deciding this wasn't my kind of party at all, or maybe fearing doing something stupid like joining in, I whirled around. Sticking to the edge of the room in search of the exit, I felt strong fingers wrap around my arm. Again.

Inwardly groaning, I yanked on my arm and turned around, coming face-to-face with none other than Winston Ashford.

My lips parted.

"What are you doing here?" I breathed in shock, suddenly feeling like I was on fire. My heart thundered against my rib cage.

"I could ask you the same thing." He sounded angry, staring at me with a furious expression that I couldn't grasp. Why was he so upset? It wasn't as if I was here for him. If anything, I came in spite of him. "What are *you* doing here?"

His eyes were blazing as I stared back. Gosh, having all this crazy sex going on around me with Winston Ashford so close was a bad idea.

My knees felt shaky, but I looked defiantly up at him. "I think it's quite clear what I'm doing here." I raised my chin, meeting him square in the eye. "I'm scanning the room to find the best group for an orgy."

Why was I such an idiot? If he insisted I join his orgy, I'd lose my mind. I didn't want anything of the kind. I was the jealous type. I liked all the attention—sexual and otherwise—on me.

He leaned against the wall casually, watching me. "Well, if you want to be fucked, I can accommodate."

I couldn't do anything but stare at him, shocked. The notes of a song I hadn't heard before barely registered through the fog in my brain, the orchestra still playing somewhere in the background.

I'll break you, just to own you.

Somehow, it felt like a warning. This man would take everything only to leave me with nothing. It'd be an unforgettable night, of that I was sure.

"What's the matter, Billie?" He waved a waiter over and picked up two glasses, handing me one. I gulped the drink down, suddenly parched. My heart hammered under my rib cage, making me feel like I'd just run a marathon. "Scared you won't be able to handle what I dish out?" he purred, lust lacing his words. The fire in his eyes could warm this entire castle or just as easily set it on fire. He downed his drink in one go too. Maybe he was as impacted as I was by the chemistry buzzing between us. "Don't you want to have your wicked way with my cock?"

The smirk on his face and his arrogant tone was all it took for my wits to come back to me. This man was giving me whiplash with his moods. "You were singing a different tune earlier. You thought I'd be too clingy, if I recall your words. I'm afraid my offer has expired, Mr. Ashford. I'd hate to be disappointed when you became the clinger."

Up this close, I could see the specks of blue and brown in his eyes and smell his cologne. Like the salty breeze rolling off a vast ocean. Fuck, it was my new favorite scent.

I folded my arms around my body and resisted the instinct to take a step forward and lean my soft body against his muscular one. Despite his asshole persona, Winston exuded an intoxicating power. Magnetic and irresistible. He reminded me of a predatory animal. Prowling and ready to pounce, full of suppressed energy.

He smiled as if he could read my thoughts. "Unless you're scared, little temptress?" he challenged, ignoring my earlier words.

Fuck, sleeping with him would be a major regret. Unless it turned out to be the most brazen, unforgettable thing I'd ever do.

This man in front of me awakened a sensation in my body that I was unfamiliar with. I watched the throbbing pulse at the base of his throat. My tongue swept across my bottom lip, yearning to lick it.

"I'm not scared," I retorted, my voice too husky for my liking. "More like repulsed. They apparently allow arrogant pricks like you to this kind of event. Regrettably, as a result, I've lost the urge to get laid."

Liar, liar, pants on fire. The chant echoed in my mind silently.

Then his arm reached around to the back of my neck and he grabbed a fistful of my hair, tilting my face up toward his.

"Wrong, my little pet," he said, and then swooped his mouth down to possess mine. He slammed me up against the wall, ravaging my lips. He tasted like whiskey and bad decisions. *Wicked.* I tried to resist. Honestly, I did. Then, I just let go and went with it. We kissed almost desperately, tongues exploring each other hungrily, hands in each other's hair and off-the-charts chemistry erupting between us.

His mouth drove me wild in a way I could never have imagined. Heat rippled through me, and every cell in my brain fizzled to a stop. My arms snaked up around his neck, my fingers tangling in his thick hair. He circled my tongue, sucking it deep into his mouth, and kissed me with such ferocity my knees went weak.

Never in my twenty-four years had I been kissed like this, and I was quickly getting drunk on the taste of this jerk that I shouldn't want.

I couldn't resist him though. There was such a thrill in his possessive hold, and something awoke in me, answering his animal call. A thrilling excitement kicked hard in the pit of my belly as I clung to him, pushing my body flush to his strong one. I soaked in his addictive heat while his hard length nudged against the softness of my stomach.

A rush of pleasure coursed through my body. Heat pooled between my legs. I had never desired anything or anyone as I did this man. I wanted—*needed*—him inside me. Now.

The kiss stopped as abruptly as it had started, with me panting and grinding myself against his thigh.

"I'm going to ruin you for all other men, Billie."

To my horror, a choked "Please" slipped through my lips.

And it was too late to take the word back. Not that I even wanted to.

Chapter 4
Billie

Much, much later, I'd remember that I never did find Tristan.

Winston took my hand and dragged me out of the ballroom and up the grand staircase that was guarded by four men. To my surprise, they let us through without a word. We walked down the long corridor before he stopped, opened a door, and led me inside.

Once inside, he turned me so I was facing him, my aching breasts pressing against his strong chest. His hot mouth found mine, kissing me roughly and with an urgent need that matched my own.

Leave me nothing when I come down.

The lyrics of the song I could still hear drummed to the beating of my wild heart. I was too far gone to fight this feeling. His large hand on the curve on my ass squeezed roughly and sent another wave of arousal to my core. At this rate, I was going to orgasm before we got to the main event.

"Are we allowed to do this here?" I panted against his lips.

"It's my place." He nipped my bottom lip. "We can do whatever we want."

Before I could say anything else, his mouth found mine again, and I was lost in the throes of desire. His hand located the zipper at the back of my dress, and soon it was a pool around my feet, leaving me in nothing but my bra, panties, and heels. He reached around me expertly and released the clasp on my bra, sending it to join the dress on the floor.

The sound of lace tearing barely registered before I found myself naked in front of him while he was still fully dressed. For a moment, he stopped and simply looked at me with an expression I swore was admiration.

Then he guided me to the gilded mirror on the wall, turning me around so we could both look at our reflection, his clothed front firmly pressed against my naked back.

"Look at you," he purred, his voice like melted chocolate. A shudder rolled down my spine as I stared at a version of myself I'd never seen before. My eyes were glazed with lust, hungry and feral. He bent his head, his teeth nibbling at my earlobe. "Your pupils are dilated. You're desperate to be fucked. Hard and rough."

I moaned, our chemistry reaching a boiling point. My chest rose and fell as we stared at each other in the mirror. He bent to bite my neck, and an electric pleasure shot through me, making my eyes widen with shock. The sensation was exquisite. Something about him and this night was making me feel reckless. Exotic. Exhilarated.

A blush stained my skin when I caught a glimpse of the two of us entangled. I couldn't tear my gaze away. His hands gliding over my body. The way he watched me like I was *everything*.

Goosebumps broke out over my skin and shudders rolled down my spine. My body drew closer to his like we were magnets. My legs parted slightly as his hands moved slower. Lower. A moan vibrated from my throat as he began to gently suck my skin, drawing more sounds out of me. His rough hands skimmed my body, leaving a burning trail everywhere he touched. I pushed my ass into his thick, hard length, yearning for it. The aching pulse between my legs throbbed in sync with my racing pulse.

He pressed a finger on my lower lip and I parted my mouth, darting my tongue out to lick it.

"Good girl." His praise did unholy things to me, and it felt liberating. "Now suck it like it's my cock."

I took his finger between my lips, sucking it gently at first and then harder with desperation and need. He turned me around, and while I sucked on his finger, he took my nipple between his teeth. With skilled precision, his hot mouth sent me into a sex-induced frenzy—one that I knew was possessing us both.

He started to unbuckle his belt, and I didn't even think. I slipped off my heels and got down on my knees, following only instinct and this throbbing desire. The hardwood cooled my heated skin as I unzipped his fly, pulled up his crisp, white shirt, and kissed his rock-solid abs. My tongue flicked out, licking the golden-brown skin all the way down to the band of his boxers.

I tugged the silky material with my teeth and pulled it down. His cock sprung free, swollen and glistening with arousal, ready for my mouth.

"Suck my cock, Billie," he murmured darkly, making my pussy throb painfully.

I used my hands to pull his boxers down his muscular thighs, then took him into my mouth. My eyes fluttered shut and a moan tore from my throat at the musky taste of him.

He drew in a sharp breath, his cock jerking in my mouth, and my insides rippled with pleasure. There was something so powerful in hearing his groans.

"Look at me," he hissed, and my heavy eyelids fluttered open, meeting the blue flames that burned in his gaze.

I relaxed my throat and took him deeper still, letting him witness every inch of his dick sliding between my lips. He pulsed in my mouth, and I should have known there was no teasing this man. He immediately took control and thrust his hips forward, jamming himself down my throat.

"Fuck yes," he groaned. His hands came to my head, his fingers tangling in my strands and keeping me in place as he started to thrust faster. "Just like that. Good girl."

God, yes.

My arousal was now soaking my inner thighs. My fingers slipped between my legs, and I couldn't resist touching myself. I rubbed my fingers over my clit, spreading my arousal, and I gasped around his cock still thrusting in and out of my mouth.

He reached down and pinched my nipple, spreading the electricity through my veins. He squeezed harder, and I mimicked the motion with my clit. My eyes rolled back as pure bliss washed over me.

"God, you're perfect," he drawled as I sucked his cock, swirling my tongue over it like it was a lollipop. I couldn't get enough of him. I was desperate for relief, craving to feel him inside me.

The sound of my slickness was as loud as our breathing. A desperate noise vibrated in the back of my throat.

"Relax your throat." I immediately obeyed. "Such a good girl. You're going to make me come." My clit throbbed in response as the wetness between my thighs ran down my legs. My body burned. My skin sang with pleasure, and I thrust my fingers inside, the need to come becoming unbearable. I pinched the swollen nub, then circled it, and my world exploded.

Sparks shot through my limbs, racing along my spine, and my pussy clenched around my fingers. I was completely drunk on him, his thrusts turning more and more urgent. With rigid muscles and a fierce groan, he threw his head back and buckled. His hot seed spurted to the back of my throat, leaving a tang on the back of my tongue as I swallowed.

My gaze locked on him, and I waited until his eyes met mine. His thumb brushed my cheek softly, almost reverently. That was all it took to get a man to worship a woman apparently.

"You were born to suck dick," he said gently, sliding his cock out of my mouth and pulling his pants back up. "Go and sit on the bed. It's time for your reward."

He didn't have to ask twice. Naked and barefoot, I scrambled to the bed, mindless to anything but having more of this feeling he was giving me.

I lowered down on the bed, my back against the abundance of pillows. He was still fully clothed and in control while I was naked and bare to him.

And yet I'd never felt more powerful.

Chapter 5
Winston

Her chest rose and fell with every breath, and she stared at me with lust and trust in those golden-brown eyes. Oh, my little pet. If she only knew how truly fucked up I was.

"I'm going to lick your pussy until you're panting with need like a bitch in heat."

She sucked in a deep breath. I couldn't keep the smile from my face as she spread her legs wider so I could see her pink pussy drip with arousal.

"Prove it," she breathed. When I went to move, she shook her head. I stopped instantly—I liked consent as much as I liked being in control. "Take off your clothes first," she demanded, her panting fucking adorable.

"Good girls don't make demands," I growled.

She chuckled softly. "Who said I was a good girl?"

"Filthy girl, then." Fuck, she was beautiful like this. The scent of her arousal made my mouth water. "How about I take care of you first? I promise you won't regret it."

She tilted her head, bringing her half-lidded, lust-filled gaze up to mine. "Okay."

I stalked her way. I put my knee on the mattress, unable to resist the temptation to ruffle her feathers a bit.

I wrenched her thighs further apart to accommodate my size. Dipping my head down, I inhaled her arousal deep into my lungs. She whimpered when I ran my nose over her clit, smearing her wetness over her inner thighs.

I dipped my head again and licked her pussy hungrily. She bucked, her back arching off the mattress with a loud moan. Reaching up, I pinched her nipple.

"Oh my God," she breathed as small shudders rippled through her body.

"Not God, my little pet." I smirked, nipping her pussy. "Winston Ashford. Remember the name because you'll be screaming it soon."

Lifting her ass with my palms, I maneuvered her as I ate her pussy like a starving man. She tasted delicious. Like summer and coconuts. I thrust my tongue inside her channel as she began to grind herself against my mouth, moaning and writhing beneath me.

Lifting my head, I smacked her pussy, partly out of anger at myself for loving the taste of her so much and partly because I suspected she liked it a bit kinky. I was proven right when she cried out and shuddered.

"What was that for?" she panted, her cheeks flushed and lips swollen.

"For being perfect," I gritted. "Now rub your pussy while I undress," I ordered. "Touch yourself while I watch."

She let out a huff.

"Making me do all the work." But her fingers were already at her clit, rubbing furiously and drinking me in as I slowly worked through each button. I undid my cufflinks and stripped out of my shirt. She sucked in a deep breath, eyes pinned on my toned abs. She rubbed her pussy faster, greedy for her own release.

"Stop," I ordered, unwilling to let her have her orgasm without me. She groaned but yanked her hand away. "Good girl."

She rolled her eyes, but there was no merit to it. She looked desperate for my cock and for her release. Her pussy was exposed, glistening with arousal and making my mouth water. I kicked off my dress shoes and peeled off my socks under her lustful gaze. She watched me, licking her lips as I discarded my pants and boxers.

"Holy shit," she whispered. She grinned, meeting my gaze. "You should really walk around naked."

I reached for a condom from the nightstand and rolled it on, reveling in the way her eyes turned a shade darker. I walked over to her and stroked my dick. Her own hand came to her clit, rubbing it shamelessly, the sound of her arousal the most erotic thing I'd ever heard. Her gaze locked on mine as she fingered herself.

"You ready for my cock, temptress?" I taunted.

"The question is, are you ready for my pussy?" she retorted, her tone sultry and so fucking sexy.

I smacked her cunt gently, and that was all it took for her to orgasm with a shudder, her flawless skin turning a deep red.

Not waiting for the wave of her orgasm to subside, I grabbed her hips and flipped her over. I gripped my throbbing cock and teased at her soaked entrance. With a hard thrust of my hips, I drove all the way into her, making her scream at the top of her lungs.

"Winston."

Fuck, I loved her voice. Even more, I loved my name on her lips.

She was so tight, strangling my cock. I slammed into her ruthlessly, nearly coming with each deep dive into her tight, hot body. She was everything I knew she would be.

Wrapping her hair around my fingers, I jerked her upright, bringing my hand around to touch her breast as I fucked her like a madman.

"Rub your pussy," I growled.

Her whimper was my answer as she started to furiously rub at her clit. I pinched her hardened nipples, and she shuddered as she came again with a cry.

Her pussy milked my cock as she climaxed, and I lost all sense of time and space. A roar ripped from me as I ground into her, burying myself deeper.

When I finally pulled out, I discarded the condom, my cum still leaking, eager for her cunt. I scooped up the cum, rubbing it over her asshole.

She whimpered, grinding her ass against my hand, which only worked to get my dick hard again. I pushed my finger into her ass, enjoying her little sounds and the way her body welcomed me. Another finger followed the first, making her squeal.

I smeared the wetness leaking from her cunt all over my dick, then removed my fingers from her hole and replaced it with the tip of my cock. She screamed as I glided in and out, barely an inch, her asshole clenching around me.

"You're doing so good, pet," I praised, my voice and muscles shaking from holding back. I didn't want to hurt her. "If you want me to stop, say the word."

"Don't you fucking dare," she panted.

I smacked her ass as I slid in further. "What did I say about making demands?"

She glanced at me over her shoulder, her blonde hair cascading wildly against the mattress. "You said good girls don't make demands. I'm not a good girl. Now give it to me."

I should have taught her a lesson and stopped then and there, but I wanted to fuck her, so I did, without remorse. And all the while, I caressed her ass and hips, her skin smooth under my rough palms. Sweat beaded down my temple and my balls tightened.

"I knew you'd be perfect," I crooned, feeling my impending orgasm. "Fucking beautiful."

She watched me through heavy eyelids over her shoulder as I fucked her. Her hand was on her pussy, rubbing her clit as she ground down, welcoming each one of my thrusts. Fuck, she might be melting for me, but I feared I was melting for her too.

She screamed my name as an orgasm washed over her. My own

release followed fast and hard, and I filled her tight ass with my cum. I leaned forward, my chest against her back, and wrapped my arms around her waist.

This woman was... dangerous for my mental state.

I gently eased out of her. Her body shuddered and she whimpered softly. I laid her on the bed and she rolled over, spent and glassy-eyed, her skin covered in a sheen of perspiration.

I walked into the bathroom and started a hot shower before I went back to the room and scooped her into my arms.

"Let's clean you up, temptress." She murmured something, eyes drooping, and I couldn't resist dropping a kiss to her puffy lips. She placed her head against my chest, clinging to me as I carried her into the walk-in shower and under the spray.

Once I set her on her feet, I took my time taking care of her. It was a fucking first for me and my movements were clumsy, but thankfully she didn't seem to notice. I washed and conditioned her hair, then I lathered down every part of her body before washing myself real quick.

I stepped out first and then turned around to wrap a towel around her. She snuggled closer, exhaling softly. As I patted her dry, she watched me with a disturbingly soft look in her eyes. Reaching for a comb, I took the next several minutes to brush her tangled mane, and with each pass through her hair, she relaxed into me more. Something about her trust hit me right in the chest.

The worst part was that I kind of liked taking care of her. Fuck, I must have drunk more than I thought.

Once we were both dry, I tucked her into bed only to see that she was already fast asleep. I turned off the lights and prepared to go find another room to crash in. I never slept in the same bed with anyone.

Yet here I was, glued to the spot and staring at her blonde hair laid out on the black silk sheet. Instead of being smart and sticking to my routine, I crawled into the bed with her, wrapped an arm around her, and buried my nose in her damp hair.

The last thought I had before I fell asleep, ready to chase my nightmares, was that I liked how her small body fit against mine.

Like the perfect jigsaw puzzle.

Chapter 6
Billie

I woke up with a soft smile and moonlight on my face.

Definitely a ten, I thought to myself through the fog of dreams and sweet exhaustion in my bones.

In all my twenty-four years, I had never experienced something so intense. My skin was cool, but my insides were still burning with the flames of passion we'd shared. I let out a giggle and muffled it into the mattress. I was completely and utterly ruined for any other man, just like he'd threatened, and I couldn't be happier about it.

Releasing another relaxed sigh, I propped myself up on my elbow and smiled at him in the darkness. His dark hair, big eyelashes, and kissable pouty lips. Out of all the men I'd met in my life, I suspected Winston Ashford would be the one to ruin me.

I lay back down, my eyes on the ceiling, and let my mind wander. Who knew an infuriating man would be so amazing in bed? Or that he would bathe me gently, wash my hair, then brush the tangles out? There were two drastically different sides to this man—the one that he portrayed himself to be, and the one that he hid.

Maybe it was that side I sensed lurking under the rough exterior that attracted me to him. Maybe it was the reason the air had sizzled around me when I first saw him. I rolled onto my side, smiling into my pillow.

I think I might have finally found my ten.

Silence bled into the dark night, and I basked in it until a tortured sound wrenched the air around me.

I startled and found Winston to my left, his body thrashing violently. His muscles were coiled tight, his skin slick with sweat. He was asleep, shuddering in the grip of what must be a nightmare as he mumbled words I couldn't decipher.

The blanket pooled around his waist, leaving his chest exposed.

"Winston?" I whispered, reaching to run my fingers down his cheek, trying to soothe him.

It seemed to work, because he instantly stilled. I let my hand trail down, stroking his strong shoulders and chest. He really was gorgeous. My eyes traveled down his chiseled body, over his abs, and to the trail of dark hair that disappeared beneath the covers.

I was tempted to pull it back and—

His hand shot to my neck and tightened. He opened his eyes, something in their blue depths terrifying, and I reached up to claw at his bronze skin. I attempted to scream, but my vocal cords kept failing me.

Horror gripped me as I stared into his blank eyes that seemed to be captured in their own hell. So much for the best sex of my life. This man had some serious issues.

There was no way I could be allowed to die after such an incredible night. After experiencing all of those mind-blowing orgasms. Destiny wouldn't be so cruel, would it?

Images of my heartbroken father after losing Maman flashed before my eyes. His grief. His struggle to carry on without the love of his life. *Yeah, destiny would be so cruel.*

Well, fuck destiny. I wouldn't succumb to it like this. I dug my fingers into his wrists, hoping at least pain would get through to him and wake him the fuck up.

"W-Win—"

He blinked once, then again, as he seemed to take in the situation. A different type of horror transformed his expression. He released me like he had been burned, lunging away from me and out of the bed with a growl that seemingly shook the entire room and rattled my teeth.

"Fuck," he spat as I started coughing, my throat burning as I inhaled deeply, desperate for oxygen. "I'm... shit... I'm sorry."

"What the fuck, Win?" I croaked, still spitting and coughing.

"I thought... Goddammit." He reached out, brushing his knuckles against my cheek, but I flinched, reeling from his touch. "Did I hurt you?" His voice was grated, his expression pained. He shuddered. "I never wanted to hurt you."

Except, he did. He all but choked the living daylights out of me. "What happened?" I rasped, my voice sounding like I smoked a pack of cigarettes a day.

I watched in amazement as that familiar mask of indifference slid over his features. "That's none of your business," he stated coldly.

I shook my head in amazement, my eyes wide with shock as we stared at each other. His thick dark hair was messy, his body a sculpted perfection. Broad shoulders, perfect posture, a jawline that could cut glass, tan skin. My eyes roamed up and down his body as I drank him in. How could someone so gorgeous be this twisted up?

"You owe me a fucking explanation," I hissed. "You nearly choked me to death."

A muscle in his jaw flexed, and I got a sense his control was hanging by a thread. It permeated the air, and I could practically taste it on my tongue. Then he rolled his lips. Fury oozed out of him, and he glared at me with such disdain I found myself reeling backward.

"You got your fuck, now get the fuck out."

My mouth just about dropped. It took all of my self-restraint not to stomp over to him and punch his beautiful face. Thankfully, I'd never been a violent person, and I wasn't about to change that now.

So, with a deep exhale, I climbed out of bed and threw on a robe.

Our clothes were strewn all over the floor, and I rushed to collect my things.

"Fuck this shit," I muttered under my breath while getting dressed. "I'm outta here. I don't have a death wish."

What a fucking scam! This douche who fucked like a ten was mentally a negative five.

In less than thirty seconds, I was out of the bedroom and making my way down the dark hallway. As I hurried out of there like the devil was on my heels, the grandeur of the castle mocked my short-lived affair. My rushed steps echoed against the perfectly polished marble hallway, stopping when I caught sight of the white lilies sitting next to a glass display.

My cell phone sat on it, and my cheeks instantly flamed with realization that the butler knew exactly where I'd ended up. Reaching for my phone, I flicked a curious look over at the display. It was the kind I'd expect to see at the Smithsonian, not here.

Just as I was about to leave, understanding sunk in. The Harry Winston necklace. The diamonds, set in a way to look like vines covered in ice, swathed the necklace until it reached a single stunning emerald. It was even more intricate than in the books I'd studied for my fashion design classes. It was this exact piece that inspired my venture into the world of jewelry design. It was mesmerizing, its sparkle capturing all my attention, sending the events of the night and the world itself fading into the background.

The story behind this piece was as enticing as the Hope Diamond's. Harry Winston designed it for the Queen of England, but he couldn't bear to let it go, so he made another piece for her while holding on to this one.

Diamonds were my passion. Yes, I could create dresses, but when it came to diamonds, it was like making love to your craft. The feeling was indescribable. It was what I saw for my future.

Heck, maybe I'd become the next Harry Winston, but with a much cooler name. A little chortle left me when the moonlight caught on the necklace. My eyebrows scrunched as I studied it. Were there rubies in there too?

I couldn't remember any mention of rubies from my studies. I leaned in closer, my hand hesitantly reaching out, and an incredulous breath left me. Holy fucking shit. The glass display pressed open. There was nothing keeping this multimillion-dollar piece protected. Winston Ashford had to be an *idiot* to be so careless with it. It was the only explanation.

My heart thundered as my fingers ghosted the piece, but then I thought better of it. Maybe it had sensors and it'd set off alarms. As I got even closer, I noted a clear film of some sort covering the stones. The light from the moon shone at a slightly different angle, and my heart froze.

Those weren't rubies. That was fucking blood.

I whipped my head around, almost expecting someone to appear behind me and whack me upside the head until my own blood splattered all over the jewelry.

I took a step backward, then another, before I bolted out of there.

Chapter 7
Winston

I continued to stand there, staring at the door long after she was gone, my jaw clenched and fists balled. Through the fog of memories that tried to break through, I heard the gong of the grandfather clock. One. Two. Three a.m. It was the longest I'd slept in years.

Finally, I closed my eyes at the memories invading my mind, hoping to shut them out completely. But I knew it was for naught. They were tattooed onto every one of my brain cells. And so, I took a deep breath and resigned myself to another night of hell.

We'd gone door to door for days, exhausted and hungry, searching for arms dealers that were spotted in this area. Another terrorist organization. Each deployment was the same. Find the bad guys. Cut the head of the snake. Move on.

But unless we found this group of mercenaries, we'd never be given our next mission. And I was so fucking ready to move on to another location. Hopefully somewhere warm with a beach, sand, and some booze. I was done with the desert and mountains for the rest of my life. The dust was stuck in my lungs, and most days, it was a fucking nightmare.

I knew my father had a hand in my deployments. He always ensured each location was worse than the last, so I wasn't holding my breath for the beach. However, my term was nearing its end, and I planned on getting out.

Assuming this other unit showed up and didn't leave us all here to die.

I was too distracted, dreaming of a better life and a cold beer, when I opened the door leading into an abandoned tunnel. Situated in the mountain range on the outskirts of Afghanistan, our intel told us it had once served as a settlement for displaced civilians.

"Winston—no—"

My buddy Leif's voice came just as an explosion detonated and threw me against the wall. I could do nothing but lie back and take stock of my injuries, the adrenaline already coursing through me and urging me to make a move. Every inch of my body howled in pain as I sat up, my eyes blinking to focus on the chaos around me. Rubble rained down in a storm of dust and sand and stone. My ears buzzed as screams echoed through the cavernous space. My fellow marines, my brothers, were trapped below, sprawled across the jagged pieces of mountainous debris.

Leif's face—fuck, was that his face? It couldn't be. I blinked again, but I was too dizzy, my head spinning. I couldn't shake off the impact to the back of my skull from when I was thrown. The world shifted around me, left, right, and back again as I fought to gain my bearings.

Ignoring it all, I struggled to stand and move on unstable feet. One step. Another. I needed to get to my men. I only made it a few more steps before I was hit again. The force of the blow knocked me out for who knew how long, the jagged mountain wall scraping at my flesh. I came to and felt the burning pain start to spread, but it was as if it was all happening to someone else. Folded over, I tucked my head between my hands, trying to make sense of the turmoil around me.

Grasp the situation so we could get out of this alive.

Something slammed into my head. Again. The hard plastic stock of an assault rifle, delivering blow after blow to my body. The blows *didn't let up as I heard someone calling my name, but I was too disoriented to respond. I needed to clear my head. I blinked against the ringing in my ears, trying frantically to clear my vision as grunts of pain and a language I couldn't translate echoed through the tunnel.*

I spotted Leif again. Instead of getting up, I used my arms and upper torso to drag my aching and damaged body across the floor.

Something hit me again, making my skull throb. I felt rage bubble inside me. I lifted my head, trying to see my attacker. Three figures came into focus. Their faces were in black masks, nothing but their brown eyes peering down at me.

A sound filtered through my brain, and I realized they were laughing. One of them danced around us, clapping his hands and hopping from one foot to the other over and around my downed men. A round of "Opa" sounded from him and his men, the jovial sound a stark contrast to the destruction around us.

If he said "Opa" one more time, I'd have to shoot him. Or myself, I thought darkly. The whole thing seemed out of place in this desert, but who the hell knew where these arms dealers were from.

As I attempted to make my way across the dirt floor to make it to one of my men, a hand grabbed me by the collar. In the next second, I was ripped from the floor and thrown back against the wall. This motherfucking wall.

I squeezed my eyes shut against the pressure in my temples and concentrated, thinking back to my training. Our lives would depend on it. My gaze flicked to where Leif was lying moments ago—or maybe hours ago—but he wasn't there.

With considerable effort, I shifted my head and found him on the opposite side of the dark space. One of the fuckers was kicking him as he continued dancing. It was enough to shoot a deadly rage through me. It fortified me with enough energy to force me upright.

Gunshots filtered throughout the cave, and I knew our backup was close. I just had to kill these fuckers and get us out of here, then I could finally pass out. I gasped as a bullet lodged itself into my shoulder, the force of it making me see stars.

The assholes were moving backward. Trying to get away from me. Fucking cowards. I didn't think, only acted on the instinct drilled into me.

I blinked up at their forms blurring at the edges. My hearing was still distorted, but I saw one of the men's mouths moving. I lunged at one and grabbed his neck, crunching his bones between my fingers. His screams pierced through the ringing in my ears.

It brought the world into focus. And my one purpose: to live and get the fuck out of this shithole.

Regaining my balance, I swiveled and scanned the tunnel. My eyes locked on Leif's slumped form, his face almost unrecognizable.

The second man dropped his gun and stopped dancing. I reached for my own rifle, now just a few steps from where I stood. He kept screaming, scrambling back across the floor with his arms. I aimed and shot him point-blank in the forehead.

The third pointed a gun at my face, and on instinct, I reached for his neck before he could pull the trigger. Shooting someone was impersonal. Killing them with your bare hands, watching the life leave their eyes... That stained your soul. It was something you could never forget. The final body fell with a thump.

I didn't waste my time pondering what I'd just done. Instead, I dragged myself to Leif.

"I thought you'd taken a nap." He coughed, choking on his blood, and I fell to my knees to push him sideways, trying to clear his airways.

"Maybe tomorrow."

He nodded with a slump of his shoulders. "Yeah, maybe tomorrow."

Because nobody woke up from naps in this hellhole.

I turned over in my bed for the hundredth time, wiping my eyes with the back of my hand, hoping to erase the memories right along with my tears. No such luck. That kind of shit followed you. Mistakes. Death. Survivors. Scars—the visible and invisible ones. Leif could attest to it, hiding from the world in his Scottish castle.

The ironic part was that I joined the military to escape my father and the blood staining his and my own hands. Only to end up in the throes of hell.

I made my way to the minibar in my bedroom and poured myself a drink. The first of many that would help me forget the night.

Including how I'd hurt the only woman I'd slept peacefully next to for the first time in years.

Chapter 8
Billie

I strolled along Villefranche-sur-Mer on the French Riviera with Violet Freud, one of my oldest friends, and tried not to roll my eyes at the obnoxious yachts peppering the coastline. It was a mecca for rich, famous, and entitled pricks, and I refused to let them see me gawk at their gaudy eyesores.

"I swear to God," I ranted, "I want to murder that fucker. Dismissing me like that." After I went home, took a shower, and forced myself to down a cup of coffee, I had to find someone to air my grievances to. Nobody was home, so I called my friend who happened to be here vacationing with her family.

Violet flicked me a glance as she twisted the pendant hanging off her necklace. An odd symbol, settled in the mouth of a skull. It was the only piece of evidence she had that related to her sister's death, and she'd never been able to part with it. She was convinced it would lead her to her sister's killer.

"You're not the killer type," she said flatly, her lips curving into a half-smile.

I rolled my eyes. "Maybe I'll become one. Then you can study me for your doctorate thesis. See? Two for one."

53

Her perfectly proportionate face lit up with amusement. "I'd rather it not be you I study." We walked down the crowded pier, remaining silent for another hundred yards or so. "What attracted you to this guy anyhow? I know you're been having a bit of a dry spell, but you *rarely* give it up on the first night."

My eyes drifted over the azure horizon. It was a good question, not that I should be surprised. Violet had a knack for getting to the root of things, always eager to understand what made people tick.

I'd been pouting to her for the past two hours. Normally, I would have poured my heart out to Odette, but she had a morning shift at the hospital. There was no way that I could keep all this bottled in until she was free.

"Because he was the best-looking man I've ever laid my eyes on. And maybe I just wanted to be a bad girl."

She chuckled. "As if you're a good girl any other time."

Her tone was sarcastic, but I didn't mind. That was who she was. When her sister died, she changed. Gone was the sweet Violet who wanted to save the world, and in her place came someone determined to make the people who hurt her pay.

This time I grinned too. "Well, he looked like he knew his way around a good time. How in the fuck was I supposed to know he carried so much baggage and would attempt to kill me in his sleep?"

She rolled her eyes. "Well, you did mention he was a dick when you talked to him," she pointed out. "And then you thought he might have a drinking problem."

I tucked my hair behind my ear. "Truthfully, I'm not sure. I just wanted to get a reaction out of him."

"Mature." She gestured to our favorite little café by the sea. "Are we going to grab a cappuccino? It might be the only thing that could make this day better."

Poor Violet. I made her come out and walk with me so I could burn all this frustration and vent about my night from hell following the best sex of my life. It was the least I could do.

I sighed. "Yeah, I guess."

"And you're paying," she remarked wryly.

I waved my hand. "Of course, of course. After all, you're trying to give me a free therapy session. Hey, wait a minute, maybe *you* should pay since I'm offering you real-world experience for your future career."

She screwed up her face. "I won't be counseling couples or fucked-up love affairs."

We made our way into the café and took the table closest to the water. The waiter came over and took our orders, and we sat in companionable silence until my cappuccino and Violet's macchiato arrived.

From the corner of my eye, I noticed a familiar figure lounging on a yacht tied to the nearest jetty, and I shaded my eyes from the sun to get a better look.

What the fuck?

Tall frame. Amazing build. His dark hair was mussed to perfection, and he looked like he just stepped off a runway, wearing clothing from this season's Zimmermann collection. I'd recognize the brand anywhere. Bermuda shorts, polo shirt, and deck shoes.

His gaze met mine and he twisted his mouth into a bored-looking smile. He began to disembark his boat, heading straight for us.

"Oh my God," I hissed through my teeth. "Don't look, but the prick is coming."

Of course she looked, and her brow shot up, unimpressed. "Ah, speak of the devil."

"Hello, Billie." He flashed a smile, studying me like I was just another acquaintance and not someone he had fucked senseless and then tried to choke last night.

"Hi and bye." *Fucker.*

Winston's jaw flexed, and he put his weight onto his back foot. What the hell did he expect? For me to fall into his arms? In his damned dreams.

He turned his attention to Violet. "And you are?"

Violet smiled like the Cheshire Cat. "Her therapist. She had a disappointing night, something about a dick not functioning, so we're having an emergency session." I wished the earth would swallow me whole. Violet rarely exercised humor. Why, of all the fucking times, was she doing it now? "Ah, that's right. Now I remember. Erectile dysfunction." She continued with her lies. "Right, Billie?"

Winston's eyes landed on me and he rolled his lips, fury oozing out of him. I could tell him my friend was joking, but there was no point. He was a douche, and he owed me an apology first.

I sighed heavily. "That's right. The guy didn't even know where to stick his limp dick either."

He glared at me, gave me a once-over, and then smirked. "I'm pretty sure he knew where to put it, but you couldn't figure out what to do with it."

Oh. He. Did. Not.

This man was arrogance personified. He gave his dick too much credit, and I'd love nothing more than to burst his bubble. I couldn't lie to save my life though, soo I remained quiet.

"What?" he challenged. "Nothing to say?"

I shrugged, taking a sip of my cappuccino before responding. "Oh, I have plenty to say, but I'm not in the mood to waste my breath." I locked eyes with him so he'd see how annoyed I was. "Also, you're ruining my view, so please find someone else to bother with your puny limp dick. Unless..." He cocked a brow, waiting for me to continue. "Unless you have something to say to me."

My parents taught me that anything could be mended with the right apology as long as there wasn't repetition of the same mistake. I'd be willing to give him another shot.

"Have a nice life, Billie."

I smiled, not at all surprised that he'd dismissed my offer. "Thank you, I will. Goodbye."

Winston stormed back onto his luxury yacht while Violet and I stared after him.

"Interesting," Violet remarked.

"What's interesting?"

She flashed me a smile. "He likes you."

I gasped, widening my eyes. "You can't be serious."

She smirked as if it were obvious. "Call it my professional diagnosis, but it's best you stay away from him."

Unfortunately, all my brain retained was *He likes you.*

Chapter 9
Winston

The concept of a "normal" family had been nonexistent since my mother's death. Losing Kingston had only sealed that fate. My father's shady deals made us a target, and Kingston ended up paying for it the most, although it left an invisible mark on all of us.

Now, my brothers and baby sister were all that mattered. None of us liked living under our father's thumb. It wasn't a safe place. It was a diplomatic battlefield full of secrets ready to blow.

So when he made his appearance this morning with an air of confidence and smugness, my stomach coiled. I instantly regretted drowning my sorrows in alcohol after the incident with Billie because I knew I'd need all my conniving wits.

Leaning back, I rolled a cigarette between my fingers, then put it between my lips and lit it. A habit that started after my mother's death. I only smoked when I was unsettled or too pissed off to think straight. Both only happened when Father was around. A cherry glowed at the end, just like this hatred I had for this man. It was strong enough that I had to choke it down.

Father's eyes shone with disdain, and his curled lips indicated he'd either just destroyed someone or he was about to. Maybe both.

His arrogant nose was unfortunately a physical feature I'd inherited from the man, and as he stood there and wrinkled it in my direction, I wished I could rid myself of the familiarity. That and my eye color.

I looked away from my old man's face and prayed for his disappearance from my life. It was so fucking tempting to make it a reality.

Standing abruptly from my chaise lounge, I flicked my cigarette and dusted the nonexistent wrinkles from my shorts. I made my way to the bar on Byron's yacht, taking my time pouring myself another drink despite the sickening feeling in my stomach.

"To what do I owe this unpleasant visit, Senator?" I finally asked.

"Aren't you going to offer your old man a drink?"

"No."

"You always have been an insolent little fucker," he sputtered, glaring at me like he'd love nothing more than to murder me.

"Kind of a requirement to be in this family."

I didn't look at him, but I could feel the heat of his glare at the back of my neck. "Maybe I'll marry you off before your brother."

My grip on the glass tightened, but I opted not to acknowledge him as I made my way back to the same chair. It gave me an unobstructed view of Billie, who was still sitting at the café. If I was smart, I'd draw the blinds.

"You've been avoiding me, son." His words, specifically the sneering way he said "son," grated on me, especially as I sensed the holier-than-thou staredown incoming. "You and your brothers haven't seen me in a year. Don't you fucking wonder if your father's alive?" That was rich, coming from the man whose own son was missing, not to mention the fact that he wouldn't bother to use his many resources to locate him.

I turned my head. "Not really." Our gazes clashed like glaciers. "I see you on the news way too often as it is. It crushes the tiny flicker of hope at seeing your cold, dead body turn up."

"You fucking—" He lifted his hand off his armrest as if he was going to smack me. Something he used to do to our mother, to my brothers and me too, until we became too big and strong for him. I'd wondered if he still had the same habit, and now I knew he did. Probably smacked around the whores he liked to bang. I stared right at that hand, daring him to hit me.

"Full disclosure," I drawled, my voice calm while my insides raged. "Touch me and I'll return the favor."

I fucking dare you.

He lowered his hand back down, knowing I didn't make empty threats. The last time he hit me, I was sixteen. The day that our little brother was kidnapped. The day that everything went to hell.

It was never supposed to happen. Father's shady dealings made our family a target in the underworld, and we all paid for it. Mother. Kingston. Our baby sister, who would cry herself to sleep for years to come and who blamed herself for our brother being taken.

We all paid for it, one way or another.

I shot Father a glare full of hate, wanting him to see it. Drown in it. There was nothing that'd give me greater pleasure than ending his life. I'd kill him, cut up his body, and bury it where nobody would ever find him.

It was something we should have done a long time ago, but we tried hard not to cross that line. It was what set us apart from Ma's relatives, the DiLustros. But that line was getting blurrier with each passing day.

He cleared his throat nervously, smoothing his expensive tie. I couldn't help but snicker at his desperate attempt to look like an honest gentleman. He was anything but, and you'd have to be blind not to see it.

"What?" he snapped, glaring at me with so much hate it warmed my black heart.

"Just admiring your tie, that's all," I drawled, shrugging. "Wondering how much it cost my brothers and me."

Senator Ashford was like a leech, and he sucked not only the blood from his sons, but also our money.

He smoothed his tie again. "I wonder what your brothers would say if they knew your part in their mother's death."

Their mother. He fucking loved torturing me, hanging that noose around my neck, ready to snap it with his truths. The woman gave birth to me too. She was my mother too.

But I kept my expression impassive as I locked eyes with him. After all, I'd had years to perfect it.

"You can give it a try and tell them," I sneered. Showing fear to Senator Ashford was like bleeding in front of a shark. Except a shark would chew you to pieces just for fun before he spit you out. My father and I both knew he wouldn't do that, not for as long as he needed money or leverage.

He waved his hand as if that was no longer important.

"Enough about that nonsense. As my second-eldest son, it's your duty to marry Nicki Popova."

"I don't eat leftovers," I drawled.

Nicki Popova was a chick my brother had a short fling with. Father latched on to it, hoping for her father's political support, and had been shoving Nicki down Byron's throat at every turn. Unfortunately, she just sealed her fate when she slipped drugs into his drink and had him suffer burns on his already fucked-up back.

It pissed my big brother off, and now he was lost to Nicki forever. Apparently my father had seen it too.

"That's such an honor," I said, my voice laced with sarcasm but also cold dread. I could still remember my parents' marriage. There was no way anyone would sign up for that hell. "But I'm going to have to pass."

My gaze darted back to the window to find Billie throwing her head back and laughing at something her friend said.

"Winston." He banged his hand on the armrest and rose to his full height, probably hoping to look intimidating. Instead, he stunk of desperation. "I need her old man's support."

"Thanks for letting me know." My eyes never wavered from Billie's form. What was she laughing about? I wanted to know what made that woman happy. I already knew how to piss her off. But fuck, I never thought someone like her would be so damn obedient in bed. The way she writhed underneath me, moaning and begging for more. "I'll let you know when I find any fucks to give."

Once upon a time, my father was intimidating. Now, I was bigger and stronger than him. I met his eyes with a bored expression while a dark shadow fell over his features, mingled with a putrid scent of menace.

"You will marry Nicki Popova." I stared him in the eye, refusing to let him get to me. He'd done that enough to last me a lifetime. I'd never let him have power over me again.

"Are you done? Because I have a busy day ahead of me." Both of us knew it was a lie, but it only made it sweeter.

"One last chance, Winston."

"I'm not marrying Nicki. Her pussy doesn't suit me. But hey, if you want her as part of the Ashford legacy, be my guest and marry her yourself. I've heard you don't mind sloppy seconds."

His face turned a deep shade of red, but my expression didn't change and neither did my demeanor. Although I knew what my father's next words would be.

He leaned forward and snarled.

"Then I'll tell your brothers your part in your mother's death." And there it was. It always circled back to that. "Marry her willingly—"

Or else hung in the air.

I leaned back in my chair and smiled.

"Marrying Nicki Popova would be a dream come true." I was lying and we both knew it. "Except, I'm already married," I drawled, grinning like a fool. Father reeled back, surprise washing over him. Fuck, what I wouldn't give to capture that expression on his face. "I'm afraid you only have one son left to pair with the charming whore."

Game, set, match, motherfucker. Now I'd just have to find a bride. And quickly.

"When? Who? Where?" he demanded, his face turning a deep shade of red.

"That's for me to know and for you to butt out of," I said coldly, my expression not changing. Even if I had a wife, I'd keep her away from this fucking bastard. He destroyed everything and everyone in his life.

"You're my *son*," he spat. I leaned farther back in my seat and looked out the window, but I could feel the heat of his glare burning a hole in the side of my head. "You think you have the upper hand, but I'll learn her name and I'll get rid of whoever pussy-whipped you."

He gritted out the words in his condescending tone, the one he used to use whenever he planned to teach me a *lesson.*

I turned my eyes his way. "You'll never get rid of this one." Because she didn't even exist. But that was just a tiny obstacle.

The vein was about to pop out of his temple. Good, I got to him. Let him taste some of his own medicine.

"The Popov family is a prominent one, and I owe—" he stumbled, surprising me by the way his face paled. He was scared. Jesus Christ, maybe I should tip off Nicki's father.

"Again, why don't *you* marry into that family?" I snickered. "Any one of them. Take your pick, I hear you swing both ways."

"You'll regret this," he hissed. "I don't forgive easily."

He turned on his heel and bolted from the room. I watched him disembark the yacht with his tail between his legs.

And they say blood is thicker than water.

Chapter 10
Billie

Feeling better after last night's mind-blowing sex—which I feigned forgetting—and Violet's pep talk, I made my way to The Swan Clinic.

It was almost dinnertime, and I wanted to spend it with my family. In order to do that, I'd have to drag my two family members out of there. My sister and dad practically lived in that building. It was a good thing that Odette studied in the States—Stanford proud—otherwise, she'd be running here every chance she got.

As I made my way through the property, my eyes darted left and right, and I frowned. The path along the shoreline that led to the hill where the hospital sat—a luxury castello, once upon a time—was lined with vehicles of all sorts. Ambulances. SUVs. Moving trucks.

"What's going on here?" I asked the nurse standing on the side.

She shrugged. "Moving patients."

I shot her an annoyed look when she didn't elaborate, my foot tapping impatiently. "Why?"

"The hospital's shutting down."

What? My brows scrunched. She must not know what she was

talking about, but obviously she couldn't answer my questions, so I went in search of my family.

Turning the corner, I spotted her. Crisp white uniform. Her hair pulled up in a ponytail. No makeup. She was directing orders in French to nurses and doctors, but her face was ghostly pale. Dread pooled in my stomach as I rushed to her.

There were people moving about everywhere, but nobody spared me a glance. Odette spotted me and I froze, the look in her eyes catching me off guard.

She left the group and made her way to me, hugging me tightly.

I swallowed a lump in my throat, fear clutching my heart with invisible barbwire.

"What happened?" My voice sounded off even to me, distorted by the heartbeat that drummed in my ears.

"We lost the hospital," she whispered. I blinked in confusion while my heart processed the words, beating in my throat and suffocating me with each breath. "The bank's taking the building."

She gripped her hair almost as if she wanted to pull it out of her tightly wrapped ponytail. Shock washed over me while I stared at her, trying to process her words.

"I don't understand," I finally said.

"It's all my fault." She hugged me, and it was then that I felt the trembling of her body. She was shaken to her core. She and Dad lived and breathed this place.

"How can it be your fault?" I rasped, a feeling of dread inching over my skin. "How much do we owe?"

She shook her head, her face still buried in my shoulder. "Millions. I don't know."

"Wh-what?" My voice cracked as my heart hammered against my ribs, bruising them with every beat.

"We're broke, Billie. There's no more hospital."

I licked my lips, feeling like I might start hyperventilating. "And our house?"

My thoughts swirled as I attempted to come up with options. Odette shook her head.

"That's safe. Dad wants us to have a roof over our heads."

My sister's anguished eyes locked with mine. Utter silence enveloped us, and each breath I pulled in crippled me another notch. The hospital was Dad's safe haven. I feared he'd fall apart without it. The panic swam through me, drowning in my eyes.

I couldn't lose him too.

"How much money do we need?" I asked again.

She pulled away slightly. "I don't know," she rasped. "I offered to quit med school, but he said it's too late. I even thought maybe we could sell Maman's jewelry, but he said it wouldn't make a dent."

My mind immediately drifted to the diamonds I'd seen at Winston's castle. Just sitting there, discarded. Collecting dust...

What if—

No, not an option. If I got caught, I'd be bringing more trouble to our doorstep. Yet... if I didn't get caught, I'd be able to take care of Dad and Odette.

And just like that, my mind was made up.

"Don't worry, *soeur*," I murmured, pulling her back into my embrace. "Everything will work out."

I had a plan.

Dressed in a skintight black suit like Catherine Zeta-Jones in *Entrapment*, I made my way through the property. A sense of foreboding lingered somewhere in the pit of my stomach, and alarms warned that I was about to do something I could never come back from.

I gave my head a subtle shake. My mood was gloomy, and pressure weighed heavily on my mind. *Yes, that's it.* People engaged in criminal activity every day, and I couldn't just sit tight and do nothing while Odette and Dad carried everything on their shoulders.

After our evening that resembled a funeral more than a family dinner, I waited for Odette and Dad to fall asleep before sneaking out. In less than ten minutes, I was back at the same place as the night before. A true déjà vu moment.

I'd taken a taxi, grateful the man wasn't interested in small talk, and requested he drop me off before we reached the laneway so I wouldn't be spotted from the property. Once I stepped onto the gravel though, I watched his taillights fade away and fought the urge in the pit of my stomach to start running after him. This place was fancy, but enveloped in darkness, it was creepy as fuck—just like its owner.

I got moving until I found a section in the fence that looked easy enough to jump. I secured my backpack on my shoulders and started climbing.

"Easy-peasy," I whispered to myself as I made the trek across the lawn and crept into the house.

No guards. No alarms. Silent as the night before Christmas. As whispers from the branches in the wind danced through my brain, I narrowed my eyes and kept my footsteps silent.

Everything in this place screamed old money. From the heavy drapes, gold-framed artwork that I didn't understand, and stone sconces lining the walls. Again, creepy as fuck.

I slipped off my shoes, my feet soundless against the marble stairs, and followed the path to... Bingo.

The jewelry display was in the same spot, and the necklace glimmered, just waiting to solve my family's financial problems.

Stealing is bad, Billie. I could almost hear Maman's voice, but I ignored it. There was no other way to come up with the money. Obviously this guy didn't need the money with the way he left something so valuable just lying around, begging to be taken.

I carefully leaned in for it, holding my breath. *There.* My fingertips met the cool surface. It wasn't until I wrapped my fingers around it and lifted it that my breath swished out of my lungs with a soft exhale. No alarm.

I couldn't fucking believe it. A twenty-million-dollar necklace with nothing to keep it safe from the hands of a regular old amateur burglar.

"I've gotcha." My blood sang with the promise of all my problems evaporating. My chest tightened at the memory of anguish on my father's and sister's faces. They lived and breathed medicine. That hospital was their life.

With the cool weight resting in my palm, I swiftly turned to leave when a voice stopped me.

"Hello, Billie."

My feet froze, and so did time. My heart sped into dangerous territory as my entire life flashed in front of my eyes, ending with me in a striped suit. *God, anything but this. Please.*

A soft snicker pulled me out of my panic. "What? Aren't you going to face the man you're stealing from?"

Closing my eyes for a moment, I gathered all the strength I didn't have and turned on my heel, coming face-to-face with the man who was as beautiful as he was damaged. His bright blue eyes shone even in the darkness, slamming into my chest with a violence that threatened to end me.

I opened my mouth, but my vocal cords refused to work.

So I swallowed and tried again, only to come up with, "What are you doing here?"

Gosh, of all the things to say.

A smirk curved the corner of his lips. Arrogant. Maybe even cruel. "I should be asking you that question."

Well, duh. "As if I would answer it," I scoffed, too brave for my own good.

"Don't worry. If I really wanted to, I'd have no trouble getting the information. You'd be screaming it while I fucked every little secret out of you, my little thief." He took a step forward, invading my space. "Or you could save us all the time and tell me what you're up to."

Well, now that he made it sound so tempting... I shook my head, inwardly scolding myself and this insatiable lust.

And while my mind frantically worked to come up with something—anything *other* than begging him to fuck me—Winston Ashford seemed to be having the time of his life, studying me with an expression that told me I was in trouble.

Deep trouble.

Chapter 11
Winston

When the alarm sounded on my phone, signaling an intruder, she'd been the last person I expected to see.

Fuck, why did I come back here? It was only last night that I fucked the wild temptress in that godforsaken room, then spent the night riddled with memories.

I was stunned to see the same woman I had been thinking of only moments before slinking her way toward my home.

The security team had chimed in and alerted me to her presence. This property was secured by a team year-round, and I'd never had an issue with nosy tourists or otherwise before. So, I warned my men not to touch the woman who crept along the wall just outside the door, curious to watch it play out. While her suit was dark and blended with the shadows, it was her golden locks that gave her away.

I'd watched her slip her flats off in order to keep her footsteps silent, her hair falling like a curtain over her face and giving me no option but to watch her ass move in that tight suit. She didn't even need to be in the same room for the air to crackle in anticipation, for my cock to throb in my pants.

There was no denying it, I wanted more of her.

That was when the idea struck.

I followed her movements, watching as she stopped in front of my mother's Harry Winston necklace. She'd stood still for several heartbeats as my own thundered in my chest.

By the time she leaned in for it, I was out of my room and down the hallway.

I hadn't approached her immediately, watching her from the shadows as she seemed to almost brace herself. It struck me again that Billie Swan had a timeless figure, with curves in just the right places.

She was beautiful. Too beautiful.

The kind of beauty that got men like me in trouble. Because... I wanted to fuck her again. There she was, about to steal from me like the cat burglar, and yet my dick ached, eager to bend her over and fuck her senseless again.

Before this night was over, I'd have her bouncing on my dick, so help me God.

That woman hadn't left my mind since she'd scurried from my room less than twenty-four hours ago. I rubbed one out in the shower this morning with images of her body writhing underneath me, her moans echoing in my brain.

There were so many ways I wanted to fuck her. I wanted her to forget anyone who'd come before me. I'd make sure she'd never want anyone but me.

Wait. What? I pushed my hand through my hair. Jesus, I *never* obsessed over women. I never even fucked the same woman twice. There was plenty of pussy around to fuck.

My attention refocused on the beauty in front of me and the necklace she now clutched in her hands.

"Put it back," I ordered, my tone icy.

Her grip on the diamonds tightened and something flared in her light brown eyes, but eventually she scowled and did as I said. To my surprise, she laid it back gently rather than throwing it into the case.

"If you don't want it stolen, you should keep it somewhere more secure."

"I do." Her brow lifted in challenge but she remained quiet. "Now, come with me."

She shook her head, sending her hair falling in bouncy waves over one shoulder. "I'd rather just go…"

"I wasn't asking, Billie. Move." She hesitated, standing there stubbornly. "Listen to me before you really piss me off."

Women usually fell all over me and lived to please me in hopes of becoming part of the Ashford world. It was interesting—and fascinating—to see a different response. Yes, Billie wanted me sexually. She didn't even try to hide that yesterday. But that was where her interest started and stopped.

She should turn me off completely. She was nothing like who I typically went for, and that made her perfect for my plan.

I crooked my finger and led her to where I first tasted this woman. The best fucking thing I'd ever had.

With enough attitude to make my cock twitch at the thought of fucking the fire out of her, she stomped, following behind me.

Once in the bedroom, I held the door open, and she passed by me with a huff.

"Why do we have to talk in your bedroom?"

"Because we're going to fuck," I drawled. "Right after we get married."

She whirled around, her almond-shaped eyes widening. "Excuse me? Did you say 'married'?" She snorted. *Snorted!* "You're out of your mind."

And I was, but it didn't matter because I held all the cards. She was going to be the solution to my little problem with my father and that Popova bitch. No way was he going to take my word for it that I was married. I was going to have to actually follow through, and Billie was the most convenient bride at the moment.

"You fucked up thinking you could steal from me, temptress." I smirked at her, relishing the flare of disdain in her eyes. "Weren't you ever taught that every action has consequences?" I watched her mouth drop open at the realization that I wasn't playing. "You acted. I'm your consequence."

She waved a hand, although her confidence was lacking. "I didn't steal from you."

"Because I stopped you." I reached up, gripping her jaw with my punishing fingers, and pulled her to my face. Her scent, a combination of coconuts and beach, filled my nostrils, making me want to lick every part of her all over again. "Do you know what the penalty is for breaking and entering? Attempted robbery?"

A shudder shook her slim shoulders, and I couldn't resist relaxing my grip on her jaw and sliding my palm to her delicate throat. I could feel her swallow, although I wasn't sure whether it was out of fear or something else.

"Answer me," I demanded as her pulse jumped against my thumb.

She licked her lips. "No."

"Let's just say you'll spend your best years behind bars." I let my eyes travel down the snug suit she wore, leaving so much yet not enough to the imagination. I frowned at the thought of another man seeing her like this. "Who saw you dressed like this?"

The sudden change in subject clearly threw her and she shrugged, attempting a calm she couldn't quite muster. "Taxi driver."

I'm going to blind him. "Which company did you use?"

Uncertainty crossed her expression. "Why?"

I grinned menacingly. "Because he's about to lose his eyeballs. And his tongue, so he can't talk to anyone about what's mine."

Her plump lips parted again. "You're out of your mind," she scoffed, rolling her eyes at me.

"You have no idea. Now give me the name."

"No," she bit out.

I tightened my grip on her throat. Not enough to really hurt her but enough to signal I was serious. "The name, Billie. I won't have some asshole blabbing around about my wife and her hot body."

She rolled her eyes once more, her makeup-free lashes batting against her ivory cheeks. "Yeah, you're definitely crazy. I won't be giving you any names. Now, either do your worst or let me go."

"No matter. I have security surveillance for miles out. I'll figure it out."

That got her attention. She chewed on her bottom lip, her light brown eyes studying me with a soft, wordless plea. Jesus, even that got me hard.

"Winston, please," she whispered. "That driver didn't do anything other than drop me off. We barely spoke. I doubt he even looked at me. I don't know what your deal is, but just punish me and leave that poor guy alone." Fuck, that was an even better idea. *Lovely.* At this rate, I'd spurt in my pants like some goddamned teenager. "But I'm not marrying you or whatever else you're blabbing about. I'd sooner go to jail."

I studied her. She seemed serious, and that spiked my curiosity. She could come out smelling like a proverbial rose if she married me. "Why?"

Her eyes darted around, studying the room we occupied last night, looking everywhere but at me. I tightened my grip on her throat. "Tell me why."

Her cheeks flamed. *Interesting.* Now I wanted to know even more.

"My parents had a good marriage. They really loved each other. I want that if and when I get married."

"And you're embarrassed about that?"

Her brows furrowed, stalling for a moment, but then she lifted her chin and pinned me with an annoyed glare. "No, I'm not. It's corny, but I don't care. I know it's possible. I don't plan on marrying anyone who can't give me the same thing, and I certainly don't see you as the man who could pull that off."

It wasn't corny. Maybe a bit naive though. Her parents probably hid their reality from her. And she's right. I could never pull that off. Nonetheless, the tiny shred of decency I had left didn't want to shatter her with that fact. She'd learn it on her own sooner or later.

"So you'll be okay if I send you to jail?" I stated casually. She immediately nodded her head. "And your family too, huh?"

"What?" Her voice came out shrill. You didn't need to know Billie to understand that her family was a tight-knit unit. I spotted it the moment her sister introduced me to her.

"If you don't cooperate, I'll put you all behind bars. Shouldn't be hard to make you look like a family of swindlers and thieves." I wouldn't, but she didn't need to know that.

"You'll never succeed," she rasped. "They don't even know where I am."

I smirked. "It won't matter when I call the police and spin my own tale. Who do you think they'll believe? You or me?" A range of emotions flared across her expression—anger, disdain, despair—but ultimately, there would be acceptance. "The deal is you belong to me."

She held my stare for a long moment before letting out a harsh, exaggerated sigh. "Definitely not a ten," she murmured.

"Come again?"

"You're a dick."

I smiled. "I know, although I'd like to point out you liked my dick just yesterday."

Her body trembled and her light brown eyes hazed over with lust. Fuck, she wanted me too. Nothing would please me more. I'd secure a marriage license, and then I'd fuck her brains out again.

Win-win.

Chapter 12
Billie

What the fuck was happening?

An hour ago I was saving my family, and now I could ruin them if I didn't play by this man's rules. I fucked up. I messed with the wrong guy. The wrong fucking family.

I'd looked up the Ashfords before coming here tonight. They were pretty much royalty in the States. In the world. They were one of the richest families on the whole goddamn planet. But their family wasn't without its own tragedies. Winston's mother was shot dead in the street two decades ago. My heart clenched at the photograph featured in one of the articles. Winston was with her when she was murdered.

That had to leave a scar. Maybe that was the reason behind the sadness and loneliness lurking behind his eyes. There was also mention of Winston's military service, and a few near-death incidents. Then there were his business ventures. Whatever the man touched, he turned to gold. It was the reason he was one of the most sought-after bachelors in the elite circles.

I also found news stories on Kingston Ashford, the youngest brother, who was kidnapped at the age of ten. There was a lot of speculation about Senator Ashford's shady deals with criminals and his affairs with women half his age, if not younger.

It would have been helpful if I'd looked into this man before I slept with him, but who knew I'd end up in his bed?

"Anything," I gritted, hating us both for being in this situation. "I'll do anything but marriage. I'll lie, tell everyone we're married if you want, but please..." My voice cracked and my lip trembled. I couldn't finish the statement.

He could have anyone, all he had to do was flash his name. It was confusing why he'd want a marriage with me. He didn't know me at all. One night between the sheets couldn't have convinced him I was the one.

Something dark flared in his blue depths. Ruthless. Obsessive. Dangerous.

"I'm going to have fun playing with my little thief," he purred.

My tongue swept over my bottom lip as my heart drummed against my rib cage. I'd seen the shows, did *some* research on ways to remain undetected, believe it or not. Stick to the shadows. In and out. Yet none of it had gone according to plan. I should have expected this from a man worth millions. Billions, even?

"I'm not a thief," I said, keeping my voice even. I couldn't show him my fear. This was a make-it-or-break-it moment for my family. Everything was in jeopardy, and I'd just have to keep playing my cards right until I could find my way out. "If I was, I'd be out there with something that didn't belong to me, and clearly, I'm still here."

I patted my hands down my body to emphasize my point. He didn't seem impressed.

"Because you were caught."

"I—I forgot something," I reasoned, jutting my chin out, refusing to give up.

He scoffed. "What?"

I desperately racked my brain for an excuse. "My cell phone," I blurted out, pulling it out of my pocket. "See, now that I have it, I'll be on my way."

I turned to leave, but his hand wrapped around my wrist. "Not so fast." I threw my head back in a frustrated groan. "You grabbed your phone when you left last night. Or I should say this morning."

I yanked my wrist out of his grasp and narrowed my eyes on him.

"I just came for my cell phone, Winston. I promise." I crossed my fingers behind my back as I uttered the lie. "I happened to see the necklace and..." I took a deep breath and exhaled. "I couldn't resist checking it out."

"And you couldn't resist trying to steal it." His voice was disinterested, though an elusive timbre soaked each word. The kind that promised deep, dark sins. "Unless you came back because you're craving more of what I gave you."

A little growl slipped from my mouth. "You wish."

He laughed. "You're right. I do. And now that you were stupid enough to try to steal from me, I have you exactly where I need you."

I crossed my arms over my chest. "I don't like you."

He didn't seem bothered, but something rippled over his features. "Maybe not, but you're at my mercy now." His voice was dark. He leaned in, the press of his lips against the hollow of my ear stealing my breath. "And believe me, Billie. I intend to take advantage of that." I shook my head, trying to clear my mind of all sensual thoughts. "You'll like it, I promise," he murmured, tracing the shell of my ear with his tongue.

A shiver ghosted through me and goose bumps ran down my arms. "I won't like *anything* from you," I breathed.

He fisted my ponytail and pressed his face into my neck. A shudder erupted through me, warmth from his touch clashing with the cold of his next words. "You won't have a choice."

My brain must have stopped working because I rose to my toes and kissed him. Messy. Wet. Every inch of my body throbbed as a rumble sounded from his chest. What was it about this man that made me delirious? Almost as if I was drunk.

"Maybe you should show me some mercy," I said. I didn't know what possessed me. Was I playing him, or vice versa? It was all blurry, and the only thing I could feel was the urge to have his hands on my body again. "For old times' sake."

He made a guttural noise, his gaze on me bitter but filled with heat. "But that wouldn't be as much fun as playing husband and wife."

I peered at him from under my eyelashes, hoping for an ounce of mercy. I suspected I wouldn't find any. Still, I had to try.

"You can play with me. Do whatever you want. Just don't marry me," I croaked, hating the way my voice trembled. I wanted what my parents had. *Life was nothing without true love*, my maman always claimed. When she passed away, I realized her words were true, because my dad had been lost without her.

"It's marriage or jail for you and your family."

Something cold settled in my stomach. I clenched my teeth, trying to prevent the vile words from slipping between my lips. I wasn't willing to risk Odette's or our father's future for my stupidity. It was in that very moment that I realized this man was beautiful and broken, but also ruthless. I imagined you'd have to be to survive in his world.

His lips curved into that arrogant smirk as he added, "If you're wondering whether I'm bluffing, don't bother. I've destroyed people for a lot less. You *will* be my wife."

Standing here, caught red-handed and at his mercy, my temper flared, and I refused to be a doormat.

"Sorry to burst your bubble, but no." I gave him my bitchiest smile. "You're a jerk, an asshole, and the last person on this earth I'd ever commit to."

"Ouch." His lips tipped up on one side in a maddeningly handsome smile that made my heart sputter in my chest. Strangely enough though, the smugness wasn't in his eyes. In fact, he almost seemed... hurt. I fought the urge to comfort him, reminding myself this monster was blackmailing me. Granted, I wouldn't be in this situation if I hadn't attempted to steal from him. Goddammit.

Before I could say anything—stupid or otherwise—he added,

"Give me your terms." His eyes were calm pools of blue. "Let's negotiate."

Tension pulled tight in his shoulders. We stared at each other in a silent battle of wills. His jaw flexed. My ears buzzed with adrenaline.

My shoulders slumped, and he must have read my surrender. What was it about him that impacted me like this? I wasn't the giving-up type. If it were anyone else, I'd have sent them to hell and been on my merry way. Yet, here I stood, every cell in my body rebelling at the idea of leaving.

Zero fucking sense.

"Explain this fake marriage to me," I demanded.

"Not fake," he said, winking at me. "We *will* be married."

Why was I still here? This man was making my head spin. He was broken, damaged. I didn't need another problem, but here I was. Refusing to move and actually considering his insane proposition.

"For how long?" He paused for a moment, almost as if he hadn't thought that far into it. *My God, he hadn't.* My spine straightened out, and I leaned in closer. "What happened? Why is it suddenly so important that you and I marry? Surely there is someone much more appropriate than me for this position." Realization dawned on me. "Are you trying to piss someone off? You picked me because I'm *not* the proper choice, didn't you?" What an ass.

He just gave me one of his looks. The kind that told me he was thinking about what I'd said. Maybe he thought the marriage was necessary, but if I learned what happened, we could find another solution. Before the flicker of hope could even ignite in my chest, a mask slid over his expression, shielding his emotions.

"Your pussy was an eye-opener," he answered in a gravelly voice, and I had the distinct feeling he was trying to throw me off. I didn't think even a pussy made of solid gold would open this man's eyes. "Have you fingered your pussy since you left my bed, thinking about me?"

A burst of flames licked over my skin. Damn him. I wished my body didn't respond to him at all. It'd be easier to fight him if he was repulsive.

"I don't need to," I snapped, angry that in fact I had. In the shower. Then in bed. Jesus. "I have plenty of men at my disposal."

He pressed his forehead to mine and inhaled deeply. "Not anymore, Billie. You fuck only me from now on."

His words caused my body to tremble. Our eyes locked as his gaze probed right into my soul. If I wasn't careful, this man could destroy me. What was worse, I would let him.

He was a hurricane. A disaster that would sweep through my life, leaving nothing but wreckage in its wake.

"If I agree to this marriage, I want it kept a secret." I'd be damned if I agreed to all his terms. Besides, when I met the love of my life, Winston Ashford would be but a distant memory. "And we need to come up with a timeframe. I'm not staying married to you forever."

He stared at me, unfazed.

"There are benefits to being married to me," he deadpanned.

I scoffed. "I doubt it. *If* I agree to this ludicrous idea, I'm only doing this shit to keep you away from my family. The moment you try *anything* with them, I'll make you wish you never laid eyes on me."

He studied me for a long moment, his gaze penetrating me in ways I secretly wished other parts of him would. Damn him. The sex yesterday was amazing, yes. Earth-shattering, yes. But it was just that. Sex. Lust.

"Fine, we'll keep it a secret," he finally agreed, much to my surprise. "But as for sex... You'll call me when you want it. You can expect the same from me."

I scoffed. "I don't give a shit who you fuck." *Liar.* "Don't call me."

His jaw clenched, but he said nothing else.

I took a moment to study the room, buying time. I was too busy to really see it last night, but this room alone was bigger than all three bedrooms in our family home. The entire back wall was made up of glass with thirty-feet-high ceilings. The remaining walls were painted a deep navy blue, almost the exact shade of his eyes.

"We can discuss monogamous sex later," he reasoned coldly. My gaze roamed over him. He was dressed down in a pair of gray slacks and a white button-up shirt. His sleeves were pushed up to reveal his muscular forearms. My traitorous pussy quivered with desire. I shook my head in an attempt to shake off whatever this lust was doing to my brain.

"Are you ready to become Mrs. Ashford?" he finally asked, his face the picture of indifference.

What *happened* to this man? It was obvious he had ghosts haunting him. Google searches gave only surface-level information, but there was obviously more to him than just that. Seeing his mother murdered would've left a mark, of course, but that happened over two decades ago. I needed something—anything—that would give me more insight into the man across from me.

"Why?"

"Why what?" he questioned.

"Why this sudden need to marry me? It's clear there's a motive behind it." His eye twitched, and I knew I was getting closer to uncovering whatever he was hiding. "Yesterday you acted like you were doing me a favor just by talking to me."

"Your pussy is that good."

I couldn't tell if he was mocking me, himself, or the world. I tried to gauge his expression, but it was as cold as a Siberian winter and as unreadable as an ancient, dead language.

"Your dick isn't," I retorted dryly. "So you'll excuse me if I need a bit more than that."

"Ah, sweetheart..." He sniffed bitterly before continuing, his drawl condescending. "We both know you loved every minute of my cock inside you."

I rolled my eyes. "I've had better." *Another lie.* "In fact, when I leave here, I'll get that better dick with a snap of my fingers."

The words had barely left my mouth before he grasped me by the throat, pushed me against the wall, and growled against my lips. Literally *growled*. The man was insane.

"Let another man touch you, and I'll make him disappear." His blue eyes turned dark enough to attract nightmares. His voice was malicious yet somehow... soft? He brushed his lips against mine. "And I promise you, it will be painful for him. *Very* painful."

I broke out in shivers, but I refused to be intimidated. *Too late,* my mind warned, but I was nothing if not proud.

"You have no right." My chin tilted at the challenge. Heat bloomed inside me at his carnal claim. Jesus Christ, where did my independence go, my reason and pride? I shook my head, desperate to clear my mind. "Besides, you're trying to distract me. Answer my question."

The temperature dipped into the negatives, the breath freezing in my lungs. The air turned harsh and caustic, like the sting of a bee, and I swallowed, my heart drumming harshly. I was determined to stand my ground, but I'd be lying if I said the look in his eyes didn't terrify me.

"All you need to know is that circumstances changed." Confusion flickered through me. Barely a day had passed since I left his bed. What could have possibly changed? "This marriage will protect you and your family."

I might have been a fool, but the vehemence in his tone pushed me to believe him. "You promise?"

His eyes grew grim. "On the grave of my mother."

I inhaled a deep breath before exhaling slowly.

"Fine," I finally said, because really, he held all the cards. I'd do anything to protect my family, even if it meant tying myself to this man for however long it took. My fate was sealed, and it was tied to his.

"I'm going to summon a priest with an expedited marriage license here in the morning. Until then, you will remain with me."

His eyes met mine, and something in their depths terrified and thrilled me at the same time.

I lowered my eyes to his bare feet. "Why can't I just come back?"

He took my chin between his strong fingers. His touch was warm and oozed power. I hated that a thrill raced down my spine, quickly followed by the hollow feeling of loss when he let go.

"Because you'll run."

"Damn fucking straight." Fuck, did I say that out loud?

"Glad to hear I was right." He flashed me a devious grin, suddenly appearing younger, and I couldn't help but stare at him. "So, how about we make the most of our last hours being *engaged*?"

I barely refrained from rolling my eyes, despite my body warming up at the insinuation. His gaze never strayed from my face, zeroing in on my lips. The way he watched me had my heart skipping nervously in my chest like never before. I wasn't sure if I liked it.

"What did you have in mind?" I heard someone ask. Jesus, it was me. God, what had gotten into me? This man, broken and probably suffering from some form of PTSD, almost choked me to death last night. Clearly he had a lot of baggage and trauma behind him... I should maintain a healthy distance from him.

We were *helping* each other.

"I'm up for anything," he murmured. "After all, I owe you."

My brows scrunched. "What do you mean?"

Anguish flashed in his eyes. "For hurting you. I don't usually sleep in the same bed with anyone. My nightmares can be..." He didn't finish the statement, and my heart clenched for him. Despite his stupid blackmail. Despite his threat to my dad and Odette. "I'm sorry. I didn't mean to hurt you."

His apology wrapped around my heart like thorny vines, puncturing holes into it and threatening feelings I didn't need to have around a man like him.

"Do you want to talk about it?" I offered, giving in to my soft side that hated to see people suffer.

"No." The steely edge in his voice was a warning. "I don't want to talk."

"Kiss?"

I'd never know if I meant it or not. It didn't matter, because the words were barely out of my mouth before his lips were on mine.

He wrapped his hand around my head and kissed me like he owned me. The last twelve hours melted away as his tongue lashed against mine, dominating me and making unspoken promises. I groaned when he palmed my ass and squeezed.

I briefly remembered that we hadn't agreed on a timeframe for his farce, but at that moment, I couldn't care less.

Chapter 13
Winston

I dominated her mouth with my own as my fingers twisted in her soft hair, controlling her movements. She moaned into my mouth. Our tongues tangled together for a fiery kiss.

"Winston," she breathed against my lips, pulling away, but I wouldn't allow any space between us. I fucking needed her like the air I breathed. Ignoring her, I trailed kisses along her cheek to her jaw and down her neck. She gasped when I suckled on the flesh near her ear. The sound was like the sweetest symphony.

I dragged my free hand down her body, the zipper of her skintight bodysuit sending a seductive echo through the room. She whimpered when I pulled down one cup of her bra, exposing her tit. I pinched the peaked nipple, twisting it hard enough to make her moan.

"I want to fuck you," I growled as I unhooked her bra and yanked it away. "Right now." I gripped her hips and sat on the edge of the bed, dragging her onto my lap. Her hot pussy against my hard dick. "Feel what you do to me?"

"It's just... sex." She whimpered when I dug my hands into her ass, kneading her flesh. "You don't know me. I don't know you."

Fuck, she was hot, but this felt like more than just sex. Something about this girl ruffled me down to my core. I pulled her bodysuit down to her ankles, exposing her body, and I couldn't help but take her nipple between my teeth.

"Ahhh... fuck."

Her tits were magnificent. A full cup, they fit perfectly in the palm of my hand. No other woman had ever made me so fucking crazy and ravenous with need. I wanted her to ride my dick while her tits bounced and she screamed my name.

I sucked harder on her nipple, grazing my teeth against her sensitive flesh, and felt her shudder against me.

Her fingernails scraped against my scalp, gripping my hair like she was holding on to her sanity, and my own.

"Fuck," I grumbled. "I want you so fucking badly."

"I want it rough," she murmured in response.

I squeezed her ass hard. "I want you to cry and beg."

We were both fucked up. I couldn't even believe she was allowing me to touch her after the blackmail I just subjected her to. Maybe she had an ulterior motive, but right now, I couldn't give two fucks. I'd let her use me and abuse me. I needed her.

"I want to hear your screams so you know who you belong to. Even before I put that ring on your finger," I crooned, running my palms up her naked back while kissing her neck. "I want to watch my cum fill your pussy, see it run down your legs."

She pulled back, chewing on her lip. "You might be crazy."

"I am," I admitted with a wolfish grin. "Are you on the pill?" She nodded her confirmation. "Let's forgo the condom."

"How do I know you're clean?" she demanded, frowning.

"I can provide the proof."

She nodded. "I'm clean too." I kissed her neck, nipping and licking her soft skin. My dick twitched at the idea of fucking a baby into her womb. Fuck, she was right; I must be goddamned crazy. Up until this moment, I did everything to avoid risking knocking someone up, and here I was excited about tying this woman to me permanently.

I shook my head, chasing my irrational thoughts away. I was getting drunk on her. That was it. I just needed to be married to keep my leech of a father out of my fucking life.

My palms roamed to her front, cupping both breasts before sliding down her flat stomach and between her thighs until I found her hot entrance. I rubbed my finger across her clit, and she whimpered, her nails digging into my scalp.

My cock was positioned against her pussy, only separated by the thin material of our clothes. She wrapped her arms around my neck, pressed her breasts against my chest.

I ripped her panties down her legs. The sound of our heavy breaths filled the space. I cupped her pussy, her hot entrance drenching my palm. "My girl is hungry for my cock, isn't she?"

She gasped against my lips, her eyes falling between us.

"You *are* fucking crazy."

"I need to feel every inch of your skin."

She crawled off my lap, giving me a glorious glimpse of her ass as she remained on her hands and knees. She glanced over her shoulder, purposely taunting me. "Then take off your clothes, Winston."

I started to undo my belt under her hooded gaze. She was naked on my bed, once again, and nothing had ever felt so fucking right. It took no time for my clothes to join hers on the floor.

"Bring me that ass," I ordered, my lips curling into a smirk.

"Come and get it, old man."

She wiggled her butt teasingly, wearing the expression of a true temptress as she smiled. It was at that moment I knew I was a goner for her. I was growing fast and furiously obsessed with her. This couldn't be good for either of us.

I grabbed her hips and pulled her closer, spanking her ass playfully, just enough to sting. "I'm hardly an old man."

She rolled her eyes. "I looked it up. You're in your thirties. I'm just about to turn twenty-four. Therefore, I'm fucking an old man."

I smacked her pussy, loving the sound of her cry as she shuddered. "Show this old man how you made yourself come, fantasizing about me. Rub your pussy and let me hear your moans."

"I never said I did that." But she was already sliding her hand between her legs and rubbing her clit furiously while I drank her in. Her eyes traveled over my abs, locking on my dick as she rubbed faster at her pussy. Precum covered the tip of my cock, and I watched her home in on it, licking her lips and making my dick rock hard.

"Stop," I demanded. She let out a whimper but yanked her hand away. "Good girl," I praised as I got closer to her, lowering my face to her glistening, needy pussy. I inhaled her feminine scent and then licked her arousal.

She moaned loudly and her thighs trembled.

I stroked my dick as I devoured her pussy from behind. Fuck, I wanted her to ride my face until I suffocated. It would be the perfect way to go.

In one swift move, I switched my position, my back to the mattress and her pussy at my face.

"I'm hungry."

Chapter 14
Billie

"*Winston.*"

He pressed his mouth and nose against my wetness, groaning against my core.

"So fucking good," he rumbled, nipping at my sensitive skin with his teeth. The vibration of his voice reached all the way up to my clit, and I knew it was game over for me.

My thighs trembled, and I feared I might be suffocating him. Attempting to shift, his fingers gripped my hips.

"Don't you fucking dare move," he commanded. "Give me all of it."

He lapped at me like he was a starving man.

"Fuck," I breathed, feeling like I was about to black out. His mouth parted the damp folds of my pussy, his tongue thrusting inside my entrance, and my back arched. My fingers carded through his hair.

I was grinding against his face, riding his mouth, desperate for the release I knew only he could give me.

"That's my girl. Show me how badly you want my tongue."

His baritone voice was rough and husky, sending shivers through me.

"Please, please..."

He dug his fingers into my soft hips, jerking me up and down, knowing exactly what he was doing. I had never experienced anything like this. The sounds and growls he made as he furiously dragged the tip of his tongue over my clit told me he was enjoying this.

His upper lip closed over my clit, his tongue never switching the pace. The friction and pressure sent shudders through me. Yesterday, the sex was great, but it didn't even scratch the surface.

"Please, Win, don't stop... oh God..."

My thighs started to tremble uncontrollably and stars burst in front of my eyes. My fingers tugged on his hair hard, drawing him closer than I imagined possible.

My thighs tightened, my hips grinding against him, and I twisted my body, chasing the pleasure. It was the most intense orgasm I'd ever experienced. Last night was nothing compared to this, and that was saying something.

But then Winston pressed his palm to my pulsing entrance and slid his thick finger inside me, finding my G-spot and applying even, firm pressure. The world faded around me. The fucked-up reason that drove us here was forgotten as my body shook against the climax rippling through me.

I stared dazedly at the man savoring me, his eyes locked on me as endless relief coursed through me, my muscles soft and languid.

Winston flipped us over, his sculpted muscles covered with a fine sheen of sweat as he hovered over me. He wiped my arousal from his mouth with the back of his hand, and then he took my mouth for a hard kiss.

The kind of kiss that shattered kingdoms. The kind of kiss that broke hearts.

"We're not done yet. I'm going to fuck you so goddamn hard."

He took his hard cock in his fist and dragged his swollen tip through my folds, stroking himself. My clit hummed again, and I was getting off on the promise of more pleasure.

I turned my head slightly, taking his earlobe between my teeth, before I whispered, "Fuck me hard and rough, Win."

With a strangled growl of my name, he slammed his mouth down on top of mine, letting me taste myself again.

It was everything. *Everything.*

"I jerked off too." His admission came through the fog. "In the shower. In my bed. In the shower again." He captured my lips with frustration. "One taste of you and I'm ruined."

Before I could ask him what he meant, his lips were back on mine. Our tongues stroked each other's mouths. Our hands were hungry. His thick shaft glided over my hot, wet entrance and we both sucked in a breath.

"You ready?" he groaned. His hand around my throat, he put his lips to my ear. "You are going to take my cock so fucking good," he whispered. His breath brushed my ear and raised the skin along my spine. "Like the bad girl I know you want to be." My eyes widened at his dirty words.

"Fuck me," I moaned, lifting my hips and running my inner thighs up and down his heaving rib cage. "As rough as you can."

My hands on his shoulders, I felt the tip of him enter me. Just as I was about to open my mouth to urge him on, he thrust to the hilt with a savagery I wasn't prepared for. The pain and pleasure mixed, and I sank my teeth into his forearm to muffle my scream.

With a hoarse roar, his hips pushed me into the mattress, his thickness taking up every inch of space within me. Then he started to move, pumping feverishly into me. My last orgasm felt like a distant memory as he drove into me, rough and fast, building up the pleasure once again. Our bodies moved in perfect union, his cock sliding through my arousal and claiming me in a way I didn't think was possible.

His big hands gripped my knees, opening me wider for him, and he pounded into me with fierce ruthlessness.

"Scream for me," he panted, raking my ear with his open mouth. "Beg for my cock. I want the world to know you're mine."

This was madness. This was perfection.

"Please, Winston," I cried, mindless with need and shaking from head to toe. The swish of air ghosted across my pussy seconds before his hand connected with my throbbing flesh. "Please fuck me. I'm so close."

His length surged into me like a hurricane, invading every inch of me. I choked on his name as I gasped.

"Such a greedy fucking cunt, isn't it? Thirsty for my cum," he rasped darkly. His hand gripped my hip with a bruising force. "Don't worry, baby, I've got you."

Winston's relentless thrusts had every cell in my body lighting up like fireworks.

"Harder," I screamed. "Oh my God. It's so good."

"Whose cunt is this?"

I bit my lip, unwilling to admit that I'd allowed him to claim it twice in the span of twenty-four hours.

His hand came up to frame my jaw, applying just enough pressure as another rush of arousal coated my sex, the sounds of slick wetness filling the space between us as he slid in and out of me.

"Whose." Thrust. "Pussy." Thrust. "Is." Thrust. "This?"

"Yours." At that moment, I knew it to be true.

He slammed into me, holding still, deep, his face dropping into the crook of my neck. "Good girl."

Fuck, his praise was doing all kinds of things to me. It sent a ripple through my core, tearing out a strangled sob, and my hands flew to his ass.

"Oh my God. F-fuck me n-now."

"Fuck," he ground out, picking his blistering pace back up, the sound of wet slaps echoing in the room. "You'll be the end of me, Billie."

My knees shot up and hugged his body, back arching. The harder he pumped, the louder my moans and screams. I ran my nails down his muscular ass, digging them in. His hips punched forward in desperation, the tendons in his neck looking ready to snap.

"Come with me."

And just like that, another orgasm slammed into me. I screamed as my pussy milked him for all he had.

"Fuck, I love your pussy," he grunted as he buried his face in the crook of my neck. The hot, grinding pulsations of my inner muscles wouldn't end, especially when he drove deeper still inside me.

I writhed underneath him when he stopped and shuddered, trying to find the bottom of the pleasure. His mouth found mine, and a dazed smile curved my lips as he kissed me like he was dying of thirst and I was the last drop of water on this earth.

Then his mouth trailed across my jaw until he reached my ear and murmured, "I want you to keep my cum inside your pussy." He showered my neck and face with little kisses. "I want you to know who you belong to."

A shiver rolled down my spine. "I have to get cleaned up," I protested weakly. "Besides, I'm on the pill. Remember?"

He wrapped me in his arms, tucking me closer to him.

I blinked in confusion as he got comfortable, pulling me closer to him. I wouldn't sleep in the same bed with him. Not after he just about strangled me last night.

"What are you doing?"

"Putting you to sleep."

I chewed on my bottom lip as I studied him. It was clear that Winston Ashford was a damaged soul. Whatever happened to him drove his behavior last night when he fell asleep. But I couldn't risk a repeat.

Instead of flat-out refusing him, I shifted to move.

"What are *you* doing?" he questioned.

"I have to get cleaned up."

Then he shocked the hell out of me. Effortlessly, he laid me back on the mattress and pulled my legs apart, staring at my pussy. "Winston—"

"Shhh," he purred, shifting and bringing his face dangerously close to my core. He stared at my pussy, at the cum leaking out of it and all over my thighs. He locked eyes with me as he gently swiped his finger through it, pushing it back inside me. Another shudder rolled down my spine at the erotic view. Then he closed my legs. "My cum is staying inside you all night."

I propped myself up on my elbows, shooting him a confused look. "I told you, I'm too young to risk shit like that, even if I'm on the pill."

He grinned, his expression relaxed, and something about it made my heart trip over its own beat. He was stunning like this. Heart-breaking, even. But I wasn't that naive.

"A man can hope," he murmured wistfully. He jumped out of the bed, disappeared in the bathroom, and was back in no time with a wet cloth. I stared in shock as he wiped my inner thighs, then discarded it on the floor.

"Now sleep, temptress." He kissed me again, this time so hard and thoroughly I forgot all about his cum, washcloth, and the world. "I'll stay with you until you fall asleep, then I'll go into the adjoining room."

As his strong arms wrapped around me, I had a distinct feeling that this was what free-falling felt like. Out of control. Irrational.

"Winston," I murmured, my voice hoarse.

"Hmmm."

"The marriage..." I felt him tense around me. "It's just on paper, right? I still have lots of things to do before I even think about settling down."

And going to jail wasn't one of them.

"Sleep, Billie."

As fatigue won out and slumber took over, it occurred to me that he never answered.

Chapter 15
Winston

Billie—my soon-to-be wife—lay next to me, nuzzling into her pillow and snoring softly as I watched over her.

I didn't sleep with women—never felt the need for it—but something about this woman made me want to make an exception. Again. I'd make sure not to doze off to sleep this time. My eyes lowered to her slim neck. There weren't bruises there, only faded red marks from last night.

Jesus H. Christ.

I was a lucky man she even let me touch her again. There was no fucking way I'd risk hurting her again. I'd hold her for a bit longer before making my way to a different bed.

I positioned her against me, her arm draped over my waist and mine hooked around her shoulders. She sighed, shifted closer to me, and hooked her leg over my hip. Lovely, now my dick stirred.

Ignoring that little asshole, I held her and stared at the ceiling through the dark as I let my mind wander. I wanted to think about all the ways I'd fuck this woman in the future, but for reasons only God knew, my thoughts drifted to that one day I hated to think about. The day my mother died.

I inhaled a shaky breath as the darkness floated back into my thoughts. To the young boy sobbing over his mother's body as her blood stained his hands and the pavement beneath them.

"Ma, please don't die." I knew she was already slipping away, yet I refused to accept it. She was the best part of my and my siblings' lives. "Mama, we need you. Please don't leave us."

Blood pooled around her as people either gave us a wide berth to avoid the scene or stopped and gawked at her. My eyes filled with tears at the turn our day had taken. How could this be happening when she was beaming down at me just minutes ago, eyes full of love?

And it was all my fault.

I blinked my tears away, desperate to make things better. Her skin was paler than ever against her dark hair. You could barely make out the emerald and diamonds on her necklace with how much blood was seeping around her chest and throat. Her blood-stained hand reached out to cup my cheek. The touch was cold. Too cold.

Her gaze darted behind me, then left and right. "You have to run, baby."

I shook my head, her form wavering under the glistening tears in my eyes. "I'm sorry, Mama."

This wouldn't have happened if I hadn't been with her today. We would've never stopped here at this stupid store. How could I be so selfish? I killed my mother. I killed my mother. The words repeated in my skull like a broken record.

"N-not your f-fault." She was fading. Her touch was getting colder by the second. "Be g-good." I sniffled, terror taking over and making my head spin. "Don't be your father."

"I won't," I cried. "I promise."

Someone's fingers dug into my shoulder blades, but I refused to leave her. I thrashed and kicked, howled in pain as my heart broke. I needed to save her.

"It's me." A familiar voice had me pausing, and it was only then that I recognized our guard.

Frantic movements. Screams and shouts, wide-eyed expressions on strangers' faces.

I shot one last look at Mama and saw that her mouth was parted, a look of shock etched onto her face. A bright red stain on her cream dress. She lay there, still and unmoving, the light completely gone from her dark eyes.

Our bodyguard shouted for an ambulance even though we all knew it was too late. She was gone. The only true parent we had.

And it was all my fault. Life would never be the same.

A soft murmur brought me back to the present moment, and my eyes lowered to the woman in my arms. Her golden hair was sprawled all over my chest, and I pushed the soft, wavy strands back, needing to see she was okay. I was met with a serene expression and a contented half-smile. I decided, right then and there, that I'd always keep her safe.

Even from me.

The buzzing of my phone on the nightstand woke me up. I squinted my eyes at the screen, barely making out the name.

Father.

That motherfucker. I glanced at the clock, noting that it was seven in the morning. I'd stayed up late into the night before I made my way into the adjoining guest room to sleep, so this sleep-in was unusual.

I ignored the call, but no sooner than I put it back on the nightstand, it started buzzing again.

"What?" I answered, rubbing the sleep from my eyes.

"We'll annul your marriage."

I growled into the phone. "No, we will not."

Someone would do us a solid if they just ended Senator Ashford. He was crooked as fuck. Cruel too. He'd succeeded in making illegitimate babies all over the world. One might argue those illegiti-

bastards were the unfortunate ones, growing up without a dad, but truthfully, they were the lucky ones. He destroyed everything he touched.

"Did you fall for this wife of yours?" I stood up and made my way to the connecting door and cracked it open. Billie was still sound asleep. "I'm sure you're blind and stupid, but whoever she is, she just wants our money."

"Not our money," I gritted into the phone. "*My* money." My mother left all her inheritance to her children, but just like the rest of my brothers, I'd ventured into business and turned it into an empire. "And no, I haven't fallen for her, but it's time I start a family."

It was the first thing that came to mind. Although, now that I'd said it, I liked the idea. At thirty-three, I wasn't getting any younger. It would be nice to have a family. A normal one. Like the one Billie obviously had.

"Have a family with Nicki Popova."

"No can do," I deadpanned, pissed off that I was even having this conversation with the man who made living in a war zone seem like a walk in the park. "I don't have a prenup."

Father might not understand loyalty and decency, but he understood money. Greedy motherfucker.

"Jesus Christ, how long have you been married?"

"Long enough," I answered vaguely. The priest should be here at nine. He'd better hurry up and get to reading the words pronouncing Billie as my wife.

"Goddammit, Winston. You're supposed to think with your head, not your cock."

I snickered. "That's rich coming from you." The bastard *only* thought with his dick. "Now, excuse me. I've got to fuck my wife. We're trying for a baby. It seems to me you'll have to marry the *delightful* Nicki yourself."

It'd be a match made in hell. Exactly what he deserved.

Not waiting for a reply, I ended the call and made my way to the bed. Billie didn't even stir when I reached out for her golden strands, twisting them around my finger.

Everything about Billie called to me. It was the oddest thing.

I couldn't fall for this woman. I fucking couldn't, no matter how easy it might seem. I did my own research the night I threw my party here. I couldn't help noting our differences, but also similarities—her closeness to her family, her love for fashion and diamond design, and especially her dedication to her father and his hospital.

She stirred, her eyes fluttering open, and smiled softly. The tenderness slammed right into my chest and stole my breath.

"Good morning," she murmured in a raspy voice.

I wrapped my arms around her warm body and squeezed until I could feel her pulse beat against my fingertips. Steady.

This woman would never have anything to worry about as long as she lived. As long as she was mine, no other man would touch her. I was the only man she would ever have between her legs. She could go wherever she wanted, because she was invincible.

Even against me.

Her eyes locked with mine, and her breathing quickened. Her response was exhilarating. So honest. It was the best kind of medicine for a man with demons haunting him.

My hand cupped her cheek, and I pressed my mouth close enough to dust her lips with a kiss. "Good morning, future wife."

Her fingers wrapped around my wrist and she shifted slightly to press against me.

I should pull away. I should end this and remain detached. But... when she kissed me like that, I felt powerless to stop it. I wanted her to keep kissing me, to keep giving me her tongue as she searched for mine.

And I never wanted it to end.

Chapter 16
Billie

Winston ran his fingers through my hair, peppering my neck with kisses.

Then, without warning, he lifted me into his arms and strode us over to the bathroom as if I weighed nothing. He fucked me against the shower wall until I screamed his name. Until I nearly fainted from how many times I came. Then he left me with a soft kiss to go get ready.

I stared at my reflection in the mirror now. A white Valentino dress came down to my knees. Elegant Jimmy Choo shoes. The whole getup was weightless and smooth to the touch, and it was exactly what I liked about it. How he managed to pull off getting these here in such a short amount of time was beyond me. And managing to get them in the right size? I didn't even want to think about why he was so good at judging a woman's size. I let out a soft snort, giddiness coming over me.

I thought about calling my sister, but how could I even begin to explain this to her? She might try to put a stop to it, because even though she was my baby sister, her instinct was always to protect me. Still, it didn't sit well. We always talked about doing this together. I thought of her face yesterday when we held each other outside the hospital and took a deep breath. This was the right thing to do. I was doing this for her. For *them*. When the time came, I'd tell her all about my wild forty-eight hours and she'd get a good laugh out of it. Probably.

And today, after the wedding, I'd talk to Winston about the hospital ordeal, and maybe I could get a loan to reinstate it back in our family's name again. That would compensate for keeping her in the dark about this marriage.

Or maybe you're being too optimistic, my gut warned. I ignored it. The man wanted to get married. Clearly he was head over heels for me. At least he was for my pussy. A freaking billionaire wanted *me*.

If anyone were to ask what came over me to agree to this, I wouldn't have an answer. When this man was around, all my marbles were lost.

With one last glance at the mirror, I left the bedroom and made my way downstairs. As I passed the halls and took in the luxury surrounding me, my heart shuddered with each click of my heels against the hardwood. The paintings—new and old—witnessed my descent, the old money promising I'd be alright. Or maybe it mocked my reasons for doing this.

"I need my family to be okay," I whispered to the empty hallways, justifying myself as the reality of what was happening bolted up my spine. My feet froze on the bottom step. Standing in the grand lobby, surrounded by portraits worth thousands—maybe millions—stood Winston in his black, three-piece suit.

My heartbeat ricocheted like a pinball. Unease drifted through me, intertwined with naivety, but I ignored it, because there was something else glimmering there too. The carnal pleasure he'd delivered over the last two nights must have overtaken my reason.

A cold whisper in the back of my mind told me that I'd regret this, but I ignored it. Instead, I went over the facts. I wanted the money to help Dad and Odette. This man had plenty of it. And he was incredible in the bedroom. Yes, he had his demons, but who didn't. He apologized. He slept in a separate room. *None of this was real.*

But the romantic in me screamed to stop this madness. Winston didn't love me, and I didn't love him. It was a secret arrangement—both of us doing it for our own selfish reasons. We simply didn't know each other enough to fall in love. Fall in lust? Yes. But fall in love? Not likely.

The idea of living in a loveless marriage where eventually he'd grow bored of my body made me feel sick to my stomach, cutting my breaths in half and sending an ache radiating through my chest.

"Maybe this isn't a good idea," I blurted, my voice hoarse with emotions.

Winston stood with his hands in his pockets as he leaned against a marble pillar, his blue gaze calm and reassuring.

"Don't overthink it." A fleeting emotion I couldn't read passed over his face. "You're mine. This will be a mutually beneficial arrangement."

Arrangement. I didn't like that word, not one bit. I swallowed the lump in my throat. Stealing would have been much less personal. Yes, I loved the sex, but eventually the attraction would fade and we'd be left with nothing.

My parents loved each other. They finished each other's sentences; they were each other's closest confidant. It was love. This... wasn't.

I suddenly knew that this throb in my heart would grow to be ten times worse if I wasn't careful. "Maybe we should stop this while there's still time." My voice was a whisper as I stared at him, handsome and cold. The heat of his stare burned right through me. "I... I... I just need—"

Money. But the word got stuck in my throat.

"Billie, we're getting married," he snapped. "You agreed."

"*Winston,* we don't even know each other. Sex is just..." It wasn't the basis for a good marriage. "Sex is not enough." And I didn't want the heartache that my sixth sense warned he'd bring along. "I don't even know your middle name."

"Ares. All the Ashford sons have the same middle name."

"Well, that's different."

He shrugged. "Now, let's do this. The priest has to leave in twenty minutes."

His phone buzzed and his face immediately turned irritated as he stared at the screen.

"A speedy wedding," I muttered under my breath. "What a perfect way to kickstart a disaster."

The front door to the castle swung open and a man strode in with all the confidence of someone who walked through life like he belonged. My gaze traveled over his tall frame and my jaw just about dropped. If that was a priest, I was ready to sin. Jesus H. Christ.

"This will be our witness. Asher. He's a captain, a pirate, whatever he wants to be."

My eyebrows shot to my hairline, only now noting Asher's clothes. A designer shirt and trousers. His tattoos played peekaboo under those sophisticated clothes that didn't fool anyone. This man was a red flag if I'd ever seen one.

Although Winston Ashford was proving to be an even bigger one. My eyes returned to him with a sigh.

"I didn't know being a pirate was a profession."

"Neither is being a thief, and yet here we are."

I shot him a glare and decided this man was an asshole. A ten at night, and only under the light of the moon. But here, standing before me today? He barely placed on the scale.

My eyes flicked to Asher, who was watching the exchange with a bored expression.

"I'm sorry you came all this way, but you can leave. There will be no wedding today."

I turned around to go back upstairs, but didn't make it one step before an arm wrapped around my waist and my feet left the floor.

"Winston!"

"We're getting married today, Billie," he whispered in my ear. My back was pressed to his front. "Don't think I'm bluffing when I say I'll use whatever means necessary to make that happen. Are you ready to jeopardize your family?"

"Jesus, talk about a declaration of love," I hissed.

"As if you'd want one," he taunted.

I elbowed him in his gut, trying to fight my way out of his grip. He grunted upon impact but didn't release me.

"Let me go." I tried to pull his arm off me, but it was like trying to pry steel.

His laugh rumbled down my back. "Never, Billie. Get used to it."

For some dumb reason, my chest grew lighter. I turned to face him, meeting his ocean blues. He looked like he wanted to fuck me right here, in front of our witness, and was barely holding himself back.

A shiver coasted through me as I clutched the hem of my dress. "I need you to hear me when I say I think it's a bad idea, Winston."

His rough palm brushed my face.

"I disagree. It's the best idea I've had in my entire life. You'll be Billie Ashford as of today."

His palm burned my cheek as I whispered, "Billie Ashford."

It tasted foreign. Strange.

And as the whole world faded around us, the slightest whisper of doom remained.

My heartbeat drummed in my ears throughout the entire ceremony. Much later, I'd remember very little besides my clammy skin and the presence of Winston's light cologne.

I barely knew the man, yet something about his presence consumed me in familiarity and broke through the thumping mantra of my pulse.

"I do."

The two simple words spoken by Winston were cold, yet his gaze burned through me like the fires of hell. He promised to love me, honor me, cherish and protect me for the remainder of his days. He uttered the words with such conviction that he almost fooled me.

When it was my turn to repeat them, I blanched.

His fingers gripped mine, not painfully, but with comfort and reassurance. Our gazes met and he mouthed, "I've got you."

The stupid romantic in me almost believed him as I repeated the words. The priest asked for the rings and my eyes tracked Winston's movements.

"It was my mother's. I can buy you a different one later," he whispered.

I stared at the ring he was holding, swallowing a lump in my throat, and shook my head. "I-it's beautiful."

A dainty yellow-gold band with glittering diamonds looked fragile in his big, strong fingers. His mama's ring for our fake marriage. It felt wrong to wear a ring with so much significance behind it. Yet, at the same time, it felt so right. Suddenly this arrangement took on a whole new meaning.

I met his gaze, the reality slamming into me all at once.

"I don't have a ring for you." A marriage wasn't in my plans when I came to rob him, but that fact, like so many others, didn't seem to matter. Winston reached into his pocket and handed me a ring. No, not a ring. A black silicone wedding band that the military and police force usually used for comfort. At least if TV shows were to be believed. I took it with trembling fingers, murmuring a soft, "Thank you."

Awkward silence filled the room and pricked my skin. The priest cleared his throat. Asher rolled his eyes. Winston slipped his mother's ring on my finger, repeating the priest's words. My heartbeats latched on to every word, burning into my chest and warming me thoroughly.

Before I knew it, the ceremony was over. He kissed me on my lips. Soft, sweet, and still all-consuming.

And just like that, I was Mrs. Winston Ashford.

"Congratulations," said our two witnesses. The priest smiled and gushed, while Asher studied us with blatant cynicism. This definitely wasn't how weddings were supposed to go.

I wanted to end this charade, but instead, I just stood there frozen in disbelief that I'd done this. A hysterical laugh bubbled inside me, but I immediately squashed it.

Winston shot me a frown, but before he could say anything, a voice boomed from the foyer. "I'm here."

I stiffened, waiting for whoever it was to appear. It didn't take long. A tall, bald man appeared with an expensive Canon camera hanging off his neck.

"Ah, finally here. You missed the fucking ceremony," Winston snapped, glaring at him.

The priest winced. I bit into my bottom lip to stop myself from freaking out.

"You could have given me more than six hours' notice." The photographer didn't seem bothered by Winston's outburst. He turned to me and extended his free hand for introduction. "I'm Sebastião, your photographer for this memorable event," he said in a heavy Spanish accent. I grimaced, taking his hand and shaking it. Memorable wasn't what I'd call this. "Congratulations on your marriage. You're the most beautiful bride I've ever seen."

I took my hand back, frowning as I studied him. I knew this guy. Well, the whole world did. He was famous, especially for his wedding and fashion photography.

Everyone's eyes were on me, and I realized they were waiting for some kind of response, so I forced a smile on and muttered, "Thank you." I turned my head and looked at my new husband. "Why the pictures?" I asked under my breath. "If it's just an arrangement and nobody will know, it's probably best we don't have any evidence."

Winston shrugged wordlessly, leaving me wondering what play he was scheming, but before I could ask another question, the photographer clapped his hands, distracting me.

"Okay, now let's get to work." He smiled wildly while we all stared at him blankly. "We'll take photos of the bride and groom first, then a group photo."

"A group photo?" I turned my head, wondering if maybe the man was delusional. "There isn't a group here."

He waved his hand as if that was a minor thing. "Okay, go over there. Our fresh husband of Bel Air—" He chuckled at his weird joke that made no sense. "Stand here. Hug her like you can't live without her."

Winston didn't move, but I felt him stiffen. Tension vibrated from him, seeping into me. It was awkward as fuck. Neither of us seemed to even be breathing. Asher, the priest, and Sebastião—who kept gawking at Asher like he was a god—waited for us to strike a pose.

"Will you hug her, for fuck's sake?" Asher finally broke the silence. "If this photographer breathes into my ear one more time like he's gonna have a heart attack at this wedding, I might have to..." He trailed off when the priest cleared his throat. "I might have to throw him out."

Finally, Winston wrapped his arms around my waist and pulled me closer. With the crystal blue sea at our back peeking through the windows, I imagined it was a pretty good backdrop.

"Excellent." The photographer started moving around, snapping happily. "How about a smooch? Some tongue action." I gasped in horror, staring at him. Maybe he was on drugs? Nobody actually said shit like that. "Give this wedding some life."

Winston's grip on my waist tightened, but he didn't look at me. "Stop talking shit. You're making my wife uncomfortable." He shot the man a death stare, muttering under his breath, "I need a fucking drink."

Unfortunately, Sebastião was either still half asleep, his brain not processing Winston's words, or too blind to see that Winston was quickly growing agitated.

But before I could ponder further about it, the photographer closed the distance between us and put his hand on my neck. "Try caressing her—"

He never finished his words before Winston just about exploded. "Get your hands off her."

His whole body leaned forward, almost as if he was ready to pummel the man. Asher pulled Sebastião back before my husband could follow through.

"Take pictures from here, man," Asher instructed. "Safer for all of us."

None of this was going to end well.

Chapter 17
Winston

I had a wife. She was mine. It might be an arrangement, but somehow it felt like... more. It could be that my mother's ring was on her finger. Or the vows we'd repeated. My mother always said never to settle, and Billie Swan—Ashford—didn't feel like settling.

She was my fucking *wife*.

Never in a million years had I imagined I'd feel what I did as I slipped a ring onto her delicate finger. A peculiar sense of possessiveness grabbed hold of me and refused to let go.

No matter what.

Something about Billie woke a foreign part of me that suddenly craved a real home and family. The kind that wasn't skewed by a fucked-up version of the marriage that I witnessed between my parents. My mother had only ever wanted love. My father gave her nothing but pain.

I poured four glasses of Gautier 1762 and handed them out.

"A toast," I suggested. Billie flicked me a quizzical look.

"Isn't it a little early for cognac?" my new bride questioned. And right she was. But when you had been losing yourself in alcohol for so many years, it became second nature. I debated putting the bottle down, but decided against it. Today was meant to be celebrated.

"Wait a minute," Asher chimed in, interrupting the staredown between us. "That should be my job." Asher took his glass and raised it. The priest and photographer joined us and followed suit. Asher grinned, and I knew the next thing to come out of his mouth would make Billie cringe. "May all your ups and downs come only in the bedroom, so you might have many little Winstons running around."

Billie rolled her eyes and muttered under her breath, "You wish."

"To love," the priest toasted.

Asher snickered. We clinked our glasses as I pulled my wife closer to me.

Tension coiled beneath my skin as I downed my cognac. Billie let hers barely touch her lips, grimacing, then she set the full glass down.

The priest made his way out, Asher making him promise to file the license we'd all signed as soon as possible. I gave in to the urge, grabbing a pack of smokes from my pocket, and lit one. I inhaled until my lungs burned and the nicotine spread through my veins in one relaxing rush.

Billie took a step to leave, and I closed my eyes for a beat.

"Don't go."

It came out too demanding, but to my surprise, she didn't fight me. I knew I was rude and far too harsh to her. There were so many words on my tongue, but they remained securely locked, knowing full well that I'd used her. I was going to change that though. I might've stolen her dream of marrying for love, but I intended to make it worth her while.

She let out a shallow breath. "Fine. But not because you asked so *nicely*."

The corners of my lips tipped up. "Of course not. Thank you."

One of her eyebrows arched. "What are you thanking me for exactly?" Her heels tapped impatiently. Billie puzzled me, whether on purpose or not, I wasn't sure. "By the way, you didn't make me sign a prenup."

"That's very perceptive of you."

"Why?" I shrugged. "It's reckless," she pointed out.

I scoffed. "That's me. The reckless one."

"What if I come away with everything?"

"It's just money. I'll make more of it."

Her lips parted in amazement. "If money means so little to you, then why didn't you let me have that damn necklace?"

"Because it was my mother's." Her eyes lowered to her hand, now wearing the wedding band that used to belong to my mother. "You can take any other jewelry, if you want. Just not that one. It was part of my inheritance."

"Ah."

I had no idea what went on inside that head of hers. Or why she'd attempted to steal the necklace. It made no difference either way, because she was now, by default, one of the richest women in the world.

Granted, she didn't seem impressed.

I watched her, waiting for her to say or do something. Instead, she reached up and took the cigarette from my mouth.

"You should really quit," she remarked as she put it between her lips and inhaled. Fuck, my dick hardened and dark amusement ghosted through me. I was starting to suspect everything this woman did was to taunt me. She exhaled, smoke smoothly escaping her parted lips. "Smoking kills."

"Many things kill." Her eyes darted to the empty glass in my hand. It didn't take having a sister who was a med student to notice the signs of my self-destruction. "Like stealing, for example, can get you killed."

She rolled her eyes. "Whatever."

"Why did you try to steal the necklace?" I asked curiously. "It doesn't seem like something that would be part of your repertoire."

She shrugged. "I wanted a change of career."

I scoffed. "Stick to fashion design." Something flared in her eyes. Surprise, maybe. "How much money do you need?" Her jaw clenched. It would seem my wife was proud, too. "It's one of the benefits of our marriage. You have access to my money."

She let out a sigh. "How much can I have?"

"As much as you need." And I meant it. That right there should have made me question what the fuck I was doing. It didn't.

Billie stared at me with those soft, light brown eyes. Seeing too much. Not seeing enough.

I reached for the Chanel catalog that sat on the table and handed it to her. She flicked it a glance, then shot me a questioning look.

"Order yourself some new clothes. Whatever you need." No reaction. Just three heartbeats as silence suffocated the room. "There's a number in there. It's a line dedicated to the Ashfords. You just give them a call, and they'll bring you whatever you want."

She gave her head a subtle shake as she flipped through the pages. I couldn't wait to see her dressed up in the clothes I bought her. I'd provide for her. I'd make her my queen. My young wife had the body of a porn star, every single inch of her utter perfection.

Especially as she held that cigarette between her plump lips, flipping through the black-and-white pages. I extinguished my cigarette in a nearby ashtray. She followed the movement but didn't say anything else.

Asher returned at that moment, his hands in the pockets of his trousers and a dark expression on his face.

"That went well," he remarked to Billie. "I got you a gift."

She snickered. "I'm surprised you were able to get anything considering this was all planned... What? Ten hours ago?"

Asher flashed her a smile. "Didn't you hear? Pirates have chests full of treasure."

Billie rolled her eyes. "Why do I feel like you're fucking with me?"

"He isn't," I deadpanned.

Asher reached into his pocket and handed her a skinny velvet box. "May you have better luck than the last owner of this bracelet."

Billie stared at the velvet box.

"Well, that sounds ominous," she muttered as she accepted the box and fumbled with it. But no sooner had the box opened than a soft gasp tore from her lips and her eyes widened. "Is that... No, it can't be."

"Can't it?" Asher had a talent for finding unique, antique jewelry. Some he got through legitimate means. Others, not so much.

Her eyes darted to me, then to Asher, before returning to the diamond bracelet in the velvet box. "But this piece... It... This belonged to Marie Antoinette."

"The very same," Asher answered. "I see your girl knows her jewelry."

I shot him a pointed look. *That's right, my girl.*

The bracelet was made up of three strands of diamonds and contained over a hundred stones. It was worth millions. It was a mystery how Asher knew that Billie had a fascination for diamonds, but clearly he'd hit the jackpot.

She shut the box with a dull thud and looked up with a determined look on her face.

"Thank you," she said, smiling at him, and suddenly, I wanted to strangle my best friend. I didn't want my wife smiling at anyone but me. All her smiles, tears, memories... they all belonged to me.

Tension coiled beneath my skin, and I gave in and shot Asher a look that promised murder if he didn't get out of here. I needed to fuck my wife. Right now.

Of course, that only seemed to spur Asher on, and he made himself comfortable.

He strode to the couch and flopped on it, crossing his legs and letting his ankle rest on his knee. Billie walked over to me, showing me the diamonds and reciting clarity, cut, color, and all the details. Needless to say, the woman knew her stones.

"I feel like I should be jealous," I grumbled.

She smiled sweetly. "Of what? The diamonds?"

I rolled my eyes. "That, and my best friend."

She stared at me, her brows furrowed. "I don't get it."

I scoffed, pressing my palms to her back and tracing her shoulder blades. I should deny it, but I didn't give a shit. I might as well let her know I wouldn't share, even something as simple as her smiles.

"Every smile, every time your eyes sparkle—" I swallowed roughly. "It's mine."

Maybe I suddenly became a lightweight and the alcohol was going to my head, or maybe it was just this woman. I didn't know. All I knew was that I wanted to hoard all of these moments. My greed knew no limits when it came to her.

"So how long have you two known each other?" Asher's voice interrupted our moment and she smiled, but she kept her eyes locked on me.

"A while," I answered.

"Not long," Billie said at the same time. I gave her a pointed look and she sighed. "What? I'm a horrible liar," she whispered so only I could hear her.

She took a half step back and turned to find Asher watching us with interest.

"Oh, young love," he drawled, his eyes shining with amusement. Fucker.

And then it hit me. Two days. Forty-eight hours. I was in so deep I didn't know the way up. What would happen when a week went by? A month?

Jesus H. Christ.

I wanted her. Her loyalty. Her good days and bad. Her everything.

When you find her, hold on. You all deserve the best, my sons. Don't settle for anything less. Don't settle like I have.

It was something Ma wanted for all my siblings, but it wasn't until now that her words suddenly came with a whole new meaning.

I'd fallen for the woman who stood next to me with soft golden eyes and long blonde hair. A renewed calmness washed over me. I would be a better man for her, and I would fucking die before I let anyone hurt her.

She was all mine. Figuratively and literally.

Chapter 18
Billie

I t was surreal.

The morning sun still crept through the windows of Winston's—*our*—castle as I watched Winston and Asher speak in hushed tones, the glass of cognac secured in my husband's grip.

I suspected his drinking was a more serious problem than I'd originally thought. But in comparison to the ring on my finger, it didn't even scratch the surface of my own problems.

Married.

I was still waiting for this nightmare to end, to wake up and realize it was all a bad dream. The bright side was that the bracelet Asher gifted me should save Dad's hospital. Help my sister pay for medical school.

My eyes flicked to the velvet box sitting on the table. A couple million dollars casually propped on a table in a seventeenth-century castle. Holy shit. If I hadn't seen it with my own two eyes, I wouldn't believe it. How was this my life?

Sensing Winston's eyes on me, I lifted my head. He was leaning against the doorframe, his tie loosened and his hands in the pockets of his dress pants. He looked every bit the businessman he was, unlike when I first saw him in Le Bar Américain.

There was a look in his eye, something possessive and dark, that set me on edge. He tried too hard to appear relaxed and unimposing, but you had to be blind not to see the killer behind that nonchalant smile. Besides, one of the articles I read mentioned that every Ashford brother had served in the Special Forces.

Was that the reason behind Winston's damaged aura?

Another few minutes and Asher departed. The quiet that filled the space with Asher gone could be chipped at with an ice pick. Winston gave his head a subtle shake, then headed for the minibar. My thoughts swirled, but I'd keep my mouth shut about it.

Discussing his probable addiction wasn't the best way to start a marriage.

"Now what?" I asked, slipping my heels off and wiggling my toes. I loved fashion—diamonds even more—but nothing beat walking around barefoot.

Winston pulled the top off the cognac bottle. "Now we relax. Or eat." He glanced at me over his shoulder. "Or we fuck. Whichever you want."

The latter was oh so tempting. *Wait. What?* The latter was the last thing we should do. We needed to talk. Come to some kind of *real* agreement. Go our separate ways.

"I think we've done too much of that already," I mused, my heart fluttering dangerously as I sat down on the chaise.

He turned around, a smile pulling on his beautiful lips. "Nah. There can never be enough fucking when it comes to you, wife."

Wife. My heart soared, singing some ridiculous love song, as a shiver ran down my back at the image of him fucking me.

"Aren't you worried that this was too rushed?" I rasped. "A mistake?"

Silence. Not that I should be surprised. This man excelled at this no-answer thing.

Winston watched me, his gaze burning like a lit match. My

maman believed in fairy tales, although I was starting to think she would warn me against this man. We had some kind of a twisted version of a fairy tale going that could potentially end badly if I wasn't careful.

Goosebumps trailed down my arms as I waited for my husband to make the first move, to set the tone of whatever *this* would be.

But he didn't even flinch. He waited with the patience of a saint.

So, like a weak woman, unable to resist, I stood up and padded toward him. We had to set some ground rules, but the lines were getting blurred by this attraction that burned between us.

Stepping into his space, I gripped the end of his tie. "So how are we going to do this?"

"Do what?"

I inhaled deeply, pulling his masculine scent deep into my senses. "This secret-marriage thing."

"How do you want it to work?" I met his gaze, my heart stilling before tugging in an unnatural way. There was a certain darkness behind his eyes. I licked my lips nervously, and his gaze followed the motion, heavy and burning. I thought back to his profession earlier about how I belonged to him, and wondered for the first time if he was feeling the same terrifying things I was.

"Why do I get the idea that there's something very important you're not telling me?" The question pushed from my lips by invisible force. "Don't you think I should know now?"

He flicked his gaze to the side before returning it to me. Secrets hid in those bottomless blue eyes, drawing heavy heartbeats out of my chest.

"Nothing important." He stepped closer, the smoky scent of his cologne reaching me. Intoxicating me. And suddenly I craved his hands everywhere. There was nothing better than the sound of his groan when he kissed me. When he came. I wanted all of it again, and suddenly nothing seemed as important as getting it.

Rising on my tiptoes, I pressed my lips to his jawline while his hard-on pushed against my stomach.

His stubble was gone, leaving his skin smooth, and I couldn't resist kissing a line down his throat, growing dizzy from his taste and smell.

He brought the glass to his mouth like I wasn't even kissing him. "We don't have to be a secret."

I shook my head, running my tongue up his throat. I dropped my palm down to cup his erection. "Probably best that it is. After all, I tried to rob you."

I rested my hand over his bulge and rubbed the entire length of him. He caught my mouth in a kiss and swallowed my moan. It was wet and rough, our tongues sliding in that all too familiar dance as a flame pulsed to life inside me.

He nipped my bottom lip. "What's mine is yours."

"Every woman's dream."

"I only care about my woman."

"Yours," I breathed against his lips. It was so addictive to think of myself as his. To know that he was all mine. "I don't share."

He set his glass down, grabbed the back of my neck, and then kissed me until I was panting and my heartbeat throbbed between my legs.

"Good," he rasped, pulling away slightly. "Neither do I."

A frenzy burned through my blood. I pressed my body to his, raked my blunt nails down his stomach, and tugged at his belt buckle. He made a rough sound in his throat, his lips devouring mine.

But soon, he was pulling away, and I moaned in frustration. "Winston!"

His thumb came to my mouth, brushing over my bottom bruised lip.

"I thought you said this was a mistake."

I sighed. "I never said the sex was a mistake," I protested. "But sex is not hard to find." Love, on the other hand, was. "Men aren't hard to find if that's all you're looking for."

"Are you saying you've had sex with another man since we met?" His growl vibrated through me.

I smiled, blinking innocently. "I never said that."

"Well, did you?"

It was best to stop torturing him, although I wasn't sure that he didn't deserve to suffer. "After I went home that first night—" He visibly tensed and I couldn't help but smile smugly. "—I made myself come... hard while thinking about you."

My blush burned through me. I was sure every inch of my skin was stained crimson now while my heart thundered like I'd run a marathon.

His body stilled for a split second. "You did?"

I rose to my toes and pressed my lips to his ear. "I did. In the shower, and then again when I got into bed. I slipped my fingers inside myself and pretended they were yours."

Drum. Drum. Drum.

Three heartbeats passed before he groaned, "Good girl. Your pussy and your mouth earned my cock." He brought his hand to my neck, placing it over my pulse point. "This." He squeezed lightly. "Your heart will beat only for me."

He grabbed my hips and lifted me, meeting my mouth with his. My legs wrapped around his waist, his hard-on pressing against my body, making me shudder with need for him. My hands buried in his hair, gripping his strands as he walked me backward toward the stairs.

He kissed me like he was trying to eat me alive, licking and biting. Like *he* needed *me*.

He trailed his mouth down my neck while I worked on his shirt buttons. I wanted his flesh against mine. I tugged the white dress shirt out of his pants and ran my hands over the hot skin of his stomach and chest. A lungful of air escaped me when he fell on top of me on the bed.

I blinked, surprised we were in the bedroom, but before I could ponder further on it, he yanked on my dress, and a rip sounded as the straps came loose.

"I liked that dress," I whispered against his lips.

"I'll buy you ten more." He pulled my bra down and took a

nipple between his teeth. I gasped as he sucked on my breast. His hands kneaded my ass, gripping it hard, and I sighed when his fingers slid inside my panties, brushing against my clit and teasing my entrance.

"Fuck, my wife's wet," he groaned. A tremor rolled through him as he kissed my cheek, trailing kisses over my jaw, and then he murmured against my lips, "You want my cock?"

"Yes," I panted. "Please, give it to me."

He shuddered. His gaze liquefied, and he watched me as his finger pushed in. I was so far gone. A flush warmed my body as I writhed, panted, and moaned under his touch. "I can feel your walls clenching around my fingers."

His breathing turned ragged and his body tensed. Two of his fingers slid in and out, and I groaned as he began to move them agonizingly slowly. He kissed my throat, and I shook beneath him as his fingers fucked me.

It almost felt like he was making love to me. My eyes fluttered shut. I fisted the sheets and dug my heels into the bed, my body shaking with intense pleasure.

"Winston... oh... God..."

"Open your eyes," he grunted. "Watch me own you, Billie."

Through a half-lidded stare, I gasped as his fingers pushed in and out of my pussy, and I came with a violent shudder. He swallowed my moans in his mouth. Wet and rough kissing with a hint of desperation and carnal desire. He sucked on my tongue.

When I came down from my high, he nipped at my bottom lip, his teeth hitting mine.

"I'm going to fuck you now," he breathed in my ear. "And I won't stop until you beg me to."

And he did just that.

I cracked an eye open, feeling a finger lazily gliding up and down my spine. I was lying on my stomach, naked, my body aching in all the right places.

His finger traced over my shoulder blades, and I shivered. I'd lost track of how many times my husband had slid that big cock of his inside me.

"I can tell you're awake." Gosh, I loved his husky voice.

"Shouldn't you be sleeping?"

He made an amused sound, his hand traveling between the cheeks of my ass. "It's two in the afternoon."

"I have to go home," I said, pushing my ass against his rough palm.

"This is your home."

I didn't answer. My father and sister were home. Winston was... I didn't know the answer to that yet. Besides, I needed to save my father's hospital, and lying around here between these sheets with Winston wasn't conducive to that plan.

He gave my ass a firm squeeze. "What's going on in that pretty head of yours?"

Taking a deep breath, I rolled over. His rugged face looked relaxed, and there was a hint of a heartbreaking smile on his lips.

"I need to help my family with some things."

His smile disappeared, but he cupped my face. "Tell me how I can help."

His words pricked at me, and I swallowed a lump in my throat.

"No, you don't need to worry about a thing." I had a multimillion-dollar bracelet to handle what my father needed. Yes, he'd offered his money earlier, but something about taking it felt... wrong. It made me feel cheap, even though he *had* forced me into this marriage. I should take the payment. Ugh, when did my life become so complicated?

His gaze traced my collarbone. "Winston?"

"Mmm?" He cupped my breast and thumbed my nipple. I was wet in an instant, twisting my legs in the sheets. His hooded gaze met mine.

"Why did you want to marry me?"

I felt the tension in his body rising as if it was being pumped into him and, just like that, his relaxed expression was replaced with a mask. The one that hid so many things.

"We should shower and get dressed," he answered instead.

I smoothed my hands up his bare chest, trying not to feel hurt at being shut down again. But then, it wasn't as if I was an open book with him either. We were a perfect fit in bed, but that was where our compatibility started and ended.

I forced a smile. *It doesn't matter*, I tried to convince myself. I got what I needed—in a roundabout way—and he clearly got whatever it was he was after.

"Winston!" a booming voice bellowed from downstairs and I froze.

"Fuck. Here we go." *What?* I wanted to ask who the man was, but the cold expression on Winston's face stopped me. He rose and pulled on jeans, flicking me an exasperated glance. "Stay here."

"Okay."

I watched him leave the bedroom. I held my breath for the next minute, listening as the raised voices became more and more heated.

"What the fuck's going on?" I whispered to myself as I jumped out of bed and dug out Winston's shirt to wear.

Cracking the door open quietly, I padded down the stairs barefoot. With each step, voices grew in pitch and words became harsher. And colder.

"My wife's a gold digger." Winston's angry voice boomed through the castle, full of venom and hate. "Is that what you needed to hear? So hear it again. My wife's a fucking gold digger. I'm using her, and she's using me. What the fuck more do you want?"

A sick feeling coalesced in my heart, suffocating and painful. The invisible thread that had started to bind us snapped, and I was falling a long way down to the hard, cold ground of reality.

"I destroyed her father. I'll destroy her too," the unfamiliar voice shouted, and I almost collapsed on the marble floor as I lost feeling in my legs. "End her, Winston. Or I will."

My hands shook with anger. With fear. Peeking around the corner, careful to remain unseen, I found Winston standing tall, facing an aged version of himself. It had to be his father.

"You won't be calling those shots," Winston said, his tone bored. Less than twenty-four hours and this fake marriage had gone to hell. How in the fuck did his father find out?

"You said it yourself, she's a gold digger. Our family doesn't need one of those."

I took deep breaths, fearing I was going to be sick in front of my husband and father-in-law, who hated me before he'd even met me.

Fury and bitterness filled me as I spun on my heel and made my way upstairs. The fragile embers of lust were extinguished, and in their place came ice and hate. This could only mean one thing: the Ashfords must have been behind Dad's destruction—behind him losing his beloved hospital. I could forgive a lot... but this?

The honeymoon was over. I'd been right from the beginning. This man was a heartache waiting to happen... but it was too late now.

Chapter 19
Winston

"What do you mean you destroyed her father?" I questioned, narrowing my eyes on my father.

"I had his hospital repossessed." His voice was smug, even proud, and I lost it.

My fist collided with his jaw. I had to exercise all of my self-restraint not to keep wailing on him. There was nothing else I'd like more.

I shook my head and blew out a sardonic breath. "See yourself out." I'd had enough of him and his poison. "Or I swear to God, I'm going to end your miserable life, Father," I spat, the last word burning my throat.

"You say a word about this shit to anyone," he said, wiping the blood off his mouth, "and I'll ensure you lose everything."

I reached for a nearby bottle of whiskey and brought it to my lips, forcing down big gulps of liquid even though it felt like needles moving through my throat. Even though the room was already spinning and sweat coated my forehead.

In one swift move, I launched the bottle through the air, aiming for my father's head and missing it by an inch. The sound of shattered glass filled the air, shards flying everywhere.

I walked out of the room and headed back to my wife without a second look. I should have known the bastard wasn't just going to quietly accept the news of my marriage. He really must have thought I was bluffing when he confronted me on Byron's yacht the other day. Not that it mattered. The vows had been spoken, rings exchanged, and promises made. There wasn't a prenup in place, so there was no fucking way to get a divorce without giving Billie half of what I owned.

While I didn't give a shit, my father did.

You killed your mother. His words seared my brain, drumming in my ears. Fuck, I was a grown-ass man, and it still hurt to hear them. I was no saint, but hearing my own father accuse me of killing my own mother always tore me apart. I should've known he'd manage to ruin a perfectly good day.

Goddammit.

The shower turned off as I entered the bedroom, the red mist from our encounter still coating my vision. I put a lock on my emotions, not willing to show my young wife how fucked up my family was.

I poured myself a glass of cognac, needing to wash off the memories and events since my father showed up. A glass wouldn't cut it, so I reached for the bottle. Just as I tilted my head back and took a gulp, the bathroom door opened and Billie made her way across the room. I found my anger slowly melting at the sight of her in my shirt. Fuck, she looked and felt like my woman.

She walked toward the pile of clothes from last night, now resting on the mussed-up bed we'd shared earlier, and discarded my shirt to don her clothes, totally ignoring me. What the fuck?

"What are you doing?"

"What does it look like? I'm getting dressed," she answered calmly. Too calmly.

"But I wasn't done with you," I growled.

"Oh, but I'm done with you," she gritted out, the shield cracking under the strain of maintaining it.

I stalked over to her only to feel her fist slam into my face. I heard an ominous crack before I stumbled back in shock.

"What the fuck, Billie?"

Blood dripped down my chin, and judging by the pain radiating from the right side of my face, I was going to have one hell of a shiner, but I didn't think my nose was broken.

"Yes, Winston, that's right. What the fuck?" she hissed.

I blinked in confusion, unsure where this was coming from.

"I knew you were a fuckup. More trouble than you're worth," she mumbled to herself as she sat on the bed and slipped on her flats, her motions jerky. "Gold digger," she ground out between clenched teeth, grabbing the other shoe and securing it to her foot.

I reached for her again, understanding finally dawning on me. She must have heard my exchange with my father.

"They were just words, Billie. Meaningless."

She barked out a maniacal laugh. "*Meaningless*," she repeated with a scoff. "You mean like this sham of a marriage? I want a divorce. And you're right. I'll clean you out, being the good little *gold digger* that I am." She stressed the words with finger quotes.

Her eyes roamed around the room until she spotted her cell phone and she stomped to it, bending over to get it.

Then she made her way over to me, her light brown eyes no longer soft but full of loathing. She was a whole head shorter than me, but at the moment, with the way she was staring me down, you'd think she was eight feet tall.

"Stay the fuck away from me and my family, or I'll be sure to make you all pay," she threatened. "These are just words too, but they're not meaningless, so you should heed the warning."

I flashed her a cold smile. "You won't like what happens to you if you try to leave me."

"What are you going to do? Destroy me like your father destroyed mine?" I could see tears beginning to well in her eyes, but she wrestled them back valiantly. "And will you dance on my grave too?" She shot me a venomous glare full of hate and disdain. "I don't give a shit what you do, *Mr. Ashford.* We're done here. I want a divorce, and you better give it to me, or I'll make you regret ever crossing paths with me."

Her hand flew through the air, but I caught her wrist before she could land another hit.

"You belong to me, Billie Ashford. End this marriage and see what happens."

"The only person I belong to is *myself.*" She wrestled her wrist out of my grip, the imprint of my fingers still on her skin.

"And the only way you'll ever be single again is if you kill me."

She gave me a feral smile, but tears burned in her eyes. The tears she was desperate to hold back. "Now there's an idea. I might just do that."

"Do your best, sweetheart. And make doubly sure I'm cold before you mark me as dead and gone. Otherwise, I'll be your shadow for the remainder of your days."

She rolled her eyes, clearly unimpressed.

"Come anywhere near me and I'll end you. And your father's career."

I was just about to warn her that messing around with Senator Ashford wasn't smart when something hit me upside the head.

The world tilted, and as I fell down onto my knees, I watched her storm out the door, flipping me the bird over her shoulder.

The world turned dark as my wife disappeared from my life.

When you find her, hold on. You deserve the best, my sons. Don't settle for anything less. Don't settle like I have.

My mother's words had to be a curse. I couldn't think of any other reason why they would keep coming back to me.

When I woke up, Billie was gone, but she must have come back while I was unconscious. She left a note and the ashes of our marriage certificate on the bathroom counter. Jesus Christ, maybe the woman was crazy.

It'd suit me right anyhow. Crazy was made for me.

I sat on my balcony and watched the rain come down over the sea. Thunder rolled in the distance, and I knew a storm was brewing. The day had started off perfectly, only to turn dreary and dark, just like my mood.

I kept going over last night's and this morning's events. The way Billie looked writhing underneath me. The way she looked when reciting her vows. The way it all made me feel. Only to end up... here.

I should have known. There was no happiness in the Ashford world. Only money, corruption, and death. The events of today magnified the situation, and it made me feel especially unhinged. My brothers and I were the product of that environment, and it was probably for the best that Billie got out when she did. Before I could corrupt her, too.

Not that I'd ever agree to a divorce. Right now, it was the only thing keeping my father and his scheming with the Popov family at bay. As far as I was concerned, our marriage was written in stone.

The rain pelted the windows in full force now, bringing me back to the moment. It was loud and angry, like all these emotions whipping inside my chest. Those glistening, unshed tears flashed in my mind, and I closed my eyes in regret.

"Your drink."

Opening my eyes, I found Asher standing with a glass extended, his own in his other hand. "I saw your bride in town. She flipped me off, so I decided to visit you." I let out a bitter laugh. "Want to tell me what happened?"

"Not really."

He raised his brow. "That bad, huh?" I rubbed my jaw tiredly and took another swig of my drink. "She was with someone. A man."

Tension rolled through me at just the thought of her with

someone else. "Kill him. Better yet, bring him to me to kill." Asher watched me with amusement. "Do you have his name?"

"No." The pressure in my chest became too much at the mere thought of Billie moving on from me so fucking easily while I was out here, drowning my sorrows in alcohol. "Probably for the best too."

I could have laughed, but I didn't find it even slightly amusing.

"What?" I spat dryly. "You're not going to crack a joke about the shortest marriage in history?"

He took a seat next to me, eyeing my shiner. "There are movie stars and singers who already hold those records. Plus, as far as I know, you're still married."

If I were a better person, I would go to her, apologize, and give her the divorce she demanded. Maybe even beg her for another chance. But what was the point? It'd be ruined later down the track anyway. Might as well cut my losses now before I got so deep I couldn't find my way back up.

"I want him dead," I said, taking a sip of the liquid sloshing in my glass. It didn't matter what it was, as long as it erased this bitter taste in my mouth and made me forget.

"Who? The man Billie was with?"

"No. Well, yes. But I was mainly talking about my father."

"Why don't I make that happen for you?" Asher offered.

"Because he'd probably make a deal with the devil and come right back." I shook my head. Father had made himself invaluable to the political world. Getting away with his murder would be hard if not impossible.

"Well, I'm the devil, so I assure you there'll be nothing he can offer that I'd accept."

I shot him a wry look. "That's good to know."

"Was the honeymoon good, despite how short-lived it was?" he asked.

The breeze swept through from the sea, Billie's soft moans riding on it. My forearm burned where she'd bitten me, branding me forever.

"Well, she set the marriage certificate on fire and left me a hate note," I remarked dryly. "So I guess you can say it was standard."

"A hate note?"

I reached into my pocket and handed it to him. He read it out loud. "This gold digger wants a full refund, fucker. I took my wedding gift. I earned it." He handed back the slip of paper, and I shoved it into my pocket. "What exactly happened?"

I shrugged. "Billie overheard Senator Ashford profess his role in the destruction of her father. There's no forgiving that. Not in her world, where family means sacrifice. Oh, and she overheard me telling dear old Dad that she was a gold digger. That went well, too."

This was for the best. Billie was better off *far* away from my family. But... I drew the line at her moving on with someone else. I was only human, after all.

Chapter 20
Billie

Odette and I sat on the little balcony of our father's home, lost in our own thoughts. The familiar dingy table sat between us as we stared out into the darkness, seeing our own demons.

Marco, the poor schmuck who pined after Odette, had already come and gone, offering his unsolicited suggestions on how we should bail ourselves out of the mess with the hospital. Meanwhile, ideas and possibilities swirled in my mind like a hurricane.

On my way out of Winston's castle, I grabbed the bracelet that Asher had gifted us. No, not us. Me. It was mine, fair and square. Yes, I loved diamonds and would love to hold on to the incredible piece, but my family was more important to me.

"Listen, *soeur*," I started, and Odette turned to look at me. "What if I got my hands on some money?" Her eyebrows shot up. Our savings were nonexistent, and all our money was tied up in the hospital. "If I could... get a loan. That would help, right?"

I'd rather die than ask Winston—my secret husband—for a loan, but I could sell the jewelry.

"I don't think a loan will help Dad and his hospital," she

muttered. "They've already started moving patients. The building is no longer ours."

"But it will help you," I argued. She'd already started talking about quitting school and getting a job to ease Dad's burdens. It was her first spring break of medical school and she was due back in the States in a week. She planned on finishing up her year at Stanford, but she still had a ways to go. "I don't want you quitting med school."

She reached over and squeezed my hand. "I don't want to quit either, but I'm not sure there's much choice. I don't want you giving up on your dream of working in Paris either. But here we are."

I waved my hand. "When you're a rich surgeon, you can front me some money."

She chuckled. "Gosh, Billie. I never knew your imagination was so wild."

I didn't laugh. In fact, I was dead serious. Yes, fashion design was my passion. Maman and I were alike in that respect. Where she made all her money from modeling and then funneled her earnings into her designs, that wasn't something I was made for. I knew I'd need financial support to get my business plan off the ground when the time came. But I couldn't exactly tell my sister that I *had* enough and then some, hidden in a drawer in my room, as we sat here tonight. I needed her to see her own dreams through first. I knew she'd do it for me if roles were reversed.

"I'll make it happen," I vowed.

"How?"

I opened my mouth to answer just as a single gunshot shattered the silence.

We ran through the house at once, our footsteps hammering against the hardwood. And dread, heavy like lead in the pit of my stomach, somehow understood what that shot meant.

I stepped into Dad's office, and my worst nightmare materialized in front of me. Blood splattered everywhere. Father's gray hair stained red at his temples. There was *so much blood*.

Unable to breathe, my lungs burned as I stared at the sight in front of me. The world stopped turning. Everything quieted, and the only thing that remained was pain.

Raw. Grinding. Unbearable.

His hand had stiffened around the gun, and his face was almost unrecognizable. My eyes went straight to the carpet he and Maman bought on their honeymoon in Cairo. So much fucking blood.

My limbs finally unstuck and I ran toward him, cursing like a lunatic. Odette showed up with towels, pressing them against his temple. The first towel soaked immediately, and she added another one. I didn't have the heart to tell her to stop.

"Is he breathing?" I wasn't sure where I found my voice.

My sister froze, meeting my eyes as if she hadn't even thought to check his pulse. Her slim fingers moved to his neck and she let out a horrified cry.

Something glinted in Dad's other hand. Bloodied rings—his and Maman's. I all but broke at the sight. With trembling fingers, I reached for it and gripped them tightly.

"Why, Dad?" My voice was hoarse from the pent-up emotions overflowing inside me. Winston's father had destroyed mine. There was no coming back from this. I wanted to make them pay, yet I had no way of making that happen. Fury and grief bubbled inside me, rising higher and higher until I couldn't hold it back anymore.

I screamed, drowning in hysterics—and guilt—as the mountains of misdeeds and secrets swallowed me whole.

Something told me even then, as I knelt in the blood-soaked carpet, that our dad's death would set us on a path that would forever change our lives.

Chapter 21
Winston

My wife buried her father today.

I stood in the back of the full church, catching glimpses of Billie. She held hands with her sister, a frozen expression stuck on her face. She looked exhausted, her eyes red-rimmed with the tears she was holding back.

I should be there with her, comforting her and taking care of her. She was mine. The thought was stupid, yet here I was, standing with my brother, who looked just as miserable as I felt.

The rain was pounding on the windows and church rooftop. The rain hadn't let up all day, almost as if the sky was in mourning too.

"They both look like death," I muttered, my heart squeezing painfully.

"They just lost their father," Byron grumbled. "It's understandable they're upset."

I shot him a wry look. "If our father died, we wouldn't shed a tear. Not one of his children would."

It made it so tempting to end the old man, but the higher he was on the political pole, the harder it would be to pull it off. Although he seemed to be capable of destroying lives all around him. Including Billie's father's.

"Was their old man kind?" I asked my brother instead. "He seems to have a huge fan base from the number of people here. Even his daughters loved him... Imagine that."

Byron gave a terse nod. "The Swan family are close." Then, remembering where we were, he added, "Were."

Were. A simple word, but it brought back the memory in a rush.

We drove in our convoy under the hot African sun. Under any other circumstance, it would be a breathtaking sight: desert sand on one side and azure sea on the other. It was one of the most beautiful places I'd ever seen. But I knew it was just another desert, a different continent, empty acres ravaged by civil wars, neglect, and pirates.

"Fuck, I can't wait to get home." Bradley was born and bred in Alaska. Joined the military to escape the freezing temperatures and monotony of a small, nowhere town. "I never thought I'd miss the freeze-my-ass-off temperatures of Alaska, but I fucking do."

"Alaska's a no-go for me," Dick, a soldier in my unit, grumbled. "Not unless there's a woman waiting for me there to warm me up."

"No Alaskan woman's going to be fucking you," Bradley snickered. "They know better than that." His eyes came to me. "They'll fuck Winston here."

"Why would they fuck him and not me?" He almost sounded offended. I rolled my eyes, stifling a smile. "I'd be just as good between the sheets."

"Because women from Alaska smell money from miles away." Bradley's tone was dry, like it was a well-known fact. I hated to point it out to him, but it wasn't.

"And here I thought you'd say it's because I'm so pretty," I retorted dryly.

"You're pretty, alright," Dick scoffed. "So is my ass. But neither is as pretty as your money."

"Well, our pretty faces and money won't do us any good here," I pointed out. "In case you forgot while daydreaming or seeing your

mirage, we are in the desert, where there are no women for at least a ten-mile radius. Stop wasting your breath."

I raised a brow, challenging them to say anything. We often shot the shit while traveling in a convoy. It was a way to pass the time while we were cooped up in a small space, restless energy coursing through us while waiting to learn what other hell we'd find at the end of our journey.

"I bet you Leif's ugly ass is getting laid in Scotland right about now." Dick's comment wasn't met with the usual enthusiasm. Instead, strained silence reigned, our worry for Leif as loud as our egos.

"Leif is strong. He'll be—" My sentence was cut off when a sudden vibration traveled through the air. The convoy swerved suddenly. I didn't have enough time to blink before we went tumbling. My head hit the roof of the vehicle, and despite the protective gear, the pain was excruciating. My head spun, tilting the world over and over again while my ears rang.

Then stillness. Except everything was tilted sideways. My buddies groaned, attempting to move. Everything was muffled. Trying hard to shake off my disorientation, I crawled out of the overturned truck.

It was then that the chaos erupted. Bullets started to fly. Making a Herculean effort to breathe, I slowly stood up. Pain roared through every bone in my body, but I ignored it.

It was a life-or-death situation.

Bullets rained down around me. On my second family. I reached for my gun and started shooting, clenching my teeth at the blinding pain I felt each time I pulled the trigger. Slowly, men came into focus. Some were already lying on the floor, clutching their wounds.

It gave me hope.

I could still save my buddies. I kept on shooting. Again and again. The enemy numbers were dwindling, hope was growing. An army-green Land Rover Destroyer appeared out of nowhere, driving toward me at full speed.

I aimed and started shooting at the windshield, only to find out it was bulletproof. I aimed for the tires next. Bang. Bang. The vehicle spun out of control until—

Boom.

A deafening explosion shook the desert. The temperature spiked, a combination of the heat in the air and the fire from the explosion. The vehicle missed me, but it hit the truck just as I watched one of my men's legs push out of the opening. The sickening screech of metal against metal.

Agonized screams.

I took a step in its direction before another explosion knocked me off my feet.

This one brought with it an eerie silence. The bitter truth yawned its black mouth: death and loss followed me everywhere.

Lightning splintered through the sky as thunder cracked the silence, mirroring the crack in my heart. The rain started to come down with a fervor, hitting the church's stained glass. Awkward silence between my brother and me suffocated the chapel, and I turned around.

I didn't stop walking until I reached the liquor store, knowing full well my brother was on my heels.

"Winston, you can't keep drowning in alcohol." Byron's voice came from behind me as I took a swig right out of the bottle.

"I know," I admitted. "But let me be tonight."

He watched me quietly for a few seconds before he nodded. I knew what I had to do. Numbness at the bottom of the bottle wouldn't serve me in the long run. Maybe—just maybe—I could get my shit together now that I was married.

Even though my wife wanted nothing to do with me.

The rest of the walk back to the yacht was silent, and an uncomfortable tension filled the space between us. It didn't help that sad trumpet tunes drifted through the air, following us from the church, its melody sickly sweet.

It wasn't until we were out of earshot of the music, Villefranche-sur-Mer in the background and our feet firmly on the yacht, that Byron and I both heaved a sigh of relief.

That night, I drank myself into oblivion, watching the storm build overhead while an invisible one raged inside me. The moon laughed as I sat on the top deck, back against the wall, eyes closed. Or maybe it pitied me. I'd had enough.

I walked into my room, slamming the door shut, and made my way into the bathroom. I shoved my pants and briefs off and switched on the shower, reveling in the warm water washing over me. Fuck, I wanted her. I fisted my dick and pumped so hard it bordered on pain. The images of my wife's tight pussy strangling my cock played through my mind. I cursed her as the waves of an orgasm took me under, drowning me.

I switched the water to cold and sucked in a breath with the first icy wave.

It was exactly what I needed.

I was too drunk to think and still unable to forget her. I figured if I was drunk enough, it wouldn't hurt as much. How fucking wrong I was. I needed to wake the fuck up.

Because I *was* drowning. Life was drowning me.

I had to get my shit together.

Chapter 22
Winston

Six Years Later

The clock was ticking.

The Atiwa rainforest's ecosystem in southeast Ghana was incredibly biodiverse—lush marshes and rivers, and a landscape that cultivated some of the rarest animals and plants.

And, coincidentally, Marie Antoinette's diamond that my wife decided to pawn off for change. Literally fucking change. Two hundred thousand for a piece worth *millions*.

I'd been tracking it for years, only to learn that it fell into the hands of blood diamond smugglers.

Not for long though.

The bracelet was mine. I bought it back from the jewelry store the day she pawned it, but my courier was robbed not two blocks away, and I'd been tracking it ever since.

I was determined to get it back.

I returned my focus to the task at hand. Tropical plants formed a dense shelter of wide, shiny leaves, and we'd hidden in the brush around a small cinder-block hut. Kingston's jaw was set, the sleeves of his tan shirt peeking out from beneath the black Kevlar vest stained with sweat, and his dark hair was soaked through. Asher and Royce were dressed similarly, and all our faces were scrubbed with camouflage markings, making the whites of our eyes glow.

I shared a glance with Asher and my brothers. We'd have to move fast or we'd lose the bracelet again. It'd been to every fucking country in Africa by now, yo-yoing us all over the continent.

Sweat streamed down my sides, and I exhaled slowly, calming my pulse. It wasn't the impending combat that made it spike. It was thoughts of my wife who I hadn't seen in six years. Who I hadn't touched, kissed, or fucked.

Who said marriage was sweet? It was fucking torture.

"You sure you want to do this?" Royce whispered, his rifle ready. His smirking eyes fell to my exposed forearm, the tattoo of my wife's bite mark clearly visible. "You might get bitten again."

He assumed I was doing this for a woman. I was, but not exactly in the way he was insinuating. I planned to return this bracelet to its rightful owner one day, assuming we ever found our way back to each other. But I wasn't naive enough to think it would solve all my problems.

I just had to hope it would help.

Despite her divorce requests. Despite her refusal to talk to me. It didn't take long for the first round of papers to be served via a no-reply email address. The second came shortly afterward. Then the third. It took about six months for them to start arriving in the hands of a personal courier. I burned them and sent the ashes to her sister's Stanford address since my intel told me they were staying together.

Slowly but surely, she got the message. The demands were less frequent now.

Eventually they'd cease, and she'd come to terms with the fact that I wasn't going anywhere. She'd give us a chance, I'd make sure of it.

"It's a love bite, you idiot," Asher remarked.

"Oh, sorry." Royce didn't sound sorry at all. "Yours? Does that make you my brother-in-law?"

Asher flipped him off, not bothering to say anything.

Nobody knew about my secret marriage to Billie Swan except for Asher, whose only giveaway was a slight twitch in his lip. And my father, who had remained pretty tight-lipped about it, to my great surprise.

My gaze met Asher's, and he gave me a pointed look. It was the perfect time to tell my brothers. Hell, I should have told them six years ago, but I didn't and I wouldn't. I'd handle Billie my way.

"At least I'm not stalking our little sister's friend," I retorted dryly. Everyone but Willow knew Royce was crazy about her. She put him firmly in the friend zone, and my poor brother couldn't figure his way out of it.

It would seem all the Ashfords were doomed when it came to love.

"When am I going to meet Willow?" Kingston asked, resolving himself to join in on our ridiculous banter. He'd only recently come back into our lives when Alexei Nikolaev, my brother-in-law, connected with Aurora. We all knew to tread lightly, given that we all still had a lot of work to do before our relationship with him was fully mended. I, as well as each of my siblings, was as determined as ever.

"I have to keep you away from her," Royce spat dryly. "You're exactly the type she goes for. The troublemakers."

Soft chuckles traveled around, and I was reminded of the hot air and how hard it was to breathe.

"Then I don't see any reason she can't be yours," Kingston retorted. "You're the biggest troublemaker of us all."

Royce flipped him the bird, drawing a grin from our little brother. Kingston was the youngest, but he'd gone through the worst shit. And for that, I hated our father even more.

"Ever occur to you, Royce, that maybe you don't love her enough?" I asked, and the look he shot me was full of horror. Honestly, it was ridiculous that we were having this conversation in a jungle, sweat rolling down our backs as we were about to attack diamond smugglers.

"What the fuck do you mean?" he demanded, his voice indignant.

"Well, clearly you have no trouble getting girls. Weren't you down in sin city for that orgy last week?" Kingston chimed in helpfully.

"I've got to fulfill my needs. I didn't sign up to be celibate." Royce sounded too defensive.

"Maybe Willow refuses to give you a chance *because* you have no problem 'fulfilling your needs' when you claim to want her. If all she sees is you banging anything with a pussy, why would she risk her trust—"

"And heart," Asher interjected, drawing an eye-roll from Royce.

I nodded. "That's right. Why would she risk any of that for you?"

His grip on his weapon tightened, and I suspected he was resisting the urge to shoot us all.

"Jesus, why are you all ganging up on me?" Then he shot me a wry look. "And since when are *you* a love expert?"

I put my hands up in a *Don't shoot the messenger* gesture. "I'm not."

"Clearly, since you're thirty-nine and still single." I didn't correct him. "Besides, you used to do the same thing. Even worse," he pointed out, "you were a manwhore."

But then Billie Swan came into my life and changed the game. If my brothers knew, they'd never let me live it down.

"Right, let's focus on our impending mission," I snapped.

"What?" Royce's voice was pouty and sarcastic. "You mean to tell me they aren't going to just hand it over?"

"Not likely," I said, rolling my eyes. Clearly, he'd been spending too much time in Hollywood, stalking Willow, forgetting how things worked in reality.

"That's not what I signed up for," he moaned.

"You're right," Kingston answered. "It's better. You love to blow shit up. Now you get your chance."

Royce grinned, flashing us that crazy smile that earned him his nickname in special ops training. Fucking berserker. One day he'd blow himself up playing with matches.

Kingston pulled out a device, its screen blinking obnoxiously with a green beacon. "We should surround the place—end them all before they get the chance to run off."

A terse nod and they all moved out, while I remained in my spot. We had them surrounded, one guy on each side of the hut.

"In position at three o'clock." Royce's voice was low in my ear.

"Coming up at nine o'clock." Asher's distinct drawl followed quickly.

"Ready at six." We were all in position, surrounding the unmarked hovel. The windows were black, uncovered holes with just enough room to push weapons through and start shooting. Anything could be hiding on the other side of those empty squares.

"No noise. No prisoners." I gave the order, firm and clear. "We take nothing but that bracelet."

They might have more jewelry and diamonds in there, but taking something that wasn't ours would put a target on our backs. Killing their men—not so much. It was an eye for an eye in the world of diamond smuggling.

Taking a knee, I slowly lifted my rifle's eyepiece, setting my sights on the front door. We'd been tracking radio signals, emails, and IP addresses, and their carelessness—or, rather, their lack of security—led us here. To the heart of the African jungle.

Royce checked in from his point, and I watched as Asher crept across the face of the structure, approaching the wooden door. His gun was at his chest. The silence that followed was deafening as we waited. Nobody breathed. Nobody spoke. He looked at me, and I nodded. I was front and center, ready to cover him.

My heart beat like a mallet against my ribs. I'd learned early on that every operation was unpredictable, volatile. As long as we kept a keen eye and sharp ear, we should have the element of surprise.

He kicked the door down, and chaos erupted. Kingston's shadow emerged from the brush at the opposite end of the house and he aimed, pulling the trigger. My little brother might not have had the same level of training as the rest of us, but he was just as skilled. If not more so, since he was forced into fighting from a young age as a means to survive.

My cheek was pressed to my rifle, the noise of cicadas rising like a chorus around us. Growing louder like a warning, almost overtaking the sound of gunfire. A man ran out of the door and I pulled the trigger. *Bang.*

Asher gave the side door a sharp kick, sending it flying with a commotion that rattled the trees. His back was against the wall again, and another barrage of bullets came. He turned quickly and stepped through the space, swinging his weapon side to side.

It was over before it really began.

We all rushed inside, stepping over dead bodies to reach the jackpot.

"There you are," I murmured, holding Marie Antoinette's bracelet in mid-air.

One day I'd fuck my wife with her wearing nothing but this bracelet and matching necklace. My dick stiffened despite the mess around me. I couldn't help it. It didn't take much more than the thought of her to get me going.

"Okay, are we ready to get the fuck out of here now?" Kingston said as he started collecting teeth from each of the downed targets. I shook my head but didn't comment. Thankfully, neither did Royce, although he did eye him uneasily. He pocketed the last tooth, meeting my eyes. "Or you planning to move in here?"

It was my brother's specialty: show up, fuck shit up, and disappear.

I nodded. "Yeah, let's roll out of here."

Just as I turned around, I caught sight of a little black velvet bag. I reached for it and found a few dozen stones staring back at me.

"Fuck. That'd be worth a fortune." Royce's voice came from over my shoulder. "Cartier would pay a fortune for it." He was right, they would. "Should we keep it?"

"We take nothing that doesn't belong to us."

Placing the velvet bag back where I found it, I tucked the diamond bracelet into my pocket and made my way out of there.

"We have to get that checked out," I told Asher, flicking a last glimpse at the cabin. He'd gotten into a knife fight with one of the guards, and it didn't look good.

"It's nothing." Asher's stubbornness would one day be his downfall.

"We don't know if the knife was clean. Don't be an idiot, see the doctor."

All in all, we came out of this unscathed.

If only I'd known how close I was to *her*. If only I'd known what I'd set in motion.

Chapter 23
Billie

His mama's ring. My wedding ring.

I stared at the elegant piece of jewelry in the palm of my hand. I should have dropped it in the mail and returned it. Instead, I'd kept it safe, lugging it with me wherever I went. It symbolized... what?

Love? Definitely not. Lust? Probably. Mistake? Certainly.

I sighed, putting it back into the hidden compartment of my toiletry bag before splashing cold water on my face, attempting to cool off.

The blistering heat made it hard to breathe, and I started to question our sanity for sticking around Ghana. We'd been here for a year, and we planned to stay for the duration of Odette's residency. I'd kept myself busy with getting certified as a gemologist, studying precious metals, and continuing my work in fashion design. Africa was a mecca for mines and diamonds, and I took advantage of being able to train with locals.

But I missed our home on the French Riviera. I missed comfort food. I missed my friend Violet, who was now a distinguished psychologist working in Italy, catering to the minds of most of Europe's underbelly. I missed goddamned sex.

Okay, the latter could be found anywhere in the world. The stupid, romantic notion that refused to die kept me from sleeping with any man who wasn't the sicko refusing to grant me a divorce.

Jesus.

It was supposed to be a temporary arrangement, yet six years later, I was still married to him. I filed for divorce using some shoddy website boasting "Quick Divorce, Guaranteed" and failed. I should've known it was a sham. All I received in return were ashes. Yes, I could file for divorce using a lawyer and make a big splash about it, but then the world would know. My sister would know.

And I was desperate to keep it a secret. It was my dirty little secret, and after everything that had happened, it felt like a slap in Odette's face considering Byron turned out to be an even bigger douche than his brother.

Once I was a divorced woman, it would be as if it never happened. The secret marriage would become the secret divorce.

I thought back to the last email I got from him. It resembled my reply when he asked for FaceTime sex, the idiot.

🖕 🖕 🖕

So fucking mature.

"Aunt Billie, are you upset again?" Ares's voice pulled me out of my wallowing, and I smiled as I crouched down to his level.

"Of course not." The truth was my nephew had a radar on our emotions, and every time I thought of Winston Ashford, I saw red. I wish I could be like my sister, who was the master of keeping hers in check.

"You had that line between your eyes," he pointed out, bringing his tiny hand up to smooth my brow.

I chuckled. "I was just thinking about a new design."

He nodded seriously. "You need to follow your dream."

At five years old, Ares was too smart and too serious for his own good. He definitely didn't inherit that from me. Maybe a tad from Odette, and certainly from his father. Another Ashford. God help us.

Although, I wouldn't trade him for anything. He'd changed our lives. During Odette's pregnancy, we read all the baby books and attended Lamaze classes together. None of it adequately prepared us for that first year. There were some days and nights where it was touch and go. When both my sister and I had broken into tears, tired and cranky, wondering how we'd make it through another day.

But Ares's smiles and cuddles were worth it. I knew it was hard on Odette to leave Ares with me while she was attending school during the day, so I started a digital journal and recorded whatever I could so she wouldn't miss any "firsts."

His first roll. His first crawl. His first word. His first step toward me. His first pedals on a trike. Gosh, *so many firsts*. They made me nostalgic.

"I think you're right," I agreed. "But first we'll go for a walk through the jungle. Maybe we'll find some diamonds here, huh?"

"Or flowers for Maman," he said hopefully.

I smiled warmly. "Or flowers. Those are just as special."

His little hand in mine, we made our way deeper into the jungle. Our feet dragged along the brush and debris of fallen leaves, breaking up the silence of the jungle. Ares, dressed in khaki pants, a matching shirt, and a wide-brim safari hat, looked very much the part of a little adventurer. While he fit right in, I was the polar opposite. I wore a yellow sundress that I designed myself and black rainboots fit for the jungle sludge. The first few weeks in Africa, I wore casual clothes to fit in, but it didn't take long for my old self to come back. I was sick and tired of neutral-colored fabrics, so I reverted to what I liked second best. Fashion.

I let out a sigh. I'd drawn so many designs—both garment and jewel—but that dream was going nowhere fast. Each one I sent in was either rejected or outright lifted, leaving me dumbfounded that those fuckers would steal my shit like that. So, without a leg to stand on legally in the middle of Timbuktu, I stopped sending them.

One day I'd have my own jewelry store and sell my designs there. Nobody would dare steal my designs then. Fuckers. I was imagining the various creative scenarios detailing how I'd get back at those assholes—I kept an extensive list—when the hum of a nearby engine shot an alarm through me.

"Do you hear that?" Ares whispered, his eyes widening.

My gaze traveled over the cocoa trees, noting a clearing in the distance with nobody in sight. I raised my eyes up to the sky, but was unable to find the source. The birds screeched ominously, and I got the sense that we needed to move out. I was just about to turn around when Ares yanked his hand out of mine and took off in a run.

"Ares," I whisper-yelled at his retreating form. "Ares, stop right now," I shouted. I picked up my pace, too focused on trying to move stealthily in the mud that I didn't notice my dress getting caught. The sound of my dress tearing mixing with my own heavy breathing made my panic surge. I was far from in shape. *Working out was not on my list today*, I thought, breathing heavily. *Not by a long shot.*

I ran after him, my lungs burning and my feet stomping against the jungle floor.

Coming to a stop in the clearing where Ares stood wide-eyed, staring at the hut filled with bullet holes, I immediately scolded him. "Don't ever do that again!"

My words were choppy. My breathing even more jagged. And all the while, I kept my wary attention on the hut, even though my gut told me we shouldn't be here.

"Look, Aunt Billie, someone was here." He pointed to the footprints caked in the dirt. Ares had become quite the tracker, living in the wild. Poor kid had nothing else to do. Our hide-and-seek games only went so far, and my nephew liked to be challenged in every area. It took Odette, myself, and the entire village to keep him stimulated.

"Stay here," I ordered him and made my way closer to the hut. The stench became unbearable as I got closer, and my heart stopped when I caught a glimpse of a foot. Fuck, there was a dead body in there.

I made my way inside. Dead bodies lay everywhere, but my eyes caught on a black velvet bag. It sat there, half open and far too tempting. I made my way to it, keeping my footsteps silent against the rickety wooden floor, my heart in my throat.

I grabbed the plush bag, then whirled around and rushed to my nephew. We had to get out of here.

"Look," Ares exclaimed, pointing to a nearby stump where he'd tracked several sets of large footprints heading south. His eyes snagged on the velvet bag I clutched. "What's that?"

He was as curious about everything as I was. I couldn't quite figure out if that was a good thing or a bad thing.

Ares reached out for it, but I stopped him. "No, we don't know what it could be," I reprimanded him softly while my grip tightened around it.

"Why are you touching it, then, Aunt Billie?"

Smart kid. Good question. Before I could stop myself, I opened the sack and was met with the shiniest stones I'd ever seen.

"Holy shit," I murmured. This could buy back our dad's hospital and kickstart my career, and we'd *still* be loaded.

"Wow," he said as my mind screamed with excitement.

I didn't have my 10x microscope to examine them, but I'd studied enough to be able to spot the clarity of diamonds. And these were graded exceptionally.

"It's a sign," Ares whispered, understanding that we shouldn't be heard nor found here.

"What is?" I asked absentmindedly, mesmerized by the shiny pouch. I should have been born a Valkyrie, since they were rumored to be enamored with precious stones.

"You should take them and start your diamond store."

My head whipped to the child. The reasonable side of me knew it wasn't a sign. The smart part of me knew it was trouble. Yet, like a fucking idiot, I was unable to resist temptation.

"You know what, buddy? I think you're right. It *is* a sign." I pecked him on his chubby cheek and hugged him excitedly. "And we'll keep this our little secret from Mommy."

"You got it, Aunt Billie."

Needless to say, it didn't remain a secret for long.

Chapter 24
Winston

I stood at the window of my penthouse and stared over Washington, D.C., the city that heaved with greed and corruption. My hands in my suit pockets, I couldn't tamp down the strange feeling burning a hole in my stomach.

Billie Swan Ashford. Beautiful, smart, and proud.

Over the past six years, I'd tried to wipe her from my mind. Sobriety didn't help. I'd come to terms with it, but forgetting her had proved impossible.

I couldn't forget her. The way she looked, the way she smelled, the curve of her breasts through her silk dress. The fire in her eyes. Now that I was sober, the attraction and need for her was even stronger.

I took a seat at my desk and mentally went over the words to say before I called her. My brothers would roast me alive if they knew how hard my heart thundered when I thought of her, but then, they weren't married, so they couldn't possibly understand it.

Except, perhaps, for Byron.

I rolled the pen beneath my fingers, back and forth, and then exhaled heavily as I dialed her number.

"Hello," she answered.

I closed my eyes at the sound of her voice... sexy... husky... so damn enticing.

"Hello, Billie."

Silence followed for two heartbeats. "Who's this?"

I rolled my eyes and let out a groan. My beautiful smart-ass. She had my number. She'd messaged me enough times to recognize it.

"Your husband," I gritted through clenched teeth.

"I'm not married," she replied icily.

"The certificate in my safe says otherwise," I grumbled. Why was she so adamant about making things difficult? I waited for her to say something, but she remained silent. "We need to talk."

"There's nothing to talk about."

My jaw clenched and my fingers tightened around my cell phone. "Yes, there is. I miss fucking my wife."

"Damn it, Winston. I'm actively trying not to be your wife anymore. It's been *years*—get over it."

"You're mine, and that won't ever change," I gritted. "Now, you can accept it and we can work on it. Or you can fight me on it, and we'll still be married. It's your choice."

"Take this, asshole." My phone buzzed instantly and I glanced at the screen.

Wife: 🖕 🖕 🖕

I closed my eyes, disappointment flooding me at her response. She was so fucking stubborn it drove me crazy.

"Billie, you cannot keep sending me middle finger emojis and demanding a divorce."

She scoffed. "You've sent me a few middle finger emojis too when you keep denying me my divorce."

"Because I don't want one."

She fell silent. That familiar feeling that only happened when I thought about her and talked—fine, emailed—with her began to seep into my bones.

"Why not?"

"Why would I?" I retorted, then immediately screwed up my face. That wasn't a good answer.

"Because I'm a gold digger." God, those words again. The first actual conversation we were having and she was throwing that damn phrase in my face. "Now, what do you want for real?" she snapped impatiently.

My mind went blank. Shit, why did this woman have such an impact on me?

"Winston?" she prompted.

"I wanted to see if you would like to have dinner with me on Saturday night."

My eyes closed in horror... What the fuck was I doing? I'd have more success kidnapping her. Besides, I wasn't even sure if she was back in the States.

She remained silent, and when she replied, she sounded surprised. "Like on a date?"

I dropped my head back and closed my eyes. "I want to start fresh. The way it should have been six years ago."

She gave me a condescending chuckle. "You have got to be kidding. I wouldn't go out with you if you were the last man on earth."

Ouch. Rejection hit worse when sober. At least the alcohol had numbed these disgusting human emotions.

"Why not?" Jesus, I was really asking for it. *Just stop talking, Winston.*

"Because you're a soul-sucking, cold bastard," she spat. "Find yourself another bimbo to entertain. I want you shoved into a deep, dark corner of my past. I want a divorce. Get it through your thick skull."

I heard a click as she hung up. I stared at the phone in my hand while adrenaline pumped through my system. I shouldn't be surprised. After all, the woman had been rejecting me for the last six years.

I should be used to it by now.

Chapter 25
Billie

I had to be the worst fucking thief on this planet.

The last time I'd stolen something, I got caught red-handed the same night. This time, it took the diamond smugglers exactly ten days to catch up to me.

"What the fuck do I do, Violet?" My best friend stared back at me through the iPad screen. She twisted her necklace in what I knew to be a nervous tic. "Don't you have any friends amongst those criminals you see on a regular basis?"

Her movements stopped for two seconds before resuming again. "Have you told Odette?" I gave her a *What do you think?* look. "Start there."

I let out a frustrated breath and grabbed the needle and thread. Sewing was the only thing I found calming. "What about some of your criminals you see? Can't they help us?"

"You don't want to get involved with them," Violet's voice was calm, as usual, and her expression was one of no-nonsense. She didn't take bullshit from anybody and was good at hiding her thoughts behind a blank expression. It was what made her an excellent therapist.

Except it wasn't helping my current frantic state of mind.

"Danso Sabir is after me," I whispered, then in case she didn't know who he was, I added, "He's a fucking contract killer for diamond smugglers."

"At least they're not flesh smugglers." I blinked in confusion, not understanding what one had to do with the other.

"You mean like that crazy guy in *Silence of the Lambs* who peeled the flesh off his victims?"

She shook her head. "No, flesh traders traffic humans." Violet looked behind me. "Hey, Odette."

I froze, then forced myself to relax and smile at my friend. "Okay, gotta go."

"But—"

"Thanks for being no help. I'll let you know if we die." I ended the call and turned around to see my sister with Ares. They both wore khaki shorts that I had designed for them with a white T-shirt and straw hat, each with a fishing rod resting on their shoulders in almost identical positions. The only difference was my sister's narrowed gaze trained ominously on me. "Hey, you two. How was fishing?"

"We didn't catch anything," Ares deadpanned, disappointment clear in his voice. "Maman kept throwing rocks into the river and chasing all the fish away."

I stifled a smile. Odette could slice into a human without flinching, but give her a fish to clean and she gagged like a baby about to puke. It was one of the things Ares and I usually did together, but today I sent them out so I could brainstorm.

"Aww, sorry, buddy. Next time I'll come along and make sure we catch something."

"Then we'll have fish for dinner," he said. I nodded, looking back at Odette. Her gaze never wavered from me. I knew that look. Trouble was imminent.

"Ares, can you put your fishing rod away, please?" Odette asked.

It wasn't until he disappeared into the other room that she spoke again. "What the fuck is happening?"

My pulse skittered, then my heart pounded harder. I pursed my lips. "What do you mean?"

Shit, why did my voice have to quiver like that?

"I stopped at the hospital on our way back from the river. Danso Sabir came in and was looking for you."

That couldn't be good. Danso came and went, depending on his dealings. Odette knew him because he had brought an injured person to the hospital more than once. The locals knew he was a dangerous man, the whispers of his connections to the Ghanaian and Corsican crime syndicates more than just a rumor.

I inhaled deeply, gulped, and spoke. "He did?"

"Why is he looking for you? For us?" she asked, the tone unwavering like her surgical hands. Her back remained rigid, alarm in her eyes. "He's bad news, Billie. I hope you're not dating him."

A strangled laugh bubbled in my throat, but I swallowed it. There was silence for a few beats before I let out a shuddering breath.

"I'm guessing he wants to kill me," I admitted in a soft whisper.

Her eyes widened. "What? *Why?*"

"I took something that belonged to his boss." I gulped. "Diamonds."

I was sure her screech could be heard clear across the village. "What diamonds?"

"The ones I found sitting around." I wasn't technically lying. Only, they were "sitting around" amidst dead bodies, in a shack I probably shouldn't have gone anywhere near. Especially not with my nephew.

"Well, give them back."

"Golly! Why didn't I think of that?" I remarked dryly.

She shot me an annoyed look. "Please don't tell me you've sold them or lost them."

"I haven't lost them," I murmured. "Or sold them." *Yet.*

"Why do I feel like there's something you're not telling me?" She put her hands on her hips, letting them rest there like our maman used to do when I got in trouble.

"Because you're paranoid?" I suggested.

"Billie, this isn't the time for jokes. Return the diamonds before I lose my favorite sister."

"I'm your only sister," I reminded her. "Besides, I can't give them back, because I don't have them on me."

Her brow furrowed. "Where are they?" Swallowing, I searched for my voice. My stomach churned because I knew full well the level of shitstorm we were in. "Well?" she pressed.

My heart thundered in my chest. The first time I attempted burglary, I ended up in a secret marriage. This time, I could end up dead. The worst part was that I'd dragged my sister and nephew into my mess.

"I shipped them to Cartier for appraisal," I rasped. "They would already be in Las Vegas by now."

Her sharp intake of breath told me everything. Silence stretched for long seconds before Odette's shoulders slumped. "I guess we have to go to Vegas, then."

And we did. For the next six months, we traveled from city to city, chasing my stolen diamonds so we could return them to the diamond smugglers and keep our lives from crumbling.

Chapter 26
Winston

Six Months Later

I walked into the restaurant in New Orleans and looked around until I found a familiar face.

It was our monthly family luncheon with my little sister and her family. No matter what, we always made a point to see each other regularly. Alessio and his family, Aurora and hers, Byron, my brothers, and my brother-in-law's entire family too.

There were times when some of us couldn't make it, and it seemed this was one of those. Royce was absent, Alessio and his family were nowhere to be found, and the Nikolaev bunch seemed to be running late as always. On the surface, the Nikolaevs were nothing like us, but somehow, we worked. We had a lot more in common when you looked at what mattered: family, loyalty, and business.

Byron spotted me and waved.

I made my way over just in time to catch Byron's grumbled words. "—he's been fucking every skirt under the sun. For decades. So why now?"

"You can't possibly be talking about me," I announced in greeting.

I sighed as Byron stood up to let me slide into the booth. Begrudgingly, I pushed my too-big body down the seat. I fucking hated booth seating. Every sane person knew the dangers of being cornered, yet in this fucking restaurant, they seemed to thrive on it.

"How do you know?" Byron said, raising his brow. "If I remember correctly, you had your share of groupies."

Not since I got married, I thought to myself.

I hadn't had sex with a woman since my wife walked out. Somehow, no other woman compared when it came to Billie Swan. Correction—Billie *Ashford*. A thrum of arousal shot through me as I thought of our time together six years ago, but I ignored it. It wasn't as if I had a choice; she wanted nothing to do with me.

She didn't fucking care that she was the only woman who made my dick hard. How many drunk emails had I sent her? For fuck's sake, I even suggested FaceTime sex. She could just look at me and I would be rock hard. My hand would take care of the rest.

As always though, the reply came in short and to the point, in the form of middle finger emojis.

There was no room for misinterpretation there. Needless to say, my dick liked that feistiness in her as well. Jesus Christ. I had yet to find something my dick didn't like about her. It wasn't healthy. But then, I'd never been big on healthy habits.

"Groupies are no longer in," I stated matter-of-factly.

Sasha Nikolaev, my brother-in-law's brother, sipped his scotch. "You're right. Not talking about you. You're practically a saint."

Byron shot me a suspicious look. It didn't escape him that six years ago I'd gone from threesomes to complete celibacy. Being married did that to you, I guess. No matter how dysfunctional the arrangement. There were years when I let myself drown in the bottle, smoking cigarettes like it was going out of fashion. I'd quit the bottle, but the cigarettes not so much.

I rolled my eyes. "So we must be talking about Royce."

Byron raised an eyebrow. "So you know?"

"Know what?" I wasn't in the mood to beat around the bush.

"Royce announced his upcoming nuptials," Sasha stated calmly, like it was the most casual thing in the world.

My San Pellegrino arrived, and I took a sip. "So he and Willow finally came to an understanding?"

Everyone knew he had the hots for her, but Sasha's smile told me it wasn't exactly the kind of understanding that would be looked upon favorably.

"That's one way of putting it."

"He didn't kidnap her," Byron chimed in defensively. "We've known Willow since she was a kid. Royce would never put her through that."

My brows shot up. "He kidnapped her?"

"He didn't, damn it. I just said that." Byron was fucking cranky. Probably worried about a PR disaster if word got out.

"Okay," I appeased him, unfazed by our big brother. "Let's say he took her on a surprise vacation."

Sasha snickered. "That sounds like him. It turns out we have a lot more in common, huh?"

We all knew Royce couldn't plan for shit. He was a fly-by-the-seat-of-your-pants kind of guy. "I swear to God, if he hurts her—" Byron pushed his hand through his hair, probably ready to pull it all out. I was surprised he wasn't bald by now. "Not a word to Aurora about this."

I leaned back into my seat casually, happy that the focus had shifted to our younger brother.

"And here I thought we could start today's reunion by announcing Royce kidnapped her best friend."

Byron's fist came down on the table, rattling the glasses. "He didn't kidnap her, goddammit."

"Someone's optimistic," Sasha deadpanned.

"Yeah, that's Byron's middle name," I drawled. "Mr. Optimistic. Ever since he fucked a pretty little doctor."

"Someone's been holding back. What's that about?" Sasha's assessing eyes held Byron's. Being that he only joined our family a few years ago, he wouldn't know about Dr. Swan and Byron's disastrous fling.

Byron waved his hand noncommittally.

"It's nothing. Just a casual one-night stand." His tone held a hint of bitterness. I didn't know if Byron even admitted to himself how far gone he was for his doctor. Probably along the same lines as my own situation. We might look like our father, but we definitely inherited our mother's romantic tendencies. "I almost forgot about Dr. Swan," he added, as if trying to convince himself.

Loud scoffs cut through the silence. "It sure sounds like it," I said.

"If you like the woman, go after her. Otherwise someone will swoop in and steal her from you, you fucking idiot."

Sasha gave wise advice.

"Don't care," Byron fired back. "Women are a headache I don't need."

"Ditto," I muttered under my breath, images of my wife punching me flashing through my mind. I was lucky my face was as tough as marble and that my shiner healed up nicely.

"You two are fucking idiots."

Sasha was right, we were. I'd gladly go for Billie. To get her out of my system, if nothing else. But the woman would sooner punch me in the balls than sign up for that logic. She'd never give me the time of day to try to *make* her fall in love with me.

The door of the restaurant chimed, and Byron rushed to greet our nephew and in-laws while Sasha and I remained in our seats, my recently found brother Kingston joining us.

"Winston, I need to borrow your jet one day soon." Kingston's voice pulled me out of my thoughts, and I shot him a surprised look.

"Hello to you too," I greeted him dryly.

He slid into the booth. "I'm not staying long."

He never did, and I couldn't blame him for it. He'd been to hell and back, and preferred solitude.

"Why do you need my plane? You have your own." In fact, he had several planes, yachts, and helicopters. He was loaded, having built an empire all on his own. On blood. Literally.

Kingston's dark eyes turned ice cold and the corners of his lips barely tipped up. "But yours can go off-radar and not be traced."

Ah, there it was. I knew he'd exact his revenge eventually.

"Whenever you need it, just say the word."

He tilted his head. "You won't tell me not to do something illegal?"

I shrugged. We were way past that point. After all, Kingston was known as Ghost in the underworld thanks to his activities. "The only thing I ask is that if you need help, you call me."

A terse nod, and no other words were needed. His eyes darted to Byron and our sister, who were approaching with the Nikolaevs on their heels. "Don't say anything to Byron."

"You got it."

Whoever Kingston had set his sights on wouldn't stand a chance.

Chapter 27
Billie

"**T**hese fucking heels," I muttered as I struggled to walk over the cobblestones of the French Quarter. Odette, ever the smart one, wore flats and looked perfectly comfortable. Ares gripped her hand, his eyes soaking in the beauty of the French Quarter. My hand shot out to grip her arm, using her to steady me.

"This better work, Billie." *Or we were good as dead.*

The unspoken words were louder than the drunks around us. Everywhere we looked buzzed with life, laughter, and good times. The scent of beignets filled the air, along with piss and alcohol. It was a... *unique* city. Nice to visit, but I wasn't sure that I'd ever want to live in it.

Elegant historic buildings surrounded us. A trumpeter played nearby, his sad tunes traveling over the breeze. The stale smell of alcohol drifted through the air. Crowds of people meandered the streets, their laughter, dancing, and colorful clothing giving this city the vibrancy for which it was known. Mardi Gras was about to be in full swing, although judging by the crowds here today, you'd think it was happening now.

I caught Odette's worried expression, the anguish she attempted to hide. She didn't want to alert Ares, our little worrier. Guilt and dread snaked through me, coiling tightly in the pit of my stomach. The last six months, ever since I gave in to stupid temptation and stole those diamonds, felt surreal. We'd been on the run ever since that fucking day. Every single day.

Why, oh why did I continue to make such careless decisions?

I should have learned my lesson all those years ago.

"It *will* work. They get their shit back, and our life will be back to normal." *I hope.* I felt my sister's wary look on me as she let out a frustrated breath.

I knew what she was thinking. At the age of thirty, I should have known better. And I did. But I saw an opportunity, and I was so fucking sick and tired of putting my life on hold.

I wanted it all. A family. A career I was proud of. A storefront with unique jewelry designed by *me*. Sex. I cringed inwardly. Fuck, would I even know how to have sex? It had been six years. Long, lonely years in the absence of human touch. I was practically a born-again virgin.

"You have everything in your purse?" Odette questioned, and I nearly stumbled again. Not from lack of balance this time. If only she knew the thoughts running through my mind right now.

I sighed. "Yes, sis. The diamonds are in the bag," I assured her. "Glittering in all their luxury."

"Why in the fuck are you wearing heels?" she hissed, watching me stumble around like a newborn fawn.

Rolling my eyes, I shot her an annoyed look. "I wanted to look good."

My sister and I locked gazes in a battle of wills. She was cranky, the lack of sleep and constant moving slowly getting to her.

"You look good, Aunt Billie," Ares said, and my expression instantly softened. With big blue eyes and dark hair, Ares would be a heartbreaker when he grew up. Just like his father, who broke my little sister's heart. Just like his uncle... well, he didn't break my heart, but he sure did hurt me.

At five, Ares knew how to capture hearts.

"Only because I wore these torture devices," I drawled playfully, kicking my foot up in the air to show him.

Odette rolled her eyes, but her expression remained soft. Once this was over, we'd get back to the French Riviera, and we'd make a real home. For Ares. For us.

"There it is." I pointed to the sign for St. Louis Street, where we were meeting Sabir.

Odette lowered to a crouch, bringing her eyes to her son's level. "Ares, when we go inside, you'll go with Aunt Billie while I deal with some work stuff. Okay?"

He dutifully nodded. "Okay."

"Good boy," she murmured, pressing a kiss on his cheek.

"Don't worry, Maman," I chimed in, trying to sound positive. "Everything will be over soon."

I should be the one meeting with the criminal, but Odette insisted on it. I guess she was worried I'd make things worse. She was probably right.

Straightening up, my sister met my eyes. "Follow the plan, Billie. Do not deviate from it. No matter what. And if something happens to—"

"Don't say it," I cut her off. "It's bad luck."

She closed her eyes, probably asking some divine being for patience. "Keep him glued to you. And stay out of sight."

I nodded. She extended her hand, and I reached into my purse, pulling out the small bag. Ten million dollars in such a tiny package. It was enough to turn our lives upside down. It had the potential to make our lives comfortable for the remainder of our days.

Oh well. It didn't work out, and I swore it'd be the last time I gave my criminal career a go.

Odette shoved the diamonds into her purse and we made our way down to the corner, stopping right at the entrance of The Sazerac Bar.

I picked Ares up and we entered the restaurant. My eyes traveled over the expansive room. It had the ambiance of old New Orleans, with walls painted in deep colors and decorated with old photographs. The sounds of the trumpeter carried through the large open windows. A crystal chandelier dominated the room.

With each passing second, my pulse thundered harder and faster, stealing my breath. I kept my composure, but on the inside, I was falling apart.

"Hello," a hostess greeted us with a wide smile. "Do you have a reservation?"

Odette and I shared a glance. "Yes," she croaked. "Blood Diamond."

Those fuckers had a sick sense of humor. To the hostess's credit, she didn't even bat an eye. "Right this way."

We made our way through the space, bypassing tables and booths, when the hostess paused. Odette gave me a faint nod, signaling it was time for us to disappear into the bathroom, when a familiar voice filtered toward me down the corridor.

"Billie?" The voice behind us sounded way too familiar. "Billie Swan."

My face paled when the voice finally registered. Slowly, I turned to face its owner. Winston Ashford. Not ten feet from us, seated at a table crowded with what I could only assume was family. My husband—my secret past—sat there with an alarmed expression, eyes darting between Ares and me.

Byron, his older brother, was here too, staring at Odette like he'd seen a ghost.

Fuck! This was not the time for my past to make an appearance.

Chapter 28
Winston

Six fucking years.

The moment I spotted her, everything came to a halt. Her golden hair shone under the glow of the chandelier. It was short now, barely brushing her shoulders. She pushed a strand of it behind her ear, and then flicked her soft brown eyes away.

God, those bedroom eyes. The image of her on her knees, on all fours, was embedded in my memory. Six fucking years, and my dick finally stirred for a woman in the flesh. About fucking time.

Abstinence was a dreadful thing—I highly recommended against it. Other women could parade around me naked and nothing. Zip. Nada. But one glimpse of my wife, and I was fully erect.

She looked just as beautiful as I remembered. Graceful. Strong. The scent of coconuts and salty air drifted through my senses, intoxicating me. My fucking cock throbbed painfully. After all this time, I still wanted her with the same intensity as the day she walked away.

"Winston Ashford," my wife grumbled, her tone full of disgust. It was clear she was thrilled to see me. "Exactly the man I never wanted to see again."

She wasn't happy to see me. Not. At. All.

"Hello, Odette," my brother greeted Billie's sister. "Or should I call you Dr. Swan?"

"Dr. Swan," she answered tightly, her tone clipped. It would seem Billie's sister wasn't fond of my brother either. I wondered if he got emails with rows of middle fingers too.

"Congratulations. But then, you never doubted your skills, did you?"

My brother could've been reciting the bible in Japanese for all I knew. I didn't pay him any attention. I homed in on Billie with a gaze that promised trouble. I told her wordlessly that this time, I'd fight for her. I'd chase her.

She turned her head to whisper something to the child in her arms, and it was like everything clicked at once.

I froze. The world tilted on its axis, and I choked down a lump in my throat as I stared at the little boy. The boy who looked like the spitting image of me when I was a kid. His blue eyes turned away from Billie and darted my way for a fleeting moment.

Christ.

This changed everything. If I were a good man, I'd have given her a divorce when she asked. But I wasn't, and now all bets were off.

Fuck everything. This time I'd write our story, and for that to happen, Billie needed to be by my side. I just needed time with her so that she'd see how good we could be together. Her path had led her back to me for a reason.

Suddenly, all the demons that'd been haunting me faded into the background. I'd fought them for her, and I'd won—for the most part. Now I had another reason to fight them. *Our son.*

My demons wouldn't get the best of me.

It was my wife who I thought about while fighting my addiction, despite the war memories that threatened to tear me apart. The therapist said to focus on something—someone—who made me want to be a better man.

That was Billie.

Chapter 29
Billie

His gaze seared into me. My heart felt close to stopping and my skin was burning up. We needed to get out of the Ashford vicinity before I did something stupid. Like jump my husband's bones.

But only because it had been so long since I'd had sex.

"Come on, *soeur*, we don't need this shit. The Ashford family is a goddamn plague on this planet. Best to keep our distance so we don't catch anything."

Like a dick.

"It's nice to see you." Of course Byron Ashford would be a gentleman. But he broke Odette's heart. There was no coming back from that shit. Maybe the entire family was damaged in an irreparable way. That had to be it. It was the only explanation that made sense.

"Mr. Ashford." Odette's eyes froze, the gold flecks in them suddenly swimming in a sea of ice. "I'd say it's nice to see you, but it'd be a lie."

That was my sister. I flashed a vicious smile at my husband, and we turned our backs on our past.

Odette nudged me away while I shot her an exasperated glance.

This hadn't started off well, and I was certain she could read the despair in my eyes.

"Just stick to the plan," she muttered, while everything in me screamed to abort the plan and run. I'd rather have criminals after me than my secret husband in my vicinity.

"Who's that?" Ares questioned, his blue eyes darting over my shoulder.

"Nobody important, baby."

My sister's eyes connected with mine, and we both knew she'd never uttered a bigger lie.

With Ares safely in my arms, I paced around the women's bathroom for what seemed like the hundredth time.

A heavy knock sounded at the door and I stiffened. Odette wouldn't be knocking. The door opened, and my heart dropped to my toes.

My husband stood in the doorway, his gaze burning with so many emotions it was hard to read them all. He looked good, even better than he did six years ago. Something about him screamed control and power on another level.

He was in a white dress shirt, his gray tie slightly loosened as if he'd pulled it one too many times on his way to the bathroom. His eyes traveled the length of me until our gazes met. His blues were clouded with something dark and exciting. Possibly terrifying. My pulse leapt.

"This is a women's bathroom," I croaked, placing my nephew down.

That didn't deter him. He entered the bathroom, shutting the door behind him.

"You kept a secret, wife." His eyes locked on me and Ares, and he followed me as I walked backward. His tone demanded a response, but I couldn't think. My thoughts were frazzled, unable to pick up the meaning of his words. "Didn't you?"

I shook my head.

"I have no idea what you're talking about," I breathed.

His gaze flashed with something sardonic. "You kept my son from me."

I swallowed as realization dawned on me. He thought Ares was his. My back hit the bathroom wall as I grasped for straws, anything to get myself out of here without spilling my sister's secret. Ares was Byron's son from their one night together six years ago. The same night—first night—that I spent with Winston.

"No more running, wife." A whisper of darkness laced through his voice as he advanced. I couldn't see straight—not with how hot my body was and how the reverence in his gaze made me feel. "Understood?"

I needed to buy time. Figure out a way to get Ares and me out of here. Odette would understand once I explained. Jesus, would this be how I finally spilled the beans to her?

"Tell me you understand, Billie." I nodded. "Good."

He pressed his hands against the wall on either side of my head. His eyes were on Ares, who was watching the entire exchange with fascination.

"Everything will be okay now."

The rasp of his voice sent the hair on my arms on end. With one hand, I reached around the smooth surface of the sink, searching for anything. I needed to knock some sense into Winston. Hadn't he fucking heard me when I told him I was on the pill?

He pressed his next words against my ear. "I've missed you, wife." I shivered at the raw need in his voice. I sucked in a breath as his lips skimmed up my neck. "I've always thought about you. There has been no other woman since we said our vows."

His admission did things to me. It made me stupid. It made me blind. It made me crave him, which was ridiculous since my nephew was right next to me.

I swallowed. "Ditto." The admission came without my permission, but it must have pleased him immensely because he let out a growl.

"You're lucky you didn't let any other man touch you, Billie, because I'd be busy hunting those men down. I really don't like it when people touch my things."

Something about his words had me burning up from the inside. He was so close, smelled so good, his body heat warming my skin, and I'd been without a man for so long.

"Don't scare him," I rasped, digging deep into the reserves of my sanity before I did something stupid.

"I'm not scared," Ares claimed, and admittedly, he didn't look one bit afraid.

"Good. We Ashfords protect our family."

"Oh." Ares's little marbles worked hard as he tried to understand that. What a damn mess. "That means you're family?"

I let out a frustrated groan while Winston smiled, watching him like a proud father with so much love and affection in his eyes it made my heart clench. I had to get out of here before the wrong secrets came out.

"Yes. And you're coming home with me."

My eyes widened. The hell he was. Even if Ares was his son, we'd never let him take him. I scoffed softly. Yeah, it looked like the Ashfords still just took and destroyed.

My fingers connected with cold glass, and I flicked a glance to the mirror. A heavy crystal vase. It was the only thing on the counter. I didn't think, I just grabbed it and swung, hitting my husband on the head.

Confusion flickered in his eyes as he let out a pained grunt. I winced.

"Sorry," I muttered, regret filling me. But I didn't have a choice.

Winston's big, strong body collapsed to the floor with another grunt just as the bathroom door opened again. My sister stood there, dumbstruck, trying to take in the scene.

"Wh-what happened?"

Her eyes locked on Winston, sprawled on the bathroom floor.

"I had to knock him out," I snapped, my voice low and too defensive. "Shut the door before someone sees us."

She shook her head. "Jesus, Billie. You'll have every goddamn person after us by the time you're done. Why did you knock him out?"

"He wanted to take Ares."

She frowned. "Why?"

"He thought Ares was his."

Surprise marred her features as understanding dawned on her. "Why the hell would he think that?"

My gaze found hers, and I released a frustrated groan. "Because I hooked up with the jerk the same night you hooked up with his brother."

My sister's eyes widened. "I... What? I thought you couldn't stand him."

I shrugged. "I can't." My eyes flicked to the unconscious body on the ground. "I still can't. Obviously."

"Step over him and give me my son," Odette ordered, her patience understandably running thin. "Then let's get out of here before anyone finds him."

Regret filled me as I took stock of his body. He wouldn't die. I could see his chest rising and falling.

"Sorry, Winston," I murmured. "You're lucky I didn't kill you, though."

We headed toward the back until we reached the emergency exit. It was the only way out, unless we wanted to risk going out through the front. So we pushed the door open, feeling the sunlight hit our faces just as the alarm sounded.

Then, we ran from the restaurant and shot down the cobblestone alley like the world was on fire.

All the while, the alarm blared behind us, promising trouble was yet to come.

Chapter 30
Winston

When you find her, hold on. You all deserve the best, my sons. Don't settle for anything less. Don't settle like I have.

The memory of my mother's voice pierced through my aching skull. I tried to focus and find the source of the chaos. It took a while to realize the alarm was going off, the shrieking sound puncturing my eardrums and seeming to shake the entire building.

I forced my eyes open and spotted the Italian marble tile, its cold surface pressed against my cheek. Fuck, why was I on the ground? Shit, maybe I blacked out.

But then all of it rushed to me. My wife. My son. Her arm raised, vase in hand.

Jesus, the woman wanted me dead.

The blaring of the alarm persisted, and I stumbled to my feet, looking for any trace of Billie and the boy, although I suspected they were already long gone.

I stumbled out of the bathroom, noting the emergency door sign flashing. Yeah, long gone. I made my way to the front of the restaurant and the commotion there.

"Take them out. I'll see you in a bit," Byron barked orders. I wasn't sure to whom, the pounding in my skull making it hard to think.

"She has my kid," I mumbled. "That was my son."

I swayed on my feet as everyone turned around. I took a step forward, my hands shaking now from the adrenaline. My wife had a mean punch.

"Your kid?" Byron questioned on a hiss. God, why couldn't he just take my words at face value and shut the fuck up. "How would you have a kid with—"

I saw realization dawn on him. The night in Le Bar Américain when he hooked up with his pretty doctor while Billie and I argued like two adolescent teenagers. Fuck, that was a good night.

"Yes, my kid. Do you not understand English?" I snapped. I was seeing double.

Byron's jaw clenched as he focused on me. I could probably guess what was going through his mind right now.

"Were you drinking back there?" Byron managed to say while Kingston grinned behind him, giving me a thumbs-up.

"She hit me upside the head," I muttered. "I wanted to talk to her about our son, but the maddening woman smashed my skull." Literally. "Then she took off. Billie and her sister set off the alarm." Byron gave me a disbelieving look, so I added frustratedly, "I didn't fucking touch any alcohol."

The truth was that I couldn't even blame him for his suspicion. I'd numbed my troubles and pain that way all too often. It was the reason I used to share women. It was easier to get lost in a sea of bodies than to let an emotional connection form.

Jesus, why was this all so goddamn complicated?

"What are you talking about?" Aurora's voice held disbelief as she appeared out of thin air. "Byron's doctor hit you?"

"No, her sister knocked me out."

"Special Forces, yet a woman manages to knock you out," Byron muttered under his breath.

But then an idea occurred to me and I grinned. I'd knock her up again and this time she'd stay with me forever. Yes, that would work. I didn't care how delusional it made me sound. I would find a way to prove to her how serious I was about making things better between us. The devil on my shoulder wholeheartedly agreed while the angel on my other remained silent, probably judging me. *Join the club, my friend.*

The look my big brother gave me told me he wanted to wipe off my shit-eating grin with disinfectant.

Kingston's eyes met mine, and I had a suspicion he knew what I was planning, but he didn't say anything. Just gave me another thumbs-up. Three brothers against one. Odds were in my favor.

Byron opened his mouth to say something, but Sasha Nikolaev showed up. "Someone exited through the emergency door, that's what set off the alarm."

Someone had finally turned it off, and the silence was almost as deafening as the sirens.

I flopped back onto the seat at our table. "Told you so. The Swan sisters escaped that way. They took my son."

And I'd get them both back. Byron would have to deal with Dr. Swan. *You're welcome, my brother.*

The restaurant was empty now, Aurora and Byron taking a seat as well, keeping their eyes on me. They were worried. They probably should be.

"What makes you think that's your son?" Byron pressed.

Sasha and Alexei sat down too, Kostya on his father's lap. Nothing fazed my nephew. If a bomb exploded next door, Kostya would glance at the damage without batting an eye.

"He's the right age and has the same-colored eyes as mine. Exact same," I said, waving a waiter over. Fuck, I'd kill for some whiskey right now. "Water. And some ice, please." I'd need a clear head to pull one over on Billie. "What do five-year-old boys drink and eat?"

The waiter gave me a blank look. Useless. "Umm, I don't know.

Nuggets and apple juice, maybe," he answered, his eyes tentative. "I don't have any kids."

Google would help me better than this moron. Or my sister and brother-in-law.

"Just bring him water," Byron said, dismissing the waiter. "Maybe a functioning brain too," he added sarcastically.

Once the waiter was out of earshot, Aurora, always the reasonable one, said, "Winston, I don't think you should jump to conclusions. Lots of kids have blue eyes."

"He looks just like us in our baby pictures." Were my siblings blind?

"Did you get any information from your woman?" Sasha asked Byron. It made no sense that they came to meet an international diamond smuggler.

"No." My brother's teeth clenched. It seemed Dr. Swan was as crazy about Byron as Billie was about me. Ah, fucking love.

"If either one of the women are involved in diamond smuggling," Alexei stated calmly, "it'll put them all at risk. These guys won't hesitate to kill the kid."

Fear unlike any I'd ever felt before shot through me.

"Byron, can't you ask your doctor?" Aurora asked Byron softly. She'd always been the romantic of the family, always wanted a big family with nieces and nephews.

Sasha answered. "She didn't seem keen on seeing him." Byron glared at the Russian, probably prepared to kill him. "Might be better to send someone else in. Someone more charming."

Judging by Byron's clenched fists, he was fighting the urge to murder the Russian. "Don't worry. I'll drag the truth out of Odette."

It didn't matter, because I'd get Billie and my son. One way or another.

Chapter 31
Billie

On the outskirts of New Orleans, the hotel we were staying at wasn't the best in the area by any stretch of the imagination. Sadly for us, that didn't mean it wasn't just as pricey. One night, never mind multiple nights, would put a real dent in our budget. Hopefully once this whole business with the diamond smugglers was behind us, we'd be back in France and back to work.

Maybe get back to normal. Ares needed normal. We all did, in fact, which was something we hadn't had since that fateful night all those years ago. My gaze traveled over the small room. Two queen beds. Our bags strewn about. Bare room. Living out of suitcases was getting old, and it wasn't good for any of us.

Especially Ares. My gaze softened on his sleeping form. He was snoring softly, his one leg hanging off the bed. Raindrops pelted against the glass window, and for the hundredth time, I paced the entire length of the small room, waiting for Odette to return.

Where is she?

It shouldn't take this long to go to the bank. Maybe getting a million-dollar loan took a lot of paperwork? She'd left when it was still daylight, and that was hours ago.

Guilt slithered through me. Yesterday, we thought we'd be free of smugglers after we returned the diamonds, but the joke was on us. Now they wanted a million dollars in interest. I couldn't get a loan. I hadn't had a real job since Ares was born. I mainly took care of him and took some odd, small jobs here and there—wedding dresses and custom designs and the like.

God, I hoped this plan worked, although a tiny voice in the back of my head was taunting me.

Ares shot up in the bed, pulling me out of my worries. He rubbed his eyes, turning his head left and right, confused. In the past six months, he'd often woken up in the middle of the night, not knowing where we were and worried about the unfamiliar surroundings.

"Maman? Aunt Billie?"

Not wasting any time, I rushed to him. "Shhh. Everything's okay."

He turned his head in my direction and opened his hands for a hug. I strode over and wrapped him in an embrace, murmuring comforting words. "I'm here."

"Where's Maman?" he asked sleepily. I was wondering the same thing, but I didn't voice it. He didn't need to worry about any more shit than he already was.

"She'll be back soon," I assured him softly.

"I don't like it here, Aunt Billie." My heart clenched. I was solely responsible for this clusterfuck, and I felt so goddamn helpless. I should be the one fixing it, not having Odette roaming from bank to bank. Yet, here we were.

"I know, buddy," I whispered. "We'll be leaving soon. Just wait until we're back where Maman and I grew up. You're going to love it."

He didn't respond, instead just tugged on my arm. "Can you stay with me and tell me a story?"

I knew that translated to "can you lie with me until I fall asleep?" and I sighed, unable to refuse him. I lay on top of the blankets of the bed he shared with Odette, and I started with "Once upon a time," mixing up facts of several fairy tales until we both fell asleep.

At least for a little bit.

A soft whimper woke me up. I blinked my eyes open, worried Ares was in the midst of a nightmare. But it wasn't him. He was sound asleep.

I twisted around and found a body slumped against the door of our room. Careful not to wake up my nephew, I padded across the floor to my sister. My gasp broke the silence as I took in her battered state.

Careful not to hurt her, I gently nudged her. "*Soeur*. Odette, what the fuck happened to you?"

She blinked, then wiped the back of her hand over her eyes. "Nothing."

Anger slowly rose inside me at her state. "Don't give me that bullshit. Clearly something happened. You're black and blue."

Her eyes met mine and she let out a heavy sigh. "Is it bad?"

"You could say that, yeah. Your lip is split and swollen. Your cheek—" I gripped her shoulders. "Tell me who did this," I demanded.

"One of Sabir's guys," she answered tiredly. All I was left with was suffocating guilt and hurt for her.

For a moment, I couldn't breathe. My throat was tight, a weight settling low in my stomach. *I should have received this beating. Not my sister.* She and Ares were innocent in all this.

It wasn't until I cleaned out her wounds and tucked her into bed hours later that I was finally able to process it all. I closed my eyes, leaning my head against the cheap headboard, and wished I could turn back time. I regretted taking those diamonds, obviously.

But even more, I regretted not seeking out Winston to help us. Maybe if I stayed and became the gold digger he claimed I was, I could have spared my sister and nephew all these years of hardships.

My eyes flit open, knowing the answer. I let myself be utterly honest with myself, reflecting on the past six years. Every moment. Every email. Every word spoken with Winston.

No more denial.

While I'd enjoyed every touch by my husband, no matter how fleeting our time together was, I knew I couldn't live in a marriage where I was less than. Eventually, I would have hated him and myself beyond repair. Beyond recognition.

My mother always said my pride would be my downfall, and I was beginning to see the truth in those words.

Chapter 32
Winston

A few days had gone by since I last saw Billie, so the news I'd just received was the last thing I expected.

I ran a trembling hand through my hair, shaken to my core. The little boy was Dr. Odette Swan's son, not Billie's. Fuck, if I'd kept better tabs on my wife, I would have known that.

Contempt spread like frostbite in my chest. At myself. At Billie. At my brother. The disappointment had a bitter taste. A mixture of fury and regret burned in my chest.

My hands shook. From envy. From anger.

I'd survived deployments to war zones, Special Forces training, living under my father's roof, and never once had anything hurt as much as this. I loved my brother—all my siblings—but I'd be lying if I said there wasn't a small part of me that was jealous right now.

"Are you okay?" Byron asked, his tone hesitant.

"Yeah, I just need—" *A drink.* "Coffee." His brow furrowed, clearly not buying it. We were downtown in his office and had just hung up with Nico Morrelli after receiving the devastating news.

I made my way to the minibar, eyeing the alcohol like my life depended on it. Fuck, fuck, fuck. I poured myself some black coffee and took a swig of it, the hot liquid a poor replacement for the numbness alcohol provided.

"You and Billie—"

"Don't," I cut him off. "My desire to talk about her matches your desire to talk about Dr. Swan. So just don't."

He nodded, and the funny thing was that he probably did understand, because Billie's sister had rejected him too.

He scoffed. "Aren't we a pair? Both of us pining after the Swan sisters, our love for them unrequited."

Bitter amusement filled me. Billie was the only woman who'd ever rejected me, ignored me, aggravated me. For six years, I'd tried to forget her. Pretend she didn't matter. Hell, I'd even pretended she didn't exist for a while when she was in Africa. I'd made myself believe her distance and remoteness could successfully erase her.

But the whole time, I knew I was lying to myself.

She was my temptation. The reason for my existence. The reason for my sobriety. Every time I thought of her or every time she was near, all I wanted to do was find a way to worship her.

"Maybe they need a bit more persuasion," I drawled, hiding behind my mask once more.

"Maybe the Ashfords aren't meant to be lucky in love?" Byron stated matter-of-factly, almost as if he'd come to terms with it. "Just look at us. Royce chasing Willow." Our younger brother had made some kind of arrangement with Willow, where she gave him crumbs and he was too happy to complain. *Fair enough.* Leaning back in his chair, he continued, "Maybe there's still hope for Kingston."

Byron's tone didn't hold much of it. The brother we knew now kept himself closed off and at bay. We'd take him in any form, but it was impossible to ignore the fact he'd gone through shit that we couldn't even begin to comprehend.

"Aurora is happily married," I pointed out before taking another drink of the black liquid.

"I didn't think you wanted kids."

I shrugged. The truth was I never thought about having kids, but seeing Billie with one, it made me realize that it could be a second chance—at life, at love. A bad reason for it? Probably. Stupid? For sure. But it felt so fucking right.

The idea that had flourished so naturally a few weeks ago returned with a vengeance. A little light bulb came on, and my mind started working feverishly. I just needed Billie in my bed and everything else would follow.

"I don't like that expression on your face," Byron deadpanned, watching me with narrowed eyes.

I smiled smugly. "But I do."

"You have an idea?"

"Maybe." Before he could question me further, I stopped him. "And no, I won't share it with you."

His chair swayed back and forth as he studied me. Byron and I were alike in some ways, but very different in others. He wasn't willing to cross the same lines I was. For the woman and family I wanted, fuck yeah, I'd cross them all.

The door swung open and Royce strode in like he was the shit, throwing himself into a chair and swinging his feet up onto Byron's desk. A vein throbbed in my brother's temple, and I smirked.

"Leave it to my big brothers to fall for sisters," he drawled lazily. Byron and I groaned out loud. You had to be a saint to deal with Royce. "So fucking boring."

"Leave it to you to fall for our sister's best friend," I pointed out dryly. "I still remember her with braces."

Royce just grinned. "Yeah, me too. She was so fucking cute."

Byron and I shared a glance.

"If you fuck it up, Aurora will never forgive you," Byron said, attempting to drill some common sense into our reckless brother.

"Yeah, she will. You know why?"

Byron and I asked at the same time, "Why?"

"Because I'm her favorite brother." We rolled our eyes while Royce's booming laughter filled the space. The two started a word match, but I stopped listening.

I had to attempt to see my wife. Maybe I'd shower her with diamonds and that would appease her enough to see things my way.

No, idiot. My inner monologue wouldn't give me rest. *You need to do better than that.*

While the two of my brothers bickered, I made myself scarce.

I pulled my Aston Martin to a stop in front of Byron's home, my fingers tapping against the steering wheel.

It had been two days since I learned there wasn't a child connecting Billie and me. Two days since Byron married Dr. Swan and they all moved into his home. Two days for my wife to avoid me. I didn't want to be staying at Byron's place, but goddammit, I couldn't stay away when she was here.

I got out of the car and made my way inside, wearing a fresh suit and sunglasses. It didn't matter how much I didn't want to be here, I wanted Billie. I wanted children, a doting mother—the whole package.

All I needed to do was get Billie on board with my plan and she'd be mine forever.

Fucking idiot. I could almost hear my brothers' voices telling me what a stupid idea this was. I was just about to head to Byron's office when I spotted a glimpse of golden hair in the gardens. A soft laugh followed, and I stopped short in my tracks.

"Your brother's in the study," Byron's butler stated, pointing to the right, like it was my first time here. I knew every corner of this house.

"I'm looking for someone else," I said, watching Billie yank on the flowers and then hand it to my—our—nephew, unaware of my eyes on her. She was speaking vividly, and whatever she was saying made the boy laugh. "You can go." I couldn't look away from her. "I know where to find her."

The butler followed my line of sight and gave his head a subtle shake. He probably *also* thought I was an idiot. It didn't matter to me. My wife was right there, prancing around with honey-golden hair gathered into a Dutch braid, wearing jeans, a white sweater, and flats that looked too tattered for her delicate feet.

I leaned against the doorframe, hands tucked in my front pockets, and observed with delight.

My nephew said something, then handed her back the flowers she'd plucked. Billie feigned surprise, a smile curving her full lips. She curtsied and took the flowers, burying her face into the soft petals.

They both burst into a fit of giggles.

"That's how you sway the ladies, Ares," she explained, a smile coloring her voice. "You're a natural. Just wait and see. Girls will be eating out of your hand."

It was only then that she noticed me, our eyes meeting across the space, her smile instantly falling.

"Aunt Billie, do you like Uncle Winston?" Ares's innocent question made her wince, looking like she might be physically ill just from looking at me.

I cracked my knuckles. "Yeah, Billie. Tell us. Do you like me?" I demanded.

If looks could kill, I'd be dead.

"I don't like him," she told Ares. She didn't even bother being discreet about it, glaring at me like I'd just killed her puppy. "What are you doing here?"

The woman was as stubborn as a mule and as proud as a queen. "This is my brother's house."

"Exactly." She put her hands on her hips, tempting me. There was nothing I wanted more than to throw her over my shoulder and take her to my bedroom. "It's your brother's place. So why are you here?"

"I'm here to see you."

"I'd rather you didn't."

"Well, it's not up to you," I gritted out while Ares's head ping-ponged between us.

She tilted her head, narrowing her eyes. "Fine, have it your way." She twirled around, giving me a three-hundred-sixty-degree view of those curves. My dick instantly stiffened in my slacks, and I groaned inwardly. This was neither the time nor the place. "There. You saw me. Now, please leave."

My pulse quickened as I tried to get a grip on my frustration. Sexual and mental. "Buddy, how about you go and play? I have something important to talk with your aunt about."

Ares took a step when Billie's voice stopped him. "Ares, stay here with me."

His foot still in mid-air, he kept looking between us, unsure who to listen to. "But—"

"Don't leave me alone with the enemy," she hissed, still watching me, animosity in those beautiful golden eyes.

"Go ahead, Ares. I promise, your aunt will be safe with me."

Ares took the first hesitant step away from us, then another, while Billie watched him longingly, shifting on her feet.

Those golden-brown eyes met mine again and my chest twisted. I fucking wanted her so much it hurt. Was that normal? Her lips pursed, and I couldn't help but picture the way they'd look wrapped around my dick. It was like I was back to being a fourteen-year-old boy, eager to explore the concept of sexuality and fucking her in every position imaginable.

Frustrated at myself and her, I reached for the cigarettes in my pocket, then lit one. Never in my life had a woman made me feel so fucking edgy.

"You wanted to talk," she pointed out, a light tremor in her voice. Good, maybe we were both on edge. Equal ground and all that shit. "Talk."

She folded her arms, staring up at me with a defiant tilt to her chin. I couldn't resist bringing my free hand to her chin and brushing my knuckles against her soft skin. A zing of electricity shot up my spine.

She lowered her lashes, licking her bottom lip, and her gaze clung to mine. As I looked at her now, a throb vibrated in my chest, bruising with each heartbeat. Was she feeling this too? People weren't usually so hard to read.

Fuck, I wanted to kiss her so bad that my fingers shook as I brought my hand to my mouth. I inhaled a deep pull of my cigarette, letting the nicotine spread through my veins in one relaxing rush and burning my lungs. It was one of the only addictions I allowed myself these days.

If you didn't count this woman, who stood tall and proud in front of me.

"Why are you looking at me that way?" Her voice was breathy, her cheeks pink. Jackass that I was, I took another step closer to her until her chest brushed against mine, and that scent I'd been missing intoxicated me.

"Because you're my wife."

Her eyes flickered around before returning to me. "Please stop saying that. Someone might hear you."

I smiled. "The world should know it." My eyes lowered to her left hand. "Where's your ring?"

She opened her mouth, undoubtedly to throw a smart-ass comment at me, but then she changed her mind, her shoulders slumping. "It's in my toiletry bag. I've kept it safe so you can have it back."

Satisfaction filled me.

"I want it on your finger."

She rolled her eyes, although her expression softened. "I'm not putting it on my finger, Winston. I only married you because you blackmailed me."

"I only married you because I wanted to make sure nobody else could have you."

She squared her shoulders, clutching on to her defiance like it was her oxygen. "I'm not an object."

"That's right. You're my wife." She let out a frustrated breath. "And as such, next time you're in trouble, you'll reach out to me." She scowled, looking adorable and so damn kissable. "When I married you, I promised to take care of you and protect you. How can I do that if you hide out when you're in trouble, huh?"

She looked shocked for a second, almost as if I had never crossed her mind. I couldn't decide if that made me mad or hurt.

She opened her mouth, then closed it only to open it again.

"You would have helped us?" The disbelief in her voice was evident. I wasn't sure what it said about me or this marriage, but I was determined to fix it.

"Yes."

Her palm came to my chest, my heart beating against it. It was such a simple, innocent touch, but it sent shockwaves through me.

"I wish..." She let out a heavy sigh. "Well, it's too late now. Odette married your brother and paid for my stupidity."

"What stupidity?"

Another deep sigh. "I found a black velvet bag full of diamonds, and I took it."

Suspicion flickered inside me. "Where did you find them?"

"In Africa, where Odette was working."

Christ. "In Ghana? In a ramshackle cottage?"

She nodded but then gasped. "Wait. How did you know it was in Ghana, or about that cottage?"

"You went inside that cottage?" I growled, remembering all the dead bodies we left behind.

"How do you know about that?" she repeated.

I cupped her face. "Billie, what were you thinking? When you see dead bodies, you turn and you run. You don't go exploring."

She licked her lips. "You're not answering my question. How do you know about it?"

"Because it was me who killed those men." I shook my head, the meaning of "small world" never making more sense than at this moment. "They stole the bracelet Asher gifted you for our wedding. I went to get it back, but you never—fucking ever—steal diamonds from smugglers."

She let out a dry laugh. "You don't say. Besides, I sold that bracelet. It wasn't stolen."

I shook my head. "You sold it. I bought it back. Those idiots stole it from me."

Her brows furrowed. "Why would you buy it back?"

"Because it's yours. I always protect what's mine, and you, wife, are mine."

And I never planned on letting her go.

Chapter 33
Billie

Two weeks had gone by since my run-in with my secret husband in New Orleans. In those two weeks, Odette was forced to marry Ares's father. To protect us from the diamond smugglers. To settle the debt and fix the mess that I single-handedly created. The guilt was a heavy burden to bear.

To hear Winston say he would have helped us made me feel even worse. I could have spared Odette from all of this.

In the meantime, I was forced to endure Winston's presence and his constant smirk while he watched me with a calculated expression in his eyes. I fucking knew it wouldn't bode well for me, especially when Winston was being... nice.

His words from two weeks ago still rang in my ears. *I always protect what's mine, and you, wife, are mine.*

Every fiber of my being urged me to run, but then, on the other hand, I wanted to ensure my sister and nephew were well taken care of. My rash decision had gotten us into this predicament; the least I could do was be here for them.

So, here I was, in my nephew's playroom. We'd been in Byron's manor for more days than I cared, and Winston's constant presence set my teeth on edge.

Sooner or later, I'd have to get the hell out of here.

"Hey, buddy. Is it okay if I play"—*hide*—"here with you?"

His dark blue eyes rose from his train set and he flashed me a showstopping smile.

"Of course, Aunt Billie." I saw him spark with interest. "But you have to be careful with it."

"I'm always careful." He gave me a doubtful look but remained quiet. Lowering down onto my knees, I grabbed a train, because really how hard could this be.

"No, not that train," he instructed quickly, and I froze. "That one is too fast for girls."

Apparently, playing with trains was a tricky business.

"Okay, then tell me which one is mine, and we'll race." He handed me the ugliest one there. Typical. Stifling a smile, I took it. "Now what?" I waited for instruction.

"Now you put it here," he said seriously. "And mine will be here. I'll let you go first because you're a girl and I'm a gentleman."

I chuckled softly, which earned me a scowl from my nephew. Lovely. Just a few days around his father and uncles and he was already adopting some questionable qualities.

"Okay, should I just run my train and you catch up?" I questioned, serious once more.

He nodded, and just as I pushed my train forward, a voice I hoped to avoid sounded behind me.

"Ah, here you are, wife." I found Winston leaning against the doorframe, his hands casually tucked in the pockets of his designer suit. I had to admit, he looked good.

Ares's eyes darted to me. "Aunt Billie didn't marry you."

I stiffened, shooting Winston a look of warning that promised retribution. "How's your head?" I gritted, hinting I wouldn't mind knocking him out again.

"Much clearer now that you're around," he answered, flashing me a grin that revealed his perfectly white teeth. Jesus, now even his teeth were sexy? This drought was fucking with my libido big-time.

"Don't get used to it." I turned my head around and titled my chin at Ares. "Your turn, buddy. Let's see if your train can beat mine."

Winston came around and lowered himself to his knees. "Want me to help you, Ares?"

Say no, say no, I chanted in my head.

"Yes, thank you."

I narrowed my eyes on them. Traitors, both of them. "Okay. If you pull the train all the way back and get traction, it will fly past your aunt's."

Ares followed the instruction seriously, and sure as shit, his train passed mine effortlessly. My nephew jumped up in excitement, his eyes shining excitedly.

"Can planes do that too?"

"The toy kind, yes," Winston answered, ruffling his hair and smiling at his excitement.

"I want to be a pilot one day," he announced with determination. "And I'm going to join the Special Forces." My brows scrunched, wondering where he'd heard that. Neither my sister nor I would have spoken about that in front of him. "I'm going to fly a Super Hornet for the Navy."

Just as I opened my mouth to ask him what that was, Winston beat me to it. "Super Hornets are cool planes, but let's wait until you're a teenager before you decide if the military is something for you."

At least he wasn't encouraging the kid.

"Did your daddy fly planes too?"

Winston's expression darkened. "Yes."

"Oh." Ares looked at the floor. "I want to be like my daddy, but I don't know him..." Regret and sorrow filled me. Maybe Odette and I should have told him about his father, but it was just too painful for her at first, and the next thing we knew, years had flown by.

"I'm sorry, buddy. We all love you, and we're lucky to have you."

Ares nodded seriously, fiddling with another train. "Now we'll have a big family, and Byron can be my daddy. Right?"

I swallowed. Fuck, Odette would have to talk to Ares sooner rather than later. The boy didn't even know Byron was actually his father, yet he was already getting attached to the man.

Winston's eyes locked on me, burning a hole in my cheek, but I kept my gaze on my nephew. "Whatever you feel, it's alright."

A worried look crossed his face as he looked at me. "Maman and you won't be upset?"

A choked laugh escaped me while my eyes burned with tears. Maybe we'd failed at this parenting thing. Ares never gave us any indication that being without a dad had bothered him.

I cleared my throat, careful not to let my voice waver. "Of course not, buddy."

He frowned. "I need to tell Maman now."

I nodded, and in the next breath, Ares bolted out of the play-room. My heart squeezed in my chest. I cleared my thick throat again and found my husband's eyes on me.

"What?" I snapped, agitated that he'd witnessed our failure.

A slight twitch lifted the corners of his lips.

"Finally alone," he purred. "You've been avoiding me, wife."

God, if I had a penny for every time he called me "wife," I'd be truly wealthy. It must be his favorite word. But he wasn't exactly wrong. Ever since Odette's expedited marriage, I'd honed the art of avoiding him. "From now on, we're doing things my way."

I rolled my eyes. "*We* are not doing anything."

I shot to my feet and he followed suit. Fuck, I just wanted to maintain space between us. Like, a whole continent. I might not love this man, but damn it, my body sure did.

His gaze slid down my curves, warming me like the hot African sun. The air pulsed, matching the flutter of my heart and the throbbing between my legs, spreading through every inch of me like fire.

Keep your distance, Billie. I didn't need the trouble that came along with Winston Ashford. I remembered his demons well. We couldn't even sleep in the same bed. And of course, he thought I was a gold digger.

I always protect what's mine, and you, wife, are mine.

Why did Winston's words wreak havoc on my peace of mind? Each time I thought of those words, my heart fluttered. Like it wanted to fly out of my chest and straight into his arms. I didn't like it.

"You cannot keep ignoring the fact that we're married."

Unfortunately, my pussy seemed to be on board with his constant reminding because it throbbed achingly for him each time he said it. My responses and feelings toward him were flighty, annoying me. Even more, they were beginning to scare me.

"I won't be your wife for much longer," I muttered, then glanced over my shoulder to ensure the coast was clear before I continued. "So can you stop calling me that? And stop smiling, for fuck's sake."

My usually happy mood had deflated, taking a turn toward grouchy. That was what six years without sex did to a person. I needed a divorce yesterday so I could find some handsome Frenchman who would fuck the memory of this man right out of me. I had no idea why I felt I needed to be faithful to this jerk, but here we were.

"What?" he drawled, still smiling. God, I wanted to wipe that smile off his face. "Can't I smile around my wife? After all, our anniversary is coming up."

"Shhh." I looked around in horror. It'd be my luck for Odette to show up at the wrong moment and hear. "Forget the damn anniversary." He didn't react, just grinned wider. "Why are you smiling at me like that?"

"Because you and I, my dear wife, are going to start this again."

"*This?*"

"Yes, this. Our marriage. We're going to do it the right way this time."

I narrowed my eyes. "Are you drunk?"

His expression didn't waver. "No. I haven't had a drop in years. We'll do the fucking without alcohol from now on."

I scoffed. "I don't think so." He opened his mouth, but I was quick to cut him off. "And don't even think about threatening me with the supposed attempted theft. That statute of limitations has long since past. I. Want. A. Divorce."

"Why?"

I blinked in confusion. "Why what?"

"Why do you want a divorce?"

I let out an irate breath. "Because you called me a gold digger. Because your father destroyed mine. He's *dead* because of him," I said, hating the way my voice trembled. I didn't want to feel vulnerable. "Because I can't stand you, and I found someone else," I lied.

His teeth clenched. "Then I'll kill him, because this"—his hand moved back and forth between us—"will never be over."

My lungs seized. My throat felt too tight. Something about his expression tore at my heart.

He took a step toward me. I took one back. He continued to stalk closer, until my back was pressed against the door.

"I'm going to run," I whispered. I didn't trust this man. Not at all. There must be a hidden agenda. "I don't want this marriage. I don't want..." *You.*

The unspoken word hung in the air.

"You can run, but you cannot hide. This time, I'll turn the world upside down to find you."

There was no emotion behind those words. Just a cold, hard fact. Yet, his eyes burned with the blue fires that promised he'd chase me to the ends of the earth.

I straightened my shoulders, intent on showing him his words didn't impact me. Unfortunately, my bravado had my breasts pushing against his chest, sending a shudder through me. It had been so long since I'd felt a man's touch.

His gaze flashed with darkness, full of lust and something I'd been feeling myself. I shivered at his heat, as if I stood near a furnace about to get burned.

"Be a gentleman and shut up, Winston," I breathed.

The tip of his nose gently brushed against mine. "Being gentle is the last thing I'm going to be."

Our eyes held each other's, some thick and unsteady feeling brewing between us. Consuming, like need. Like something I'd seen only once before. Between Maman and Dad.

A part of me knew this couldn't—wouldn't—end well. But I gave in to the urge to feel him, just one more time. I closed the space between us, and it was all he needed.

To feel him against me was like coming home. It ached, but in a good way. It tore at every cell in my body, leaving something desperate behind. The idea of walking away, back to the cold, color-less life I'd lived before him stirred unwelcome emotions in me.

"I'm never letting you go again. That's a vow, Billie." A whisper of darkness laced through his voice as he pressed his hands against the wall on either side of me. Alarms should be blaring. They didn't. I couldn't focus—not with how hot my body was.

"I'm going to fuck you now." The rasp of his voice sent the hair on my arms on end, and I sucked in a breath as his lips skimmed up my neck. "Six years is a long time to go without sex, without your pussy." I shivered at the insinuation. Did this mean...?

"A-are you telling me you haven't had sex in six years?" I whispered.

"You think I'd fuck another woman after tasting you?" he grunted.

"Yes."

"You'd be wrong." His eyes bore into mine. "And remember this. I. Don't. Cheat." I swallowed. "And I'm going to find every man who touched you and end them." It was a growl that lowered into a threat.

"Who touches me is none of your business."

"It's *my* business, because you're mine." Something about his words—his claim—was burning me up from the inside. He was so close and he smelled so good. I knew it was pointless to fight it.

Heat bloomed beneath my skin, tightening in my breasts and burning a lower path.

"I..." My heartbeat dipped between my legs, throbbing with desire. I dropped my head against the wall, drawing half-lidded eyes up to his. "I didn't cheat either."

My lips parted as he ran a thumb across the seam. As his hands slid down my waist, my hips, skimming the outsides of my thighs. The caress was slow, reverent, as if he was remembering the map of my body.

His possessive gaze watched me as he eased the dress up my legs, exposing the lacy fabric. My body shivered in anticipation. He dipped his hand beneath and roughly pushed those fingers inside, drawing a strangled sound from me.

"Fuck, you're wet," he groaned. I clutched his waist, and my hips started to rock against his hand of their own accord. "Still eager for my cock, I see. Don't worry, you'll get it."

The beginning of an orgasm was already stoking a fire inside me.

He pulled two fingers out of my pussy and brought them to my lips, stopping my protest.

"Suck," he ordered. Any sense I had left evaporated, overwhelmed by a pool of lust. I drew his fingers into my mouth and sucked, his gaze darkening and promising me the fuck of my life. I tasted my arousal and that familiar scent of him that I somehow hadn't forgotten.

I scraped my teeth against his fingers as he pulled them back out and dipped his hand between my legs again. A flush warmed me as I writhed, panted, moaned under his touch. He slid his fingers in and out, slow and lazy, draining all my sanity. And then he rubbed against my clit a final time, and spots exploded behind my eyelids.

He lifted me by the waist and carried me out of the playroom while his mouth devoured me. I couldn't say whether he walked three steps or three miles. A gasp escaped me when he swept everything off the bathroom counter, then dropped me onto it in a rough motion. Glass shattered. Products clanged. Clothes flew.

He ripped my panties down my legs, and with trembling fingers, I worked on his belt buckle. Reaching beneath his waistband, I took him in my hand. So hot and hard. So familiar.

He spread my legs before he pushed inside me in one deep thrust. I choked. He hissed, his eyes focused where we were connected. His hands clutched my hips, the grip sure to mark me.

"Oh God, more," I begged, clutching at his arms. He didn't need me to ask again.

We both shook as he thrust back inside me. I moaned as pleasure burned through my veins. We were both shaking as he eased out, only to drive back inside. I ran my fingers up his chest and held on to his shoulders as he fucked me slowly on the edge of the counter.

We both watched his length disappear in and out of me. It was erotic. It felt better than I remembered.

His lips skimmed against mine. "Who's fucking you?"

"You," I moaned. A noise of satisfaction rumbled in his chest, and then with heavy breaths, he continued to fuck me with violent thrusts that tore even more gasps and moans from my throat.

He lifted me off the counter, pressed me against the mirror, and fucked me deep and hard. On the opposite side of the wall, a faded reflection of us in the window stared back. With every one of Winston's thrusts, the muscles in his body contracted, sending goose bumps scattering up my spine.

His hand on my throat and my legs wrapped around him, I slid a path down to his ass and squeezed. Every sliver of contact between us was maddening, and I knew I needed to be wearing less clothes.

"Are you watching me own you, wife?" he rasped, his kisses sloppy and distracted, his hands hungry. "I'm never letting go." *Thrust.* "Mine."

Something unraveled in my chest. I didn't understand it. It was just sex. I loved sex. Yet, with each word whispered against my skin and every claim, I melted like butter for *this* man.

And that terrified me. But before panic could flicker to life, the orgasm hit me hard, shooting stars between my eyes and knocking the breath from my lungs.

I tightened a fist in his hair, lightly biting down where his shoulder met his neck. With a rough noise, he came inside me.

It wasn't romantic in the least, but something about this whole thing—or maybe it was the mind-blowing orgasm—brought out a tender part of me. With my legs still wrapped around him, I placed a kiss on his neck, soaking up his smell.

He rested his hands on my hips, breathing hard while I kissed his jawline, his cheeks, his lips.

Something slid down my thigh, and my eyes shot open. My sex-high evaporated and turned to ice in my stomach. He must have felt it, too, because he tensed.

"What's the matter?"

"No condom," I breathed. "I'm not on the pill."

"No access to birth control in Ghana?" A suspicion snuck into my mind, poking at it, but like an idiot, I ignored it.

"No, it was too hard and—" And it was pointless since I wasn't having sex with anyone.

He smiled, those lips that could bring so much pleasure curving with a hint of smirk to them.

"Perfect." His hand caressed my back, never ceasing its movement while every fine hair on my body stood at attention. "My wife." He murmured the rough words against my lips, and I knew he saw the blush that arose when he ran a finger across my cheek. "It's about time."

And then I saw it. The look in his eyes that told me he planned this. The fucker wanted me pregnant.

"You bastard," I breathed. "You didn't even think to ask me what I want?"

This was the last straw. It was time to get out of here for good.

Chapter 34
Winston

Billie shoved at me, her expression furious.

I let her go, rougher than I intended, as anger brewed inside me. But instantly a twinge of regret followed.

The woman had no idea how deeply I was committed to this marriage—a visceral need to make her mine, to make this work. It was a hunger that roared in my chest and bled into my veins.

My wife had stoked the fire of my obsession for years. The farce might have fended off my father, but it didn't stop me from wanting the real thing.

"We've been married for six years." I ignored the soft curves of her body as she leaned back on the mirror that I'd just fucked her against.

"Not a real marriage," she spat, like the whole idea gave her nightmares. Contempt spread like frostbite in my chest. How much time had we wasted when we could've been getting to know each other? Building a life that meant something?

"The certificate and the church say otherwise." My eyes fell to her bare finger. "You better put my ring back on your finger, because I intend on announcing to the world that we're married."

Anger roared in her eyes. "Fuck. You. We are not married. I only agreed to it because you blackmailed me."

"I don't understand why you're making it all such a big deal." I leaned down, my lips brushing her ear. I closed my eyes, inhaling her scent. "You belong to me. Forever. And you *will* give me children."

I felt rather than saw her take a step back. With her head tilted up and her spine stiff, she shoved me, her breath ragged and stilted.

"There's more to marriage than just having kids," she said, her tone clipped.

"What is it that you're saying, Billie?" I snapped, a grim smirk slashing across my face.

She took another breath that shook her entire body.

"I'm not having kids with you," she hissed, then whirled around, leaving me alone. Again. No matter though. I'd give her the night to cool off, and we'd start again tomorrow.

One more day and the announcement would be out. Then, if need be, I'd kidnap her and lock her up until we came to a mutual understanding. I grinned.

Great plan.

"Wake up!"

I felt a steel-toe boot kick me in the gut. I attempted to curl up into a ball to protect my ribs, which were surely broken. Another kick and I clenched my teeth to keep a sound from coming out.

"Are you sure that's the man the senator wanted?" one of them asked, causing me to stiffen.

"Yes. He wants us to teach him a lesson."

There were a hundred U.S. senators, but only one made it his life's mission to teach me a lesson. Over and over again. I knew my father ensured I was given the shittiest assignments, but this... It was unfathomable, but I should have seen it coming.

My father was a bastard through and through.

I was in a cell, lying on the concrete floor. I bided my time, assessing how many guards were in this shithole. The layout of the compound was pretty basic, since these guys were idiots. They'd never blindfolded me to conceal my location. They probably assumed I'd never get out of here alive. Others hadn't been so lucky.

My stomach lurched remembering the frail and battered women and children in cells on the way to my own. It made me rage, made me want to fight. And I had—letting my emotions rule me before we'd even reached the wrought-iron bars.

I might have made a mistake when I let these men take me prisoner, but so did they. Without a blindfold or a hood, I was able to check out how many cells surrounded me and where the exits were.

After a few days of torture, they'd taken the bindings off my arms and legs, thinking they'd broken me. Amateurs.

Another swift kick followed, and I sat up slower than I needed to. The guard shoved me and pushed me down the hallway when a bullet sounded, immediately followed by a scream piercing through my skull.

My eyes found the dead body of a woman, her face hidden behind a burqa. I didn't recognize her, but the boy... the boy I recognized. He often came to the compound to sell outdated magazines and fresh fruit.

"You bastards," I hissed. "He's just a kid. Pick on someone your own size."

The guards didn't care, their cold expressions unmoved as they glanced at the dead woman and the bleeding boy.

"Traitors. They help you," one of the guards spat the word, immediately sitting on the filthy floor.

"Mama," a little boy yelled, lying in the pool of blood. Images I'd hoped were forgotten flooded my own mind. "Mama." His screams were hauntingly familiar.

Nobody helped. There were battles and wars waging all over the world—some visible and others not so much. Back home, my war was invisible—against my past, my father, and the mistakes that led to my mother's death. Here, in the desert of an unfamiliar country, we fought a different war, but I wasn't sure who was winning. The women and children certainly weren't.

His face was bruised, his eyes black and blue, salty tears making him wince as they drenched his cheeks.

The cruel guard was laughing. Fucking laughing. And a switch flipped inside me. It triggered something, and it wasn't until I was standing among piles of bodies and bad men that I saw her. Another woman. No, not a woman. A girl. She couldn't have been more than fifteen. A bomb, blinking an angry red, tied to her waist, and her fingers wrapped around the slim pencil-looking device.

"Let me help—"

Boom.

I shot up, drenched in sweat and whispers of nightmares still on my mind. Cold sweat covered my skin as I sat in the comfort of my bed in Byron's manor while deafening silence encircled me.

I jumped up, my feet making no sound on the floor. As I stumbled to the closet to put on some clothes, my mind replayed the images I was desperate to forget. I didn't have scars on my body like Byron, but the constant reminder was still there, pressing against every corner of my mind.

It was the reason I never spent the night with anyone. It was also the reason I was unable to form attachments. I didn't want witnesses to my closet full of fucked-up ghosts. Billie had come close to seeing it. I didn't need a repeat.

I threw on some pants and a T-shirt, making my way out of the room and down the stairs, until the cold air hit me. It seeped into my bones and stole my breath, but I still found solace in it.

The darkness gave me the space and solitude I needed. It was a surefire way to chase my nightmare from my scattered mind.

I sat on the terrace of Byron's manor, looking up at the stars. It was well after midnight, and despite being tired, I couldn't sleep. I never slept well, but I at least slept better when I was in my own home.

The deck chairs by Byron's pool sat ready for use. He insisted on everything being perfect, any time of year.

"Are you sulking?" Kingston's voice came from behind me.

"Aren't you too old to be sneaking up on people?" I lay back against the deck chair, closing my eyes.

He took a seat next to me. "Never too old for that."

I yawned, fighting sleep. My guilty conscience worked its thing, and Billie's words kept echoing in my skull, making it hard to turn off my brain. Maybe I should have spoken to her about having a baby *before* I took matters into my own hands.

You think? Fuck, now my own brain was mocking me. I knew it was wrong when I decided to have sex with her without protection. Dammit, I was supposed to make her forget about everything. The plan was to get her into my bed and keep her there.

For days, weeks, months. Forever.

"You look like you need company," Kingston deadpanned.

I tilted my chin toward the bar setup at the corner of the pool area, stocked with all top-shelf brands. "Want a drink?"

He shook his head. "No, I'm not one for alcohol."

"I wish I could say the same," I muttered. I stood up and made my way to the bar. "Want a snack?"

"Like Twinkies?" he teased.

We used to eat that shit like it was going out of style before he was taken. We'd sneak it by our cook and nanny, then devour them like the dirty little secrets they were.

"Yeah, that'd be good right about now."

He yawned. "Better than what you're about to do."

I found myself by the bar, whiskey in hand. I gripped it like my life depended on it. The reasonable part of me knew I should stop while I was ahead. It was a slippery slope with a single taste of alcohol on my tongue, but I craved the oblivion.

I fucking craved it.

"One glass can't hurt," I said as I poured whiskey into a glass.

"Famous last words."

I didn't listen. I tipped my head back and downed the liquid in one go, the bitter alcohol burning down my throat.

It felt good. It felt bad. *Fuck, fuck, fuck.*

I stared at the night sky, wondering if Billie liked to stargaze like I did. No matter where she was in the world, I thought about her. About... everything. Her touch, her taste, her scent. The world outside could explode, and I wouldn't care.

I replayed the last few hours in my head. I might have fucked up in my delivery, but what did she expect? For me to just give her up?

I shivered at the image of the expression on her face. Her realization that she'd risked getting pregnant, and that I planned it. The condom was the furthest thing from my mind; although I couldn't say with a straight face that I'd completely forgotten it. I was totally elated by the possibility of a child, of someone tying her to me.

We'd spent less than a day together during our "marriage," and it was high time that changed.

She told me once that she wanted to marry for love. Maybe that was the missing piece. Growing up, love wasn't something I witnessed between my parents, but she did. She had a front-row seat to what a picture-perfect marriage looked like. And I walked into that picture with a hand grenade, blew it to pieces, and then set those pieces on fire when I blackmailed her to marry me.

Love. The word rang in my ears.

Maybe if I wanted to make amends and get her back, I should start there.

A shudder rolled down my spine. Everything about my life had led me to where I was today. *Who* I was. What if she peeled my layers back and found them ugly?

I took another swig of the drink, the brown liquid tasting as bitter as the promise of a life without her.

For decades, I'd felt restless, but around her? The world stopped turning. The buzzing in my ears ceased. The ghosts hid in the shadows, almost as if they were scared of the light she brought.

My lips curved into a smile.

They *were* probably scared of her. She'd punch them too. Goddammit, I needed her with me—in my bed, in my home, near me. Everything seemed pointless without her. I slowly shook my head, still not willing to believe she'd rather get a divorce than see what we could build together.

"Slow down, Winston." I poured myself another drink, slamming the bottle down and almost cracking the bar top. I seized the chance to plant my seed in her. Why couldn't she see how right it was? *Because she has goals, you idiot.* My brain had no qualms pointing out flaws in my thinking. Obviously, I wanted to start a life together, but stripping Billie of her independence and happiness wouldn't earn me any points. "You won't get her back if you're drunk."

I could feel my brother's eyes boring into me as I made my way to him, bottle in my hand. Clearly, I ignored him.

"What happened that's got you so rattled?" he questioned. It wasn't as if I was going to admit to him I purposely tried to impregnate my secret wife. *Not secret for much longer.*

"I'm not rattled."

He smirked. "Not even our asshole father makes you touch the drink. But a few minutes around a woman and you're ready to empty Byron's aged collection."

"Why are you assuming this has something to do with a woman?" I questioned.

He shrugged. "Usually the way it goes."

I found his eyes. Dark brown like our sister's and Royce's. "Speaking from experience?"

He snickered. "Fuck no. I've seen enough trouble coming from it to know it should be avoided at all costs."

"So you don't need my plane for a woman?"

He didn't answer, choosing to stare off into the pool. "Define 'woman,'" he answered, uninterested. "I need some ice cream."

"You're going to turn into fucking ice cream."

"Probably," he replied, clearly not worried. I glanced up at Billie's bedroom window. All the lights were off. Nice to know *she* wasn't having problems sleeping. *Infuriating woman.* "What are you looking for?" he asked.

"Checking something out."

"What's something?"

"Nothing."

He chuckled softly—a rare sound these days. "Are you sure it's nothing? Because I could have sworn you were obsessed with Byron's new wife's blonde sister?"

I narrowed my eyes as I homed in on him. "What makes you think that?"

"Maybe the way you can't look away from her."

"And how do you figure that? You haven't even met her yet."

"Maybe I'm stalking you both," he deadpanned.

I smirked at his insinuation. I knew for a *fact* he was stalking—just not Billie. He'd perfected it so well that you never heard him come or go.

I shot to my feet, drink still in my grip, and began to pace. "The woman hates me. I waited six years. Six fucking years, Kingston. Do you know how long that is to go without sex?"

"I can guess."

"I got blisters on my hand from wanking so much. I didn't want to be like our father." Kingston stared at me. I walked back and forth on the patio as my mind raced. "She plays me like a fucking fiddle and doesn't even try. And all she keeps demanding is a fucking—" Christ, it almost slipped. Not that it would matter in a few days. "She wants to break up." Kingston's brows furrowed in confusion. I imagined it wasn't lost on him that there wasn't much to break up in the first place. "It's like the only word she brings up with me."

Kingston thought for a moment, then stated, completely unfazed, "You should expand her vocabulary."

"You know what she is?" I pointed at him. "Infuriating. Stubborn." I pushed my free hand through my hair. "So fucking gorgeous with a pussy that makes me forget everything." I dropped to sit down and exhaled heavily. "Fucking everything."

"So what are you going to do about it?" My eyes darted back to the window. "Wank some more?"

I rolled my eyes, so many ideas playing out in my mind. "Probably."

I glanced up at the stars again, dreaming of a pregnant Billie. I'd stop at nothing to tie my wife to me. I should have done it six years ago. Now that she was back, a life without her was unthinkable. Something about her just clicked for me—just as it had six years ago. I let her go then—for both our sakes. I had some *issues*, as my family liked to call my addiction and PTSD, to work through. I continued staring at the stars, willing them to give me solutions. Maybe something along the lines of what my brother had with Billie's sister.

A shuffle of a chair beside me dragged my gaze away from the constellations. Kingston studied me with a concerned expression.

"Why the relapse?" Kingston broke the silence.

I let out a frustrated sigh and let my head fall back. "I think my wife is spooked."

Silence.

"Your *wife?*"

I turned my head to look at my baby brother. The brother who should have had a carefree life, yet ended up in the pits of hell. I knew he wasn't done with his revenge. Not that I blamed him. Fuck, if he asked for help, I'd be right beside him, helping him get it. But much like all of us Ashfords, Kingston liked to work alone.

"Yes, I married her six years ago to avoid Father's insistence that I marry Nicki Popova." Acid rose from my stomach at even the idea of having that bitch a part of my life. "Billie happened to show up at my home, attempting to steal something. One thing led to another, and it was either go along with my plan or go to prison. So a deal was struck."

Kingston let out a whistle. "Okay, I didn't see that coming."

"I didn't see Billie coming," I muttered. "Or maybe I did, but I was too blind to it. That sassy mouth of hers. That fire."

"So you two have been secretly married for six years." I nodded. "Did you meet up once in a while or—"

I scoffed. "I wish. For six years, I've been getting emails from my wife demanding a divorce."

Kingston shook his head. "Sounds to me like you didn't give her much choice in the first place."

"No, not at first. But then we..." *Fucked like rabbits.* "Worked it out."

"So what changed?"

"She overheard me calling her a gold digger to Father." He grimaced. "Yeah. Exactly how she felt about it," I muttered.

"Did you mean it?"

I shrugged. "To be frank, I didn't give a shit what she was back then. Although now, I know for a fact that she isn't."

"How so?"

"Well, in six years, she hasn't asked me for a dime. She just wants a divorce."

"Which you refuse to grant."

"Damn straight," I gritted. "I'm no quitter."

He shot me a "you're a dumbass" look. I hated to admit it, but he wasn't far off.

"And now she's back."

The corners of my lips tipped up bitterly. "Yes."

"Well, she must be happy about it if you two ended up in your bedroom tonight." The smirk on my brother's face didn't escape me, although the amusement never quite entered his dark eyes. It was rare for Kingston to smile with his eyes anymore.

My wife had felt as amazing as I remembered. No, scratch that. She'd felt even better. I'd never experienced a connection so strong. Fucking ever. Maybe it was the fact that she was my wife. Or maybe it was her admission that she hadn't strayed while we were apart.

It had to count for something. Right?

My jaw clenched, my molars grinding painfully. If only she

hadn't started thinking about damn birth control. She was adamant about having nothing tying her to me.

"Oh no, I know that look. What have you done?" Unlike Kingston who had learned to keep his expression a blank, cold mask to survive, the rest of us were open books. "What have you done, Win?"

"Nothing," I lied, then relented. "We didn't use protection."

"On purpose?"

"She forgot. So did I... sort of. I want her pregnant."

"Jesus Christ, Win. You're really into her, huh?" I ran my hands through my hair. "I'd preach to you about the wrongs of knocking up your wife on purpose, but I have a pretty good feeling you already know them."

"It's not like either one of us are getting any younger. I'm almost forty. She's thirty. We've been married for six years." Although none of that time was spent together...

"Jesus, man. Pull yourself together."

I shot him an exasperated look. "You're not helping."

He shrugged. "How in the fuck would you like me to help?"

"You can't." I gave my head a subtle shake. "I'll talk to her in the morning. Maybe we can come to some kind of agreement. Have kids in exchange for whatever she wants from me. Keep having sex as long as I give her whatever she wants."

"Even a divorce?" Of course Kingston would ask the logical questions.

"No divorce. I don't need Father or Nicki Popova in my life." I rubbed my eyes and moved my neck from side to side to relieve the tension in my shoulders. I truly didn't understand why Father didn't marry her himself. The two were a match made in hell. Perfect for each other.

"Winston."

"Hmmm," I answered absentmindedly.

"What does Father hold over you?" My head whipped to the side, meeting my brother's gaze. "If you want to be rid of him forever, you can't keep it a secret. Whatever it is."

"What do you know about it?" I demanded, my voice sharper than intended.

Kingston shook his head.

"Nothing, but I know he's blackmailing you. The money you've given him could have bought him a private island somewhere tropical." It was worth it not to lose my brothers and my sister. I'd have signed over my entire fortune. "I can tell by the stubborn look on your face, you won't talk."

"You don't talk about certain things either," I pointed out. "None of us talk about our scars."

Kingston's expression darkened. "Touché."

His demons were carved into his skin, every tattoo and every nightmare.

"Where is Royce when you need him to lighten the mood?" I muttered under my breath. Royce was the comedian in our family. Whether he tried or not, he always managed to make us all forget about the fucking shit that weighed this family down.

"Who knows?" he retorted dryly. "Although I'd bet my life he's probably wherever Willow is." Kingston shook his head, sardonic amusement on his face. "What is it with the Ashfords always wanting what they can't have?"

"Maybe it's to do with the fragment of DiLustro blood in all of us." I snickered. The DiLustro men were greedy, but always for love. The women they couldn't have. The women that weren't theirs. Bottom line, they searched for love in all the wrong places. Just look at the clusterfuck our cousin Basilio created when he kidnapped his bride.

Our mother was a DiLustro, daughter to a kingpin who was married off to our father. She loved him. It was a mistake, because all our father knew to do was take and take and take until there was nothing left of a person.

"Maybe," he agreed pensively. He stood up abruptly. "I have to go."

"Where?"

"Somewhere."

He was never very talkative.

"Why does it feel like you're up to something?"

He shrugged. "I am. I found some information on the dark web."

There was a beat of silence before I answered. "Okay."

"It mentions someone I thought was dead. And a flesh auction that Perez Cortes plans to host sometime in the future." I stiffened. Flesh trading was one line nobody in our family crossed, even in the criminal underworld that we were now connected to through Aurora's marriage to Alexei Nikolaev. "Word on the street is that my enemy will be here."

Fuck.

"Your enemy's a woman?" It was usually women who were traded, although not always.

Kingston nodded. "Sofia Catalina Volkov." A cold smile flashed across my brother's face. The kind that promised cold retribution. "I found her weakness." I remained quiet, watching my little brother, whose eyes seemed older than mine.

"What's her weakness?"

"Her kid."

Well, double fuck. I could tell him innocents should never pay, but unfortunately, it was the way of our world. The only thing I could wish for right now was that the old Kingston would re-emerge when the time came. The little brother who was fiercely protective of the vulnerable kids on the playground and in school.

"Is that why you want my jet? To stay under the radar?" I asked him quietly.

"Someone's got to pay," he answered, his tone icy. "About your wife... If you want her in your life, you'll have to learn to talk to her and include her in your decisions. Whether to get her pregnant or negotiate the terms of your marriage. Whatever. Nothing else will fly."

"Great, my baby brother is wiser than I am."

Kingston slapped me on the shoulder. "I've always been smarter than the rest of you."

Lost in my thoughts and my gaze drawn to the stars, I said, "You're not wrong there, little brother."

Then, true to his nickname, Ghost disappeared into the night.

Chapter 35
Billie

Boom, *boom, boom.*

My heartbeat drummed in my ears, hurt like never before. Actually, once before—by the same man when he called me a gold digger. My eyes welled with stupid tears, and there was an odd pang in my chest. I felt... used. The look in Winston's eyes betrayed him. The man was trying to impregnate me, and being the idiot I was, I fell right into his trap.

I shook my head in disgust.

I marched toward my room and slammed the door behind me, locking it just to be safe. I wouldn't put it past him to sneak in here while I was sleeping and catch me off guard.

What the fuck was he thinking?

I angrily swiped my stupid tears away. I hated that I was crying, my face screwed up. I made my way into the bathroom, and for a moment, I stood still, at a loss for what to do. Or maybe hoping to hear Winston run after me to apologize.

But I knew he wouldn't. He never apologized back then either.

The earth moved beneath me at the reminder, and that familiar pain lanced through my heart. Then without a warning, a sob tore through my lips and my heart cracked. I swore I could hear the sound bouncing off the fancy tile of Byron's home.

I had no idea how I'd gotten into the shower. I stood there under the hot water with my head in my hands. My sobs refused to cease, my heart beating fast and hard in my chest. It hurt.

I couldn't even bring myself to go to my sister. Byron looked at her like Dad looked at Maman, and all Winston wanted from me was a baby. First a secret marriage, then calling me a gold digger, and now an heir.

How much more did he expect me to put up with?

I put my hands over my mouth and tried to trap my heart-wrenching sobs. The pain in my chest throbbed, a gaping hole growing with each heartbeat.

All this time, when he'd rejected my request for divorce, he did it with the intention to one day use my body and get me pregnant.

I screwed up my face and slid down the tiles until I hit the floor of my shower, the hot water pelting my back, alone and heartbroken.

I let him make me cry again.

Knock, knock, knock.

The soft sound echoed through the darkened hallway, the sun not yet ready to creep over the vast windows.

My sister opened her bedroom door, looking disheveled.

"Billie." She blinked a few times. "Is everything okay?"

My eyes fell to the necklace she was wearing. The very same necklace that I tried to steal from Winston six years ago. The very piece that had gotten me into trouble, the reason I was blackmailed into a secret marriage and a night of honeymoon sex.

"Billie, you're worrying me."

Odette's voice pulled me from my reminiscing, and I immediately forced a smile.

"Yes, I just wanted to let you know I'll be gone before you wake up in the morning." I pushed my hand through my blonde strands. "Well, in a few hours, I guess."

Her eyebrows shot up in surprise, then she glanced behind her before stepping out into the hallway.

"Isn't it too soon?"

I shrugged, lowering myself and taking a seat on the rug, my back against the wall.

"I'm almost thirty. Definitely not too soon to be on my own." She smiled tiredly, then sat next to me on the plush rug. "Besides, I can't just sit here and wait."

"I understand."

I wasn't sure if she did or not, but I didn't have the energy to get into my crazy, temporary, secret marriage to Winston Ashford, or his sneaky way of trying to impregnate me.

"You look... good. Thoroughly fucked," I said, and Odette's cheeks turned crimson, drawing a soft laugh out of me. "It's a good thing."

She tilted her head, watching me pensively. "I feel like you're running, *soeur*."

I rolled my eyes. "I'm not." It was exactly what I was doing, but I couldn't divulge my plan without getting into all the stupid details of getting blackmailed into marrying Winston and everything else that went with that.

"You never explained why Winston thought Ares was his?"

My cheeks burned as I let out an exasperated breath. I guess we were going there. "I slept with him."

"I figured that much..."

I raised my hand, waving it up and down. "Then why did you ask?"

"Because I think there's more to it."

"Of course there is," I hissed. "The guy is trouble."

"All men are," she muttered. "But he seems to only have eyes for you."

"And he's a blackmailer." Her words finally sank in. "Wait. What?"

She smiled. "He watches you like Dad used to watch Maman. Like he'd die without you."

I blinked, immediately shaking my head, dismissing that possibility. "Winston is nothing like our dad. He manipulates, blackmails, and... and... he calls women gold diggers!" The last words came out of me a few decibels above normal, and from the odd look she was giving me, she'd noticed.

"Hmm, he has probably been surrounded by gold diggers for much of his adult life given how wealthy he is."

I shrugged as I tried to act like those words didn't bother me. I didn't like thinking about Winston with other women.

Six years is a long time to go without sex, without your pussy. His words hummed through me with each heartbeat, repeating them like a bad love song. There was nothing romantic he'd said or done.

It's time we get pregnant. Yeah, let me jump right on that crazy train. *Not.*

But a part of me believed there was more to it than his sudden desire to knock me up.

Then there was everything I watched my sister go through. I couldn't just forget the way she'd screamed and howled in pain during labor, and her broken heart afterward. At least she'd accomplished something in the past six years. I hadn't accomplished anything, and my husband... He'd become even richer.

"He called me a gold digger to his father," I murmured, hating the way my voice wavered. It made me feel vulnerable.

"Senator Ashford's an asshole."

"Who destroyed our father."

I stiffened, but before I could say anything, she waved her hand. "Don't get me started. I'm all for saving people, but even I'd love to murder that man."

"Same," I muttered.

"So what I'm trying to say, Billie, is go make your mark on

the world. Make your dreams come true, but if you've found what our parents had, don't let it go because of your stubborn pride."

The lump in my throat grew. The last six months had been stressful, our main objective being to avoid the drug smugglers and to survive. Now that her husband had gotten us out of that mess, life could get back to normal. Only, I wasn't sure what normal was anymore.

"I just need to do something of my own," I murmured. "I feel like I haven't accomplished anything."

After I helped Odette raise Ares while she finished her degree, then followed her to Ghana where she completed her residency, it felt like I lost purpose. My dream was on hold for a bit, and maybe this was my sign to get back to it. Open a jewelry store and combine it with my fashion aspirations.

Her face fell. "Don't say that. I would have never been able to finish med school without you. Ares wouldn't have had an amazing childhood if it weren't for you."

"Sorry, I probably sound bratty."

She shook her head. "No, no, absolutely not. I understand, and whatever you want to do, I support you, Billie." I knew she did. She always had my back. "I want you to go after your dreams. I just want you to know how much the past six years have meant to me. You've done so much. For me. For Ares."

"That's what sisters are for," I murmured softly.

"I want you to use the money I got from Byron."

"Are you sure? It feels kind of wrong."

She shook her head. "It's not. I asked him and he was good with giving you that money." Her husband gladly shared his black Amex with Odette and my sister didn't hesitate to withdraw a substantial amount. It would be enough to fund my trip and allow me to stay in Paris.

The door opened and Byron stepped out, wearing nothing but gray sweatpants. Shit, there really was something about men in sweatpants. And his abs. Jesus Christ. Did all the Ashford brothers have rock-hard abs?

He looked between us. "Everything okay?"

I jumped to my feet, brushing the nonexistent dust off my pajama pants. "Yes, we were just talking."

Odette smiled. "Sister stuff." He nodded, then gave us back our privacy. "We can talk more, Billie. It's not like there's a job I need to run off to tomorrow."

I smiled sympathetically. My sister loved working in the hospital, the mayhem of emergency rooms. She breathed that shit, and I knew it wouldn't be long until she was back into it. If Byron was smart, he'd recognize that she'd need it to be truly happy. If only he could give his brother the same advice.

"I know, but my flight leaves early."

She pulled me into her arms and hugged me tightly. "Nothing— not the money I was finally able to give you because of Byron or anything else in this world—would ever be enough to repay you for what you've done."

I smiled. "Just be my sister. Always. That's my only ask."

Chapter 36
Winston

Apounding headache lingered in the back of my skull.
That familiar feeling—dry mouth, stiff joints—was definitely a sign of my hangover from hell. I forced my eyes open, the sun high up in the sky blinding me. The blurred surroundings slowly came into focus while my ears continued to ring.

Byron's house. Empty room. My clothes carelessly discarded across the bedroom floor. A knocked-down bottle of whiskey.

Fuck, fuck, *fuck*!

Instant disappointment washed over me at my stupidity, but I couldn't dwell on it because someone barged through the door. Before I could contemplate throwing something at their head, the man in question came into view.

My father.

An air of smugness filled the room as his eyes coasted over me. His dark blue eyes shone with pure evil and arrogance. He was the poster child of corrupt politicians everywhere.

Shifting my feet off the bed, I reached for a pair of clean jeans and pulled them on, leaving my feet and torso bare. Taking my sweet time, I turned to face my father.

"To what do I owe this unpleasant and unwelcome visit?"

His lips curled in distaste. "You're an ignorant little fuck."

I shrugged. "I do what I can. As long as I'm nothing like you, I'll rest easy at night."

His glare practically burned a hole through my skull.

"You think you're so much better than me, don't you?" Evident was the tone he used on anyone he considered beneath him—which was ninety-nine percent of the population. "But you're not. In fact, you're *just like me*." He smoothed down his ugly burgundy tie while I imagined strangling him with it. "In fact, it would seem your little secret wife can't stand you, just like my wife couldn't stand me."

"Shut the fuck up," I hissed, my fingers twitching by my side and wishing for a gun so I could empty its magazine into my father's body. "Don't you fucking compare my marriage to yours," I said with the most calm I could muster. "You humiliated and cheated on my mother at every turn, which is a low I'd never stoop to."

A dark shadow fell over his features. Ever since Ma fucked him over and left her fortune to her children instead of her cheating husband, he'd been holding it against us. Sometimes I wondered if he held something else over my siblings' heads like he did mine.

A long time ago, when I could barely walk, I wanted to be like him, but that was short-lived. Father lived to use and abuse, worried only about people that could benefit him or that he could take advantage of. His children were no exception.

"Last chance, Winston." Father attempted to sound threatening, but all he managed was to come out desperate. There was panic lurking in his eyes that he tried to contain. "The debt to the Popov family cannot be pushed off anymore. It's time to pay up."

"That sounds very much like a personal problem." I didn't give two shits about his debt or his problems.

"Well, I wish I could say it was pleasant chatting with you, but..." I shrugged, staring him in the eye and refusing to let him see the turmoil and damage inside me. He'd be quick to take advantage of it. "It wasn't. You know where the door is."

His face turned a deep shade of purple, but my expression remained impassive.

"You should have come back from the desert a stronger man." I guess we were going there.

"Yeah, yeah. We all know about the strings you were pulling." I reached for my phone, noting it was already almost midday. Fuck! I had to find Billie. "Now if you could kindly get the fuck out of my sight."

His jaw clenched. "I tolerated you for years, but even my patience has its limits."

I scoffed. "Senator Ashford's patience is running out. Imagine that. Just fucking admit it, Father. You're disappointed I came back from my deployments. You didn't want to make me a stronger man; you wanted me dead. You tried your hardest, but looks like I'm harder to kill than you thought."

His upper lip curled in a snarl. "You might be hard to kill, but I bet your secret little wife isn't."

In the next breath, I was on him, my hand wrapped around his neck and his body slammed against the wall, shaking the foundation. The sound of glass shattering filled the space. The whole of my attention was on the bastard who gave me life.

"You even so much as *look* in her direction and I swear to God, I will end you."

The door to my suite swung open, but I didn't bother looking to see who it was. I kept my attention on my father as I contemplated murdering him. Right here and now.

He looked over my shoulder and smiled that condescending smile. "Ah, Byron. The slightly better son."

"What the fuck is going on here?" The tone of Byron's voice told me Father's ass-kissing got him exactly nowhere. I released my grip from his throat.

"Nothing. Your brother and I were just *bonding*." Father patted my shoulder before ducking under my arm. "I'm on my way out."

I let the fucker into my head. He now knew Billie was my weakness. I only hoped he knew how serious my threats were. Anger pulsed in my eardrums and I grabbed the nearest object, pulling it back and taking aim but stopping myself before I hauled it at his head.

Instead, I met Byron's worried gaze.

"Is everything okay?" Byron asked after he left.

"He threatened Billie." He stiffened, knowing full well our father was capable of following through with his threats.

"Maybe it's good that she left," he grumbled. "But I can put someone on her tail to ensure she's safe."

My brain was stuck on his first statement. "What did you just say?"

"I can—"

"No, the other thing."

"Billie left." This time, the object in my hand did fly across the room, the ceramic vase nearly hitting Byron's thick skull. "Jesus Christ, Winston. What the fuck? Are you trying to kill me?"

"How could you let her leave?" I shouted, pulling on my boots.

"Well, I can't exactly tie her up and keep her prisoner." Actually, that sounded like a good idea. "What's the deal with you and her?"

"No deal." He looked at me like I was certifiably crazy, not bothering to hide that he knew there was more to Billie and me. The nosy fucker probably knew the truth anyway. "We're married."

He narrowed his eyes. "If I didn't know you better, I'd say you were in love with your wife."

The words slammed into my chest with a force that had me reeling back. *In love with my wife?* No, it couldn't be. We'd spent six years apart, barely knew each other. Was this how love worked?

I didn't fucking know.

I was so fucking broken that I couldn't even sift through my own feelings. All I knew was that she felt like home.

A violent shudder ran through me, along with a shocking revelation.

Somehow, I had fallen in love with my wife. Maybe that was the reason I needed her so much and was willing to trap her by any means necessary.

"Yeah, that's dumb. Although, I have to admit, I would have done the same." Byron's voice pulled me out of my thoughts.

I blinked while he looked at me with that big-brother smile. I wanted to wipe it off his face. Or hug him for it.

"What?" I asked. Did I say all that shit out loud?

"You won't trap her by impregnating her." Fuck, maybe I was still drunk. "The Swan sisters grew up..." Byron searched for a word, then finally shrugged. "Normal, I guess. Their parents loved each other and actually wanted to be together. They were nothing like ours. I think that's what the sisters are after."

My heart was in my throat.

It beat, loud and fast.

Hard and strong.

Alive.

"There'll be an announcement in the paper about my marriage to Billie," I finally said, emotions reaching new levels. "I want everyone to know." My brother nodded. "When did she leave?"

His eyes darted to the grandfather clock that now showed two in the fucking afternoon.

"At the crack of dawn."

I felt empty at the idea of my wife roaming the world by herself, running away from me. My brain and my heart craved blissful numbness, but not the kind that alcohol provided. Not anymore. I needed her.

"Shouldn't you be with your family?" I asked, something about it slashing at my chest. I should have a family too, yet somehow destiny kept throwing wrenches my way.

"I *am* with my family." He grabbed my shoulders, grunting something underneath his breath.

"Stop," I protested, feeling like a shitty brother. "This hangover is a bitch."

Byron's attention flickered to the empty bottle in my room, but he didn't comment on it.

Instead, he narrowed his eyes on me.

"That won't happen again," I gritted, beating myself up over it again. If I hadn't touched the alcohol, maybe I would have heard my wife leave this morning.

"Winston, you're my brother and will always be my family, but I swear to God, I cannot watch you punish yourself anymore." I blinked in confusion, and he let out a string of frustrated curses. "Do you think I'm blind?"

"Maybe."

"Well, I'm not." He reached and shook me by my shoulders. "Ever since Ma died, you've been on this path of self-destruction." He clasped harder. "Her death wasn't your fault."

The relief at his words didn't come. He didn't know my stupid ass dragged Ma off the course just for a stupid game.

"It is," I said monotonously. "I insisted we go to that game store, knowing full well the security wasn't checked out."

His eyebrows furrowed. "Yes, it was."

I shook my head. "No, it wasn't. We were never supposed to be there."

Byron locked eyes with me. "I looked over the schedule for that day. Father anticipated her taking that route home, and the only thing on that whole street that any of us visited was that game store."

The significance of his words slammed into me. All these years—

"He blamed me for it."

Byron shook his head. "Not. Your. Fault." Suddenly, I felt just a tad bit lighter. My breaths came out in great big gasps. "But if you lose your wife, that will be your fault."

And reality sank in. I had to fight for her. "I have to go. Don't forget, tomorrow, every major newspaper will have my marriage announcement in it."

I had to ensure every corner of this earth received the news.

Byron smiled. "Go get her, brother. Smother her with love."

If Billie was after love, she'd get it. Because she deserved the world.

Chapter 37
Winston

Six Weeks Later

After I woke up hungover and found Billie gone, I had even less idea what I'd do with her once I found her. Pound my chest and growl "Mine"? Tie her to my bed? Lock her up in a tower and fuck her into oblivion? The irrational thoughts swirled, but none of them came even close to what I was actually doing.

Stalking her. Keeping her safe after my father's threat.

I'd been at this for six weeks, two days, and twelve hours. She sat on various terraces at cafés, despite the cold weather sweeping through Paris. She ate a lot of chocolate croissants. She walked the Pont des Arts and the Pont de L'Archevêché—the two bridges that embodied love—multiple times. She met with bankers, over and over again, determined to get a loan and open her custom-made jewelry shop. Each time she was rejected, and when I looked into it, I found that the reason was always the same: insecure funds. Basically, since she didn't have the means to procure the diamonds and other gems to actually put into the jewelry she designed, she was seen as an unfit candidate.

So, I bought the bank and made the manager who rejected her call her back and offer her a business deal. Of course I would finance my wife. I'd even gone and settled the matter of resources—by buying her a diamond mine. Now, I just had to get her to talk to me.

Billie might be stubborn, but I was determined.

I'd tolerate a lot coming from her, but celebrating her loan with another man? No. Fucking. Way. Sure, there was another woman there with them, and Billie looked bored out of her mind, but the fucker was flirting with her like it was going out of style.

I sat at the very back of the bar, monitoring their interactions. Billie wore a dark burgundy dress that hugged her curves as she moved and her eyes shone with excitement while she explained something. The fucker sat next to her while her other female friend sat across from her. I didn't like it one bit. Her two friends looked familiar, although I couldn't quite place them. Not with this jealousy flowing through my veins at seeing their proximity.

Billie brought a forkful of pasta to her mouth and started eating at the same time as the fucker lifted his finger to the corner of her lips, wiping the sauce from it.

My fingers gripped the glass, threatening to shatter it. I thought of creative ways to murder the man. He looked all too eager. I'd dig out his eyeballs. Then cut off his ears. Then I'd slice his fingers. Maybe even his tongue, because I was certain his screaming would get on my nerves.

I grinned menacingly, imagining the blood that would flow, when my buzzing phone distracted me.

Dr. Tristan Bennetti and Dr. Violet Freud.

Then it clicked. I'd seen both of them six years ago at Billie's father's funeral. They'd been there for her when she was at her lowest... Okay, putting a pause on the murder, but I'd still get them kicked out of here.

I sipped at my drink, the sparkling water bubbling over my tongue. Sometimes being sober was a bitch, but it'd be worth it. For Billie. For my family. For *our* family.

I thanked the waiter and left him a generous tip, then I turned and made my way to Billie's table. I wasn't sure what I'd do once I got there, yet here I was. I needed back in her orbit. I was tired of stalking her from a distance. I hated that there was another man closer to her than me. I wanted to share her celebrations and accomplishments.

I needed all of her—her light and her smiles—all for myself.

I grabbed a chair and shoved it in between her and Dr. Bennetti.

"Hey, what are you—"

Billie's eyes widened when she realized it was me. "Hello, wife," I whispered against the shell of her ear, sliding my arm around her waist. "Miss me?"

I watched with delight as goose bumps erupted over her skin.

"Not one bit," she replied dryly. "I'm sorry, but this is a party for three."

Her friends watched the exchange with fascination, and when she became aware of it, a blush tinted her cheeks.

"Good, then this fucker"—I gave Dr. Bennetti a pointed look—"can scramble and get the fuck away from my wife."

Billie rolled her eyes. "Ex-wife."

I flashed her a cold smile. "Not yet."

She scooted her chair away from me, almost landing in her girlfriend's lap. "Soon. Since you were a dick and announced to the world we've been married for six years, I filed for divorce the normal way the very next day."

Ah, right. I purposely ignored that bit of fucking nonsense. She'd started the procedure with some pro-bono lawyer that mine would chew up for breakfast. Besides, she'd been unsuccessful in properly serving me, so the process hadn't officially kicked off.

My eyes fell to her left hand, eyeing her ringless finger. While she pawned off the bracelet, I knew she'd kept my mother's ring, even though she'd yet to wear it. Still, I took that as a good sign. Pathetic? Maybe.

I needed to hold on to every little sign of hope I could.

I leaned over, biting the flesh of her earlobe—hard—drawing a small whimper from her.

"There will be no divorce, temptress. Not while you might be carrying my child," I rasped, my dick throbbing against my slacks. *Fuck*, couldn't the little brainless fucker just chill for a bit?

Billie let out a shaky exhale. "I... I already got my period."

I glanced at the two distinguished doctors gaping at us. "Will you two excuse us, please?" I said, smiling. "Go fuck, eat, whatever you want. Just get lost so my wife and I can have a private conversation."

Dr. Freud flicked Billie a hesitant look. I knew that determination in her eyes. If Billie asked her to stay, she would. Dr. Bennetti wasn't far off. They'd need an incentive.

"Unless you want your careers destroyed and your revenge plans fucked up, I suggest you get lost." Violet and Tristan shared a fleeting look. Shock plastered on Billie's face, confirming that she knew something about Violet's mission to avenge her family. Since nobody moved, I shot them a firm glare, adding, "Right. The. Fuck. Now."

Tick. Tock. Tick. Tock. Silence pulsed like a ticking bomb.

"It's okay," Billie finally said, reassuringly. "I can handle him."

I smirked, even though I doubted her definition of *handling me* was the same as mine. If only she knew how much power she had over me. All she had to do was smile, and I'd be on my knees at her mercy.

"But—"

"Just go," she cut her friends off. "Now."

They stood up and left the restaurant, glancing over their shoulders one last time as they disappeared from view.

"Ah, finally alone," I announced.

"You are such a dick, you know that?"

I grinned. "But you love my dick, wife."

She narrowed her eyes. "I love any dick. Yours is nothing special."

My mouth found her neck, nipping and sucking, while my fingers played with the hem of her dress. "Is that why you remained faithful?"

She shuddered and a soft moan escaped her when my hand skimmed up her thigh. "I... God, I... hate you."

"You claim you hate me, but I bet if I reached beneath this dress, I'd find evidence that proves otherwise."

"I don't love your *anything*." The tremble in her voice matched the tremor in her fingers. She was determined to resist me. That was unacceptable.

"Keep telling yourself that." Her breath hitched as my free hand tightened around her nape, my fingers drawing small circles over her silk panties, right above her clit. "Now, we're going to have a talk. If you resist or lie, I'll make you come, right here in the middle of the restaurant, screaming my name so every person in this city knows you belong to me."

She whimpered, the sound passing her lips a most delicious melody. "Stop."

"Now let's go back to discussing your pregnancy." I couldn't get distracted by her soft noises or her warm body. We'd talk first, and then we'd fuck. "But let me warn you, each lie will result in me finger-fucking you. Right here in this restaurant."

Hooking my finger on the hem, I emphasized the words by releasing the elastic with a snap.

She hissed. "Sicko."

"You like it." Her blush spread down her neck and disappeared underneath her dress.

"So have you actually started your cycle since we last had sex?" Silence. I grazed my teeth against the sensitive flesh of her earlobe while my fingers inched closer to her hot entrance. I was suddenly glad she and her friends had chosen the most secluded table in the restaurant.

"No." Satisfaction filled me. I would have loved to follow through, but knowing it'd been almost two months and she still hadn't gotten her period was even better. "That doesn't mean anything though." Another shudder. "I could just be late."

I wasn't sure what I'd do once we talked about all the things that went wrong in our marriage—or whatever you called this *thing* between us. I just knew that I was desperate to make it work. My baby brother was right. I'd have to include Billie in my—*our* decisions, so we could give this a real chance.

"I'm sorry," I said, and her eyes darted to me in both surprise and confusion. "I'm sorry for not talking to you first about wanting children. It was wrong."

Her delicate neck bobbed as she swallowed. "Okay." She still seemed hesitant to trust me. It wasn't as if I'd given her any reason to.

"I want to start anew."

She shook her head. "We never started anything, Winston. It was just one night... three nights," she corrected herself quickly, calling to mind the last time we had sex, right before she took off like a bat out of hell.

"Then let's start this—" I gestured between us. "Let's start our life together now."

"The bottom line is we don't know each other. I still don't understand why you forced this marriage."

"I have a proposition for you."

She let out a sigh and rolled her eyes. "The last time you had one of those, it didn't turn out so great."

I ignored her comment. "Let's date." She kept staring at me, almost as if she didn't understand my English. Maybe I should repeat it in French? "I'd like a chance for us to get to know each other. No more lies or hidden agendas." She scoffed softly. "There had to be a reason you walked over to my table that night at Le Bar Américain."

She shrugged her shoulders. "You were hot, and I was horny."

Okay, it wasn't exactly what I hoped to hear, but it was a start. "We have chemistry."

She shook her head. "And you almost choked me to death that night."

I stiffened at the reminder. It was one of my most shameful moments, laying a hand on a woman. The image of when I finally came to my senses and saw her horrified expression had been seared into my mind.

"I had—have some things that..." Fuck, I didn't want to lay out all my weaknesses. I wanted her to see me for my strengths, and then once she was completely in love with me, *maybe* I'd let her see my fucked-up side. My invisible scars. I cleared my throat. "I'm working through some things."

She tilted her head pensively, and I wondered what she was seeing when she looked at me. A mistake? A mirror image of my corrupt, greedy father? Or something else entirely?

"Your alcohol problem?" Goddammit, this was too much.

"I got it handled." For the most part. I hadn't had a relapse since my conversation with Kingston. Before that, it had been months.

"That never goes away, you know." I didn't take her for someone who had experienced addiction. "Why do you drink?"

"I don't. Not anymore."

She wouldn't let this one rest, I could tell. "But what made you start?"

I reached into my pocket for cigarettes and tapped them against the table. "I wanted to forget."

Just when I thought she'd pry further, she stopped and steered the conversation in a different direction.

"Why did you call me a gold digger when you're the one who forced me to marry you?" Her bottom lip wobbled, which only worked to make me feel like shit.

"Billie, you know you're not. You haven't tried to take a dime since you walked away." Her eyes shone with tears that threatened to spill, and my chest tightened at the sight. My father always made my mother cry. I refused to be like him. "Hear me out—"

"I don't want your apology. It means nothing coming from someone who wouldn't know the first thing about feeling remorseful." My stomach roiled at the possibility that I might have lost her before even being given a chance. I was tempted to say something snappy and lash out, but I held back.

"Okay, maybe I'm not sorry for trapping you into a marriage. Or trying to get you pregnant. But I am sorry I didn't come after you sooner. I'm sorry I was too drunk and dumb to see that by some luck I was given a beautiful, smart wife. I'm sorry I didn't work on getting you back sooner. Instead, I fixated on the bracelet you pawned off just to get that piece of you back."

Fuck, I was laying it on thick. For the first time since my mother's death, I was all in. I no longer wanted to pretend I didn't care.

"We needed the money. And I figured your father owed us so..." Her voice was small, almost shameful, but she refused to cower. That was who Billie Ashford was. A fighter. "Everyone knows that the bride keeps the gifts."

"Is that right?"

She narrowed her eyes. "It is. Your father ruined mine."

Guilt charred inside me, simmering like a geyser. My father ruined a great many lives. "Is that the reason you want the divorce?"

Her lips thinned. "One of them." Taking a deep breath before she exhaled, she continued, "My family's everything to me, and your father destroyed that. Money from the bracelet was supposed to get my dad's hospital back and take care of my sister."

I wished she'd come to me. I would have helped her, signed away my entire fortune if need be.

"You pawned it off for way too little." She didn't answer, staring at her fingers. Why did it have to bother me that she wasn't wearing my ring? I wanted to brand her so the world knew she was off-limits. "So what do you say, wife?"

"To what?" She raised her hand and flagged over a waiter for her check.

"To us dating." I didn't want to be the guy who lost the girl before he ever really had her. The same one who hid behind a bottle and nightmares. I hated the crippling loneliness that hit me every day. I wanted to feel like I did every time this woman was around me—like a worthy man. I was choosing to be better with her. I would keep trying until she saw us the way I did. Meant to be.

The waiter placed the check down and she reached for it. "What are you doing?"

She pointed to her plate that was licked clean and her sparkling water glass. Yet another confirmation that had me suspecting she was pregnant.

"Paying for my dinner."

Chapter 38
Billie

A look of horror dawned on Winston's face.

"When you're with me, I pay for everything," he growled. "I pay the bills. I take care of you. I touch you."

"Wow, I didn't realize you were from medieval times." Not that I usually minded my date handling the check, but this wasn't a date. He crashed my celebratory dinner.

"You have a little something right here, by the way," he said, reaching a hand toward my face.

"Where? Here?" I was reaching for the napkin in my lap when he leaned forward and licked the corner of my mouth.

"It's gone now." My eyes darted around the restaurant while my cheeks burned with embarrassment. This man had no shame. I felt his fingertips on my cheek, and my eyes fluttered shut for a moment. I opened my eyes and found his mouth so close to mine. "Don't let another man touch you. It makes me do crazy things."

He was jealous, I realized. Of Tristan. The notion was ridiculous. Tristan was more Odette's friend than mine, but since he was in Paris and I didn't know many people here, I figured I'd reach out to him. After finishing med school at Stanford, he committed to doing his residency in Paris. He was really digging the European lifestyle, and he seemed to get a real kick out of my stories from Odette's residency in far-less-glitzy Ghana.

"He's a friend," I said quietly. "Nothing more."

He nodded as if satisfied with my answer, and it was only then that I realized he took the check and was handing over his black Amex to the waiter.

"Winston," I scolded. This version of the man I met six years ago was even more attractive, which was scarier because I could see myself easily falling for him. Only then, he'd have a better chance at shattering my heart. I'd seen what happened to Dad when Maman died. This would be like that, maybe even worse, because he'd still walk this earth. "It's not fair for you to pay when you didn't even have dinner."

"But it's fair for me to pay for my wife's celebratory dinner."

I opened my mouth but immediately closed it, narrowing my eyes. "Why would it be a celebratory dinner?" The smirk on his face was my answer. "What did you do?"

"Nothing much."

I watched him, trying to read his smug expression. Then with horror, I thought about how I'd suddenly been approved for a loan after being rejected so many times. "What did you *do*?" Before he could answer, I added, "Remember, you said 'no more lies' earlier."

He chuckled. "And here I was worried you hadn't heard a single word I said."

"Winston, are you or are you not behind my loan approval?"

And with a half-smile that wrecked me, my husband answered, "I am, but only because I believe in your vision." I narrowed my eyes at him while my traitorous heart shuddered with delight. "I really do, Billie. I had the thought to venture into jewelry six years ago, but deviated from the path. Now, I want to help you succeed."

I sat there, considering him, trying to decide what ulterior motive he might have for helping me. I wasn't stupid. I knew he'd do anything to keep me chained to him, but for some reason, I believed him. I wasn't sure why since he hadn't really earned my trust, but I didn't think he had a hidden motive to help me. He didn't need my expertise. I was certain he could find the best in the field and get his jewelry line off the ground before I could say "peekaboo."

"Why a gold digger?" I asked again. I couldn't explain why it bothered me, but it did. Maybe I was being immature or too sensitive, but I couldn't be okay living with a man who thought of me as anything but his equal. And the gold digger label really irritated me. Truthfully, it hurt like hell that he thought of me that way. "Your father did what he did, and you *still* made me out to be the bad guy."

The anger that used to gnaw at my insides whenever I thought of Winston was silent. It turned out my friend Violet was right. It felt good to bring the things that bothered me for so long to light.

"You're right," he said. "And that was wrong. I should have ended him right there and then." We had lost six years, and I was starting to think maybe it was all in vain. "My father is toxic," he continued. "One day, it's inevitable that he'll be dealt with." His hand grasped mine in a tight hold. "But one thing I know for sure was that six years ago, I was toxic too." I considered his words, surprised by his admission. I still remembered the demons and vices I'd witnessed during our short time together. "Fuck, I still have shit to work on, but know this, Billie. You were *never* the bad guy. You were never the gold digger. I've known my share of those, and you don't even come close."

I sniffled silently, refusing to let tears flood my face. "Then why call me that?"

His deep blue eyes met mine, siphoning all the oxygen from my lungs. "You noticed I didn't make you sign a prenup." I nodded. It was dumb on his part, to be frank, but I didn't mention that. "I did it on purpose. My father is a greedy fucker and was forcing me into a marriage that would help push his political aspirations. First, he started with Byron, and then he moved on to me. Through whatever twist of fate, I'd already told him I was married when you happened to show up that night, attempting to steal my mother's necklace."

"So you took advantage of the opportunity."

"Yes." He flashed a boyish smile. "That's what I am, Billie. An opportunist."

"You don't say," I said wryly. "So I gather you and your father aren't close?"

I regretted the words, because his smile was immediately wiped off and replaced by a stormy, dark expression. "None of us are close to our father."

"I'm sorry." I couldn't imagine having anything other than a loving relationship with my parents. Dad took his own life, but I knew he loved us. When Maman died, he was lost and sad, but he hung on for us. "Forgive me for saying this, but you don't seem like a pushover exactly. How could your father force you to do anything?"

"He held something over my head." My heart broke for him. "Something that happened when I was a kid and I..." He swallowed hard, clearly upset. "It's something I couldn't let my siblings know, although it seems he manipulated me. My father's always been remarkable at that."

I reached out and covered his big hand with mine. "I'm sorry. Want me to kill him?" I said it to lighten the mood, but the scary part was that the idea didn't bother me as much as it should.

His lips curved into a small smile, the vulnerability in his eyes gutting me. "Want me to kill my father for calling you a gold digger? It'd be justifiable."

"You'd go to jail."

"Only if I got caught," he answered semi-teasingly. "Besides, you'd be worth it."

I smiled at his reasoning, something romantic about it. But only in theory. His father manipulated him for decades. It was high time to stop giving him power over our lives. But I didn't want to harp on about it and ruin the evening that suddenly seemed promising.

"What if I really was a gold digger?"

He shrugged. "Then I'd have deserved it if you'd wiped me clean. It would've been worth it for me not to have to marry Nicki Popova."

The name sounded familiar but I couldn't quite place it. "She's a model. She comes from a very influential family."

Then I remembered. She was the woman who'd tried to get between Odette and Byron. Who did she think she was, moving from brother to brother like that?

"That bitch needs to be taken down," I muttered.

Silence fell around us before I realized what I'd just said. Winston, on the other hand, smiled like he'd won the prize of his life. Big enough that his dimples made an appearance. Fucking gorgeous.

"I like when you stake your claim."

I rolled my eyes. "I didn't."

His eyes flicked over to me. "Don't keep me hanging, wife. Are you willing to give us a chance?"

I looked at him, considering his words. He was right when he said we had chemistry, but was that enough? The fact that I couldn't even begin to *think* about sex with another man had to mean something. I'd have to be careful with this one though. It was like making a deal with the devil. I needed to put every condition I could think of in this contract, even if it was a verbal one. Putting my hand on his thick thigh, I said, "If I am, any sex we have would have to be protected sex."

His eyes widened as if he couldn't believe his luck. "You'd have sex with me while we're doing this dating thing?"

I squeezed his thigh. "Well, a girl's got to have sex, and we get along well in that department. And sex is part of any healthy relationship."

His blue eyes dropped to my lips, and then, as if remembering where he was, he jumped up, taking my hand and practically pulling me up to my feet and dragging me out of the restaurant.

"Let's go home."

I giggled at his reaction when a voice stopped us from behind. "Sir. Sir, your card."

Winston didn't even bother glancing at the man when he took the proffered card and shoved it in his pocket.

A romantic stroll through the most romantic city in the world.

We spent the rest of the day talking, laughing, and kissing our way around Paris. Somewhere along the way, I started to feel more at ease. Maybe it was his ocean-breeze scent. Or maybe it was his vow to do this the right way. I wasn't sure what it was, but it felt so damn right.

"By the way." I turned to face Winston. "We have to set some boundaries."

He let out a chuckle. "What did you have in mind, temptress?"

Butterflies erupted in my stomach upon hearing his endearment. He was the only one who had ever called me that.

"When I'm having lunch with friends, you can't just crash it. You can't be grouchy and abrupt to the people in my life." I counted on my fingers. "No more blackmailing, and—"

"Sold." Well, that was too easy. "One caveat. If a man's attending your lunch, I need to run a background check."

The tension in his shoulders was palpable. Winston's jealousy was cute, but misplaced. I wasn't a cheater.

"I can work with that," I agreed, smiling. "And in turn, you won't be trying to impregnate me without discussing it with me first. In fact, we'll discuss all aspects that relate to me."

He smiled, letting out a sardonic breath. Gosh, when this man smiled, he made my heart flutter in a weird way. "You're a tough negotiator."

"Let's shake on it." He accepted my hand into his big palm. "Now tell me, what have you been up to for the past six years?" I asked, wanting more glimpses of the real Winston.

My hand safely in his big palm, he flicked me a glance. "Getting sober." His hoarse baritone voice and admission reverberated through me. Our gazes locked and his nostrils flared. "It's not something I'm proud of. Once I was in the military, drinking became my way to... forget."

I squeezed his hand in comfort. "Forget what?" I asked, peeking up at him to see his jaw tightening.

"My fuckups. My father's." His nostrils flared at the mention of his father. "I joined the military to escape my father, and I ended up in hell. It turned out death followed me everywhere because he controlled everything, even while I was serving my country."

Senator Ashford sounded more and more like the biggest jerk on this planet.

"Maybe you put too much on yourself," I finally said. I couldn't fathom the shit he'd been through.

He let out a chuckle, but it had no warmth. "Maybe."

I eyed him, strained silence reigning for a moment. There was a softness buried behind his eyes, and my heart tugged in an unnatural way.

"You know what always makes Ares feel better?"

The corners of his lips curved up. "What?"

I stepped closer, until his suit brushed against me and his cologne seeped into my lungs. It made every cell in my body tremble with anticipation.

"Ice cream," I breathed, tilting my head and brushing my lips against his. "Let me treat you to the best ice cream in town."

I pulled him along, both of us chuckling and leaving the gloomy past behind us. At least for a little bit.

We made it two hours before Winston was pulling me down a quiet alley and slamming me up against the stone wall. He might've struggled to pull my dress up over my hips, but his mouth had no issue ravaging my neck. I knew then it was time to make our way back to my apartment.

The past and his father's wrongdoings would have to be placed on pause while I deliberated on how to maneuver our "new" relationship. I knew I'd do anything to shield him from pain. It should have alarmed me, but Winston was hurting, and there was nothing I wanted to do more than go back in time and protect the little boy who Senator Ashford hurt so much.

But there'd be time for that. For now, we'd do this. Date, fuck, try to find some common ground. I didn't know.

"Door, wife," he panted. "Open the damn door."

I fumbled with the key, but he took them from me when it became obvious we were getting nowhere fast. His hands must've been slightly steadier because we stumbled into my little studio apartment in the next breath. The air crackled with electricity. My whole body throbbed, needing to touch him.

"Take your shirt off."

He licked his lips and followed my demand as his eyes roamed over my body. My breath caught as his broad, muscular chest came into full view. God, I could have drooled over his abs alone. Every ounce of him pulsed with power and had me aching.

His olive skin. His muscular biceps. Those corded forearms.

My eyes widened as he twisted out of the thin cotton shirt, showing off a group of circles inked at his forearm. I reached out and traced each tiny circle that made up the oval mark, then noticed there was something else there too.

A date.

Butterflies took flight in my stomach, soaring in my chest. "Did you..." I inhaled a big breath before exhaling. "Is that..."

No, it couldn't be. Only... I was fairly positive it was. I'd had to give it to the attorney at least ten times over the last month when I demanded a divorce.

"It's your bite mark," he rasped. "And the date we were married."

A strangled laugh rushed to fall from my lips, but for some reason, it mixed with so many emotions that it came out as a cry. I sniffled and paused, unused to sifting through so many feelings at once.

I suspected I knew the reason behind it, but I wasn't ready to admit it.

Tracing my finger over it, his heat seared through me, warming my bones. I admired the work with a feather-light touch. My heart fluttered so fast it drowned out everything but one feeling that I didn't dare identify. *Bu-bum. Bu-bum. Bu-bum.*

"Your pants. Off too," I breathed, pulling my hand back.

A brilliant blue, his eyes locked on mine as he unzipped his fly and pulled his dick out. Thick, hard, and ready for me. My chest rose and fell as I watched him, my heart beating wildly. There was no mistaking who was in charge here, despite me handing out the orders. Something about this man screamed pure male domination.

The chemistry between us—raw, honest, all-consuming—was hard to deny. It had been there from the first moment we met.

He began to slowly stroke himself, and there was something so damn sexy about it. The muscles in those shoulders and arms flexed as he jerked himself lazily. My insides rippled in pleasure, my sex throbbing with need for him. This was like watching my own personal show. Actually, scratch that. It was so much better. I was ready to explode, and he hadn't even touched me yet.

"I need you fucking naked," he growled darkly, never ceasing his pumping. His jaw clenched, his movements faltering as I grabbed the hem of my dress and pulled it over my head. I was left standing only in red panties and a matching lace bra.

His precum glistening, I licked my lips, needing to taste him. I could feel my core clench, my pleasure hovering right at the surface. In one swift move, he was next to me, dragging my panties down my legs, letting them fall on the floor. My bra joined soon after.

Then he stilled, dropping his gaze down my body. I was naked and vulnerable once again. But so was he.

"One day," he murmured darkly, "when you're ready..." His hand skimmed over my flat stomach. "Your belly will grow big with our baby."

There was an undercurrent of darkness fused with tenderness rippling between us. I didn't understand it; I'd never felt anything like it.

"And if we don't have a baby?" I questioned on a whisper. "Will what we have be enough?"

He took me in his arms and kissed me deeply as he held my face in his hands. "It is for me. And if it's not for you, tell me what you need. Anything," he whispered softly, which eased my fears. He took my mouth in his, his tongue slowly sliding through my open lips with just the right amount of exploration. "I'll be whatever you want me to be. Just let me be yours," he murmured.

My entire heart threatened to disintegrate in my chest at his words ghosting my lips.

He laid me down and spread my legs, kissing his way down my body.

"Look how wet you are, Billie. You're going to ruin these sheets."

A shudder rolled over me as I stared at the ceiling, my breathing loud in the otherwise quiet room. He lifted my legs and hooked them over his strong shoulders. I was completely open to him, and he wasted no time as he bent his head and sucked hard.

I bucked off the bed.

"Ohhh... God!" I cried out.

He drove three of his thick fingers into my sex and began to pump me while his tongue worked my clit, sucking on it. Digging my fingers into the sheets, each sweep of his tongue sent shivers through me. Heat erupted inside of me, liquefying in my veins. He licked me from entrance to clit, a growl of satisfaction vibrating through me.

My body began to quiver, just like it always did for him. It wasn't long before I convulsed violently as an orgasm rippled through me.

"Good girl," he whispered, seemingly pleased with his own efforts. He leaned in and kissed me again. His tongue stroked mine, and my legs opened wider, inviting him in.

He went to get up when I wrapped my arms around his neck. "Where are you going?"

He couldn't be done with me already. "Condom," he reminded me softly. "Until you're ready."

My gaze found his eyes, flickering with something heavy. After the shock of his attempted entrapment, I realized I didn't hate the idea of having a baby with him. I hated the idea of what I would forfeit just to be with him. But Winston listened. My heart tripped over itself, pounding in my ears.

I lifted onto my elbows, my breasts pressing against his hard chest as I pecked him softly on the corner of his mouth. One of his hands pushed into my hair, and he wrapped the long strands around his fist as he deepened the kiss.

"Hurry up," I panted against his lips.

My period was never late. So either I was already pregnant or I was about to get my period, but it was important to me that we made big decisions like this together. He rolled on a condom and slid his hard cock along my drenched folds, then gave me another searing kiss. The world tilted off its axis, or maybe my head grew dizzy, as I trailed kisses down his neck, sucking on his rough skin.

He fell onto his back, pulling me over him and dragging my face to his.

"Ride my cock, wife," he murmured against my lips. "Then I'll fuck you. You owe me six years of moans and screams."

I smiled against his mouth as I straddled him. His thick cock pressed against his stomach, and he guided my hips to settle over his.

"Ahhhh," I moaned. It was no wonder I could never quite manage to move on from him—it felt like he was made for me.

"You're soaking my balls like such a good girl," he praised.

"Winston," I breathed, shuddering with his cock halfway inside me. With heavy breaths, we both watched as I slid down the length of him. "You feel so good."

"You missed my big cock, didn't you?" he rasped.

"Stop bragging," I whimpered.

He let out a dark chuckle as he cupped my breasts. He still knew exactly how to touch me. I rocked against him, adjusting to his size. Six years was a long time to go in the absence of such a well-endowed man.

"You'll take all of it, wife," he rasped, grabbing my hips, slamming me down, and filling me to the hilt. My mouth fell open in pleasure and I shuddered around him, my nails digging into his shoulders.

He fucked me deep and hard, meeting each thrust with a devastating brutality. I'd never felt closer to anyone than I did to him right now.

"So fucking tight," he ground out. He slowly moved me up and down, letting me feel every single inch of his thick, throbbing shaft. His eyes were hooded as he locked eyes with me.

I leaned forward and kissed him messily, licking his open mouth.

"Your cock is the best," I whispered, causing him to shudder and his eyes to roll back in his head. "You ruined me for anyone else."

"Because it's you and me, baby. Forever." He picked me up by the hips and slammed me back down, and I whimpered at the overwhelming sensation of being manhandled. "I'm going to fill you with my cum."

"Please," I begged. "Give it all to me."

He was losing control, and so was I. I dipped forward and sucked hard on his tongue as I rode him.

He hissed before his control completely slipped. He bucked me off, pulled out, and threw me onto my back. He slammed in, knocking the air from my lungs.

"Harder," I moaned. "I need your cock."

"Is your pussy weeping for me?"

"Yes, *yes*." I clenched around him and he pumped me harder. "Oh... God... yes!"

He lifted my hips again and drilled deeper. My body reached new heights of pleasure, throbbing with the promise of a new high.

"Who's fucking you?" he growled, thrusting into me, each one sending a wave of heat twisting up my spine. We were flush against one another, his hand on my throat, my legs wrapped around his torso.

"You."

"Who do you belong to?"

"You." He hit just the right spot, and I cried out. His every touch felt like perfection. He was tearing me apart at the seams only to put me back together. "More," I begged. "Fuck, I need more."

He pumped into me at a piston pace. I grabbed on to his shoulders as I convulsed around him, crying out his name. With one last punishing thrust, he held himself deep inside me and shuddered into my neck. I could feel his cock jerk as he orgasmed, his length twitching inside me.

We panted as we clung to each other, soaked from the exertion. He peppered kisses along my throat and down my chest, nuzzling against me.

"Mine," he murmured against the soft skin there. "Nobody compares to you."

Something warm unraveled in my chest, and I knew I'd let him in. And I couldn't imagine a scenario where I'd slip from his orbit unscathed.

Chapter 39
Winston

She was fast asleep. Completely dead to the world. I tired her out—both from the feral way I'd fucked her and the bath I drew for her when we finished.

She blew my mind with her willingness to give this—*us*—a try. She was so small and soft, yet so fucking strong and stubborn. Sprawled on her back, her golden hair fanned over the pillow and her eyelashes casting shadows over her cheeks, I couldn't stop staring at her.

My eyes fell on her left hand, her fingers lightly curled over her soft belly. She was naked underneath that blanket, tempting me, but I knew she needed rest. I watched her for a few seconds because I couldn't take my eyes off of her, but then I straightened away from her.

Careful not to make any noise, I rose to my feet. My training had conditioned me to function on very little sleep. Sometimes we'd go days without it. Tonight would be one of those nights. I couldn't risk drifting off and hurting her.

Especially if she was pregnant from our night together when no protection was used.

I exhaled as I stared at her ringless hand. I knew I was being para-noid. That she'd disappear and never come back before we had the chance to put our compatibility to the test. We could be—no, would be good together. I wanted a baby, children to spoil. I wanted to leave a trace of Billie and me behind so when we were gone, the world still had proof of our love roaming this earth.

Okay, maybe not our love. My love. But if she gave me a chance, I'd be the man she needed me to be. I wasn't decent enough to let her go, so I'd work for the rest of my days at being someone deserving of her.

With restless energy coursing through my body, I roamed her sanctuary, taking note of her apartment. It was small but cozy, with a direct view of the Eiffel Tower and its glittering lights. I wondered if she knew we had a penthouse in this city, and every other major city in Europe.

Probably not.

The hardwood flooring was spotless, albeit on the *vintage* side. Countless fashion and jewelry drawings hung on the walls. The furniture was minimal, but something told me she wasn't much into home décor.

I opened her nightstand drawer and my breath caught in my lungs. The wedding ring—my mother's ring—sat in there next to two others. I reached for it and turned it over, examining them, and spotted the faded names. *Her parents' wedding rings.* Something inside my chest tightened.

Maybe I should have killed my father decades ago. It would have spared my wife the pain of losing a parent to suicide. It would have left me and my siblings orphaned, but at least we wouldn't have his looming, evil presence to deal with.

Taking a seat in the only armchair in the apartment, I watched Billie sleep as my thoughts drifted back to the day when everything changed.

"Why were you and your mother downtown?" Father had been asking the same question for days. The funeral was this morning.

Aurora and Kingston hadn't stopped crying, and Byron, Royce, and I were taking turns comforting them despite our own shattered hearts.

All Father cared about was why Mama was downtown.

"I asked you a question, boy."

"Shopping," I gritted, hating my father now more than ever.

"There isn't a store on that whole block she liked," he spat out, grabbing my arm. I was almost as tall as him. Another year or two, and I'd be bigger and stronger. Byron already was, and that was the reason he didn't fuck with him anymore. I couldn't wait for my time to come.

"Was she seeing a man?"

I blinked in confusion. It was no secret Father had mistresses. He made zero effort to hide it, and there were a few times he even dared to bring them home, which had never ceased to infuriate Mama. She wouldn't stand for it, and their screaming matches would echo through the house.

His grip on my arm tightened, and I yanked it away. "No, she wasn't. That's what you do."

"Then why was she on that block if not to meet a man?" His fury over the matter was incomprehensible. Mama was dead, and all he was doing was degrading her memory. "I'll have every piece of surveillance on that block delivered to me."

"She took me to a game store, okay?" I bellowed. "I wanted the game that just came out. Are you happy now?"

Suffocating silence matched the guilt that had been swallowing me from the inside since the moment my mother was shot, bleeding out on the filthy pavement of downtown D.C.

A manic laugh that grew louder and louder.

"So she's dead because of you?" I blinked my burning tears away, refusing to let them fall. I couldn't even remember the last time I cried. Yet I couldn't deny this blow. Something about the way Father uttered those words felt like a whip across my face. "You killed your mother," he said, laughter still lingering in his voice. "Your siblings will hate you when they learn."

I stiffened. My brothers and baby sister were my world. I couldn't lose them too.

"Please, Father, don't tell them." The look on his face told me he would, and desperation clawed at my chest. Byron would never forgive me. I'd selfishly wanted to go to the game store, knowing full well our security detail was planned to a tee and didn't include that stop. Our guard had even warned Ma against it.

I didn't care, the newest edition of my favorite game was the only thing on my mind. And because of that, my mom was dead. Because of me.

"Don't you know, son, every secret has a price?" My heart iced over, the look of the man who gave me life cold and calculating. "Are you ready to pay it?"

I swallowed hard, knowing this man had never been a true parent, and now I risked losing my siblings if I didn't do whatever he demanded.

A whimper yanked me out of my memories and into the present, where the warm body in the bed mere steps away writhed in distress.

I stood up and made my way to her, turning on the bedside lamp.

"Too much." Billie twisted on the bed, her face pale. "Dad, wake up."

My heart wrenched at the pain in her voice. Pain caused by my father. Everything that man touched, he destroyed. I brushed my fingers over her damp hair, combing them through the silky strands.

"Shhh. It's okay." She choked a sob, cracking my heart at what she must have felt. I'd felt it too once, and it stayed with you forever. "I'm here," I murmured, pressing a kiss to her forehead.

Finally, she quieted, then shifted and buried her face into the pillow.

I remained close by as I thought back to my father. For decades, I'd wanted nothing more than to get away from him. Yet, now that I knew he manipulated and used me in such a cruel and unforgivable manner, I wanted nothing more than to seek him out and end him. He made it impossible to live without this guilt when I was in fact blameless. If anything, I suspected my father might have had some-thing to do with it.

Fuck, I joined the Special Forces to get away from him. I was all in no matter the mission... never mind that he was the puppet master responsible for sending me into the eye of the storm. But then, anything was better than being on the same continent as him.

My priorities had finally shifted. This woman was all I wanted, and I'd protect her with my life. I'd lay the world and my love at her feet.

Chapter 40
Winston

The last few days, Billie and I alternated on initiating dates. I'd taken her to a fashion show; she'd taken me to a war museum. The following day, I'd taken her shopping in Paris for all her heart's desires. We visited the Place Vendôme and Boulevard Haussmann.

After that, I took her to Les Galeries Lafayette Haussmann to shop for clothes. It wasn't the most original date idea, but she loved clothes and complained about nothing fitting her, so here we were.

I scrolled through my phone, reading emails and taking care of business, while a train of sales ladies paraded more dresses her way until she finally stopped them. It would seem my wife loved designing, but trying clothes on wasn't her thing.

A grumble came from her dressing room and I shot to my feet, making my way to her. Pushing the curtain aside, I noticed her struggling to zip her dress up.

"Shit, I think I'm gaining weight," she muttered, the crack in her voice doing stupid things to me.

Without thinking, I joined her in the changing room, closing the curtain behind me.

Billie's head snapped up. "What are you doing?"

"Judging for myself," I said, studying the beautiful curves hidden by a timeless, black-and-white Chanel dress. Billie didn't follow the latest trends, which made her stand out. It was what I loved about her.

"You're breathtaking," I said, ignoring the way her neck flushed pink. My balls instantly tightened as a subtle cloud of floral perfume hit me, our close quarters working to accentuate her scent. It didn't matter how often I fucked my wife, it was never enough. Even now, I felt like I'd die of blue balls.

"Is that so?" She smiled.

"Yes." Stepping forward, I grazed my knuckles over the soft skin of her collarbone, pushing her long blonde strands out of my way and causing her to shiver.

My cock instantly leapt. "Sit on the bench."

She held my gaze and shook her head. "They'll hear us, Winston."

Hesitation flashed over her features before determination settled over her and she lowered onto the bench.

I kneeled down in front of her and wrenched her thighs apart.

"If we weren't already married, I'd think you were about to propose," she taunted. I stilled for a moment, then quickly got back to business.

Dipping down, I inhaled her cunt. Fuck, her arousal was the best kind of aphrodisiac. I ran my nose over her clit, drawing a whimper from her.

"My wife's pussy is drenched," I crooned. "Always so needy."

I licked her opening through her lacy panties and she bucked, her head falling back against the wall behind her. Reaching up, I inched the material down her slim legs. I tongued her everywhere but her clit.

She squirmed, crying out loudly enough to draw attention. I reached a finger up to her lips and gave her a look that I hoped would remind her of our surroundings.

"I need more," she breathed.

"Not yet." Lifting her ass with my palms, I ate her pussy, lapping her juices like a starved man. Her thighs tightened around me, her fingers gripping my hair. She was close, shuddering under me and moaning my name.

I nipped at her clit and kneaded her thighs, finally bringing her to orgasm. She ground herself against my face like the greedy temptress she was.

Once she was sated, I rose to my feet and pressed my mouth to her parted lips.

"My wife is the best kind of dessert."

The next day, it was Billie's turn to decide on a date, and I couldn't do anything but stare at her, lost for words.

"Get in, Winston." Billie wore a wide grin, wiggling her eyebrows in challenge. "Unless you're scared."

As if to accentuate her words, the beast of a horse whinnied. The coachman pulled on the reins, trying to control the big-ass horse who probably wanted to rise up on his hind legs and knock me out.

"You can't be serious," I stammered, my eyes scanning the beat-up carriage. It looked like it dated back to the fifteenth century. "We're going to stink like horseshit."

Where in the fuck had she found a horse and carriage to rent? I wanted to go and torch that business down to the ground. As if the gigantic horse heard my thoughts, he neighed his protest.

"Stop whining and get in. You said to pick a date, and this is my date."

"Billie," I groaned. "I meant dinner on a yacht or a stroll beneath the stars. Not riding around in a decrepit carriage."

"Isn't it great!" She beamed as she looked up at me, then noting my not-so-thrilled expression, she added, "If you play along, we can get freaky between the sheets back here."

The crowd around us gathered closer and kids screamed, unused to seeing a horse with a fancy carriage in the heart of Paris.

Music started to play, and to my surprise, it came from inside the carriage. "Where is the radio?"

"Don't worry about that, old man." Billie laughed, her grin stretching even further as she extended her hand. "Come on, or I'll have no choice but to tell everyone you're a chicken." A snowflake landed on my nose, and she leaned over, brushing it away. "Come on, husband. This is my date, and you have to play along."

More flurries followed. Kids started to squeal and run around as they attempted to catch the snow with their tongues. Billie laughed up to the sky, attempting to catch one herself, and I couldn't help smiling. It was like the woman I met six years ago had slipped away, and a more content version had taken her place.

I climbed up and slid into the seat next to her.

"Is it legal to do this in Paris?" I asked her. "I have no desire to spend the night in a French jail."

She threw her head back and giggled, carefree, while her eyes shone like diamonds. I had to admit, I loved this version.

"Don't worry, I'll bail you out."

My face screwed up. "That's comforting. Take my black Amex. The PIN is—"

She covered my mouth with her small hand. "Don't worry. I got you. I married rich, therefore I don't need *your* money. I have my own."

Another easy giggle escaped her, and I fucking loved the sound of it.

I reached out and tugged her closer to me, wrapping my wool overcoat around us. Her hands came to rest against my chest, and her eyes held mine hostage. She fit perfectly in my arms, tucked in and safe, where I could protect her from the cold and all the darkness in the world, including my own.

A piece of her hair fluttered in the wind, dragging across her face.

I fingered the strand and tucked it gently behind her ear. Without fail, every time I touched her, my skin buzzed.

I was so fucking smitten with my wife, and I didn't know how to show it to her. I wanted to shout to the world *I love Billie Ashford*, but I suspected the words alone wouldn't be enough. I cupped her cheek, her golden eyes sparkling with delight.

Everything around us slowed as I lowered my head. She met me halfway, and our lips brushed. She shuffled her soft body over, snuggling against me. Energy crackled around us. Her body trembled, her fingers clawing into the fabric of my suit as I kissed her like it was my last chance.

My tongue teased hers as she wrapped her arms around my neck. She tasted like she was designed for me. Made for me. Meant for me. Swallowing her little moans, I fed off them like an addict. I groaned as she pressed into me, wishing we were anywhere but here, wishing—

"*Achoo!*"

She pulled away and looked up at me with swollen lips. "Bless you," she said, smiling.

Another sneeze.

"Bless you again." She let out a soft chuckle. "If you sneeze a third time, I'll assume it didn't take and you're a demon who must be destroyed."

"*Achoo.*" Suddenly my skin started itching. My face felt... off. Two more violent sneezes followed.

Fuck, my eyes were beginning to close of their own accord, the sensation so odd—like someone had punched me.

"Winston, are you okay? You're not looking so... good." She cupped my face, her cool hands soothing. Someone must have set my skin on fire. "Fuck, I think you have allergies."

Her voice was distant and distorted as every part of me felt like it was about to explode from the inside.

Chapter 41
Billie

An hour later, we sat in a hospital room, Winston pumped full of the French equivalent of Benadryl.

By the time we arrived at the hospital—in a fucking *carriage*—Winston was barely conscious.

Thankfully, the coachman helped. We each took an arm and carried Winston's big frame into the hospital while I screamed for a doctor. Thank God Tristan was there.

"He's out of the danger zone," Tristan repeated as I stared at Winston, sleeping soundly in the hospital bed, still wearing his boots and coat. I wanted to crawl into the bed with him and never let him go. "It's probably wise to keep an EpiPen on your person at all times, and stay away from horses."

I smiled sheepishly. "I thought it'd be romantic."

"I didn't think you were into all that," he remarked, amused. I shrugged nonchalantly, not bothering to elaborate. When you grew up watching honest romance blossom between your parents, of course you strived for it. "And how long have you been married?"

I knew that question was coming. In truth, I was surprised it took Tristan so long to ask.

"Six years." I rubbed my eyes tiredly. "Don't ask for details because you won't get them."

He raised his hands and chuckled. "Okay, I'm not asking, but I sense a story there."

I rolled my eyes. "It's a good thing you're not a writer, then."

He hugged me. "You're right. I suck at writing anything but prescriptions. Try to get some rest." A page came through the speakers, the sound muted in the room to keep patients resting. "If you need me, just ask any nurse to call me."

I squeezed his arm. "Thank you again."

He left and I made my way to the bed, running my fingers over Winston's face. Then, against policy and probably sanity, I crawled into bed next to him and wrapped my arms around his large body.

"I'm sorry," I whispered for the millionth time. My heart clenched every time I looked at him. At least his face wasn't swollen anymore. "So, so sorry."

Winston's eyelids cracked open. "You couldn't have possibly known I was allergic to horses," he rasped, his speech slurred. "I didn't even know it myself."

I swallowed, my stomach twisting into knots. "I could have killed you." Just the thought sent a cold sweat across my skin. It wasn't until this very moment that I realized how lost I was for him. I was a fool to think I could live without him. His hold on me was invisible granite from day one.

The corner of his lips twisted. "And you would have been a very rich widow."

"Don't even joke about something like that." I shook my head, burying my face into his chest and thanking whichever higher being was up there pulling the strings.

"Reach into my pocket," he murmured, and I shot him a glare.

"I'm not jerking you off!"

"No, but don't tempt me. My *jacket* pocket. You have a dirty mind, woman."

My cheeks heated but I rolled my eyes and played it off. I reached into his jacket pocket, pulling out a long velvet box.

"What's this?" I asked, twisting it between my fingers.

"Open it and see."

I shifted, then slowly pried it open. "The bracelet," I breathed, my hand coming up to my heart. "My wedding bracelet."

He nodded. "I've wanted to give it to you at the perfect moment, but I figured I'd better do it now. In case I die of allergies." A strangled laugh escaped me as he took my wrist and clasped the bracelet around it. "Now you're mine."

He claimed me, and it did things to me. I wanted to straddle him and kiss every part of him, tell him he was mine too. That I missed his touch more than I was willing to admit. Not a man's touch, no. *His* touch.

But this was not the time.

"We have to talk," I said instead.

His arm hooked around my waist, his hand gripping me tightly. "No time like the present."

I shook my head. "You almost died, Winston. Tomorrow, when you're rested."

"I'm better now." His nose brushed against mine, his whisper warming me from the inside. "Besides, you're the best medicine."

His hand lowered to my inner thigh and a choked laugh escaped me. "Don't even think about it. You almost died. No sex tonight, no matter how cheesy your lines are."

His mouth brushed my cheek. "But we can fool around."

I pulled away, narrowing my eyes on him. "We can *talk*." He released me with an exasperated breath, and I couldn't help but smile at his reaction. Boys would be boys forever, I guess. "I had to fill out documents."

He nuzzled his face against my neck. "That sounds sexy."

"It wasn't," I muttered. "There was a questionnaire, and I realized I know nothing about you. I didn't know if you were on any medications."

"I'm not."

"Or if you have a history of heart disease."

"I don't."

I took his face between my palms and held his gaze. "The point is that I didn't know any important information. I couldn't even fill out an admission form. We're supposed to be *married*."

"So you want my medical records?" he teased.

"I guess we can start with that," I told him, dropping my head back and blowing out a raspberry.

"Okay, I want yours too." He pecked my cheek, hugging me tighter. "I'm guessing your sister has it."

He was frustratingly composed for a man who, less than an hour ago, was on the verge of being put on a ventilator, but I wanted him in all his raw, exposed vulnerability. I wanted to know what made him tick. I wanted to know what he loved and what he hated. Aside from sex, of course. In that department, we were well-matched.

"Winston?"

"Hmmm."

"Do you think we'll ever be able to sleep together?" He stiffened, and I pushed my nerves aside before I continued. "In the same bed. Like this." He lay there like a mannequin as I tried to tamp down my nerves. I couldn't tell if he was upset by my question. "I really want this to work," I whispered.

Not just because I suspected I was pregnant, but for me too. I was tired of fighting this attraction, tired of pretending I didn't want him.

I walked my fingers over his jaw, down his back, over the tattoo with our wedding date on his arm. It took some effort, but he eventually relaxed.

"I don't want to hurt you." His voice was so low I almost missed it.

"Maybe it was a onetime thing," I murmured as hope whispered through every fiber of my being.

"It's not. My nightmares... They take me back to war, to being tortured, and I forget where I am. I've attacked my own siblings when they've tried to wake me. I could have—" A quivering breath heated the space between us. "I'll never forgive myself for hurting you."

Something about the way his shoulders slumped broke a dam inside me, sending hot tears down my cheeks. I chewed on my bottom lip, so many emotions piling on top of one another.

"My parents..." My voice cracked, so I cleared it and forced the words past my lips. "They were so happy. And in love. It was almost a curse to witness because it made my sister and me want the same thing." The words fell from my lips as tears wet my cheeks, dampening his pillow. He wiped a tear away with his thumb, the tubes attached to the top of his hand reminding me that I really *should* let him rest. But all the gentle caress did was pull the truth from my throat. "I want what they had, and I'm starting to see their love and happiness was a joint effort. Something they strived for and fought for together. So whatever ghosts you have, Winston, let them be mine too. Otherwise, the possibility of a happy future will only remain that... a possibility. An unrealized dream."

I could avoid all these feelings that seemed to stack up high and keep myself guarded by ten-foot walls, but I would regret not having told him the truth. I would regret acting as if I didn't care.

"You might not like me as much."

I'm afraid to let myself think about how much I do, actually.

"Try me," I murmured softly. The look in his eyes almost launched me off the edge of the steep cliff I was teetering on. Silence stretched as ghosts marred his expression. "Please talk to me, Winston."

Bu-bum. Bu-bum. Bu-bum.

"My actions led to my mother's death." A sharp inhale, mine. A release, his. "It's what my father holds over my head. It's the reason I joined the military. To escape. Part of me didn't expect to survive, and the other part wishes I hadn't after everything I've seen."

The utter despair in his expression gutted me. I pressed my palm to his cheek.

"Why do you think your actions led to her death?" A weighted pause. I reached for the second blanket and wrapped us in it, then hugged him tightly.

"Because I insisted on going to that store."

"And your dreams?" I questioned quietly, remembering the news clippings I'd read. "Are they about witnessing your mother's murder or—"

He shook his head.

"When I dream, it's all over the place. War. The day my mother got shot, bleeding in the middle of the street. Shit that happened to women and children when I was fighting overseas."

I never would have imagined his issues went so deep. Suddenly, guilt at how I reacted to him shook me to my core. Maybe I should have tried harder to work things out six years ago instead of abandoning him, but the truth was that everything came crashing down— my father's suicide, Odette's pregnancy, trying to overcome our financial and mental struggles. There was no space for Winston and me six years ago. He had issues he had to work through, and so did I.

"I have a friend," I murmured softly. "She's a therapist, and I'm pretty sure she'd call those night terrors. She's seen it mostly with ex-military guys." He remained silent. "Winston, if this is going to work, we need to be honest with each other. You can't hide from me. I want it all—the good, the bad, the ugly."

His shoulders dropped. It was as if he was struggling with himself, so damn intent on keeping everyone at arm's length.

But I wouldn't let him. I'd show him that this time, I wasn't going anywhere.

Chapter 42
Winston

I wanted to spit it all out, but I couldn't risk her knowing all the shit I'd done. She'd walked away from me when she got a tiny glimpse of how fucked up I was. If she knew the extent of the darkness, she'd surely run and never look back.

"I'll tell you everything on one condition." I was a bastard, but I *needed* her to stay.

She pulled away slightly, running her fingers over my tattoo. She seemed obsessed with it, and I'd be lying if I said I didn't love that.

She stared up at me with eyes that glimmered with yearning. "Anything."

"Stay with me for the rest of your life." A raging possessiveness had taken hold of me, and I pulled her into me with a hand glued to the small of her back. She didn't resist, simply pressed her cheek against mine.

"And what happens if you don't end up wanting me for the rest of my life? What if you eventually tire of me?" She looked so vulnerable.

"It will never happen. Say you'll stay."

She searched my face until she found whatever she was looking for. "I will."

"Promise me."

She kissed the corner of my lips. "Why do you need a promise?"

"Because I can't bear to live another day without you." The last six years had felt like centuries. Now that we'd had days and weeks together, giving this a real go, I was fully addicted. To go a day without her was to age a decade.

"I promise, then, but I have a condition of my own."

"Anything, temptress."

"Whenever you need help, we'll be there for each other. No matter what. I don't care if you commit the most horrific crime, you don't keep it from me." I felt her mischievous smile on my cheek. "And same goes for me."

Her lips pursed, almost as if she had a specific crime—and target—in mind, and I turned my head to lick them. "If you want someone killed, you tell me and I'll handle it."

She chuckled, lifting her chin. "Your father's close to topping that list, but for now, no need for murder." I nodded my agreement. "Okay, we've got ourselves a deal, Mr. Ashford."

"Mrs. Ashford."

"Now let's get back to our discussion," she demanded. I should have known she wouldn't get distracted. "I suspect your father did something foul."

"My mother was shot in front of a store," I told her. "It was our last stop, an unplanned one, before we were supposed to go get Byron. All I cared about was the release of whatever the latest video game was. I had to have it. It was because of me that we went to that store, and the killer anticipated it. My mother was clearly the target, and I suspect I know who ordered the hit." Her brows creased in a line, confusion splashing her delicate features. "My father let me believe it was my fault, used it against me for years, and threatened to tell my siblings I'd killed her. The guilt ate at me."

"*Jesus.*" Fuck. This was exactly why I didn't want anyone to know. "How old were you?"

"Twelve." *She'll leave me.* The thought shook me. Even the knowledge that my father twisted it all didn't erase the guilt, the shame. It had been my identity for so long, it was impossible not to think it. "It's hard to ignore that if that spoiled boy hadn't insisted on going to that game store, I could have saved my mother's life."

I slowly sat up, and she let out a frustrated breath as she pulled me back onto the dingy little hospital bed. "Where are you going?"

"Don't you want space now?"

Her grip on me tightened. "No, I don't. Winston, you were a kid. There was no way you could possibly know what would happen." She gripped my shoulders, her eyes locking with mine. "Don't you see? It could have happened at any time, in front of any store. And your father should have told you that, not held it over your head. He's a manipulative bastard, and you know that."

The grown-up version of me understood that, but it still didn't banish nearly three decades' worth of guilt. It was impossible. It became a part of my existence, just like everything else.

"The nightmares are about that?" she asked quietly. Fuck, I'd give anything for a stiff drink right now. Maybe it was a good thing we were in the hospital. "That night you thrashed in your sleep and wouldn't wake up no matter how many times I called your name?"

The nervousness in her voice got to me more than anything.

"It's a mixture of things. No rhyme or reason, really."

"Have you gone to a therapist?" she whispered, sorrow filling her face. I didn't want pity; it made me feel less than. I already knew I was plenty fucked up, through and through.

"I've seen a therapist on and off. He says it's PTSD bullshit."

She smiled sadly. "It probably is. I'm guessing you no longer have sessions?"

"No." I got tired of just talking about problems and not coming up with any meaningful solutions. "I stopped drinking. Apparently it was my coping mechanism. You saw for yourself how destructive it was."

She nodded. "Not the best one," she agreed, but there was no judgment in her eyes. "It might be worthwhile to talk to a therapist again."

"If you want me to see a shrink, I'll see one. If you want me to burn down this world, I'll do it. I'll do and be whatever you want me to be. Just let me be yours, Billie."

I didn't give a shit that it made me sound like a pussy-whipped wimp. I was in so deep I didn't know the way out. Even worse, I didn't *want* to find it. This was exactly where I needed to be.

She interlocked her fingers with mine, her thumb brushing the inside of my wrist. I could lie here and let this woman touch me all day long.

"You're mine, Winston," she said quietly. "And I'm yours. Both of us, together. Get that through your head, okay?"

I stilled, certain I hadn't heard her right. "Say it again." My voice was hoarse.

"You're mine," she whispered. Then, taking a deep breath, she looked into my eyes. "I haven't taken a test, but I'm pretty sure I'm pregnant. I'm never late. My appetite's been all over the place and I've gained weight." She sniffed, her misty eyes meeting mine. "I'm yours, and so is this baby—if that's what ends up happening. If you'll have us."

A smile tugged at my lips as relief slammed into me. My lips pressed against her ear, and I made a promise. "I'll have you with all my heart." I didn't miss the hint of a smile on that pretty mouth of hers, nor the way her eyes glistened with emotion. I pushed a strand of her wild hair from her face and draped it over her shoulder. "You and our family. That's all I want."

"How do I know you're not just saying that because of the baby? Maybe you just want to continue your bloodline."

I cupped her cheeks, my eyes reaching into hers. "I don't give a shit about my bloodline." She smiled softly, and the sight of it pierced my chest. "Byron or any of my brothers can continue the damn Ashford line. I'll take your last name for all I care."

She cocked a brow. "But we've been married for six years."

"And I noticed you kept your last name," I pointed out. "Maybe I need to take yours so everyone knows you're mine. I want the ring on your finger, my name tattooed on it so it can never come off."

"So it doesn't matter to you if we have a girl instead of a boy?" Her insecurity was something different. She'd always been a spitfire with a smoky voice and tempting body. Now, Billie was showing a completely different side of herself. Maybe it was the pregnancy hormones, or maybe she had been hiding that side of herself all along. I didn't know which it was, but I loved this part of her too.

"Give me daughters with your stubborn streak and mind any day." My blood thrummed in approval of a bunch of little girls looking like Billie running around us. "Give me daughters with your beautiful, warm brown eyes and golden hair. I want the world to know that you walked this earth a hundred years from now and see the traces of you in our daughters."

She stilled for a moment before whispering her own promise. "Then it's you and me, baby. Forever."

Then and there, I knew we were in this together. For better or for worse.

Chapter 43
Billie

Life was good. The only way to keep things going was to live fully. No fears, no regrets, no pride. And with all my heart.

Just like Maman told me.

Winston had his driver bring his Rolls-Royce to the hospital in the early hours of the morning. He insisted on driving, then made his way through a sleeping Paris. He pulled over at a lookout and parked the car, and as we snuggled in blankets, we watched the sun rise over the city of love while "I Don't Want This Night To End" by Luke Bryan played from the vintage speakers.

It was old and new, past and present. Our future.

We didn't talk. We just sat there, his arms wrapped around me, and watched as the city slowly stirred to life.

"This one's the best date yet," I whispered. My hand on his chest, his strong heart beat in sync with mine.

Twenty-four hours had gone by since our fiasco with the horse. I tended to Winston even though he was fully recovered from his allergic reaction—I suspected he craved the attention. We spent a ridiculous amount of time dreaming up many names for our hypothetical girl or boy. It might not amount to anything, and I truly might just be late, but we'd be prepared in any event. All that really mattered to me was that we were on the road to mending our relationship.

"How about Fifi for a girl?" he asked.

I cringed, meeting his eyes in the reflection of the mirror. He was already dressed in a tux and being more secretive than usual about our plans tonight.

"How about we put a pause on names until we take a pregnancy test," I suggested, laughing. "We might be way crazy here." Although, women's intuition told me I wasn't. I couldn't ever remember a time when I had laughed, only to immediately start crying.

Coming up behind me, he wrapped his arms around my waist. "Okay, no more names until we see that pink plus sign on the plastic stick."

I chuckled, a flight of butterflies taking off in my belly. The promise of a bundle of joy had us excited and nervous. We were both at the perfect age to start a family, yet it was hard not to be nervous. I was with Odette every step of the way while she was pregnant, but it felt different now that it might be happening to me.

"I love you," I whispered. The words had barely left my mouth before he yanked me toward him and crushed his lips to mine. It wasn't a sweet kiss. It was fierce and consuming. Everything I needed.

"You have no idea how long I've waited to hear those words," he rasped.

"I'm sorry it took so long for me to realize," I said sheepishly.

"You better love me even when the hormones leave your body too. There's no getting rid of me now," he warned. "Not that there was a likelihood of it before."

I smiled, responding to his touch. "That's fine by me."

"I'm keeping you forever." I tried to blink back the tears beginning to form, feeling overwhelmed by emotions. *Again.*

"You better," I murmured.

"We're finally in agreement." He let out a soft chuckle as he tilted my chin up. "Are you ready for our adventure today?"

I nodded.

"Do I look appropriate for whatever you have in mind?" His eyes roved over me. The silky golden material swept over my curves, shining under the dim lighting of my studio apartment. I took a step back, the slit down my thigh revealing just enough. It wouldn't do much to keep me warm, but it was too beautiful not to wear it. When he remained quiet, I murmured, "You said wear something fancy."

"You're stunning. I won't be able to look away from you in the car. It's more than a little dangerous." My cheeks warmed, the look in his eyes full of that indescribable affection that every woman wished for from her man. He headed into my closet and returned with a garment bag slung over his arm. "You'll need this."

I yanked on the bag's stiff zipper and my mouth dropped to the floor. "A fur coat?"

He nodded. "Where exactly are you taking me?" I asked, as excited as I was curious. After yesterday's disaster, I was more than happy to let Winston take the reins, so to speak.

He chuckled at my enthusiasm. "You'll see."

The truth was that I loved surprises and gifts. Maybe that was the reason his use of the term "gold digger" had gotten to me. It was something I was always teased about growing up because I loved nice things.

Maman said there was nothing wrong with it, as long as we strived to achieve those things for ourselves. And that was exactly what I was trying to do.

Since we decided to give "us" a shot, there wasn't a day we hadn't spent together. He'd taken me on dates. Surprised me with lunch. Walked along the Seine with his arm wrapped around me while I told him my deepest fears.

We made our way out of the apartment and down the street. His every step matched two of mine as we strolled through old Paris. We hadn't grown by leaps and bounds, but we were moving in the right direction.

People passed by us, flashing us smiles, almost as if they knew something major was afoot.

"I've always wanted to take a walk through Paris in the warm spring rain." I laughed at the silliness of ever finding that romantic. I'd freeze and catch pneumonia if we were to do it now, but a romantic heart refused to see reason. "Maybe a drizzle, so my boyfriend and I didn't get sick. And then he'd kiss me senseless and make me forget all about the cold."

He took that as his cue to open his long wool coat and wrap it around me. My hands snaked around his waist as a few passersby threw us fleeting glances. We looked like a couple on our honeymoon.

"Somehow, I feel like being called your boyfriend is a demotion."

Something about today felt different. I couldn't pinpoint it. Winston's touch was possessive, more so than usual. His hands constantly roamed my body, and his lips were never far from my skin.

"Okay, then I'll call you my not-so-secret husband, who I wish would kiss me senseless in the rain."

I felt his lips against my forehead, and I sighed. It was unreal how much I loved his touch. His everything. For the past week, it felt like we were really dating. No, not dating. It felt like we were an everyday married couple, and I was loving every minute of it.

He stayed with me at my studio, never once complaining about the lack of space. He still slept in the chair, but I was ready for the next step. Him sleeping in the bed with me. Maybe tonight.

We talked. We planned. I ran my ideas by him, and he threw in a few of his own. I was getting excited at the prospect of opening the store of my dreams. He knew exactly what he was doing.

Holding Winston's hand, we strolled through the lamplight-lined streets, and despite the cold air, I felt warm because of the man next to me.

"How many kids do you want?" I blurted suddenly, the question coming out of the blue.

He ran a thumb across his bottom lip pensively. "How many do you want to give me?"

I raised a brow. "It's up to me?"

He nodded with a serious expression. "You hold all the cards, baby. Whatever you want, it's yours."

I paused. "I guess we'll need to have a lot of sex," I remarked pensively, barely holding a straight face. "Because I might want a whole soccer team."

"As long as my daughters are into soccer," he said, reminding me of our conversation not too long ago. Happiness bloomed in my chest as I beamed at him.

He looked at me reverently, those deep oceans pulling me into their depths, and we resumed walking. "Life with you is..." He trailed off, seemingly to collect himself. "Happiness. Peace. Contentment."

I cocked my head, frowning at him. He was acting a bit weird today. "Is that a good thing?"

"The best." I turned to face him and he took my lips for a quick kiss, his tongue brushing mine. "It's what I've been searching for my entire life."

He urged me on. Like he couldn't wait for what came next.

Suddenly he stopped, and my eyes darted around, noting a luxury boat waiting for us.

"A speed boat?" I asked in surprise. He nodded and I stared at him. "But we'll freeze."

He laughed. "Don't worry. I won't let that happen."

Then he nudged me forward, unwilling to say anything else.

"Winston..."

He hopped in then scooped me up with little effort. "I don't think I can handle two disastrous dates in a row."

Still holding me in his arms, bridal-style, he bent his head, his rough voice in my ear. "Trust me, Billie. We're starting over." I exhaled beneath his intensity. "Do you trust me?"

I nodded, surprising myself. His eyes lit with satisfaction before setting me on my feet.

I couldn't stop looking at him as he issued orders to our captain. I wanted him in every way I could have him. But what I wanted more was to give him what he needed. To be what he needed.

He returned to me with a champagne bottle and two glasses, causing me to burst into laughter.

"Where did you find that?"

He grinned. "It's for us to celebrate."

I glanced at the bottle suspiciously. "A bottle of Champagne brut Goût de Diamant?" I didn't know much about vintage wines, but I knew this bottle was expensive. I chewed on my lip nervously, unsure if I should state the obvious, but then couldn't hold back. "Is it smart to have alcohol?" I whispered.

"I hate champagne, so it's safe." He poured us two glasses, handing me one. "To us, wife."

I took it and we clinked our glasses. "To us," I repeated.

I took a sip of the bubbly, watching him do the same. His tongue barely touched it.

I rose to my tiptoes and kissed him, so happy I felt ready to take on the world. When I pulled back, something feral and possessive lit in Winston's blue eyes. It was everything I needed to know to be certain I was—we were—doing the right thing here.

"I have something for you," I started when the boat came to a stop. I glanced around, the sudden silence surrounding us when our boat driver jumped into the water. "What the fuck?" I yelled, grabbing Winston's hand and shaking it hard. "Our captain wants to kill himself. Jesus, Winston. Do something."

Winston groaned. "He's not killing himself."

The man resurfaced from the dark waters of the Seine, soaking wet and smiling wildly.

"*Au revoir*," he yelled, waving, then took off swimming.

"He's going to freeze," I mumbled, turning around to find Winston on one knee, a velvet box in his hand. The man in the river forgotten, all I could do was stare at this man in front of me, wondering what was going on. Maybe the bubbles got to him after all.

A soft melody drifted from somewhere in the air. The Eiffel Tower's lights flickered in perfect harmony to the tunes of the song that might have sounded familiar if my brain wasn't so dumbfounded.

"Billie Swan, would you do me the honor of becoming my wife, a second time?" Winston's deep, husky voice made me tear up as the truck-size diamond sparkled. "I can't imagine this life without you. I should have done it the right way from the get-go, because the moment I saw you, I wanted you. It just took me a bit longer to figure out that I *needed* you too."

"Oh my God," I croaked, my voice distant. I lowered down and chanted, "Yes. Yes. Yes."

Then I reached into my pocket with one hand and opened my fingers, showing him what was in my palm. "I wanted to give you this tonight." For a moment, he stared at it, frozen, and insecurity snaked its way through me. "It was my dad's, but—"

He stopped me with a kiss. The most perfect kiss ever. "Yes, it would be my honor." I breathed into his mouth, and our bodies brushed against one another. When he broke the sensual dance of our lips, he leaned his forehead against mine. "Put it on my finger, Mrs. Ashford."

I took his hand in mine and slid my dad's ring onto his finger. "I, Billie Swan, promise to love you for the rest of my days. I promise my fidelity, and all my love, in good times and bad."

It fit him like a glove. It was meant to be.

"My turn," he rasped, holding the most beautiful engagement ring I had ever seen and sliding it next to his mama's ring. "With this ring, I promise to love you, cherish you, and stand by you for the rest of my days."

He lifted his head, his eyes hooded, and he kissed me like he couldn't breathe. Like I was the source of his oxygen, and he needed me to survive. Just the way I needed him.

He ran a thumb across my lips, smiling. I'd never seen him so relaxed. "How about we buy the pregnancy test and find out together?"

"I'd like that." I smiled dreamily at him before remembering our driver, my head whipping around. "Where is our boat captain? Did he freeze?"

Winston took my chin in his hand. "He had a diving suit beneath his clothes. I promise, he's fine."

I breathed a sigh of relief, then chuckled softly, burying my face into his chest. "Winston Ashford. Who'd have thought my husband would end up being such a romantic?"

For the next hour, we enjoyed the light show and music Winston had arranged for the event. We even had our dinner delivered. Yes—on the boat.

When we wrapped things up and he docked the boat, a woman appeared out of nowhere. She was breathtakingly beautiful with long blonde hair and blue eyes, wearing an expensive Valentino dress and... holy fuck, were those Christian Louboutin Daffodile Strass pumps in red? A tiny green monster sat on my shoulder, urging me to knock the woman out and steal her shoes. The angel on my other shoulder told it to shut the fuck up. I was married to Winston Ashford, we could afford the shoes. But that little girl who used to flip through her mother's fashion magazines wanted to buy them for herself.

"Winston, darling," she purred as she sauntered forward, completely ignoring me. It was right then and there when I decided I didn't like her. Her cold-as-ice smile was a dead giveaway though—this woman was trouble.

She ground herself against Winston and smiled up at him, her hands wandering too freely for my liking. I was ready to teach her a lesson. Winston blandly stared at her, not encouraging her but apparently too shocked himself to stop her.

It would seem I'd have to take matters into my own hands because this bitch needed to back the fuck off.

"Get your filthy paws off my man."

Chapter 44
Winston

I blinked and Billie was pushing Nicki away, causing her to stumble and fall right on her ass. I just stood there staring, my smirk speaking for itself.

"Oh my God!" Nicki screamed. "She assaulted me."

Billie cocked her head, challenging me to say something, and all I could do was smile. Finally! My wife had finally laid her claim. A few pedestrians rushed over to see what was going on.

"Winston, aren't you going to help me?" Nicki cried, pretending to struggle to get to her feet. "This woman's an animal."

"This woman is my wife," I said, my tone a clear warning. "So you better watch your next words."

Maybe it made me a pussy, but I couldn't pretend that Billie's actions didn't make me happy. I'd been waiting for it, and hallelujah, it was finally here. I wanted to throw her over my shoulder and run her home, then fuck her nice and slow as a reward.

Fuck, that was a good plan.

Nicki rose to her feet as she continued to shout profanities.

"Can't you see it, Winston? She and her sister are thieves. *Criminals!*" The woman was certifiable. I didn't know how I was still surprised after all these years. She took a step toward Billie, sputtering, "I'm going to end you for this." Her finger shoved at my wife, but I caught it before she had a chance to touch her.

"That's enough," I warned. "You should be happy you didn't touch her, or I'd have removed your hands from your body."

Nicki, the dumb bitch that she was, didn't comprehend the severity of my threat. "They're destroying everything. Our fathers will never accept your marriage. They'll destroy her and her sister."

She screamed like a lunatic. None of it mattered to me. She dared to threaten my wife. *That* I'd never overlook.

"The next time you dare to threaten Billie, I'll end you. And if you end up behind bars, it will be a mercy."

"Take that, bitch," Billie hissed. "And find a single man to harass."

Nicki muttered shit about going back to D.C. as I hooked my arm around my wife and we stepped around a fuming Nicki. "Tonight was perfect," I drawled.

Billie's shoulders slumped. "I'm sorry. I just couldn't stand there and watch her grind all over you."

I chuckled. "You misunderstand." Her eyes flicked my way, questions filling them. "*That* was part of the perfect."

She grinned. "And—"

I stopped her by pressing my lips to hers, relishing the curve of her smile.

Suddenly the world felt just right. Perfect as it should have been all along.

Chapter 45
Billie

The moment we got back to the studio apartment, Winston stopped dead in his tracks.

"Fuck."

"What?" I faced him, worried something was wrong. After the run-in with Cruella, we walked home in silence. Hand in hand. The way he'd stood up for me. And that proposal... I'd tell our children about it for years to come.

It was the most romantic proposal ever.

"The pregnancy test."

I winced at his reminder. "How could we forget?" I muttered. "What does that say about the kind of parents we'll be?"

He chuckled. "Well, we did get sidetracked." He cupped my face, pressing a kiss on my forehead. "I'm sorry about that. I wanted tonight to be everything and more."

"It was," I assured him quickly. "I... I loved it." Damn it, I was getting choked up again. He bent his head, brushing the tip of his nose against mine. "Tonight *was* perfect," I breathed against his lips, and his tongue swept over my bottom lip. "Will you want me when I'm big and fat?"

He threaded his fingers through my hair. "I've wanted you since the first moment I laid eyes on you. Your first snarky comment, and I was smitten."

I laughed at his sweet admission, a single tear rolling down my cheek. "Ditto, husband." My stomach chose that moment to growl, breaking the moment, and a fierce blush colored my cheeks. "Oops."

"I'm going to get you something to eat," he murmured against my lips. "And a pregnancy test."

"You're the best father ever and the baby's not even born." My stomach growled again. "Can I have gummy bears, waffles, and ice cream, please?"

"Anything my woman wants, she gets."

I grinned. "You're the best."

"Just know though, I plan on being the best husband ever too."

"It's good to have goals," I murmured, chuckling. Gosh, was it legal to be this happy? Another kiss, then he was out the door with the promise of returning quickly.

With Winston out to grab us some snacks, I headed for the shower. Once I was in and standing under the steaming water, letting it trickle down on me and wash the night away, the anger I'd felt earlier swirled down the drain. He was my husband.

Mine.

It would seem I was just as possessive of my man as he was of me. My lips pulled into a soft smile at the memory of how he'd defended me. I could only imagine how he'd be once we really got the confirmation of our pregnancy.

I'd just turned the water off and wrapped myself in a soft robe when I heard the door open.

"You're back already?" I yelled out. No answer. I wrapped a towel around my head and made my way out of the bathroom and into the bedroom.

My steps faltered and I stood frozen, staring at the stranger in my bedroom. I didn't recognize him, but it didn't bode well that he'd gotten through the locked door—never mind that Winston was probably at least a half hour from returning.

I wanted to run. I *needed* to run. Except, he stood between me and the only way out of this room. *Bathroom!* I'd lock myself in the bathroom and buy myself some time before Winston got home.

But before I could move, something heavy came crashing down on my head.

Everything turned black.

Chapter 46
Winston

The wide-open door was my first clue. The dead silence when I entered the apartment was my second.

"Billie?" No reply. Just ominous silence. My footsteps echoed throughout the small apartment. Kitchen. Bedroom. Bathroom.

Something glittered on the ground. *Her rings*.

My heart fully stopped before it started again, thundering in my ears. Did she run? Was she just lulling me into a false sense of security so I wouldn't think she'd leave me?

I shook my head, my gaze falling to my finger. She wouldn't have given me her father's ring if that's what she was planning. She wouldn't have discarded it so carelessly. It left no other option. She'd been taken.

But by who? How?

There was only one answer that came to mind. My father. My pulse thundered in my ears, and despite being in the middle of Paris in the warmth of Billie's home, I suddenly felt like I was back in a war zone.

Where women and children always paid the price.

The images in my head started spinning, and I knew I didn't have time for them. I'd been gone for at least forty minutes. Every minute counted if someone had taken her. And I didn't doubt that to be the case.

My phone vibrated in my pocket.

> Unknown number: I'm done fucking around with you Ashfords.

I couldn't process the information fast enough. Another message buzzed.

> Unknown number: Pay up or your wife will pay the price.

The ground shook beneath my feet. My brain fogged up, the images of all the dead women I'd witnessed in my lifetime mocking me. I hadn't been able to save a single one so far.

The phone vibrated again. A picture of my wife lying on a bed. Her hands and legs tied. She was out cold. An angry lump on her head was clear as day through the grainy image. My blood turned to ice.

Fear consumed me. It started in my heart and spread to my lungs and soul like venom, until it was the only thing drumming through me.

The sound of the city was a distorted, background noise. The shopping bag slipped from my fingers, its contents spilling onto the floor.

My eyes locked on the pregnancy test, and I fell to my knees.

I clasped my hands over the unrestrained thunder of my own pulse ringing in my ears, fighting to regain some semblance of control.

I fisted my hands and closed my eyes, but regretted it immediately when the images of death returned.

The blood pooling on the pavement, the scent of copper, the gunpowder, the desert—all the distorted images mixing together until they spiraled out of control.

I'd never felt a fear like this, but through it all, a voice came through.

"Pull yourself together, Winston." I raised my head, my brow furrowing. What was Asher doing here?

He helped me up from where I was kneeling on the floor. I needed to get a fucking grip. I couldn't fall apart. There was no time. I needed to act fast before that fucking psycho sent another picture.

"What are you doing here?" My own voice sounded off.

"I came as soon as I heard."

"Heard what?"

"Your father struck a deal with the Popov family." I stiffened but didn't say anything. "This dumbass talked while I was at their..." He trailed off for a moment, clearing his throat. "At their party, some event for... stuff." Silence stretched between us, punctuated by his mention of *stuff* and my knowledge of his extracurricular activities. "Anyhow, your father made an agreement with Nicki's, but the old Popov is no longer the head of that organization."

"So he officially relinquished it?"

Rumor was that he ran it all. Over the past twenty years, criminal groups from the Western Balkans had become key actors in the global drug trade. Balkan networks were involved in heroin, cocaine, and cannabis production and trafficking from Latin America into ports in western and southeastern Europe. And supposedly, Danil Popov was behind it all.

"No, his son, Danil, took over and calls all the shots now." Asher tsked. "The old Popov was prepared to let your father's debt slide a while longer, but Nicki ran to her brother. She's desperate to marry into your family."

The crazy woman had no idea how fucked up this family was. Maybe even more so than her own.

"What kind of deal did my father make?"

"A union between your families."

I scoffed. "That will never happen."

"Or give up the Ashford diamond mine"—which I owned, and

thankfully, I was smart enough to put it in my wife's name—"and give up his spot in politics, endorsing a Popov-designated family member as his replacement."

"There is only one thing my father likes more than money, and that's power. It seems he made a bad deal, because none of his sons will marry Nicki Popova."

Asher nodded.

"Anyhow, Danil Popov, Nicki's brother, issued an order to either kill your old man or get his daughter-in-law who's in Paris. He somehow learned her name was on the deed of your diamond mine. Considering your wife's in Paris—"

Fuck, why couldn't Danil just end my father? Goddammit.

My hands balled into fists, and I locked eyes with my good friend. "Why didn't you call?"

"I tried. You weren't answering." My jaw locked, the muscles in my body crying out. I'd turned my phone off for our night on the river.

I wouldn't let my wife down. I'd save her if it was the last fucking thing I did. One breath. Another. Three deep breaths, and I squared my shoulders.

"I need all the information you have," I spat out as I typed a message back to Danil.

> Me: One bruise, one hair out of place, and you'll have a war on your hands.

The reply was almost instant.

> Danil: You're in no position to be calling the shots.

"He wants the diamond mine," Asher interrupted.

"Why?" I'd need all the leverage I could get my hands on and as far as I knew, the Popov family wasn't into mining.

"The diamond mine is his way into controlling the underworld in Africa."

I shot him a surprised look. "He's aiming high, huh?" Asher shrugged his shoulder. "How did he learn I own it?" I questioned. I hadn't exactly been advertising the fact that I bought the mine. In fact, I hadn't shared that information with anyone but Kristoff Baldwin, who secured the purchase through his company. And I'd stake my life on the fact that he wouldn't share that information with anyone. "And how do *you* know about it?"

He grinned. "I was at the auction."

I let out a sardonic breath. Asher, just like Danil, had an agenda.

"If that fucking diamond mine is what he wants, he can have it." I'd give him my entire fortune if it meant getting Billie back unharmed. "But I swear to God, I'm gonna murder him for coming near my wife."

Asher grumbled, "Can I have the diamond mine, then?" under his breath, but I ignored him. We needed reinforcements. I dialed Royce first, and he answered on the first ring.

"I'm not in the mood for another round of preaching, Winston."

"I need you," I said. "My wife has been kidnapped."

"The wife you've had for six years? The one I had to read about in the paper?" he deadpanned.

"One and the same, yes."

"Are you sure she didn't leave you?"

"Christ, Royce. She was kidnapped by the mafia because of Father." Silence, deafening and suffocating. "Can you get your ass here or not?"

"Where is *here*?"

"Paris."

"Fuck." That didn't sound promising. "We just landed in Australia and my pilot left. It might take a minute to get to you." My mind worked furiously, but best-case scenario, Royce wouldn't be in Paris until tomorrow afternoon. "But Kingston's in Paris."

I shot a look at Asher. "Kingston's here?" He shrugged. "What's he doing in Paris?" I asked my brother.

"Fuck if I know. Something about a girl."

I didn't have the energy to worry about whether it was Sofia Volkov's daughter. He should just kill her mother and call it even. Not that I could blame him for needing that revenge.

"Stay in Australia," I finally said. "And don't fuck things up with Willow, or our sister will have your balls strung."

I ended the call and dialed Kingston. "Not now, Winston."

Why did all my brothers have to choose *now* to be in the middle of something? I bet if I called Alessio and Byron, their greeting wouldn't be far off what I'd gotten so far.

"My wife's been kidnapped. Balkan mafia. Danil Popov has her. I need your help."

"Fuck, they couldn't have done this yesterday?"

"They might have planned it for yesterday. I was busy having an allergic reaction to a horse, so we spent the night in the hospital."

"You're allergic to horses?"

Asher snickered. My eyes shot to him, and he quickly wiped a hand across his mouth in a poor attempt to hide his amusement. My gaze darkened, ready to go on a rampage.

"Long story. Can you help or not? It'll be just the three of us, Asher being the third wheel."

My friend rolled his eyes and flipped me the bird.

"Sure, pick me up."

He recited the address and I memorized it as I headed out the door, Asher right beside me.

I'd save my girl if it was the last thing I did.

Chapter 47
Billie

My eyes shot open and a fresh wave of dread washed over me.

I was curled in the corner, hugging my knees. A towel lay next to me, and I recognized it as the one I'd wrapped my hair in. I lowered my gaze and found myself wearing nothing but a robe. The events of last night slowly trickled in.

My icy hands roamed my legs, my thighs, but I didn't feel any abrasions. I sighed in relief, but fear still remained.

"Hello?" I called out, my throat dry. No answer. Maybe this was a case of mistaken identity.

It was dark, the only light coming through the slit under the door. I slowly turned my head to survey the room, immediately wincing in pain.

"Ouch," I whispered, bringing my hand to my temple and trailing my fingers over my skull. There was a goose egg there, but other than that, it seemed okay. I shifted slowly, gray stone surrounding me. The room reeked of urine and mold, making me feel nauseous.

What the hell was going on?

I rested my forehead on my knees, exhaustion taking over. Maybe this was nothing but a bad dream. A nightmare. After all, you saw shit like this in movies. The average person didn't experience kidnappings. Marrying into the Ashford family with a shady-as-fuck father-in-law? Yeah, definitely not an average family.

Footsteps sounded outside the door, bringing my thoughts to a stop. My heart started to race, my instinct urging me to make a run for it. I squeezed farther into the corner, unsure what to expect. A cold shiver rolled through me as I started to tremble.

I jumped at the sound of the keys rattling. In the next moment, the door opened with a loud creak, allowing a bright light to filter into my prison.

My state of alertness heightened at the sight of him. He was tall and muscular without being overly buff, and was not the picture of a stereotypical criminal. Aside from tattoos that crept from underneath his crisp white shirt. He looked like military.

Kind of like Winston.

"What's going on here?" I demanded, my gaze shifting to his face, and for a moment, I felt struck. *Jesus Christ.* His features were striking. Dark, sharp, and terrifyingly blank.

He was good-looking in a clean-cut sort of way, but there was an unmistakable beast lurking inside of him.

He extended his hand, and I eyed it suspiciously, refusing to take it. He didn't seem to take offense to my snub.

"I'm Danil." He pushed his hands into the pockets of his dark trousers, almost as if trying to appear non-threatening. *As fucking if.* Even looking more like a sophisticated businessman than a criminal in that three-piece suit, you couldn't mistake this man for a nobody. "I'm taking you somewhere more comfortable."

"For me or for you?" The words shot out before I could retract them. Wasn't the first rule of being kidnapped not to taunt your jailors? Or, wait. Was it to taunt them so they'd become exasperated and dump you somewhere?

The corner of his lips twitched, and I got the distinct impression that this man rarely smiled.

"For you," he deadpanned in a cold voice. "Don't worry, Billie Ashford, I have no plans to lay a hand on you." His icy blue eyes roamed over me. "Not unless you ask for it."

I scoffed. "Don't hold your breath." Another twitch of his lips. I accepted his help and stood up, careful not to expose myself. "It would have been polite to wait until I got dressed to kidnap me."

"I'll consider that for next time."

My eyes bulged. "There's not going to be a next time. You're going to regret this."

"Highly unlikely." His voice was cold, controlled, and confident.

I swallowed hard. "You plan on killing me?"

He turned around. "That depends on your husband and father-in-law." *Senator Ashford?* Yeah, that sleazeball would happily let me die. Winston wouldn't though. He was coming for me, I just knew it. "Follow me." He didn't wait, striding away from me with long, even strides. "Unless you'd prefer to stay here where any of my men could get their hands on you."

That got me going. I ran after him, my three steps matching his one.

We made our way down the hall, then up the stairs, where men were bickering in a foreign language—Eastern European, if I strained my ear correctly—traveling down the hall.

"Holy shit," I muttered, spotting a Mona Lisa painting, and struggling to understand what it was doing here. It should be on display in the Louvre museum. I'd just left a moldy, smelly prison cell and this world-famous painting was one of the first things I ran into. I struggled to wrap my head around it as I noticed the *fleur de lys,* the symbol that referred to the French monarchy. Then I spotted the planets and deities depicted on the ceilings and I knew exactly where we were. Although it made absolutely no sense. "Are we in Versailles?"

315

"We're close." Danil flicked a glance over his shoulder. "Smart girl."

"Not a smart man," I muttered. Why wasn't he worried that I'd attack him from behind? *Maybe because I'm naked under my robe, and there are no weapons in sight.* "I'm surprised this place isn't swarming with police yet."

"It won't be. This is the rented part of the Versailles grounds."

"But Mona Lisa—"

"Isn't in its usual spot on display," he deadpanned. "Obviously."

"Obviously," I agreed dryly.

His phone buzzed, and he lowered his gaze to it. His brow creased as he read whatever message was on his phone.

He raised his head, his expression a reserved mask. His features were too bold, his face too sharp, his eyes hooded. He was darkness dressed in an Edwardian suit and wearing an expensive Rolex, inviting trouble.

Yes, that was it.

Suddenly, he stopped in front of an ornately decorated door, covered with golden motifs and royal crossed letters. He swung it open, motioning for me to enter. With a thundering heart, I entered the room with Danil right behind me.

He looked over to the three men in the room, who stared at me like I was their ticket to something big.

"I have something urgent to take care of." He turned around and faced the other men. "Keep her safe."

And just like that, he left me alone with the wolves.

Three muscular enforcers surrounded me, eyeing me like I was a piece of candy.

They each took a step forward and I took two back, intent on keeping a distance. Apparently though, these men were from a culture that didn't respect personal space. I gave my head a subtle shake at such a stupid thought. Every bad man, no matter the culture, refused to respect the privacy and space of a woman.

Another guy entered the room, and I groaned inwardly. One more threat to worry about.

He was a lot better looking than the buffoons trying to intimidate me. In fact, he was gorgeous, despite the scar that ran from his left temple down to his jaw. Where had I seen him before?

Then I remembered. He was the man in my apartment.

He spat something in a language I didn't understand, causing the other three to stand back. The bald guy spat something back, causing the other two to laugh.

I was cornered.

Two of the men pounced on me, each grabbing an arm. I screamed and kicked, thrashing against their hold. The third one started to undo his pants, but before he could take a step forward, the fourth guy rammed into him, causing him to stumble.

"Get the fuck away from her," he growled in perfect English.

The incident startled the other two, and I took the opportunity to jerk out of their grip and kick the one on my left in the shin right as the other one pushed me onto the floor. My head hit the hardwood and pain exploded in my skull. I sunk my teeth into my bottom lip to stop a whimper from escaping.

I thrashed wildly, screaming at the top of my lungs. The blond man reached for his crotch and straddled me, his bulge pushing into my stomach. He leaned over, licking his lips, and I stilled.

"I'm going to make you bleed," he grunted, smiling viciously. Holding my breath, I waited. One second. Two seconds. Then I headbutted him with all my strength. Blood exploded from my mouth, but his yelp was so fucking worth it.

The fourth guy was now fighting two men, and by the looks of it, he was winning. I just had to fend them off a bit longer. I bucked and kicked, but he still managed to rip open my robe. On the verge of being assaulted, I lost my shit.

I wailed on him, screaming so loud it pierced my own eardrums.

Bang. Bang. Bang.

Blood exploded in my face. A body fell on top of me, and I kept on screaming until the heavy form was pushed off of me. I scrambled backward, my naked body exposed.

There was only Danil and the other guy who'd tried to stop them. They both averted their eyes while my teeth chattered.

"Mrs. Ashford, I'll need you to get covered up before your husband barges in here." I lowered my eyes in a daze, then with numb, trembling fingers, attempted to fasten the ties on my robe without much luck.

With a sigh, Danil came up to me, his hands expertly twisting it tight.

"Th-thank you."

He took two steps back but remained close, eyeing me warily. "This is my friend Soren." He tilted his chin at the three dead bodies surrounding us. "I apologize for this. It wasn't supposed to happen."

I opened my mouth but closed it immediately. My brain had stopped functioning, and I was unable to find a single thing to say.

Pulling out a handkerchief from somewhere, he handed it to me.

When I remained unmoving, staring at him blankly, he explained, "You have blood on your face." He took the matter into his own hands when I didn't budge. He brought it to my face, and I flinched. "I'm just going to wipe it so your husband doesn't have a heart attack when he sees you."

When he sees you.

That finally got my limbs moving, and I combed my fingers through my tangled strands. "D-do I look okay?"

Danil's lips twitched.

"You look like you've been to hell and back," Soren answered from a few feet away, giving his head a subtle shake.

My hand came to my stomach and rested there. Both men's eyes followed the movement, then shared a wordless glance, after which Soren mouthed a "Fuck."

The sound of an alarm signaling a break-in followed right after.

318

Danil and Soren came to stand beside me, sticking me between them, each one putting a gun to my temple.

"Sorry about this," Danil drawled. "But this is the surest way for us all to get out alive."

I didn't know what he meant, but it didn't matter.

Because Winston was coming for me.

Chapter 48
Winston

Asher turned his attention to Kingston, his restlessness setting my teeth on edge.

"I'm so glad we all coordinated our clothes," he drawled casually. Kingston shot him a dry look, then flipped him off. It was a coincidence, all three of us dressed in black, blending into the night. My brother looked out the window, like he was expecting an ambush. He had barely spoken a word since he agreed to help me.

Royce vowed not to tell our other siblings anything—not that it was a hardship since he was avoiding them. I didn't want Byron to get wrapped up in this. Not when he just finally got the woman of his dreams. And then there was that small thing of his wife being Billie's sister.

Yeah, better to leave him out of all this.

So here we were. The three of us against who knew how many. Jesus, this sounded like a three musketeers movie. Cheesy and about to end badly.

"How'd Nicki pull this off?" Asher asked as he peered at the castle from the window of the SUV.

Kingston, Asher, and I were crammed in the vehicle, my brother's hand resting atop the rifle on his lap. He appeared calm and unperturbed, but it was just a facade. I knew, because I was sporting the same one.

We were parked in the shadows of the tree line on the outskirts of Versailles. The fairy-tale setting would have been charming if not for the fact that the bastards were holding my wife prisoner.

Fuck, if they touched one hair on her golden head, I'd murder that entire family. Fuck the possibility of war with a powerful criminal organization. I'd burn the entire world for my woman.

"She didn't. Her brother did," I muttered. Nicki was dumb; her brother was a savant. He was the head of the Popov family and was well known in the business world, but it'd always been said that the men of that family were connected to the Russian mafia. Nicki's brother took it a step further and expanded their empire to include the Balkan mafia.

"What? Did they rent all the grounds of Versailles?"

I shrugged. "With the company they keep, I wouldn't be surprised."

I shot a quick message to Priest—aka Christian DiLustro—to infiltrate the security system. The guy was a genius, and normally, he didn't like to fuck with anything French since he'd established a peace treaty with the Corsican mafia and the latter vacated the Philadelphia territory. The deal was that they stayed away from each other's territories.

But Versailles was hardly anyone's territory.

My phone vibrated in my hand before I had a chance to put it away.

Priest: You owe me.

It wasn't ideal, but Priest was the lesser of two evils, considering he was my cousin.

I briefly closed my eyes, trying to purge the haunting images of what Billie might be going through in there, even knowing she was a fighter. She'd get through this, but what would it mean for her in the long term?

I stared out the window, my gaze laser-focused on the movements around the castle.

Bang. Bang. Bang.

Gunshots rang out, and the silence that followed had my breath catching.

It was time to move. To get back what was mine.

My hand tightened around my weapon.

"Everyone's earpieces working?" The three of us shared a look, and with terse nods, we exited the vehicle. "Stick to the shadows."

With my gun loaded and in my hands, I ran toward the building, swearing to everything that was holy that I would murder the whole Popov family if they hurt her. The fuckers. How dare they go after her?

Making sure the path was clear and there were no guards to ambush us, we used the trees as camouflage and inched closer to the location.

"Why is nobody attacking?" Kingston's voice came through my earpiece. "I can feel their eyes on me."

Asher's voice came next. "It's probably a trap."

That was the wrong thing to say to Kingston, but my brother's steps never slowed down.

"Nobody's taking me prisoner," he grumbled. "I have to go to Brazil."

"Vacation?"

"You two! Stop chitchatting," I snapped. "Asher, check the thermal imaging device. We need to know where they're keeping Billie."

Something was fishy about this whole thing. Someone should have fired at least one bullet at us by now. Nothing. I knew it was too easy, but I couldn't worry about that.

I ran the length of the property until we reached the door. No matter what happened, Billie was my priority.

I knew my father's choices would lead to another devastating end, but the Popov family made one terrible mistake this time: they involved my wife.

Chapter 49
Billie

"Are you two sure someone's coming?" I asked after what seemed like hours of standing with two guns pointed at my head. "I'm not hearing a thing."

"He's coming, and he brought reinforcements." Soren's voice was full of conviction, his eyes never straying from the door.

"What kind of reinforcements?" Maybe he brought the entire army. After all, Winston was ex-military.

Danil smirked. "The dangerous kind."

I scoffed. "Are you saying you're not dangerous?"

This conversation was ridiculous.

"Of course I'm dangerous." I snorted and Soren rolled his eyes at me. "And pray you never find out just how much."

I didn't think he was boasting, his tone was practical and matter-of-fact, which in itself was terrifying.

Something beeped and Soren checked his phone with his free hand before nodding at Danil.

"Here we go. Finally."

My hope ignited when the door opened and Winston entered the room. He and the two men trailing after him had their guns trained on Danil and Soren.

Winston's blue eyes landed on me, appraising. I looked like a mess and couldn't even imagine the thoughts that were running through his mind. When he reached my face, his jaw was clenched so tight, I was surprised it didn't snap.

"I'm not hurt," I quickly said. "It's not my blood."

That must have eased some of his tension because the corners of his lips lifted into a heart-stopping smile. I returned the smile, my heart melting even as tears burned my lids. I just wanted to run to him and hug him, let him take me home.

Winston turned to look at Danil and Soren, his expression morphing into a cold mask.

"The Ashford brothers and the pirate," Danil drawled. That was his brother? "Sounds like the title of a bad novel."

"More like some hot smut," I muttered under my breath. Soren choked, attempting to stifle a laugh, his eyes crinkling with amusement. Maybe I'd hit my head too hard. "Just don't shoot me by accident."

"You got yourself quite the woman here," Danil announced.

"I know," Winston gritted.

"There'll be no coming out of this alive," Winston's brother drawled. "So let's save ourselves some time and let me shoot you, collect your teeth—"

"Kingston, please stop with the fucking teeth," Asher deadpanned. "Your sister-in-law is about to pass out. You're scaring her. At least wait a day or two and let her get warmed up before you start with the teeth."

Kingston just shrugged a shoulder. Maybe he was a tad bit... crazy. Unhinged. Murderous? Fuck, what was the word I was looking for?

"I like collecting teeth, fucking sue me."

I paled, suddenly not sure who the bad guys were here.

"Ummm... can we stop talking about teeth?" My throat filled with bile and my limbs started to tremble. "I don't feel so good."

Then, as if to prove the point, I retched, folding over and throwing up what little there was in my belly. Winston ran over, ignoring the guns Danil had trained on him.

Winston pulled my hair away from my face as I heaved over and over again. Luckily, it didn't last long, and I straightened, wiping my mouth with the back of my hand.

"You know, Odette puked her guts out when she was pregnant with Ares," I blurted out, my observation misplaced considering the situation we found ourselves in.

Danil let out a sardonic breath, and said, "You don't say," while Winston's eyes roved over me, his hands following the path, checking for any injuries, stopping once again on the blood. "It's not mine," I murmured again, taking his palm and pressing my cheek against it. "You came for me."

"Didn't I tell you? Always." Winston pushed me behind him, facing Danil and pointing the gun at him again. "Kidnapping my wife was a shitty way to get my attention."

Danil smiled coldly, clearly unbothered despite the fact that he and Winston had guns pointed at each other. Chances of one of them dropping dead were fifty-fifty.

"Actually, I wasn't trying to get in touch with you," Danil answered calmly. "Just collecting a debt."

Winston's vein throbbed and he looked like he was about to explode. "Work out this debt with Senator Ashford. I don't owe you shit."

Danil remained quiet, his eyes locked on Winston, and something passed between the two of them. Something that made my heart hammer with trepidation.

"It's best if we discuss it in private," Winston finally said. He turned around and kissed me on the cheek. "Go with my brother." I shook my head. "With Asher, then."

I swallowed. "Okay."

With that, Winston and Danil strode out of the room. Soren remained, lowering his gun, although he kept it in his hand.

"So now what?"

Soren shrugged. Asher rolled his eyes. Kingston tilted his chin at the three dead men. "Will someone grab their teeth?"

Chapter 50
Winston

I shut the door behind me, the luxury of the room a stark contrast to our current situation. I still held the gun in my hand, ready to pull the trigger if need be. Danil wasn't fooling me by trying to appear relaxed. He was anything but.

"If I didn't know you liked pain, I'd be making you hurt right now, Danil. Dare to touch my wife again, and I'll make it my mission to tear you apart, limb from limb."

Danil walked past, sliding his one hand in the pocket of his trousers while keeping the other loosely gripped around his gun.

He let out a sardonic breath, turning to face me. "Considering your father started this mess, you should hold on to that anger and aim it at him."

I laughed. "I hear your old man isn't much better."

"I handled that problem, and he knows that one foot out of place, I won't hesitate to slit his throat." I raised a brow with reluctant admiration at his admission. Danil was a ruthless bastard, but I couldn't say that his father didn't have it coming.

And so did my own father. Danil was right. My father had been the root of all the things that went wrong in our family. It started with him, and it could end only with him.

"Let's get to business, shall we?" I steered the conversation away from my own fucked-up parent. "Nobody in our family will be marrying Nicki."

He rubbed his jaw, leaning casually against the table probably worth millions.

"Fair enough." He didn't seem surprised. "Then I'd like the deed to the diamond mine you purchased."

"I bet you would," I muttered.

His eyes narrowed. "Or I can get your wife to do it."

"You won't fucking speak her name." The threat escaped me, so calm and deadly it stilled the air.

Danil watched my face, let out an amused breath.

"You have it bad for her." I gritted my teeth, refusing to answer. He didn't know the half of it. I'd give up my balls for her, and I was pretty attached to them. Fuck, my life for hers was a no-brainer. I'd refuse to walk this earth without her in it. "Okay, so the diamond mine it is?"

I nodded. What were diamonds compared to Billie's safety?

"My wife has plans to start a jewelry designing business, and she'll have the first right of refusal on anything you dig up."

He nodded his agreement, and I moved toward the door, eager to get back.

"One more thing." His words stopped me with one hand on the doorknob. I drew my gaze to him. "About your father..."

The meaning touched the black part of my heart, and a twisted smile pulled on the corner of my lips. "Consider it done."

I shut the door behind me.

Chapter 51
Billie

Home sweet home.

After all the men settled their scores and glared at each other for a while, Winston finally hauled me into his arms and brought me back to Paris.

"I need a shower," I muttered. When he went to move, I placed a palm on Winston's cheek. "Alone, please."

He nodded, and the moment I entered the bathroom, I turned the shower to scalding, discarded my ruined robe, and stepped inside. Slowly, the events of the last twenty-four hours rushed through me, and the terrifying what-if scenarios played through my mind.

I swallowed hard, attempting to take calming breaths. "Nothing happened," I whispered to myself. "Everything is okay."

I chanted the words over and over again while I stood under the stream of the shower longer than usual, scrubbing every inch of my skin. But it'd been close. So fucking close. A shiver rolled down my spine, and despite the hot shower, I felt cold.

Thank God Danil was a decent criminal, if there was such a thing, but I still felt filthy.

I expected Winston to object to leaving me alone in the bathroom, but surprisingly, he sat down on the bed and said to call him if I needed him. That simple gesture just about sent me into an emotional tailspin.

Once done, I dried off, and since I no longer had a bathrobe, I stood at a loss for what to wear until I spotted a neat pile. Winston must have brought them in for me. I slipped on the panties and nightie, wishing I had stocked up on some pajamas that covered a bit more.

Thank God I wasn't wearing my silky nightie when I was kidnapped. That would have been an invitation for those delusional animals to touch me.

I shook my head to chase away the thoughts. My husband came for me. He saved me, and I hadn't even thanked him yet.

Once dressed, I made my way into the bedroom and found my husband still seated where I'd left him. His expression was one of worry, but I could now see the mask he wore, trying to hide his feelings. He didn't want to upset me.

I didn't think about my next move. I just threw myself into his arms, uncaring how weak or silly it made me appear. Worse things could have happened, but I was still shaken to my core. No woman should ever be subjected to bullshit like that.

"Thank you for saving me."

"I'll always save you, Billie. I promise to find you in every world and every lifetime." His words sent a ripple through me, taking hold of my heart. I trembled in his embrace, soaking up his strength and reveling in his familiar scent. "Tell me what you need," he murmured. "Tell me what to do. I hate seeing you upset."

And it was all I needed. This. Him.

"Just hold me," I said, burying my face into his chest. And as he held me and whispered comforting words, the nightmare slowly faded away.

"I was so scared," he admitted, his tone raspy and full of emotions. "I've never been so fucking scared."

My palms on his back, I gripped his shirt and pressed my cheek against his. "You saved me."

He took my chin between his fingers and brought our faces inches from each other. "You're my wife. My woman. I'll always come for you. I'll always protect you."

I pushed myself further into his warmth. I just couldn't shake off the cold licking my skin.

"What is it?" he asked. I shook my head. "Billie, I swear—" He cut himself off, softening his tone. "You can tell me anything."

"I thought that was it," I choked out, ashamed of my cowardice. "I thought they were going to rape me."

His face tightened. "And... did they?"

I shook my head. "No, Danil came in and killed the ones who tried." His hold tightened on me, and it was exactly what I needed. "What did you give up to save me?"

His blue orbs met mine. "My father and the mine I recently purchased."

My brows furrowed. "A mine? What type?"

"Diamonds." He shrugged as if it was nothing.

I gasped. "Why would you do that?"

He cupped my face. "I'd give it all up a hundred times over for you. There's plenty of riches in this world. There's only one of you."

Our eyes locked. His look was full of rough whispers, late-night promises, and sinful deeds.

"And your father?" I asked. "How do you feel about cutting ties with him?"

"I've been done with him for a very long time."

I nodded, although it was hard to understand such a cold relationship. I'd have laid down my life for my father, but then Senator Ashford couldn't be compared to my caring and kind father.

"Won't that be a betrayal to your family? What will your siblings think?"

"I'd make a deal with the devil for you." A soft gasp slipped between my lips. "Giving up Senator Ashford is hardly a hardship.

My brothers and sisters have been done with him for years too. He is not our family."

And just like that, I knew this man would kill for me.

A sharp pain pierced my back, waking me from my sleep. I must have cried out, because Winston's face was inches from mine, his brows furrowed and his hand on my forehead.

"You're burning up," he said, panic lacing his voice. "You were crying, and I couldn't wake you."

Another shot of excruciating pain blazed through me, and I bit into my lip, tasting blood.

"Something's wrong," I rasped. The pain in my lower back reminded me of the first days of my period but at a strength I had never experienced before.

"Fuck, we've got to get you to a hospital."

I attempted to sit up despite the stabbing pain in my spine. The intensity shot stars into my vision. I focused on Winston's blurry face, unable to hold back a whimper. Pressure built and I felt warmth trickling down my inner thighs.

Winston pushed the blanket off me, ready to scoop me up, and froze when his eyes locked on the red stain on my nightie. I fixed my eyes on the growing stain, and we froze for a moment, knowing exactly what was happening.

"Fuck," he muttered, desperation unlike any I'd heard before marring his expression. "Fuck, fuck, fuck."

"W-Winston," I breathed as another round of pain plunged into my lower abdomen. My hand started to tremble and nausea filled me. I didn't get to say the next words before his strong hands lifted me, every step toward the bathroom sending waves of pain through me.

We got in the shower and he threw towels onto the tile, lowering me carefully onto them.

"W-Win—" My voice broke. My heart cracked. There'd be no

baby. We'd never even taken the pregnancy test. "P-please, no. Please, please, please."

"It's okay," he whispered. "I've got you."

He produced a cell phone from somewhere and dialed with shaking fingers.

"We need an ambulance." His voice was firm, his command clear as he recited the address, but it wasn't enough to keep the veil from slipping.

A scream tore from my lips. My inner muscles quaking and cramping.

Winston threw the phone carelessly across the tiled floor and reached for the showerhead. The spray of warm water soaked me, running down my legs in a river of red. His big body wrapped around me, his chest at my back, I buried my head into his bicep as another round of stabbing sensations had me screaming in pain. I wasn't sure how long it lasted. Maybe a minute. Maybe an hour.

He took my hands in his. "Hold on to me," he murmured. "Don't look."

"I'm sorry," I croaked, my throat raw.

He cupped my cheek and his blue eyes locked with mine. "It's my fault, temptress. So let me bear the pain." My heart twisted, knowing his pain was no less than mine. Just a different kind.

Sobbing, I nodded, and he held me tighter. My hands fisted in his, my nails digging half-moons into my skin, and I sunk my teeth into his collarbone, stifling my screams.

And the whole time, Winston whispered soft words, promising he'd never leave. Promising he had me. I panted against him as beads of sweat formed on my forehead.

Finally, the physical pain subsided into a bearable throb, but inside, the pain lingered. The hollow emptiness. The promise of something that had been so close to grasping.

I turned my head to see whatever this could have been, but a hand gripped my chin, holding it firm. "Look at me, baby. Just me. It's just a heavier period," he murmured. "Just focus on me."

A sob tore from my throat and he scooped me up.

"I swear—" His voice cracked, and I heard his despair. "We'll get through this, Billie. I promise."

The first echoes of the ambulance sounded nearby, but it was too late.

Chapter 52
Winston

The minutes turned into hours.

Billie passed out just as the medics came. I suspected from the loss of blood. I promised God, the devil—anyone who was listening—anything and everything, as long as she pulled through.

We'd been in the hospital for the past three hours. Billie was out cold, likely from the pain meds they'd administered.

It had taken less than thirty minutes, but I almost lost my mind in the waiting room. I'd refused to leave her side since they wheeled her out. Not during the vitals measuring; not during the doctors' visits.

The miscarriage.

The whispers.

Pitying gazes.

A sonogram. Another one. Murmurs of second opinions. Shadows of people checking her, coming and going, throwing me fearful glances as they walked by me. I was about to snap if someone didn't start talking.

My loafers squeaked along the hospital floor as I strode around the hospital bed where my wife lay unconscious.

Fuck, I'd kill for a drink or a cigarette right now. No, not that. I'd kill to see my wife's golden-brown eyes open. I wanted to see her smile. Hear her voice.

"Why is nobody talking?" I snapped, tugging at my hair desperately. "What are the whispers about? I swear to God, start talking or —" I couldn't threaten murder. They'd kick me out in a heartbeat. Fuck, I felt so helpless.

"You and Billie just can't keep away from the hospital, huh?" A familiar voice came from behind, and I whirled around, coming face-to-face with Tristan. The nurses cast looks full of admiration his way, then scattered once he gave them a subtle order.

"What's going on?" I repeated, stopping in front of the hospital bed. Billie's complexion was whiter than the sheets she was lying on. "I'm going out of my mind here."

"You look like shit," was his answer.

I caught a glimpse of myself in the window reflection. Bristles along my jawline. My hair was a mess from all the times I had pushed my hands through it. My eyes were red. I had only enough time to slip on shoes and a shirt before we were wheeling out of Billie's little apartment, so I was still wearing the same pants from earlier.

"I just want to know what everyone's whispering about," I said tiredly. "I want a promise that my wife will be okay." Before I lost my shit.

Tristan took a deep breath and then exhaled.

"Billie will be okay." I let out a relieved sigh. I could handle anything else. She was the most important thing to me. Tristan remained quiet, the silence heavy with something ominous.

"But there's something else," I stated, much calmer this time.

He nodded.

"Billie has one ovary." My brows furrowed. She'd never mentioned it—not that we'd ever discussed ovaries much. "It's a healthy ovary, so there shouldn't be issues getting pregnant in the future, but the chances are slightly lower."

"So Billie's going to be okay?" I asked. If there was even a slight risk of endangering her life, I'd get a vasectomy. We could adopt babies. As many as she wanted, if that's what she wanted.

"No more than if she had two ovaries," he stated calmly. "Although, you'll have to minimize stress and certain triggers. I'm assuming you two will try to get pregnant again?"

I shook my head. "No." Tristan's eyes flashed with surprise. "We'll take it slow. I want her to recover first and maybe take a long honeymoon, then we'll talk. I'm going to let her take the lead here, Doc."

It was the first sincere smile I'd ever gotten from Billie's friend. "I can see why she fell for you now." He rubbed his chin pensively. "Strange how she never mentioned you over the last six years. I didn't even know she was married."

I rolled my eyes, not willing to go down that road.

"When can I take her home?"

"Tomorrow. We want to keep her here for observation a little while longer."

I nodded. It was just enough time for me to ensure my penthouse was fully stocked for us. We'd been staying exclusively in Billie's apartment, but I knew once she got settled in with me, she'd appreciate the extra space and luxury, not to mention the round-the-clock security.

"Anything else I need to be made aware of?" I asked.

"No. Just have her take it slow. Keep an eye out for any signs of depression, and bring her back for a checkup."

With that, he left, and I made my way to Billie's hospital bed. I brushed her hair out of her face, and she shivered against my touch. I reached for another blanket and pulled it over her, then lay carefully against her.

"I'm never letting you go again," I whispered against the silence.

I placed my palm on her chest, the beating of her heart a comfort and security against me losing my mind. She felt so small in my arms that it had my heart shuddering in my chest at any and all possibilities of someone hurting her.

Including me.

It was right then and there when I knew that I'd keep my word to Danil, no matter the consequences.

Chapter 53
Billie

O nce again, a hospital bed was bearing the weight of the two of us.

Winston's strong embrace while I was in and out of consciousness was the only thing I allowed myself to feel. I gave myself over to it, desperate to soak in his strength.

Don't fall apart. Don't fall apart.

And so, I let him ground me. His arms around me. His fingertips on my forehead. The soft scent of his cologne. The warmth of his skin. And his soft murmurs of how much he loved me. How much he needed me.

He traced the shell of my ear, tucking a piece of hair neatly behind it. "I just need you to be okay, Billie. Please... for me." His voice cracked, and with it, my heart did too.

I loved him. The crazy, intense, devastating kind of love.

My eyelids peeled open, and I found him watching me with a furrowed brow.

"You okay?" My voice came out raspy.

He let out an anguished laugh. "Am I?" I nodded slowly, my head heavy. "Baby, I'm only okay when you're okay. Are you? Tell me what you need."

"Just you," I murmured, the room around me coming in and out of focus. "And some water maybe."

He was quick to move off the bed and bring a glass with a straw to my lips.

"Suck," he ordered.

"That's what she said," I said, attempting humor, but it came out flat. The corners of his lips tipped, but there was no amusement in his eyes. He was hurting too.

I drank the water, and with each swallow, the lump in my throat grew bigger and bigger. I wanted to suffocate. I didn't want to feel this emptiness.

I broke. The first tear broke through, then another, and a dam was opened.

"I'm sorry," I sobbed. He put the glass on the table with a thud and was back in the bed with me in the next second.

He wrapped his arms around me and held me tight. "You have nothing to be sorry about, Billie."

"But you wanted—" A hiccup. "A... a b-baby." Another hiccup. "And my one... s-stupid... ovary—"

I never got to finish because he silenced me with a kiss. Then he cupped my cheeks and kissed my forehead, my nose, each cheek, then my lips.

"Your ovary is perfect and didn't cause any of this." He pressed another kiss on my lips before he continued. "Yes, I wanted a baby, but I want you more." There was firmness in his voice. "We can have a baby later. When the time is right and you are better. If you want to. If it's not meant to be, we'll adopt one. Or whatever you want to do. Just don't leave me."

His touch on my cheek felt good. Reverent. Warm. I needed it like I needed air to breathe.

My heart twisted in my chest, desperate to believe his words. "R-really?"

Another hiccup left my lips and my nose tingled, threatening to set me off on a full-blown sob session.

"Yes, really." There was such conviction in his voice that I had no choice but to believe him. "You're all I need. Don't you see, Billie?"

"Wh-what?"

"I love you," he murmured, his big hand caressing every exposed inch of my skin in a worshiping, comforting kind of way. "My heart is yours, and I don't want it back." A sob tore from my throat, but he didn't stop, his thumb wiping my tears away. "I'm yours, wife. All my imperfections. All my demons. All my love."

"I love you too." My voice was barely a whisper, but my heart screamed the words from the top of the Eiffel Tower. "Probably from the moment your sexy ass walked into that bar six years ago."

He pressed his lips against mine as we lay together on the stiff hospital bed, me safely in his arms as I cried into them.

"We've just gotten engaged," he said softly. "We'll take it slow. First we need you to recover, and then I'm going to spoil my girl for the rest of my life. I'll probably drive you crazy."

I shook my head. "You won't."

He chuckled. "I will," he whispered reverently. "I have my demons and my vices that threaten to resurface. But compared to my need for you, those are just small bumps in the road. As long as you're with me, I'll happily watch the world go up in flames and not blink an eye."

"That's... not good, Win," I croaked, but amusement filled me nonetheless.

"I never said I was good." Silence enveloped us before he continued. "You tell me what you need, and I'll make it happen. You want babies, we'll have them. You want diamonds, they're yours. You want the world at your feet? Consider it done. You want revenge—"

I stopped his next words with a kiss of my own. "You," I murmured, my lips against his. "I just want you."

"You have me, Billie." It was a vow. The most beautiful promise in my husband's deep, gravelly voice. "You have all of me."

"Ditto," I breathed with a strangled sob. Winston's knuckles stroked my cheek gently, and I closed my eyes. I belonged to him, me and my one ovary. It was curious how something that I had never even given a passing thought to suddenly became so important, simply because I wanted to give Winston everything.

It might just be us for the remainder of our days. Maybe we'd have a baby—through adoption or of our own. I didn't know what the future would bring, but we'd take it a day at a time. *Together.*

Yes, together. I liked that.

As the abyss pulled on my consciousness once more, I knew he'd be here, waiting for me when I woke up.

Chapter 54
Billie

"What is this place?" I asked as he pulled up in front of a building that definitely wasn't home. I gazed through the tinted windows, his hands firmly on the steering wheel. He turned his head, watching me with that guarded expression on his face.

"It's our building."

My brows furrowed, and I returned my gaze to the lavish, manor-style high-rise that looked like it dated back to the fifteenth century. The entrance even had a doorman adorned in uniform there, waiting for Winston's signal to open the door.

"Our *building*?"

"Yes." He took my hand into his and squeezed it gently. "I should have talked to you about it before bringing you here. I have an apartment on the top floor. It's safe, and nobody comes in and out of this building without my approval." I sighed, thankful that he'd thought of it. Truthfully, I didn't want to go back to my apartment. First the kidnapping. Then the miscarriage. "Is that okay?"

I nodded, and he sighed in relief. "What about my clothes?"

"Already here. I had all your stuff moved here."

"Thank you."

He cupped my cheek. "This is your place as much as mine, Billie. It's ours. Understood?" I nodded. "There'll be no more shit happening to you, or so help me God, I'll climb up to the heavens or down to hell and have a word with those assholes."

I smiled tiredly. "It's good. It's just been a bad month. It can only go up from here."

He hummed his response and unclipped his seat belt. Someone was already at my door, but he yelled, "I got her."

He stepped around the car and opened my door, unclipping my belt before scooping me up into his arms. I let out a small squeal. "What are you doing?"

The doorman smiled. "Mr. Ashford. Mrs. Ashford. Welcome home."

Breathing deeply, I inhaled my husband's scent and leaned into his formidable wall of muscle. He was my strength right now, and I soaked it in greedily.

He didn't lower me down in the elevator that took us to the top floor. Or when we entered the penthouse. Not even when he started giving me a tour of the place.

"You know I can walk." Although it felt good being held. It was all he'd done for the past few days.

Staring down at me with love and entwining our fingers. "I know, baby. But I need you close." I sighed, pressing my head against his shoulder. "Let's start with the living room." There was a beautiful chandelier that was clearly a luxury item, which would have normally taken my breath away.

"It's a beautiful view of the city."

"Here's the kitchen. I have someone come in twice, sometimes three times a week to cook and freeze food for the days she's not here."

"She?"

He smiled. "Yes, she. Mrs. Pierre."

"Is she hot?" I asked.

"Totally. Her great-grandchildren are probably hot too." He grinned. "I like you jealous, wife."

I smacked him playfully. "You're the worst."

He continued down the hallway, his strides firm and confident.

"Okay, this is our bedroom." He opened the door and a small gasp left me. The space had furniture that belonged in a castle. A crystal chandelier looming over the mahogany four-poster bed.

"The most important part of the house," I muttered in awe.

His brows drawn, he met my gaze. "Do you want to have a room to yourself for a bit?"

"No." He watched me with a guarded expression, his eyes traveling over my face for any signs of distress at sharing a bed with him. I had none. After all the shit we went through, I needed him. He slept in the bed with me last night in the hospital, and while I knew he didn't get a lot of sleep, he hadn't hurt me. The same happened when he had his allergic reaction. Neither one of us noticed it until now. "I want to sleep in the bed with you. It's safe."

Glowing eyes the color of the ocean on a cloudless day softened as they watched me, full of the same emotions I was feeling. "You're my cure, wife." A somber look passed his expression. "You're what I've needed all along."

He strolled us around the master bedroom—me still tucked in his strong arms—toward the floor-to-ceiling glass window.

My head tilted up at the artwork on the wall and my lips parted. I couldn't resist saying, "At least there'll be something to look at while you're fucking me."

A strangled laugh escaped my husband, and I had to admit, I loved the sound of it. Like a flicker of light in the darkness.

"Wife, you'll be looking at me while I'm fucking you, not at a damn ceiling. I catch you staring at that, I'll have the whole thing repainted."

I chuckled. "Or you could bend me over and fuck me that way."

He pressed his mouth to my temple. "That's a good idea too. But before we get ahead of ourselves, you have to heal."

347

"I know." I chewed on my bottom lip.

"What is it?" he demanded. I shook my head, unwilling to say. "Billie, tell me or I'll drag it out of you."

"Will you be able to wait?"

"Woman, I waited six years for you. Six months will be a piece of cake."

I winced. "Six months?"

He nodded. "I researched it. It's best to let you heal for six months."

I frowned in confusion. "But Tristan said we can have sex whenever I feel ready."

Winston stiffened, his steps halting. "You talked to Tristan about sex."

My cheeks flushed. "He said it's best to wait three months before trying for another baby, but we can have sex whenever I'm up for it."

"When I see that man, I'm going to punch him," he muttered, resuming his steps. "Safety first, Billie. All medical journals recommended six months."

"Jesus, Winston. That's half a year."

"This is our closet," he said, changing the subject. "Feel free to rearrange it any way you like."

Our clothes hung in a walk-in wardrobe, our shoes placed together, and something about that small detail made me feel warm inside. In my apartment, our clothes were crammed in a tiny dresser, and Winston frequently had to leave to go get more of his things. This was so much better.

"How about a bath?" he suggested, and before I could open my mouth to ask if he'd join me, he added, "I'll keep you company."

"Actually, that sounds really good."

Within five minutes, I was submerged in steamy bubbles. The water lapped over my breasts, and I couldn't resist releasing a long sigh. I leaned my head back against where he sat at the edge of the bathtub and closed my eyes. So many conflicting emotions swirled inside me—love, fear, the need to be held, the need to be alone.

"Better?" Winston asked when I sighed in relief. His hands were on my shoulders, kneading the tension out.

"Yes, thank you," I answered, opening my eyes and glancing over my shoulder at him. He was fully dressed, his suit jacket thrown over the lounge chair and his sleeves rolled up to his elbows, revealing corded muscles.

He started to lather a sponge with soap, then brushed it over my neck, shoulders, and my back. It felt divine.

"What do you think about getting away for a bit?" he asked as he continued washing my body, his touch careful and attentive. It wasn't sexual by any means, and something about it made me feel even closer to him.

"We just got home," I murmured. "I don't want to leave yet."

"A honeymoon."

I smiled as I peered at him from under my lashes. "It wouldn't be much of a honeymoon if you intend to refrain from sex for six months."

A grin coasted across his beautiful lips. "Six months," he agreed, the stubborn tilt to his chin.

"What are we going to do for six months?"

"Talk. Eat. Talk some more. Sleep."

That night, we cuddled in bed together, his body wrapped around me while we watched my favorite comfort movie, *The DaVinci Code*, together.

It was the first night of forever sleeping together in our shared bed.

I sat on the windowsill of the penthouse, staring at the landscape of the city. Tilting my face up to the winter sky as a lone cloud glided lazily above the sun, I soaked up the heat. I'd been feeling cold all day, despite the cozy clothes and thick socks Winston pulled onto my feet before running out for a quick errand.

I missed hearing Odette's and Ares's voices. Aside from a few texts here and there, I hadn't really talked to them. I reached for my cell phone, which was devoid of any calls or messages.

A lump formed in the back of my throat.

I didn't want to call my sister only to cry to her. Not after she'd sacrificed so much for me. Guilt pierced my chest remembering I'd started it all with those stupid diamonds. I was a terrible sister.

The vibration in my hand startled me, pulling me out of my pity party. My eyes fell to the phone, and as if the universe had read my mind, my sister's name was flashing on the screen.

"Hello?"

"It's your favorite sister." Odette's voice warmed me more than the sun pouring through the large window could.

"You're my only sister," I pointed out, smiling.

"Just a minor detail," she replied breezily. "Winston called." I sighed, suddenly feeling tired. "I won't ask, but I need you to promise me that you'll tell me what you need."

My throat closed, emotions clogging it. "You've done a lot for me already. Maybe I deserve this after the clusterfuck—"

She cut me off. "Don't you dare put the blame on yourself." It was stupid. I knew it, but I couldn't shake off the feeling that if I hadn't been so reckless, it could have been prevented. "Did you ever think that it's thanks to you that we have finally gotten the men we love?"

"How do you know I love him?" I asked instead.

A soft chuckle filled the phone line. "How do you know I love Byron?"

"You're my sister."

"Exactly."

"Although I fail to see your logic at how you having Byron could be attributed to me."

She sighed, and I could almost picture her rolling her eyes at me. "Well, if you hadn't stolen those diamonds, we wouldn't have made our way back to the States. We wouldn't have run into the Ashford men in New Orleans."

"I'm hardly Cupid."

"Everything worked out, Billie." Odette was always more rational than I was. "And I know you're hurting about losing the baby."

"It just wasn't meant to be."

"Maybe, but it doesn't make it hurt any less." She was right, it didn't. I'd managed to fall inexplicably in love with that little bundle of joy. "I just know that you're strong, and you will have a baby one way or another someday."

"You sound sure," I muttered.

"I am. Ares needs a little cousin to play with."

"He already has that," I pointed out. "Your marriage to Byron gave him multiple by default."

"True, but they refuse to live in France." My brows furrowed at the odd comment, but I didn't ask her to elaborate, sidetracked by her next comment. "Women often withdraw into themselves after a miscarriage, but I've found it's helpful to talk. Don't keep it all in. No matter how silly something is, just talk about it. It'll hurt and upset you, but it will also help you to move on."

I cleared my throat, this sense of vulnerability a novelty. Although I had to admit, she was right. I couldn't keep sulking and examining every little thing I could have done differently.

"I miss you and Ares," I murmured.

"We miss you too. Is there anything you need?"

I shook my head, then remembered she couldn't see me. "No. Tristan said it just has to run its course, and Winston's taking good care of me."

"I know. He's been calling every day. Soon, he'll be calling himself Dr. Ashford." A choked laugh escaped me. My husband had gone overboard a bit, but it was sweet. "I told him to listen to you and what your body tells you."

"He's convinced we have to wait six months for smexy time."

Her laugh rang over the phone. "That might be going overboard."

"You think?" I retorted dryly.

"You just do your thing, and when you're ready, you'll know."

"Yeah, then I'll jump his bones."

We laughed with a lightness that had been absent for a while, until slowly the amusement lapsed into an easy quiet.

Something told me life had better things in store for us. It was just taking its time.

Chapter 55
Billie

It had been twenty-eight days of ups and downs. Tears and smiles. Dates and sleepless nights.

Nobody had ever talked to me about miscarriages, so I didn't know what was normal. The worst part, I didn't talk about it either. Winston tried to tiptoe around the subject, assuring me he was here for me.

And I knew he was.

I knew it was silly to grieve something that had barely taken root. I'd barely been pregnant a month.

"Gosh, I love all these baby designs, Billie." Violet gushed over my latest drawings that were about to go into production. "Makes me want to have a kid."

I chuckled despite the light twinge in my chest. "I never thought I'd hear the good doctor claim that she wants to have a kid."

She shrugged. "I could be persuaded." My eyebrows met my hairline, but I said nothing. If there was something she wanted to share, she would. "Could I reserve this one? I'll give you anything."

She pointed to the bracelet adorned with little elephants. "Anything, huh?" I teased.

Her grin was my answer. "Anything."

I penciled her name at the bottom so I wouldn't forget. It was another thing that had been suffering. My damn memory.

"It's yours," I said with a smile.

She glanced around the fancy penthouse. The view of Paris stretched in front of us, and I couldn't deny it was a dream come true.

Except I couldn't find the strength to be excited about it. About anything, really. I threw myself into work in hopes of moving on, but I feared I'd achieved the opposite. I was losing my passion for diamonds and fashion. In fact, I feared that if someone left a bag full of diamonds in front of me, I wouldn't even attempt to steal it, which was... unlike me, you could say.

"Do you want to talk?"

My attention returned to my friend, and I forced a smile. "About?" She tilted her head, not falling for my aloofness. "No, I don't want to talk about it," I said, sighing. "Please don't go all shrink on me. I'm not a criminal."

She chuckled. "For the most part."

My abdomen throbbed dully with another reminder of what I'd lost. It had been twenty-eight days since the hospital, and my period came in like clockwork, which according to Tristan was an excellent sign.

I would have been excited if this sadness wasn't clouding my mind, drowning all my other thoughts. I remembered the days when my nephew was just a tiny baby and the feelings that filled my chest as I held him or when he fell asleep in my arms.

I let out a heavy sigh. It was a pointless line of thinking.

"Where's your husband?"

I wondered that myself. He was strangely mysterious before he left. Usually, I had to push him out the door, or when he had to take care of something, he'd give me a rundown of what he was doing and how fast he'd be back.

"I don't know," I admitted. "He had something to take care of."

I glanced back out the large windows in an effort to look unbothered, but Violet continued to stare at me. She was relentless like that.

"He's been so good," I whispered finally.

"But?"

I swallowed. "No buts. It just makes me want to cry because he's so wonderful, and I keep thinking if maybe I'd just fallen into his arms without the runaround, I wouldn't have been"—*kidnapped*—"stressed. And I'd still be pregnant."

"You're smart enough to know that's not true."

I nodded. When I said it out loud, it sounded ludicrous. "I know. Tristan said it was just the nature of things. Something wasn't right." My voice cracked. Fuck, I hated feeling so vulnerable. I didn't like feeling this sadness and tightness in my chest.

"It just means it wasn't meant to be," she stated, all business. "And when it's meant to be, it will be even better. Heck, you might end up with triplets."

I sighed, my lips curving into a smile. "Triplets would be a lot."

"Twins?" she said teasingly.

"I'm not greedy, I just want a healthy baby." Not that it would happen soon. Winston was adamant about letting me heal. He'd read every article there was about miscarriage and recovery time.

"When do *you* think it's safe to have sex again?" I blurted.

Her eyes widened before she started to chuckle. "Okay, now I feel better."

I stared at her, waiting for her to expand, and when she didn't, I let out a frustrated breath. "About?"

"First, I'm not a gynecologist or a physician, so it's probably best to ask Tristan about that. And second, the fact you're asking about it at all is a good sign of your healing."

"Oh."

"Listen, Billie. Everyone's different. Trust yourself. If you feel like having sex, do it. If you need to be sad, be sad. If you need to cry and scream, cry and scream. Just don't hold it all in."

My sister had said the same thing, and it made sense. "No

wonder you're so good at your job." She flushed, and I couldn't help but think there was something else going on with her. "How about we eat a whole gallon of ice cream?"

Her eyes sparkled and she opened her mouth when the doorbell sounded. With a sigh, I went to open it.

My mouth dropped open when I saw my sister and Ares standing there, smiling wildly.

"Surprise!"

"What? How!" I could hardly form a sentence before my nephew threw himself into my arms. "How's this possible?" I whispered as I felt Odette's arms close around me.

It wasn't until we were all in a tight embrace that I realized how much I missed them. We were a unit, a family, and yes, Winston was part of that too, but it wasn't one or the other. It was all of us together.

"Winston called Byron and said you needed us. So, here we are," my sister explained.

My throat squeezed and I tightened my grip on them. "I've missed you so much."

Odette kissed my cheek. "I'm sorry I wasn't here for you. I wish—"

I shook my head. "You're here now. This... Everything's perfect now."

I glanced behind them to see Winston and Byron standing in identical poses, hands in pockets. My eyes connected with my husband's, and I mouthed a silent "Thank you."

No amount of diamonds or money in the world could buy this. My family.

"I missed you, Aunt Billie," Ares mumbled into my stomach.

"Me too, buddy," I rasped. "You've grown at least five inches."

He giggled, his eyes shining happily. My sister glowed too. I didn't even have to ask whether they were happy. It was written all over their faces.

"I'm going to be bigger than you soon," he announced proudly, earning him chuckles all around.

"Don't rush it, little man."

We walked into the penthouse as Violet stood up and headed toward us. "Hey, Maddy," she said, using my sister's old nickname. "Long time no see."

"Jesus, Violet. I didn't know you were still in Europe."

She smiled. "More interesting criminals in Europe," she deadpanned. The Ashford brothers' exchange didn't escape me. "Anyhow, I have to get going."

"Are you sure you can't stay for that ice cream?"

"Yay," Ares exclaimed. He was always in the mood for sweets.

Violet shook her head. "No, unfortunately not. I just got a text requesting an impromptu session." She leaned over and pecked my cheek. "But text me if you need me. I'll see you soon."

Ares's hand still in mine, I hugged her close. "Thank you," I whispered into her ear.

Ares got distracted and made his way to the window. Violet strode out, and Winston walked toward me. "Missed you," he rasped against my hair.

"Missed you too. The best surprise and gift you could have given me. Thank you," I breathed. "Besides your glorious self," I added quickly.

He smiled. "I'm glad you think so."

It was then that I realized the cards I'd been dealt didn't line up for our first pregnancy, but I was surrounded by more love and better off than so many others in this world. I had Winston Ashford, the man of my dreams. I had a family. I had everything that made me rich in all the right ways.

And for the next few hours as we cooked, laughed, and watched a sappy Hallmark movie, I knew this was where I was meant to be all along. Among family, with the man who looked at me like I was his whole world.

Because he was mine.

Chapter 56
Billie

S afe and warm in my husband's arms, I stared at the dark
ceiling and the flickering city lights that poured through the
windows. Several months had flown by, and we'd kept busy,
all the while a feeling warned something big was about to happen.

My sister, brother-in-law, and nephew had been with us for over
four weeks now. It was great, but I couldn't shake off the feeling that
something was about to happen. Something big. It was in all the
secret calls Winston was taking. All the secret messages he'd been
sending. When I overheard him talking to Byron about giving me full
access to his assets, my suspicions were confirmed. I knew it deep
down, and the fact he brought Byron and my sister over confirmed it
for me. He wanted to ensure I was taken care of while he went on a
"business" trip.

I had a bad feeling that the trip had something to do with what
happened with Danil.

After tossing and turning for another half hour, I finally couldn't
hold it in anymore. I reached out for the bedside lamp and flicked
it on.

The lamplight cast shadows over my husband's sleeping face. I hadn't forgotten what happened the last time I tried to wake him up, but he didn't seem to be in the throes of a nightmare this time. He slept peacefully, his stubble making him appear younger and messier.

I pressed my palm against his cheek.

"Winston," I whispered, guilt slithering through me for interrupting his sleep. When he didn't move, I bent over and brushed my lips against his. He groaned, and my body shivered as lust awakened right along with my husband. "I have to talk to you."

His hands came around me, one gripping my ass and the other grabbing my nape. "I have a better idea."

God, he smelled so good, his body heat warming my skin. He'd been resisting all my sexual advances, and we were approaching the third month of his self-imposed, no-sex rule. I'd done my own research and provided him with evidence that said it was safe.

But Winston was stubborn as fuck.

His rough, warm palms roamed my thighs, touching me like a starved man. So I just went for it. I shimmied my panties down my legs, leaving me exposed underneath the oversized shirt of his I was wearing.

I grabbed his hand and brought it to my hot core. "God, that feels good," I breathed, my pussy throbbing with need.

"We said no sex for six months," he rasped against my lips.

Grinding myself against his hand, I murmured, "*We* didn't." My hips rolled, matching every thrust and glide of our tongues. I moaned, pressing tighter against him, running my nails down his biceps. "I need you so bad. We'll be careful." He stilled, and I thought he'd stop. "I promise, it's safe. Please, Winston."

He let out a rough breath, and I knew he'd given in. He started off slowly. Touching me. Caressing me. Whispering sweet nothings. Leaving a trail of fire everywhere his fingers trailed across my flushed skin.

My lips parted as his hand lowered on my ass, his finger inching into a different hole.

"Winston," I gasped.

My palms on his chest, I felt a tremor roll through his body as he kissed me slow and sweet. A pulse throbbed between my legs as I panted against his lips. My body shivered in anticipation as his finger pushed further inside me. I writhed and moaned under his touch, growing hotter than ever before.

Two of his fingers slid inside me while one still filled my ass, and I whimpered with delight when he began to move them in and out slowly. Each slide of his fingers was slower, like he was worshiping me.

The fullness was so delicious and intense. His strong body underneath mine. His hard erection pressing against me.

Then he rubbed my clit, and I shook against him. I mewled, and he swallowed the noise in his mouth.

"Who fucks you, wife?" His lips skimmed against mine, the finesse of the kiss gone as he ravaged me. "Tell me."

"*You.*"

Another brush of his finger against my clit and stars exploded behind my eyelids as I came. Satisfaction rumbled in his chest as he lifted me by the waist, his fingers digging into my hips.

A gasp escaped me as he pushed inside me in one deep thrust. My breaths turned erratic. I was filled to the brim.

He groaned in satisfaction, his eyes glued to where we were connected. "Fuck, I love being inside you. It's like entering heaven."

"Fuck your way to heaven," I choked, clutching his arms. He eased out and then back inside, both of us shaking with the intensity of our love and desire. "Oh... my... God."

He fucked me slowly, and although I was on top, he had all the control. With heavy breaths, I watched him fuck me while I straddled him. Pleasure burned through my veins as he lifted me up, then watched his length disappear inside me. In and out.

I ran my fingers down his chest, loving the wall of muscle underneath my fingertips.

"I love you," I murmured.

He peered up at me, so much love in his eyes that it made mine burn. "I waited my whole life for you." His pelvis ground against mine, molten heat spreading through my body. "I'd kill for you. If there was ever a choice between you and anyone or anything else, it would always be you."

A throaty moan escaped my lips. "Ditto. Now fuck me, husband."

And he did. He fucked me deep and slow. Hard and fast. Each thrust sent a wave of heat through me, my toes curling with the intensity of it. The pressure built, and I leaned over and licked the corner of his lips, tasting him.

My fingers tightened in his hair as the orgasm hit me hard, knocking my breath from me. He fucked me through my orgasm as I held on to him, moaning and panting.

"Come inside me," I begged, my forehead against his. His fist in my hair, our bodies grinding together, he thrust one last time and came inside me with a rough noise.

Our heartbeats thundering as one, my husband's fist still in my hair, he lifted my head and took my mouth for another kiss. Slowly, I pulled away and locked eyes with him.

"I wanted to talk," I murmured softly.

"But we ended up doing something much better," he said, his voice filled with admiration. He sat up, and when I went to move, he stopped me. "Stay like this. Just for a little bit longer."

Why did it feel like goodbye?

"Winston." My voice was a whisper, panic wrapping around it like fear around my heart. "I'm worried."

His fingers tightened around me. "You're safe. I won't let anything happen to you."

I shook my head, swallowing. "I don't want you to go tomorrow." Tension pulled his shoulders taut, but he didn't say anything. "Please tell me you're not doing anything reckless."

He smoothed a hand through his hair. "Don't worry about anything, Billie."

"See, that makes me worry even more," I said stubbornly. "Remember when you said we'd talk about everything. No secrets."

This marriage was a partnership. I didn't want him keeping me in a bubble.

"It's safer if you don't know anything."

I released a shuddering breath. "No."

He blinked. "No?"

I shook my head. "I don't want to be safe. I want you. For better or for worse, Winston. That's what we promised. They weren't just empty words. Not to me."

He stared at me and my heart beat in an anguished rhythm.

"I have to *take care* of my father," he finally said, and realization settled upon me. He wasn't just cutting his connection to his father. He was going to kill him.

I swallowed, unsure how to feel. It wasn't that I cared about his father, but I was worried about the consequences. *Thou shall not kill.* Truthfully, his father deserved it, but Winston didn't deserve to go to jail for it.

"I... I can't lose you." A heaviness tugged at my chest. I ran a hand into his hair, needing to touch him, and a rough noise sounded low in his throat. "I can't live without you."

It wasn't a lie. Even during the six years that we were apart, there were so many days I thought about him. So many nights I made myself come while picturing him touching me and loving me.

"I will come back to you, Billie. One way or another, I'll find my way back. Even if I have to break out of prison."

I sighed into his mouth, knowing I couldn't convince him to abort this mission. But I could make him a vow. "I'll be waiting for you with my bags packed, ready to run."

His gaze filled with something as dark as sin as he cupped my face with his palms and ran a thumb across my bottom lip.

"I am yours. All my imperfections. All my demons. All my love."

It was the vow he'd give me for the rest of our lives.

Chapter 57
Winston

Washington, D.C.

I was about to do something that could blow up in my face big-time.

The risk was significant, but the benefits outweighed them. Even if I got caught, the knowledge that my wife and siblings would spend the remainder of their days safe from this man was worth it.

The iron gates slid open, and I drove through the long driveway lined with weeping willows—my mother's favorite. Midnight was quickly creeping up, but the mansion was lit up like the damn White House.

My father's house stood tall behind the trees. I'd like to say I never knew it'd come to this, but I really did. From the day my mom died, I knew things would end badly with my father.

All I had to think about was my wife's face filled with pain and sadness, and I had to fight the urge to torture the fucking bastard who managed to destroy so many lives.

I'd settle this unpleasant affair.

The house was empty. Thanks to Priest and his hacking skills, all the surveillance had been shut down on this block, and every single member of the staff had gotten called away.

So the old fucker was nice and alone.

I found my father in his bedroom, smoking a cigar and watching the news. The curtains were drawn, casting the room in near darkness. The room reeked of stale sex, blending with the walls and secrets this house had seen.

He had three whores in his bed—my mother's bed—less than an hour ago, according to Priest.

I hit the light switch, causing the corrupt senator to blink against the harsh glare. The bed creaked under his weight as he shot upright to see who dared enter his domain.

"Winston, what are you doing here?"

A smooth smile rested on my lips as venomous rage raced the length of each limb.

Of course the fucker was naked. My lips curled in distaste as I strolled to his bedside, one hand in my pants pocket and the other hanging nonchalantly at my side. I had to fight the urge not to lunge at him and wrap it around his neck.

"I've come to let you know my wife's still alive." His wrinkled hand gripped the thin sheet. The look in his eyes said it all. An admission that he was willing to sacrifice her for his own fuckups. Not sure why I would ever be surprised; after all, he'd used every one of his children for his own gain. "But my baby isn't."

I made sure he could see the hate in my eyes. The promise of retribution. The promise of sending him to hell prematurely.

"You'll thank me one day."

"Never." My voice hardened.

"In our world, tough decisions need to be made," he drawled with that cruel smirk on his face. "I liked fucking your mother—in fact, she was the best pussy I ever had—but she was in the way. I would have never been able to become a senator with her and her baggage by my side."

Hate like nothing else bubbled inside me, searing my veins. "What do you mean?" I asked in an icy tone.

He smiled maliciously. "I knew you'd want to go to that game store. You're nothing if not predictable, Winston."

"You had her killed." Saying the words out loud rattled my bones. His cruelty. His nonexistent morals. His greed.

Realization at how far this man was willing to go put the devil himself to shame. All these years, he'd used her death against me, and it was all a fucking lie. He ended her and left my siblings and me without a mother, and he didn't have an ounce of remorse.

"Why?"

"I needed the help from the mafia to secure my seat. She kept blocking my path, running to her family and blabbing that I was willing to get into bed with the Russians. Our family's destined for greatness, not pettiness."

He'd cost my mother her life. I spent years hating myself. The familiar gnawing pressure in my chest grew, remembering the day my mother died.

"Do you think you achieved greatness? Your children despise you. The fucking world despises you. My wife's too good for me. Too good for the filthy Ashford name."

I closed the distance, and with each step, the strong scent of his cologne prickled my gag reflexes. Or maybe it was just the idea of him.

"Not fucking true." He just smiled, thinking he had the upper hand. "Our connections with the underworld are far-reaching. Not just Russians. Not just Italians. Not even just the Balkans. There's no stopping us." He had gone too far. His greed would destroy us all. "You're an Ashford, not meant to associate with the likes of that Swan scum. It's bad enough your brother fathered a bastard." I leaned over, and he just smiled, too stupid to see he had pushed me too far for the last time. "Our blood is better than theirs."

I shook my head. "Enough."

He had made every single one of his children into an object to use and abuse. Just as he had with our mother. No more.

"You said it yourself. That hussy is a gold digger."

"Shut. The. Fuck. Up."

He smiled. "I did you a favor. I hope they fucked her bloody."

I grabbed his neck and stared into his soulless eyes. "Danil had the decency not to let her get raped." I tightened my grip, causing him to start choking. "You ruined a life for the last time, Father." He coughed and sputtered, clawing at my wrist. With each passing second, his grip on me weakened. "I hope you burn in hell."

He coughed, gasping for his next breath. I didn't look away or even blink, relishing every fucking second of his misery. The look in his eyes turned haunted and his dying breath became a raspy melody.

It was glorious.

It wasn't until he stared blankly ahead that I finally released my grip.

Now, it was time I returned to my wife.

Chapter 58
Billie

A whole two weeks had gone by since Winston went on his "business" trip.

We agreed on no phone calls and no texts, and I regretted that now as I made my way through Villefranche-sur-Mer and down the promenade until I got to the sea. This was where my sister and I mourned our mother's death, then later our father's.

After Winston left, I grew restless and came back to where it all began.

After days of constant check-ins from my sister and brother-in-law, I needed space. They'd been a wonderful support, and Ares a good distraction, but I needed some alone time. Byron, much like his brother, had a gift for business. He helped me roll out production of pieces using first of the diamonds from the mines. It turned out Winston had made a deal with Danil for right of first refusal of all diamonds coming through the mine he gave up.

I sat down on the beach, the cold breeze sweeping off the sea. The sun slowly descended behind the horizon of the hillside village, the sea glistening with its last rays. Each minute extinguished another until dusk closed in on me.

Where are you, Winston?

The news of Senator Ashford's death dominated the media, but there hadn't been a word of foul play. I watched daily for updates, and the story was always the same. Senator Ashford died peacefully in his sleep.

The funeral was yesterday. Byron flew out for the day and came back first thing. The disappointment when he came through the door without Winston was heavy.

"Is this seat taken?"

My heart stilled at the sound of my husband's voice. I swallowed, scared I might be hallucinating. Slowly, I turned my head and met his gaze. *Blue.* Full of devotion and love. Full of promises for our future.

"It's a free beach," I said quietly. He lowered down next to me, his knees touching mine, and pulled me into his arms. "I missed you," I croaked.

His jaw tightened. "I know. I just had to be sure."

Sure they wouldn't pin it on him. Sure that it wouldn't come back to me. I didn't ask for details, and I knew he would never tell. Whatever he'd done, it was for his family. *Our* family.

"Welcome home."

"You *are* my home, wife."

I felt the intensity of his love in his words. In the way his fingers shook as they touched me. It made my heart clench.

"Are you sad?" he murmured, wiping a tear from my cheek with the pad of his thumb.

"Happy. I'm so happy you're home."

He pulled me closer until all I could feel was *him*. He lowered his forehead against mine, cocooning me in his heat and his familiar scent.

I tilted my head and he kissed me as he held my face. Soft and deep. Slow and consuming. It made my heart tremble and sing with happiness.

"I love you," I breathed against his lips.

"And I love you, wife."

As we stared out into the sea, I wasn't sure how the future would play out. But I knew we'd face it with grace.

Together.

Epilogue - 1
Billie

Four Years Later

"You look like you're about to burst."

Odette giggled at my nephew's honesty, and I narrowed my eyes on both of them. I wanted to strangle them, even though Ares's words couldn't be more true.

Objectively speaking, I looked like an inflated balloon. I was forty-one weeks pregnant, and Christmas was fast approaching. It was obvious that my son had adopted his father's stubbornness. I would have found it adorable if not for my body that could barely wobble from one end of the room to the next. My breasts were the size of steroid-fed watermelons, my back could barely support my weight, and my hormones were all over the place.

But no matter the moaning and groaning about being past my due date, I was happy for the fashionably late entrance my son had opted for. It'd given me just a bit more time with him, knowing that it would be my last pregnancy.

I wasn't sad about the news when the doctors broke it to me—I was lucky enough to have experienced pregnancy at all.

"Could I claim hormonal insanity if I murder someone in the late stages of pregnancy?" I pondered aloud.

"We can give it a try." Violet was nothing if not a supportive friend during these difficult times. Odette snorted, while Ares rolled his eyes.

"Dad will never allow it. Neither will Uncle Winston."

"Don't fool yourself, Ares. Uncle Winston would kill us all for Aunt Billie," Odette said, deadly serious. "Let's just pray that her mood swings pass."

Violet snorted. "Maybe he can claim insanity too."

Ares scrunched his nose, rolling his eyes. "I'll never be whipped like that."

The three of us shared a glance and chuckled, knowing full well one day a girl would have him smitten and wrapped around her little finger. She'd better be worthy of my nephew though. Violet was standing at the window, admiring our little haven in Southern France. Our permanent home by the sea.

Winston and I frequently traveled to Paris, but with our baby approaching, I wanted to be where we first met so our baby could be born here. I wanted to be close to my sister and ensure she delivered our baby. There was nobody I trusted more.

He made his way out of the living room of Winston's castle by the sea, clearly done listening to women talk.

"He's going to be a heartbreaker one day," I told my sister.

"Honestly, it's alarming how good-looking every Ashford is," pointed out Violet.

"What's alarming is how this baby is still inside me." I pointed at my huge belly.

"What's this nonsense about someone killing us all?" Byron drawled as he and my husband strolled in, both cool and collected in their designer suits. Winston sauntered in my direction and leaned down to press a lingering kiss to my lips. "Ares called Winston pussy-whipped."

A gasp tore from my sister's mouth, and she glared at my brother-in-law. "He must have heard that from Royce. That man will be the sole reason for our son's foul mouth."

"Fucking right," he agreed, grinning, and Odette let out an exasperated breath.

"How are my two favorite people doing?" Winston murmured against my lips, ignoring them all.

I smiled, rubbing my belly. "Fully cooked."

He rubbed my stomach through the dress I'd designed as part of my latest maternity line. "And the little guy?"

I grinned. "Too stubborn to make his grand entrance."

Winston smiled. "He loves his mama too much."

Groaning, I grabbed the tip of my husband's tie and tugged him to me. "We've got to have some wild sex tonight so this baby will come out."

"Of course," he said eagerly, his eyes shining with amusement. We both knew wild sex at this stage was impossible. We'd been limited to oral sex, lots of porn, and mild petting over the last few weeks. "Whatever my wife wants," he said, grinning.

I shot him a look. "Are you mocking me?"

He laughed. "Never. I know better than to do that at this stage."

Our audience chuckled softly in the background, and I reached my hand up. "Can you help me out of this chair, please? I need to stretch my legs." He scooped me up in his arms, and I squealed. "Winston, put me down. I'm huge, you'll break your back."

"It'll be worth it."

I smiled and then stiffened as I felt warm liquid trickling down my thighs.

"Umm, Billie," he hedged. "Any chance that you... peed yourself?"

His eyes darted between my legs and we both froze. "I think my water broke." We both looked at each other. "Ready for us, Daddy?"

"I was born ready for you two."

Epilogue - 2
Winston

Five Months Later

My wife's small hand slipped into mine. Her long blonde hair was loose and wild, falling down the back of a white lace Givenchy dress. The diamonds around her neck that I designed for her matched the bracelet I'd retrieved from the smugglers.

Despite being jewelry-crazy, my wife only ever wore that neck-lace and bracelet, as well as her wedding ring. It was the best sight ever. My wife was the best gift ever, and I would never take it for granted.

Woof. Woof.

"Fifi," she scolded our little puppy—a chocolate-colored French bulldog—for barking at a passerby. "You'll wake up our little boy." As if our five-month-old son knew he was being mentioned, he stirred in the baby carrier I wore, cooing. My wife's eyes lit up, and I grinned at the sheer happiness in her gaze.

My chest grew fuller every time I was around my family. The past five years had flown by, and this was a new chapter for us. The one we'd been waiting for, and I knew life would only keep getting better.

There wasn't much I liked to do more than spend time with my family. Billie had kicked her award-winning label off all those years ago and was welcomed into the industry with open arms. I couldn't be prouder.

"Ugh, she's not listening to me at all," Billie muttered when our puppy refused to stop barking.

"She's protecting us."

Billie chuckled. "I guess size doesn't matter."

"Not when it comes to loyalty." I pressed a kiss to her forehead. She sighed against me, and satisfaction hummed in my throat. It was impossible to resist her—her smiles, her golden-brown eyes, and the love she had for our family. For me.

Amongst the fading sound of sirens, the scent of the Seine, and the taste of urban air, spring was in the air. The overcast sky darkened and the first drops of rain fell from the sky.

I reveled in my good fortune.

My steps halted and so did hers. I turned her to face me, cupping her cheeks. The rain was warm and light, and she blinked it off her eyelashes.

Her pulse fluttered, her breaths filling the space between us.

She stepped forward, our baby boy's hands gripping both of us, connecting us. I wasn't worthy of her or this life, but the thought of letting my wife and son never existing without me in the picture wasn't possible. We were meant to be. She was mine, and I was hers.

"I love you, Billie Ashford."

She lifted her hand and pressed her palm to my cheek. "And I love you, Winston."

After years of searching and battling demons, I found peace as I kissed her in the rain. Like it was our first kiss. Like it was our last.

THE END

Acknowledgments

I want to thank my friends and family for their continued support. To my alpha and beta readers - you are all amazing. You put up with my crazy deadlines and even crazier organization. I couldn't do this without you.

My books wouldn't be what they are without each one of you.

To the bloggers and reviewers who helped spread the word about every one of my books. I appreciate you so much and hearing you love my work, makes it that much more enjoyable!

And last but not least, **to all my readers**! This wouldn't be possible without you. Thank you for believing in me. Thank you for your amazing and supportive messages. Simply, THANK YOU.

I get to do this because all of you.

XOXO

Eva Winners

What's Next?

*Thank you so much for reading **Secrets of a Billionaire**! If you liked it, please leave a review. Your support means the world to me.*

***Reign of a Billionaire** is the next book in this series, and it will address our very own Ghost that appeared in Thorns of Omertà, Kingston's book https://bit.ly/3Ot7Ilw.*

If you're thirsty for more discussions with other readers of the series, you can join the Facebook group, Eva's Soulmates (https://bit.ly/3gHEeoe).

About the Author

Curious about Eva's other books? You can check them out here. Eva Winners's Books https://bit.ly/3SMMsrN

Eva Winners writes anything and everything romance, from enemies to lovers to books with all the feels. Her heroes are sometimes villains, because they need love too, right? Her books are sprinkled with a touch of suspense and mystery, a healthy dose of angst, a hint of violence and darkness, and lots of steamy passion.

When she's not working and writing, she spends her days either in Croatia or Maryland, daydreaming about her next story.

Find Eva below:

Visit www.evawinners.com and subscribe to my newsletter.
FB group: https://bit.ly/3gHEeoe
FB page: https://bit.ly/3oDzP8Q
Insta: http://Instagram.com/evawinners
BookBub: https://www.bookbub.com/authors/eva-winners
Amazon: http://amazon.com/author/evawinners
Goodreads: http://goodreads.com/evawinners
TikTok: https://vm.tiktok.com/ZMeETK7pq/

Made in United States
Orlando, FL
04 October 2024

52354417R00243